THE COMPLETE ADVENTURES OF HENRY CHALK,

PEDESTRIAN TOURIST

To my granddaughters;
Scarlett,
Patience
and Clover

THE
COMPLETE
ADVENTURES
OF
HENRY CHALK,

𝕻edestrian 𝕿ourist

by

Nick Cowen

First published in the United Kingdom in three volumes in 2005 (Chalk), 2009 (Flint), 2013 (Gold). First published in this complete edition in 2020.

by The Hobnob Press,
8 Lock Warehouse, Severn Road, Gloucester GL1 2GA
www.hobnobpress.co.uk

British Library Cataloguing in Publication Data
A catalogue record for this book is available from the British Library

ISBN 978-1-906978-89-1

Typeset in Doves Type 12/15 pt
Typesetting and origination by John Chandler

Contents

INTRODUCTION

This book celebrates the once popular exploration format of two hundred years ago, the domestic travelogue. At a time when the Napoleonic War caused a hiatus to the continental excursion, the established Grand Tour, intrepid travellers were forced to explore their own backyard by visiting the more remote quarters of Britain. These journeys would be recorded in a steady succession of letters to a friend or a family member and at the conclusion of the tour this correspondence would be gathered together, illustrated, embellished to make it more exciting and then published, often anonymously. In some cases, flagrant plagiarism took place with authors claiming their own tales of adventure but in reality, cribbing from the many accounts already in circulation.

Having studied this forgotten format and purchased a number of examples, I then began to research one particular anonymous travelogue that had been published in 1811. This book turned out itself to be a fascinating spoof of the domestic travelogue genre but it included very real references to South Wiltshire and its antiquaries, who were actively investigating the great many ancient round barrows that populated the chalk landscape. After two years of trying to unravel the threads in this one book, I then contemplated some sort of orderly and academic study on the now forgotten domestic travelogue. I soon realised that I am not built that way and the many disorderly historical tangents that I had pursued could not be beaten flat into a straightforward and scholarly piece. Instead I decided to write my own adventure story in the style of the domestic travelogue and very quickly the correspondence from my young fictional pedestrian, Henry

Chalk, accumulated on the page before me. I was now able to weave my haphazard research into the tale and populate the adventure with real characters, preserving accurate chronologies and events whilst the wandering pedestrian tourist provided the glue to hold it all together. John Chandler at Hobnob Press then read "A Tour in Search of Chalk" in manuscript and it must have struck a chord as he informed me that he would like to publish it. Being true to the genre that I had recreated, I wanted to publish it anonymously, as was the custom, and John obligingly agreed. "Chalk" came out in 2005 and two further volumes of the trilogy, "Flint" and "Gold" were completed and published over the next eight years, all penned by "A Pedestrian". Now seven years on since "Gold" was released, John suggested that the trilogy should be compiled as one volume. From the outset, it was always planned as an adventure story in three parts and so, with little alteration, it is now presented as "The Complete Adventures of Henry Chalk, Pedestrian Tourist" and, to break with tradition, I have put my name to it.

Things do not readily happen in a vacuum and my curiosity about domestic travelogues was born out of a deeper immersion into the history of a very specific area; South Wiltshire, where I maintained the public rights of way for 30 years. Described by one local farmer as a 'round peg in a round hole', the paths that I was entrusted to look after, to protect and improve, were the trails of previous human activity, etched into the chalk, ranging across history and prehistory. Today, on one level, these are routes for healthy pursuits or somewhere to walk your dog and they should be 'fit for purpose', to meet modern demands. Scratch beneath the surface and these are paths across an ancient landscape, walked and ridden into existence and born out of necessity. Paths have always led me back to previous eras, even in my early teens growing up in the Wylye Valley where I naively craved the past, imagining it a better place that the present. As I got older, this rose-tinted view became tempered by reality but my thoughts often still roam somewhere between the recent and ancient past.

I have frequently reinvented my explanation of the Chalk trilogy and previous attempts have suggested that it is a book of books; a young man's rite of passage; a deeply immersive tale amongst the soils and rocks of very specific and real places; a bloody obsession; a thesis dressed up as an adventure story; a sharing of my fieldwalking experiences; a roll call for the unsung participants in Sir Richard Colt Hoare's magnificent 1812 publication Ancient Wiltshire vol.1; a tensioning mystery about love, money, greed and murder; a classic adventure story. It could be all of those things, but ultimately it is what the reader gets out of it in terms of entertainment and pleasure. Over to you.

KEY:

Part One: A Tour in Search of Chalk,   >>>>>>>
commences from Salisbury

Part Two: A Tour in Search of Flint,   ooooooo
commences from Shaftesbury

Part Three: A Tour in Search of Gold,   XXXXXX
commences from Marlborough

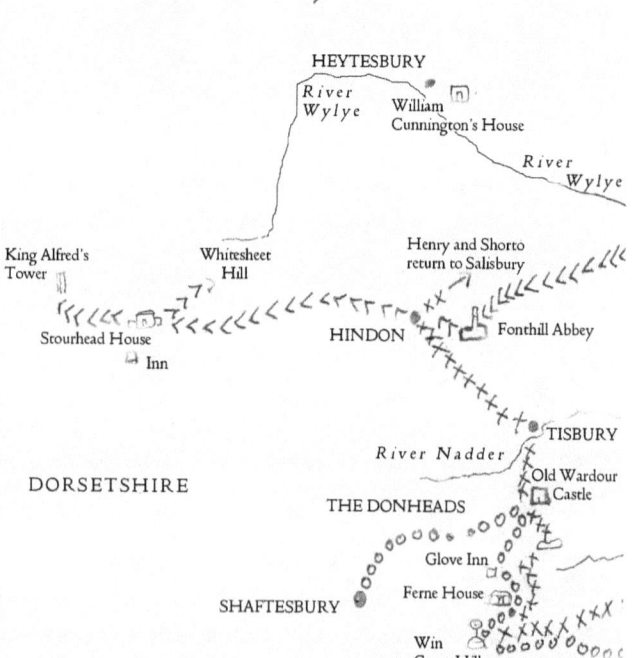

SOMERSETSHIRE

SALISBURY PLAIN

HEYTESBURY

River Wylye   William
            Cunnington's House

River Wylye

King Alfred's   Whitesheet   Henry and Shorto
Tower   Hill   return to Salisbury

Stourhead House   HINDON   Fonthill Abbey
        Inn

TISBURY

River Nadder

DORSETSHIRE   Old Wardour
                    THE DONHEADS   Castle

                    Glove Inn

                    Ferne House
SHAFTESBURY

Win
Green Hill

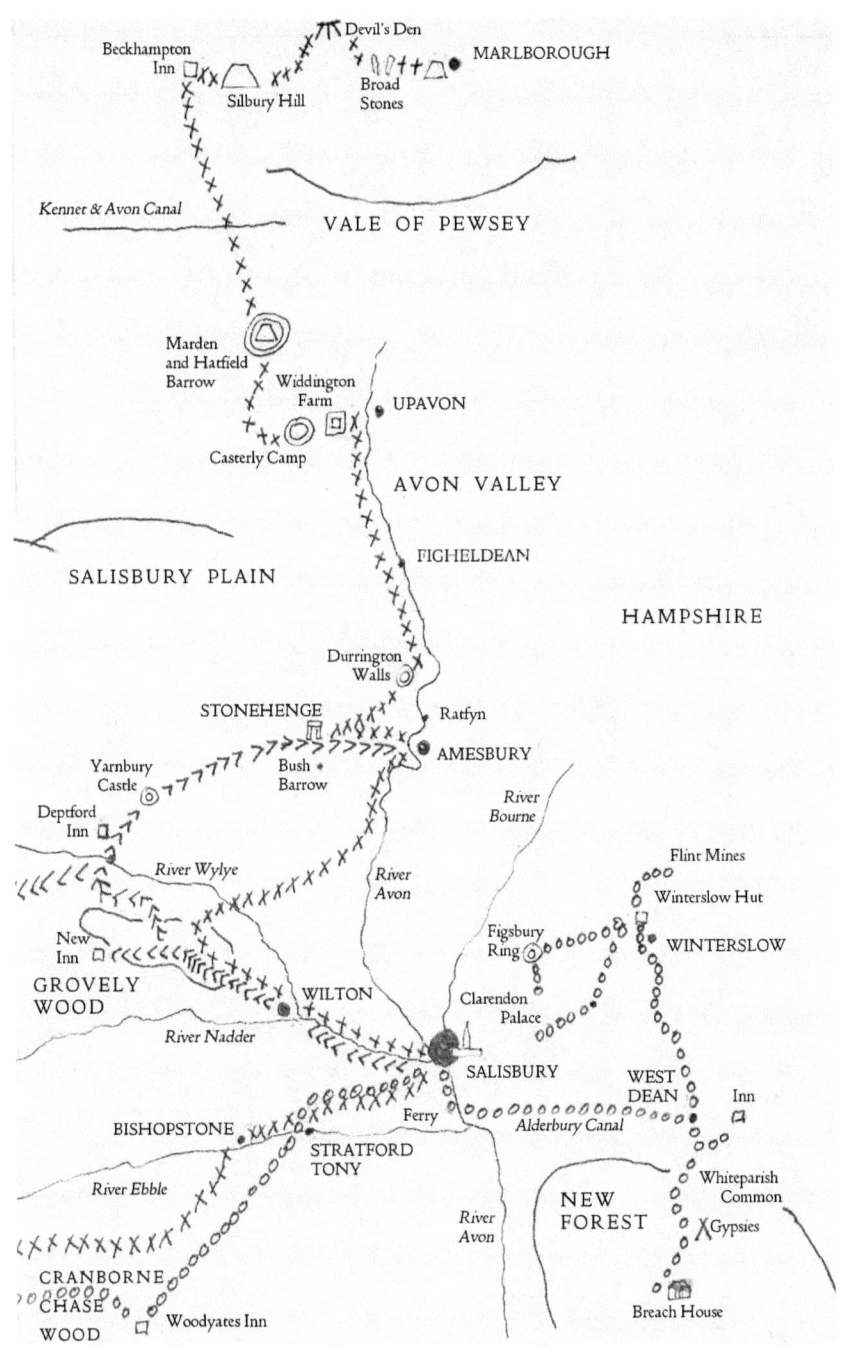

PART ONE

A

TOUR

IN SEARCH OF

CHALK

THROUGH PARTS OF

SOUTH WILTSHIRE

IN

1807

WRITTEN IN

A Series of Letters

ENCOUNTERING ON THE WAY; A CHARCOAL BURNER,

TOGETHER WITH A VISIT TO

STONEHENGE, FONTHILL ABBEY
AND STOURHEAD,

INTERSPERSED WITH VARIOUS ANECDOTES,
ANTIQUARIAN OBSERVATIONS AND BOLD VIEWS ON
THE PREHISTORY OF THIS LAND.

BY

A PEDESTRIAN.

LETTER TO THE EDITOR

As the recipient of the following letters I hold myself entirely responsible for encouraging my young nephew to venture forth on such an undertaking when so inexperienced in life into such uncertainty and danger.

Had I realised that my own recent work; "A Pedestrian Tour of North Wales, 1805" would have inspired my dearest nephew so, I would most definitely have resisted the small vanity that its publication provided. It was with increasing horror that I received and read the steady succession of correspondence knowing the extent of the sham on which his livelihood depended. The knowledgeable reading public will no doubt be aware of the plethora of published journals that proclaim adventures to all parts of our British Isles when in reality their authors set foot no further than visiting the tired accounts of others and in the event of any shortfall let their own limited imaginations complete the task. Let it be known that I am guilty of just such a crime for crime it will be if my own nephew suffers harm on his own naïve quest.

It is with some desperate hope that this publication, in the form of my nephew's letters to myself, will somehow fall into the hands of its young author and remind him of the trust he once placed in me and that in response he might again take up his pen to give even the smallest indication of his wellbeing.

Yours faithfully
J. CHALK
November 1807

Thursday 8th October 1807

MY DEAR UNCLE,

Your surprise in receiving this correspondence can only be matched by my own in the writing of it. I find myself engaged on a pedestrian tour in South Wiltshire and when time permits I will divulge the circumstances which lead to this undertaking but suffice to say it did not suffer long in the formation of a plan. Your own published account of a Tour of North Wales has these past two years been an inspiration for me to leave London and see with my own eyes the world outside that overcrowded and stinking metropolis. I hope one day to follow your own path and visit Lake Bala and Beaumaris and also to ascend Cadir Idris to contemplate the importance of the human race from that great elevation. Now I have before me John Cary's map of Wiltshire that I obtained from a bookseller in Salisbury and across this sheet my own adventures lay in store.

I reason that you will not be offended if I were to record my present activities, whatever they may be, in a series of letters to you my dear uncle and you can do with them what you will. However, I flatter myself indeed that I can compete with you with either the pen or the pencil.

Travelling on the outside of the London to Exeter coach I have suffered the most severest shaking of my life. The inside of the coach being full I shared the roof with a cheerful Irishman and a not so jolly officer who is to sail from Falmouth when conditions permit. From amongst the jostling luggage I had watched Salisbury Cathedral spire grow slowly from the gentle folds in the landscape and with every revolution of the wheels I was willing it to rise up and tower above me knowing that only then by finding myself in its shadow would there be an end to the torture.

Finally we halted in the centre of Salisbury and after sliding down from my perch I found that I could not put one foot in front of the other and my left leg may as well have been constructed of wood such was the use of it, which is not a desirable way to begin life as a pedestrian tourist. The only remedy for this condition is to walk and so, I hope sir, you will forgive me when I tell you that having longed to reach the base of this great gothic spike, I then turned my back on it and purchasing from a bookseller my new map I then stumbled my way out of the city. Surely Mr Camden and lately Mr Britton can furnish you with all the pertinent details regarding Salisbury Cathedral: the height, the width, the length, how many windows and when the spire last caught ablaze etc..etc..etc.. Indeed, I would be more pleased to encounter the quarries themselves from which this rare stone had been won in a county so renowned for its chalk rather than be conducted on a weary tour of the building itself. Please forgive my impertinence for I do not really mean so. I promise to return to Salisbury but I feel as a narrator my spirit should be free to explore the unexplored, to see with new eyes and to record exactly all that I witness. You will know well enough, my dear uncle, that to follow the trail of another over old ground is not the way of the adventurous pedestrian tourist. I may as well sit in the comfort of an old worn armchair and blow the dust from the yellowing pages of the accounts of others before reaching for my pen to concoct my own. That was not your way, nor shall it be mine.

At the miserable landmark that is Fisherton Gaol my thoughts and direction were distracted by the sight of the gibbet, occupied by some poor wretch who by the attentions of various carrion was made to swing and turn gently in the windless evening. Having missed the handpost, I found myself on the road to Wilton rather than my intended destination toward the Avon Valley and Amesbury. At Wilton lies another target for the persevering tourist, Wilton House. Sir, I refer you in advance to Walpoole's New and Complete British

Traveller to acquaint yourself with the complete list of paintings contained within and also to determine exactly which tree Sir Philip Sidney reclined against whilst dreaming of Arcadia. But what kind of account is this that skirts around the obvious and dwells even less on describing the incidental?

I had barely left the city boundaries when I took a fall. I had halted at the entrance to a brickworks to observe a cart load of fresh bricks leaving the yard for the city. Here was the source of the material for those fine new red brick buildings I had just observed in Salisbury. The ruts in the road outside the entrance to this industry had been loosely filled with some large and incommodious nodules of stone and it was amongst these that I first stumbled and then fell, twisting my ankle and grazing the palms of my hands, with the pack on my back adding to the weight of the fall. As I lay there at the side of the road facing downwards, at first not a soul came to my assistance. A dog showed some interest in my pack, sniffing at the cheese and ham and another cart pulled around me. I hauled myself up into a sitting position and inspected my ankle, moving it slowly to and fro and I brushed off the loose grit from my grazed palms. You may wonder, my dear uncle, why I am giving you an account of my fall and its aftermath when surely a fall is a fall is a fall and is to be expected by the pedestrian tourist. It was not the fall that interested me but what made the fall, the large ochreous nodules were, I believe, flint and were in the main rounded and natural looking yet one caught my eye as it was almost porcelaneous in appearance, flattish and very regular in shape like a large flat bottomed leaf. I picked it up and immediately felt the keenness of its edge which extended around all sides, yet the base of the piece was broad and blunt. You will know my amateurish peculiarities when confronted with interesting geological examples and here I sat in the road turning this stone around in my grazed hands noting how it fitted well into the palm as if it had been made so. The next cart out of the pit stopped before me, the heavy horses were blinkered but able to look down on this miserable wretch in the road, obviously wounded in his understanding of the world. The driver held his team back as two passers-by, a man and a boy, cheerfully assisted me to my feet and dusted me off but hastily departed before I could offer them something for their trouble.

Walking was now difficult, but curiosity regarding the provenance of this unusual stone led me to inspect the excavations within the brickworks. The working day was now drawing to a close and a huddle of pan-faced smokers in the yard observed me as I hobbled about the place. I found a pile of flint nodules of the same type that caused my fall and beyond these the pit itself, cut in ledges at different stages of excavation. I could determine the top soil and beneath that perhaps ten feet of earth suitable for the manufacture of bricks. This whole depth concluded on a bed of chalky rubble and on this evidence it seems as though the strata of clay and brickearth lay above the native chalk. A closer examination revealed a seam of the ochreous flint nodules that were obviously deemed superfluous to the brickmaking process and fared little better as road material but here I am certain was the source of the crafted piece that had first caught my ankle and then my attention. As I picked at the face of the excavation, I did not unearth another fashioned flint but instead what seemed like a large and weighty bone that was certainly animal in origin but I had neither the tools or the time to continue with its investigation. With only the benefit of seventeen summers on this earth I do not know the answer to the mystery of how a piece of stone that appears to have been shaped by human design can be buried naturally at such a depth and to lie in combination with animal remains. These are indeed questions for a mind much greater than my own and perhaps I will in time meet such a person, if fate can but arrange it. I then left the brickyard with a vow that I should return someday and study the curious strata in greater detail and also to interview the workmen here to establish whether the brickearth has yielded other faunal remains which even the most unobservant should surely recognise.

I struggled on for a good mile with my ankle now burning and the sun which had been present throughout this long day was now making its departure with spectacular effect. Nothing was deemed too lowly for the great wash of its golden pigment; the grazing beast, an old gatepost and even the tumbled down roadside cott seemed to relish the final benevolence of the day.

I found no small surprise in the way that this small town of Wilton had been given over to the weaving of cloth and carpets. The innkeeper at the Bell Inn, for that is where I now write these pages, informs me that as many as one thousand people are employed in this trade. (I recall your wisdom that landlords are prone to exaggeration so you can make your computations accordingly.)

Certainly the air is thick with the smell of dyes and the acrid stench of the fulling process. My arrival at the Bell Inn near the market place was coincident with an incoming stage and I believe the landlord mistook me for a passenger as he enquired as to my comfort on the journey, for my part I felt in too much discomfort from my fall to correct him. I ate a modest supper of mutton, sitting at a table in the parlour with a couple from Somerset, Mr and Mrs William Handsome, who were irrepressible in their anticipation of a visit to Wilton House in the morning, Mr Andrew Staples, a clothier from Bath on business and Mr Nicholas Cowen, a very tall gentleman from I know not where who seemed to enjoy his pipe before, during and after the meal. I then retired to my room to begin this account of my first day as a pedestrian tourist and thankful for the speed that I am able to write, one blessing available to the simple clerk. I will bid you goodnight my dear uncle but before I am able to sleep I intend to seek out the landlady to see if a little laudanum will relieve the painful throbbing in my ankle.

Your ever faithful nephew and servant

HENRY CHALK

P.S Having no notion of the hour but finding that I am caught somewhere between sleep and waking dreams I have relit the candle and again taken up my pen. My ankle pains me still even after the draught which only seems to have brought about wild and cataclysmic visions. I have been dreaming of great seas washing across a wild landscape and as tides recede, all at a furious pace, huge rivers converge to shift and scour the hillsides with alternating warmth and great coldness yet this seems like no biblical catastrophe presided over by an angry God, these are natural forces at work. I sense that these horrifying events are somehow of this place and have occurred at a junction of river valleys that are now gentle and subdued but it was not always so. Somewhere in this tumult I saw my flint nodule repeatedly turning through the air, cutting skin, flesh and sinew, the edges bloody, the nodule then falls into clear water the blood reeling away in pale red ribbons with the flow of the river until the silt blows across the stony bed and its shape is lost. I want to retrieve the piece from my pocket to see that it is not lost but my eyes are straining and I must close them.

Friday 9th October 1807

MY DEAR UNCLE,

I realise now how thoughtless I must appear having not enquired after your health when I have selfishly dedicated pages to my own circumstances, although perhaps it is the nature of the traveller to be absorbed so. As I write these words I am crouched in a woodland clearing where a primitive of times unrecorded would feel at home. Indeed, it is as if I have been thrown back into an age where the luxuries of modern life have not yet even been imagined. But I am jumping ahead of myself and must begin the day at the Bell Inn when after breakfast on reaching for my purse to pay for my accommodation I found it not about my person. I searched my pack and the room but all to no avail. I can think of only one circumstance when this loss could have occurred and I believe that it was the event of my fall yesterday evening and more particularly the assistance offered by the man and boy who so cheerfully helped me to my feet and it appears cheerfully helped themselves to my purse. Their hasty departure should have alerted me and the moment having passed I can only make a lesson of it for the future. I am again indebted to you my dear uncle for I followed your example of keeping safe a single guinea piece for just such a disaster.

Unwisely it seems, I confided in the landlord that my pocket had been picked the previous day which combined with the fall was ill luck for this pedestrian tourist. His already landlordish complexion grew more so until I produced the guinea piece but he made it clear that that he was not disposed to pedestrian tourists and had he realised that I had not arrived aboard last evening's mail then no room would have been made available and he bid me a "Good marnin' young zur".

However before departing I submitted yesterday's letter for posting and sought out the maid and tipped her one shilling as you instructed in your journal but "boots" was nowhere to be found and I spent his sixpence on a loaf of bread from the bakery in the town.

The streets were teaming with the comings and goings of those connected with the cloth and carpet industry, dyers with their overshirts flecked with every hue and wagons stacked high with woolsacks turning slowly at the crossroads. The broad burr of Wiltshire voices could be heard from the greetings and partings of workmen and gentlemen alike, much different to the harsher London tongue of which I must class my own speech. With my ankle swollen, but at this stage in a tolerable condition for slow walking, I made my way along West Street. I had already decided, after an earlier consultation with Mr Cary's map, to explore a tract of woodland called Grovely and see whether autumn had yet taken a grip, with a desire to be free of the hustle and bustle of even this small town of Wilton as it puts in mind too much of aspects of London.

A pedestrian is able to pass through a tollgate without expense and has the pleasure of being able to walk on a good road for nothing. As I exchanged the time of day with the gatekeeper I wondered whether my simple form of travel would one day become an acceptable pursuit and so the landlord at the Bell Inn, for the sake of his livelihood, would have to amend this prejudice and welcome the pedestrian tourists. It is certainly the best way to witness every passing detail for as I climbed up towards the wood I was amazed at the industry of the spiders here with their webs binding the hedgerows, each delicate thread glistening and sagging under the weight of the morning dew. Flocks of birds I feel ashamed that I cannot name were massing out on the stubble fields, feeding on the remnants of the harvest until as one they would turn their attentions to the wayside bushes that glowed red with berries and squabble over these until another charge is called and back to the fields they go. I told myself that I had no right to be so full of cheer as I hobbled on with the sun at my back and I even began to sing aloud to the spiders and the unnamed flocks. As I entered the shadows of Grovely my ankle again pained me greatly and I now followed uneven woodland trails with many halts along the way. At every turn grew regular clumps of the same bush, these stunted trees had no one single trunk but many straight shiny brown rods that looked ideally suited to providing me with a walking support. I clambered in amongst one of these trackside bushes and as I was in the act of twisting and thrashing one such pole in an attempt to detach it, I heard a loud curse from behind me. I turned at once to find a small man whose skin was so darkened with grime that one may have mistaken him for a chimney sweep, although we were some distance from the nearest chimney. I could see by his agitation that he was not pleased by my actions although he might have been speaking another language as I could not comprehend a single word he uttered. I explained my own predicament but the little man appeared to be equally uncomprehending, I then hopped on my good leg until I eventually tumbled over and sat on the soft forest floor. The man grunted at my lame demonstration before setting down his large leather bag and from beneath his coat he produced a heavy hooked knife and with a few swift blows in the midst of the bush he extracted a stick with a fork at one end and a curious barley twist in the middle. I hauled myself to my feet and received the walking stick and it was indeed a handsome aid for any man with my thumb fitting perfectly into the cleft at the top. I thanked him and he nodded approvingly but did not stand aside to let me pass, instead he rubbed his thumb and forefinger together before my face. I was happy to pay for my new stick out of my diminished funds but in temporarily giving up my support to reach into my pocket I again lost my balance and returned to the forest floor but on this occasion I cried out in pain for I had tried to put weight on my weak ankle. The man from the woods gestured for me to remove my boot and stocking and the swelling was plain to see. He then gathered up my boot and stocking and slung his own bag across his shoulder and hauled me upright. Supporting me with a strong arm he indicated the direction we were to follow and although not of great stature I felt his immense strength as he guided me between the stunted bushes. His hands are large and blackened and have seen a lifetime of rough work and he has a strong odour of bonfires and soot about his person. After some labouring by my human support and some helplessness on my part we approached a clearing in the wood and the trade of my new acquaintance became apparent, he is a charcoal burner and all about lay evidence of his woodland craft. My dear uncle, I must now set down my pen for I have a curious duty to perform at the request of my host which in time I will describe.

*

Having now brought me to his camp I sensed that the little man was now ill at ease and knew not what to do with me. In the centre of the encampment was positioned a large smoking heap that I took to be charcoal in the making and he began the business of tidying and tending to his livelihood but would then falter and look about to where I sat observing his every action out of my own curiosity. In time a boy appeared of perhaps ten years of age who shared the same grimy countenance and viewed me with equal suspicion from across the woodland clearing. The charcoal burner now departed and the boy began a task of tying up bundles of small branches and stacking them aboard a cart. I could do little but take out my writing set and all was silence in the camp save for birdsong and the nearby rustlings of small woodland creatures. In time the master of the smouldering heap reappeared and in seeing me at my writing scurried away to his primitive hut and returned with a book which he took no time in pressing towards me. I took the volume and opened the cover and to my surprise I found it to be "Robinson Crusoe". The little man

stabbed his short, blackened finger at the illustration in the frontispiece
of Robinson and his negro Friday on the shores of the desert island. It
is a book that I read not a year ago and the story was still with me, so
striking was the adventure and the telling of it. After my inspection
I was for returning the book but the charcoal burner made it very
apparent that he expected me to relate this tale to him on the spot with
his face a picture of anticipation. Having no other tasks to perform
with my ankle not permitting any further distance I put aside my pen
and began to read aloud the tale of Robinson Crusoe. I had not read
more than a single page when this small man's dirty and furrowed
brow knitted together as it had when we first met and I knew this
to be a clear indication of his dissatisfaction. I gathered that he was
not comprehending the words or language or even my own unfamiliar
speech and so I began to recite slower and with more plainness but still
the man grew restless. As the story was fresh in my mind, I decided to
take a different action and make a simpler model and even a drama of
it as best I could. With the volume in my left hand to remind me of the
order of the tale and importantly I believed to give the impression of
recitation from the book to its unlikely owner and so I began.

My dear uncle, you will well remember the tale yourself and I
shall not repeat it here save for the moments when I judged the success
of my dramatics by the interest on the faces of my audience of two, for
the boy had now abandoned his work to stand open mouthed beside
his master. After leaving Hull, Robinson first encounters the full force
of the sea and sorely regrets his actions and for not heeding his father's
pleas to remain at home. Of the severe storm at Yarmouth when the
ship is at anchor and the captain prays with the crew for their very
lives and they are saved while the ship flounders. You will well imagine
my actions of wind, storm and boiling seas for the more I made of it
the wider grew the eyes of man and boy. How long I continued in
this manner I do not know until I required a rest from it and placed a

fallen leaf between the paper leaves to keep place and closed the book. Both were vocal in their resistance to this halt in the proceedings but I explained that it could not be done at one sitting and there were many pages to follow and a fellow must keep his strength up by eating and drinking. I shared with my new companions my bread, cheese and ham and with little hesitation they devoured all my carried provisions offering me in return a hard, flat and tasteless substance that I believe is called "barley bannock". They also drank deeply from an old flagon which Tam then passed on to me and I found it to be a sour beer, of which I drank little.

There is now an opportunity while the smouldering heap receives further attention with the careful adjustment of the surrounding lattice wooden panels that screen an almost imperceptible wind from affecting this slow conflagration and in this interval, I can again take up my pen. I would dearly like to be able to give some account of the language of these people for the man has I sense an impediment to his speech where he cannot make a word without forming a straining from his nose which is an affliction that must have caused him great difficulty for all of his life. The boy though appears to understand his master's every command whilst he himself is all "burrs" and "aarhs", as I find customary here in South Wiltshire, with words that I can hear but do not always comprehend for there must be a local vocabulary. I sense that I will be required shortly to resume the tale of Robinson Crusoe and I cannot disguise my enjoyment of this role and the effects that my words and actions are bringing to these Wiltshire faces. I should also like, if the opportunity permits, to try out my skills with my pencil to see if I can capture this woodland scene for it is filled with interest and there is a tidiness and order here that belies the appearance of its blackened occupants. I find myself of a sudden in a stranger's world and I can do little to affect the situation and I know not where I shall sleep this very night for I cannot leave even if I wish it, which I do not,

and I am content to open my eyes and mind and become myself a part
of this place.

*

Having just eaten the greasiest of stews I can now report, my dear
uncle, that I am no longer in the heart of Grovely wood but that I
have been installed in the lowliest of inns which makes the Bell Inn
at Wilton appear a most respectable establishment. As dusk began to
creep in amongst the trees the charcoal burner signalled that I must
leave the woods and at first I did not know to what destination. I
then departed with the boy aboard a horse and cart on a journey along
woodland tracks. As we rattled along, I established that the boy's
name is Tam and his master's name is Peter Winter. I told him my
name and from thereon he referred to me as "Master 'Enry". There
were strange hootings that Tam explained as being "a nowl" and
he mimicked this earie sound exactly causing great confusion with
the originator of the call and, I suspect, with any other nowls in the
district. In time we emerged into open country with the great wood at
our backs. The evening was cold and clear and the sinking sun made
a great blood red mess above the distant tree cloaked hills across the
valley with the clouds all scratched and torn about. Interrupting the
far horizon I noted a structure, perhaps a spire or tower that must
be of some considerable height to announce its presence from such a
distance. When asked to identify this curiosity Tam shrugged his
shoulders and then whistled merrily until we reached our destination,
a low building beside a trackway with blue woodsmoke creeping up
pencil straight from its chimney. Before I could climb down from the
cart Tam had already entered the place and explained my circumstances
to the landlord. An old board on the face of the building named this
establishment "The New Inn" which I could just read in the failing
light and it is indeed not a new inn at all. After a consultation with Mr
Cary's map I see that its position is recorded to the south of Grovely

wood and as a consequence I now have some idea of the position of
Peter Winter's camp. Tam unloaded the "vaggits" of bundled wood
that he had prepared earlier and was soon departing back up the track.

"Boi master 'Enry, oil zee thee n' the marnin'," called out the
boy, over his shoulder.

My accommodation takes the form of a small loft, situated
directly above the parlour and it was with great difficulty that I
negotiated the vertical ladder with my ankle still painful and weak.
The loft has a narrow cot on one side and a shuttered window on the
other and through the gaps in the bare boards I could see the activity
below in the parlour. Supper was served in this room below and I have
already remarked as to the content of my evening meal. I sat at the
only table in the place and around the walls sat men on benches dressed
in long overshirts with pots of ale in hand, fuming on long clay pipes
which they had jammed between their whiskers. I gauged that my
presence in this building was a source of great amusement, sitting as
I was in my London clothes, for there were many nods and glances in
my direction from these fellows and some laughter also. I judged that
this place was like a stable, not for horses but for rough countrymen
and workers of the land for there was straw spread about the floor
and it mingled with the mud from these working men's boots. After
the completion of my meal I knew not what to do other than to retire
to my loft for the night and again take up my pen. I am sitting upon
the course grey blankets of my cot and I hold a great apprehension as
to what I might find between them when I muster the courage to lay
down for the night. I have spied a small hole in the roof tiles that frames
a bright half moon and there is a growing coldness in this place to
which I am bracing myself for a desperate night. I recall from earlier in
the day the tale of Robinson Crusoe who regretted on many occasions
the loss of his family and home and that steady middle ground through
life that his father did his utmost to guide him towards, rather than

the peaks and troughs of adventure. As you are only too aware sir, my parents are no longer of this earth yet I could still take that middle ground that my father, your brother, would have dearly wished for me.

I shall now prepare for bed and wish you a goodnight my dear uncle in the hope that you will not tire of the accounts of my deeds, as I fear there is no other possible recipient for my scribbles.

Your faithful and errant Nephew
HENRY CHALK

P.S.

I fear that I must test your patience further with this postscript.

I have in my hand your own publication of "A Tour of North Wales 1805" which has greatly informed and inspired in equal measure. I refer to your comments on the essential preparations required for such an excursion, and an item that you consider indispensable, "a crisply starched white nightshirt". As always, I have followed your advice with strict attention and having dressed for bed I stood holding the candle before me and looked about the place and also down at myself. Here I am in this damp and dirty loft, in this world where whiteness plays no part, enveloped in rank tobacco smoke from the parlour below and about to enter between grey and filthy bedding. I can inform you that I am standing in my nightshirt, shining as brightly as if I were a visitation of the Angel Gabriel himself. I sincerely intend no blasphemy sir, but it is a situation that has warmed my heart and brought me no small amusement, for which I thank you.

Saturday 10th October 1807

My dear Uncle,

I awoke before day break with the crowing of a cockerel in the yard and dogs barking also. In the night I dressed myself in my day clothes and returned to bed in the hope that I might become warmer but if I am to stay another night here, I will demand more of these filthy blankets. After hearing movement downstairs and the crackling of a new fire in the grate I arose and descended carefully with my ankle not yet repaired and warmed myself for some minutes before the blaze. Presently I drew a pail of cold water from the well and carried out my ablutions as best I could and I am still required to use my new stick for even these smallest of tasks. There has been no indication of how I should break my fast although I can report that I have drunk a cup of milk that was still warm from the brown cow that appears to wander freely here. At first I thought it content to browse from the hedges and eat whatever grass exists beside the muddy track although as the boy heaved the hay down from the loft above the stable, the beast has grown wise to this event and now feasts contentedly on the horse's breakfast. The chickens are picking and scratching out on the track below my window and here comes "cock-a-doodle-do" who has just trampled on the back of one poor bird, to which she took great offence in clucking noisily and flustering her feathers back into order. The stable boy has now spied the antics of the brown cow and has slapped its rump to drive it away from the stable door with a loud curse. Observing life from the open shutters of my loft here at the New Inn is not without interest but I should like to be reunited with Peter Winter and the boy Tam as I feel a kinship growing which I cannot readily explain. I am curious also as to how a simple woodsman can possess a book that he can never hope to read yet he appears to derive some pleasure from my foolish rendition. I believe it is a grave mistake to underestimate any man for they are always sure to surprise.

*

I am now sitting near the smouldering heap in Peter Winter's camp for Tam was true to his word and appeared at the New Inn to fill up the water barrel on his cart from the well and we slowly rolled back up into the shadows of Grovely, with the water slapping against the insides of the barrel. Tam has informed me that his mother's sister is the landlady of that inn to which he supplies the "vaggits" of bound wood in return for milk and eggs. In a blackened bowl I have just eaten a meal of "mushroons n' cheddies" of which the former are gathered from the fields nearby and the latter is but the simple potato. It was a warming dish if not providing much taste to the palate and I was thankful for it. I was fully prepared to read aloud Peter's book but both he and Tam are busy at their tasks. The boy is sat with a heavy hooked knife cutting these walking stick poles along their lengths to produce bundles of these "zpars", as he has named them. Tam then made the shape of a roof with his hands to indicate their purpose and perhaps they are used to affix the shaggy straw that is so common hereabouts.

I have a series of small bites about my skin which I can only attribute to those "dancing legions of the night" to which you so eloquently refer on your travels in North Wales. I can confirm that they also abide in great number at the New Inn. Peter has gestured for me to join him aboard the horse and cart and I shall not keep him waiting.

*

Our destination was unclear, but I was content to observe the many activities that take place within this great wood. There are a minority of other charcoal burners at large here with their own smouldering heaps and some that have reached an advanced stage of production where the finished charcoal has cooled sufficiently for it to be exported from the wood. I saw no heaps as yet unburned and I am wondering that the charcoal burning season in Grovely is almost at an end. It appears that charcoal production is not the primary task of these woodsmen for their skills are many and indeed the woven panels are stacked high in these clearings and must be in great demand as pens and fences. There is one industry here of which I cannot establish a purpose and that is the stripping of bark from certain trees and it appears as though it is the bark itself that is the important commodity and not the timber. This bark is then loaded high in great wagons and taken I know not where and it is on these occasions that my inability to understand Peter Winter's grunted explanations that frustrates. We passed a wooden hut that was fully draped with the dead carcasses of birds and small mammals and on this occasion we halted. Peter then took a bulging sack from our cart and emptied it at the feet of the occupant of this morbid dwelling and amongst this pile of unfortunate creatures were a number of the red bushy tailed tree rats that I had watched with great fascination during my short time within this wood. In a flash from their position on the ground they could ascend to any position and pass from branch to branch and tree to tree as swiftly as any bird on the wing. A count was now made of all these limp and lifeless corpses and with some form of agreement settled upon we were again on our way.

At the far edge of the wood, where a long ditch seems to mark the boundary between Grovely and the outside world, we again halted and Peter gestured for me to disembark also. He then took a digging tool and entered a deep pit and I observed from above his hacking and scraping at the ground. From this thick reddish brown soil, Peter prized out a number of large irregular flints which he then hurled in my direction. I did not realise his purpose as he sat down on a timber out of the shadow of the wood and from the bottomless pocket of his black coat he withdrew a small hammer wrapped in a piece of course leather. He then draped the leather across his lap and began striking these nodules with the hammer. I sat down beside Peter Winter and noted that he was smiling to himself, seemingly enjoying the mystery and knowing now my curiosity and hunger for explanation. With sharp taps of his hammer he first quartered the blocks and I could see how the leather was required for protection against this action. With further deft blows and with a great speed that he employs in all his activities, the pieces were reduced further until they resembled the size and form of a segment of an orange. Peter then turned his hammer to utilise the pointed end and struck a careful blow to this segment, detaching a small flint wedge which he then held up for my inspection. To emphasize its purpose, he mimed the aiming and firing of a gun and then laughed whilst I acknowledged that I now understood that his many skills extended to the production of gunflints. The charcoal burner indicated that this was not the finished article as there was further trimming required but for now Peter dropped the piece into a bag and the spent orange segment was tossed to the ground. I now realised my part in this procedure as Peter again reached into his coat pocket and produced Robinson Crusoe and I had for competition the splitting of flint ringing about my ears.

There was a further distraction happening in the open field where a gang of labourers were digging a great pit from which cart loads of fresh white chalk was being extracted and spread about the surface of this field. The rich brown clay soil, the same as was clinging to Peter's flint nodules, had been drawn to the sides to gain access to the underlying chalk and I would have dearly liked an explanation on this matter. Peter simply shrugged when asked, as if what went on beyond the bounds of Grovely was of little concern to him. The sight of this bright white substance in the morning sun took my mind further away from the desert island and to the instance of the digging of the great well in the brewery yard in Southwark. It is perhaps the occasion of the last contact between us sir before this current flood of correspondence and you will recall, at that time, my eager anticipation of this project for it was indeed undertaken at my suggestion. You will I hope forgive me, my dear uncle, if I now inform you of the circumstances of the digging of the great well as it prays on my mind often for it was completed shortly before the death of my father, your only brother. I somehow believe that it is chalk that has guided my destiny and it is perhaps a quest for chalk that has brought me here to Wiltshire. You will I gauge believe these to be foolish words from a foolish youth but please, I pray, firstly let me attempt to justify these words and my actions by explanation.

I believe I told you of the contamination suffered to the water at the brewery from the old shallow well and the need to somehow remedy the situation. On my visits to the British Library I found a publication by the Board of Agriculture relating in part to the digging of wells and I proposed this to my father as a solution. I warned of the great depth that would be necessary, perhaps as much as six hundred feet, and I made calculations as to the cost of materials and labour and these he then presented to the bank. It was surely a great investment as no other brewery in London would have such a fine source of water and beer is not a commodity that will decline in its public demand. The bank deemed it a sound proposal and work commenced immediately. Two men were employed to the task and cart upon cart load of London bricks were required to line the well and mountains of spoil were drawn up and hauled away from this core into the earth beneath London. At any opportunity I would leave my desk to observe the changing nature of this extracted material as it appeared, with month upon month of sand, gravel and clay. Despite my calculations as to the depth and cost of this operation my father became more agitated with every passing week and would then scold me for suggesting such a venture. I recall the afternoon when my father was on a visit to the bank and I was able to stare from the office window and noted how the spoil had changed from a pale clay slop to great pure white lumps of chalk and of a sudden this brightness made the yard an exceedingly dull and dirty place. I ran down the steps to inspect this magic white material, tipping out the buckets and pushing around in the heap and I cared not that my hands, boots and clothes became white in an instant. It was at this moment that my father returned to the brewery with a representative from the bank to assess the progress of the investment. I shall not forget the look on my father's face if I live to be one hundred years, to find his only son and heir at play in a spoil heap, covered from top to toe in chalk dust when he should have been working at his desk. As my father trembled with rage the gentleman from the bank merely shook his head as if he were witnessing the antics of a simpleton.

"In name and nature, Master Chalk," he said solemnly.

I will not recount the extent of my punishment save to say that no effort was spared, with the lesson that I must be fixed in my ambition to one day be the owner of a fine brewery and not a simple labourer. I was also forbidden my weekly visit to the British Library which pained me more that any beating. As the weeks passed my father only addressed me on matters of business where my duties as a clerk demanded his attention and I dared not go near the well, even in his absence, least I should get a speck of this chalk on my clothes or shoes.

You will imagine my frustrations when water was finally reached. At first there were raised voices of alarm as the excavator of the well signalled that he should be drawn up at once and it was feared that he would be drowned in the cradle such was the ferocity of the water emerging from the deep. In only three hours the water rose to more than three hundred feet and over the next two days it rose one foot in the hour. The relief on my father's face was palpable as his deepening investment finally bore its rewards and Chalk's beer could now be renowned for its purity above all other London breweries. At no time did he give any recognition that it had been my idea or did he permit me to join the cheering and celebration in the yard.

If my handwriting trembles it is not through the telling of this tale but of the cold here at the New Inn. The candlelight flickers in the gentle night breeze as there is little to halt its progress as it passes through this building.

I must return to the travails of the one-legged pedestrian tourist as I left him near the dank flint pit with Robinson Crusoe in hand if not in mind. Whilst Peter Winter filled his bag with gunflints, I did my best with the book but was sorely distracted by the activity before me, the piles of chalk in the field and my own wandering thoughts. At one time I put my hand in my coat pocket and felt the fashioned flint from the brickearth pit near Salisbury. I pulled it out, half in the hope that it might draw Peter's attention away from the activities of the castaway which indeed it did. He demanded to view it and turned it around slowly in his hand, the dark brows converged as the storm clouds gathered but not in anger or frustration on this occasion, only I believe, out of curiosity. I carefully relayed the details of its provenance, not knowing how much of this information would interest the charcoal burner. All the while he turned it around in his hand and held it for a moment between thumb and forefinger then moving it from side to side. In an instant he was back in the pit and returned having prized out another flint nodule. He then embarked on the same reduction process as before but on this occasion he stopped short of reaching the orange segment and instead worked on a larger, flatter piece. One attempt was flung to the ground with a loud grunt but the second proved more successful and he then worked around the circumference of the shape, striking small shards of flint from both faces. Whilst Peter was engaged in this work, I hobbled about to get the blood moving in my limbs. Littering the soil all around the pit amongst the autumn stubble were the discarded orange segments from previous gun flint manufacture. Some were as dark and fresh looking as those of today yet many were clouded, perhaps affected by weather and the passing of time. These may be the residue of gunflint workers from earlier generations and I do not know how long it takes for broken flint to turn from dark to cloudy. Peter held up the finished piece for my inspection and immediately returned to his gunflints as if enough time had been wasted already. It was slightly smaller than my original but cleverly made and fiercely sharp. He snatched it back and easily cut through the corner of his leather protector to prove its efficiency. He smiled at the success of his craftsmanship and then returned it with a nod towards Robinson Crusoe to which I could only agree to oblige.

I feel that as long as I keep the pen in my hand, I will not have to enter between those dreaded blankets but I sense a heaviness in my eyelids. I must relate also that from our position at the edge of Grovely wood near the flint pit and beyond where the workers dug into the field, lay in the distance a great tract of land that Mr Cary's map confirms as Salisbury Plain. It is an open vista on such a grand scale that I have never before witnessed. When my ankle is repaired, and it feels better with each passing day, I shall set my coat tails and enter upon its gently rolling surface in search of that lost island they call Stonehenge. I believe, my dear uncle, that Mr Robinson Crusoe has greatly affected my mind for I now see water where there is only land. Sir, I bid you a cold and scratchy goodnight.

Your faithful nephew
HENRY CHALK

Sunday 11th October 1807

MY DEAR UNCLE,

I have cabin fever for I am confined to the environs of the New Inn. Tam again kindly returned me to my lodgings here last evening yet as we parted I recall now that he made no reference to a meeting today. It is after all the Lord's Day but without my woodland friends, time passes slowly. I have hobbled about this place observing the occasional passer-by and I feel like some wayside simpleton who has no other task to perform. I have drawn this building as it is not without interest as a simple establishment but the light is poor and there has been rain with the clouds as grey and dirty as the blankets in my loft.

I can report sir that last night did not pass without some drama and surprise. The parlour was full of noise and rising tobacco smoke which did choke me and after attempting sleep I resolved to remove to the hay loft above the stables where I gauged I may have a warmer and more peaceful slumber. I know not at what hour but I was awoken at first by dogs barking and then by voices in the empty stall below. In a lamp's light I observed two men, who were earlier this very evening in the parlour and indeed were now heavily influenced by liquor, as they struggled between them with the carcass of a large deer. With one end of a rope attached to its hind legs, the other was then cast over a beam and with great exertion the two men eventually managed to raise and suspend upside down the unfortunate beast. The stable door was closed yet evidently with a third character outside on the track keeping watch. There then began a display of intoxicated butchery which my eyes were drawn to observe for not being one to turn from the sight of such things. With a freshly whetted blade, the first man, who had now removed his long shirt and under shirt, placed the horse's water bucket beneath the animal's head and then slit its throat. As the pail filled with the steady flow of thick dark red blood he stood back and the two men passed a flagon between them. The butcher then returned to the task and made a deep incision into the belly of the beast with the second character stood behind the carcass to hold it as steady as a drunken man was able. The three-quarter full pail was removed and the first man, with his bare hands, began to scoop out the innards onto the straw below and of a sudden there was a bang on the stable door. The lamp was fumbled for by the second man who in doing so released the deer to swing forward and strike the butcher who already had his hands full with knife and entrails who then tumbled over backwards to the floor. The voice from outside reassured the two men that all was well and there followed a succession of curses from inside the stable that I could neither fully understand nor wish to repeat. In summary however it was agreed that "stoopid Mart'n ee did vall azleep agin' thik dur". The animal was then crudely skinned and the apportioning of the meat began. At one stage I sensed that I would sneeze from the dust in the hayloft but I kept as silent as I could for fear of discovery as I knew not what these drunken men would do to me if they but realised that there was a witness to their criminality. My dear uncle, I only relate this event to you in the strictest confidence for as I was contemplating on the penalties that would befall these deer stealers if apprehended, I felt a chill at the mention of a name known to me. It was evident that these characters were to meet young Tam at a prearranged location, to only one end that I could perceive and that was the passing on of illicit meat. One parcel of venison was concealed in a dark corner of the stable and I began to suspect that everyone from the landlord to the stable boy was to benefit from the oversight of this night-time butchery. Even the dogs here at the New Inn were complicit in removing the evidence as they were finally let in to clean up the entrails from where they lay in the straw. The men departed and I heard a cart draw way. I wondered at my own position, should I attempt to return to my bed and perhaps alarm the household or should I remain in the stable and risk detection in the morning? I must have spent too long considering this issue for the next I knew the stable boy had thrown open the doors of the hay loft and I awoke to see the surprise on his face and his readiness to pierce me with the long fork. I explained to the boy that I could not sleep in the inn for it was too noisy and that I had had a very comfortable and warm nights rest. The stable boy viewed me with caution as I could not have failed to witness the proceedings during the night. The landlord beckoned me as I was at the well and asked if I had "Zlept zur?". He is a nervous man with a quick eye and a strong odour of onions about his person. I replied that I had never slept better, which was indeed true, and that this evening I would be looking forward to a hearty meal. At my response the landlord smiled weakly and retreated swiftly from whence he came. Perhaps I am playing a dangerous game but I feel that it is very much in the spirit of this place and I have received enough thin and greasy stews to date.

*

My words to the landlord did not go unheeded for when I sat at the table in the empty parlour, my greasy stew was supplemented by a moderate portion of the illicit meat. The cook had somehow contrived a toughness that gave considerable exercise to the jaw and teeth but I welcomed the challenge nevertheless. I had barely pushed aside my plate when there was a knock at the door to which the landlord feigned some alarm. It was apparently a visit from the parish constable who took a deliberate look about the place to ensure that the sanctity of the Lord's Day was being observed. Having satisfied himself in this respect he then confirmed with the landlord that I was indeed a guest and was therefore entitled to enjoy the custom at the New Inn on this day. After clearing his throat this lean gentleman, who did not wear

The Charcoal Burner

The New Inn

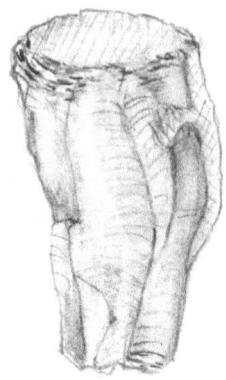

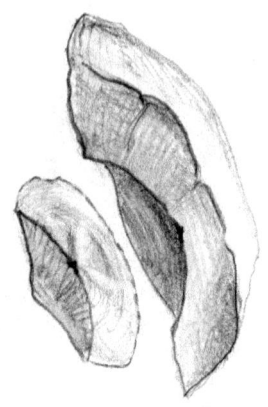

Flint Nodule,
Stourton

Gunflint, Grovely Pit

Flint Butchery Tool, Fisherton Brickearth

the ubiquitous embroidered overshirt but instead a simple black coat, then presented himself before the solitary table to address me in person.

"Zur, gent'man zur," began the constable, "you wud be the gent'man zur thas been abroard n' the wud zur?"

I introduced myself and explained my purpose as a pedestrian tourist and my predicament also, having taken a fall and was therefore resting until sufficiently recovered to continue. This information was greeted with the blankest of blank expressions.

"Yus zur, n' I spec youm be makin' yur way presently, beggin' yur pardon zur?"

I could only imagine that this apparent contrivance had been at the initiation of the sly landlord, as he had not the wit to be discreet in his surprise and simply nodded his agreement to the parish official's every word. I informed both gentlemen that I would indeed be departing in the morning and I felt that there was little to be gained from any form of protest. I do feel, my dear uncle, that I shall be able to make some slow progress tomorrow and it will be a relief to vacate the New Inn. Having carried out his duty the parish constable was then invited to stay for a pot of beer, to which he feigned persuasion, whilst I excused myself to take the air outside in the lane before I retired. I shall lay fully clothed on my cot for this my final slumber as I do not wish to provide easy nourishment for those "dancing legions of the night". In the parlour below I can still hear the low rumble of conversation and through the gap in the floorboards I have witnessed the landlord presenting the parish constable with a small package, which he quickly secreted in his coat pocket.

I would like to make acquaintance again with Peter Winter and the boy Tam before I depart from Grovely. I shall have to forsake Robinson Crusoe, marooned still on his desert island but I do not feel that the charcoal burner is concerned with the book's completion. He requests over again the same passages; the shipwreck, the discovery of Man Friday and any episodes with the firing of muskets and the hunting of foul or game.

I shall now bid you a goodnight and I hope tomorrow to be able to post the accumulated pages of correspondence that will, I fear, now arrive in one large flood rather than a steady trickle.

Your faithful and repaired Nephew
HENRY CHALK

Monday morning 12th October 1807.

SIR

It is now the following morning and I have a little time available before sealing my correspondence and I shall therefore continue whilst I can. Tam arrived at the New Inn with a cart load of "vaggits" and kindly transported me to Peter Winter's camp in Grovely, as I desired. You will not be surprised to learn sir, that neither he nor I made reference to the activities late on Saturday night. He will depart shortly to Wilton where he has agreed to meet the post. I opened my shutters at daybreak to witness a pack of hounds as they made their approach to the inn led by their master and another gentleman, dressed for the business in hand in their scarlet hunting jackets. The landlord brought out two pots of ale for these gentlemen who remained mounted whilst the steaming dogs with their tails wagging descended into the murky pond that lies to the side of that place. The master, on his necessarily large steed, was cursing loudly a gentleman called Mr Beckford who would not it seems permit hunting on his land.

"If the abominable fellow would only let us across his acres, we'd have a straight run through to Wardour."

The second gentleman then speculated on how many foxes found safe harbour in this forbidden territory and they both drained their pots with a grimace and a curse at the sourness of the ale. The master blew his horn and the whole noisy affair continued on its way with the pack responding with yelps of pleasure at their morning exercise. I then settled up with the obsequious landlord and felt under no obligation to leave a tip, with a promise to myself never to return to that place.

We did not proceed on our usual route into Grovely but instead we continued along the trackway to the south of the woodland for some distance. In time at a crossing of the tracks and where a milestone was situated, we turned and began our slow climb for every way into the wood requires an ascent. Before the fringe of woodland was reached, Tam instructed the horse to halt and he jumped down and carried with him a woven basket. At first I could not see his purpose until, amongst the longer tufts of grass, he plucked out a number of the field fruits called "mushroons" and laid them in his basket. I joined him in this task and he indicated which were desirable. The best have a flat creamy top with their undersides a flesh pink and they have a freshness in smell that makes the juices run in the mouth. Tam picked more than could possibly be eaten at one sitting and he informed me that he transports them to Wilton where he has some demand there. As we moved from tuft to tuft, I noted that there were many rabbit throws across this open grassland and amongst these black soil heaps lay a quantity of broken pottery pieces. I indicated as much to Tam who calls them "panshards" and I pocketed an assortment and in addition I collected also some small coinage which when scraped clean has a silver appearance. Once I had established these signs of former occupation, I recognised that there were many banks, hollows and sub-divisions all across these slopes on this southern aspect. It is an area that Tam refers to as "Amshill".

As Peter Winter returns to the camp from viewing his traps, so Tam can now depart to Wilton, for there must always be one of the pair in attendance to safeguard the smouldering heap least it should misbehave. I must seal my letter and bid you good morning my dear uncle. I fear my ink runs low and my well is near dry.

Monday afternoon 12th October 1807

MY DEAR UNCLE,

I am on the move once more. My walking companion is my thumbstick and the stimulation of thought and slow pedestrianism is the perfect pace to view and ponder. My ankle is tolerable and today I have walked the farthest yet since my first shaky steps in this county. I have had many halts along the way but it suits me so as there is no urgency to my ramble and it will take more days yet before I am fully repaired. I am careful where I place my feet least I should turn my ankle again, which would be nothing short of a disaster. Peter Winter has shown me how I should strap it up to walk and I shall repeat this method until I feel no discomfort and it is strong once more.

If the landlord of the Bell Inn at Wilton felt ill disposed towards this pedestrian tourist when I was at my cleanest and least travel worn, I feared how I should be received at the respectable Deptford Inn now with the grime and aromas of Peter Winter's conflagrations strongly about my person. My duration at the New Inn did little to preserve

a tidy appearance having slept in my day clothes for three nights and
not once meeting with hot water. All was strangely silent when I
made my approach to the inn yet I need not have reached such a state
of apprehension as I was warmly greeted, the landlord and landlady
being kindly and I believe they show a respect for all, gentlemen and
common workmen alike. I have located boots and requested a bath in
my room and whilst this is being attended to, I have taken up my pen
in the parlour now that I have obtained a fresh supply of ink from the
landlord. It is a pleasure to be sitting at a table and chair after days of
crouching in Grovely wood, furniture not being a necessity to the life
of a charcoal burner there being only rough stools and stumps for the
purpose of sitting down.

I did not leave Peter Winter's camp until late into the morning
and I was pleased that he chose to escort me for some distance. As
Tam returned from Wilton and so we could now depart. I said a fond
farewell to the boy Tam for I should have dearly liked to instruct him
more in reading and writing. I wished to warn him also of the dangers
of complicity in deer stealing with a great fear that one day he may
get apprehended, but it is a consequence of making an existence here of
which, as a Londoner, I can know but little nor pass judgement over.
When the smouldering heap finally grows cold perhaps that will signal
a departure from this place to endure a long and barren winter until
their season begins over again and with Grovely comes opportunity.

Peter seemed as glad as I to skirt the fringe of the wood and as
I have now become accustomed, he spoke little and kindly tempered
his ferocious pace. We now witnessed the first signs of nature's slow
decline towards winter with the rattle of dry leaves and a trace of ice in
the wind. A conspicuous and noisy bird then crossed our path which
displayed a most impressive variety of coloured feathers with a white
ring around its neck and a long tail and I believed it to be some form
of exotic chicken. Peter mimed the aiming and firing of a gun and then

cupped his hand to his ear and indeed we could hear distant cracks of gunfire and my guide then indicated that this strange bird was the intended quarry for this form of hunting. I did not wish to disturb the creature into flight lest it should head towards the battery of firing guns and certain death whilst the charcoal burner observed my attempted stealth with obvious amusement.

As always Peter has a purpose to his actions and he led me to yet more signs of ancient occupation where great ditches and banks have been laid out on these ranging northern slopes. Our inspection revealed many more humps and bumps continuing around the hill and indeed into the wood itself and again, as in the rabbit throws at Amshill, I have found small coins lying together with broken pottery. Earlier I had shown Peter the "panshards" from Amshill that I had collected this morning with the mushroons and I thought him little interested. Again, I am at fault in my estimations for the charcoal burner now swept his arm across this area to suggest that if it was broken pottery and small soil encrusted coins that I desired then I was not to go wanting here. I have tried to establish the objects on this currency and there is I believe a head on one side and it is perhaps a galloping horse on the reverse. That these ancient peoples who made their settlements on both sides of this ridge lived in an age of metal there can be no doubt. If coins can be forged then tools and weaponry can be manufactured. Metal though cannot be extracted from chalk or flint so metal must be obtained from other regions for this purpose, whereupon the elements of trade and transportation must be negotiated, which are considered to be modern practices and not the activities of the barbarous savage. The habitations in this area are of grand proportions, perhaps on the scale of a small town when combined with Amshill and its defences reveal a fear and a vulnerability from the north. Indeed, there are further indications of this insecurity with a ringed entrenchment that I have also visited today further west along the ridge, named "Castle" on John Cary's map and also "Badbury Camp", which is situated on the downs above the small village of Wylye. I believe sir, that this ridge was once a frontier, though who was feared and which battles were won and lost I cannot judge.

I have just heard a distant horn signalling an approaching stage and of a sudden the quiet here is broken with the bustle of preparation; the grooms busying themselves in the yard and the maids a' clattering in the kitchen. I wonder that my bath has been forgotten as until now this place has been asleep but I shall continue with my pen until I am disturbed by new arrivals or my appointment with hot water is due.

After our foraging for coins and broken pots my friend and guide indicated that he was to return to his camp and for a moment the tempestuous brow that I had feared at our first meeting cleared itself of all deep furrows and Peter Winter smiled. It was a brief affair that passed over like the weather on this October day, with a flash of sunlight between a flotilla of dark and heavy bottomed cloud. The charcoal burner, with a mischievous glint in his eye then tapped my hand as it clasped the handle of the walking stick and gave a quick rub of his thumb and forefinger to remind me that I had not yet paid him for his handiwork. There was so much that I should like to reimburse Peter for; his hospitality and kindness, the instruction in woodland craft and flintworking, his local wisdom and a deal more besides. I had not enough for all these things and I emptied my pocket of all coins into my cupped hand and this miserable pile of copper and silver was now all that I had left. I had given Tam two shillings this morning for the price of the postage of the letter and instructed him to keep the small remainder. Peter grunted and picked out threepence from the pile in my hand for his stick and then turned without ceremony and quickly vanished into the wood. I wondered whether I would ever have the good fortune of meeting Peter Winter again yet I believe such is the way with travelling, brief relationships are made and then left behind but with a memory here that I shall always cherish in my heart.

*

I am now sitting up in my bed here in the Deptford Inn as the candle spits and sputters and I see that I have wax upon the page. With my bath awaiting, I was finishing the account of my departure from Grovely wood when the passengers from the newly arrived coach filed through the parlour. First to show were two smart and fashionable young ladies who I now understand to be twins although their identical appearance suggested as much on my first impression and they were travelling with their chaperone. In close pursuit were two gentlemen who I also correctly gauged were father and son, such were their facial similarities. Instinctively I ceased my labours with the pen and stood as the ladies entered and extended this courtesy to the two gentlemen. The elder of the two gentlemen, and the last in the line, then halted to bid me "good evening". He smiled and studied me more closely as I stood with pen in hand and I felt obliged to comment on the wretched sight before him.

"Good evening sir, please excuse my appearance, I am a pedestrian tourist engaged on a short tour of the south of this county and I can inform you that I am due a bath very shortly."

"Indeed," he replied, "I have met with pedestrian tourists before but never one who travels under the guise of a chimney sweeps boy. I am afraid sir that I will not have our paths cross without discourse and explanation on this matter and I would therefore like to extend an invitation for you to join my son and I at dinner, when I am certain that every part of this conundrum can be satisfactorily resolved."

As you will know my funds have diminished to the extent of expecting only the most simple of meals and I did not wish to put upon a stranger or cause embarrassment to myself or another and so I politely declined with an explanation that I had already made my arrangements with the landlord. The gentleman was not easily dissuaded but finally we

agreed that once stomachs had been satiated, I should be very welcome
to join them. I can inform you that this gentleman's name is Mr Richard
Fenton and he is travelling with his son Mr John Fenton. The gentleman
then departed with a smile and a farewell gesture.

"I bid you a good evening and wish you an enjoyable repast, Mr
Henry Chalk, pedestrian tourist."

My ablutions were undertaken in barely three inches of cold
water and I am gratified that I should feel no guilt when I leave this
place without a tip for boots for I have found him tardy and surly in
his manner towards me. He is a young man yet older than myself and
I suspect a degree of contempt in perhaps serving one younger than he
and I have witnessed his ingratiating manner towards others. I shall
also clean my own boots and dispense with his service entirely.

After my meal, which although simple was a veritable feast
to one who has suffered the hospitality of the New Inn, the landlord
approached my table and asked whether I would now like to join the
two gentlemen in the front room. More introductions were required
for the benefit of Mr John Fenton and myself and before I had even
become seated the same gentleman had pressed a large glass of wine
into my hand and a toast was loudly proclaimed.

"To Mr Henry Chalk, pedestrian tourist and no longer a
chimney sweeps boy."

On the insistence of these two irrepressible gentlemen I now
gave a full account of my journey thus far although I refrained from
relating the encounter with the pickpockets outside the brickyard near
Salisbury as I did not wish them to know my current embarrassment.
They asked about my family and expressed sincere feelings regarding
the death of my father, your brother, in the summer of this year and
my mother's passing away almost ten years ago now. I would not
permit this to dampen the degree of amusement and interest that these
gentlemen seemed to derive from hearing of my every twist and turn

and indeed if there were ever two people capable of raising the spirits then I soon discovered it to be Mr Richard Fenton and his son John.

I revealed that my attention was now drawn to that most mysterious of destinations, the magnet for every insatiable tourist, Stonehenge. This news could not have pleased the two gentlemen more as this was the very purpose in spending the night here at the Deptford Inn so that they might make that identical excursion in the morning. It was made very clear that no protest on my part was going to be sufficient to dissuade them from extending an invitation for me to join them in this venture. Mr Richard Fenton informed me that I would be required to suspend my pedestrianism for the day as they were to place themselves entirely in the hands of "the pilot of the plains" their good friend and fellow antiquary, Mr William Cunnington. This learned gentleman would be arriving shortly after breakfast in his carriage and the order of events thereon would be undertaken solely under his direction. I had no choice but to agree to this arrangement, so forcibly was it proposed and it would also give my ankle a further degree of rest after today's exertions.

Mr John Fenton had by now excused himself to ensure that the two identical ladies with whom they had shared a carriage earlier this evening were not wanting for some company after their dinner. His father suggested that a singular offspring of that family would have been sufficient in attracting his attention but to multiply this vision by two would only serve to hasten the process and double his efforts. As the night was clear and cold, we were glad to draw our chairs up to the fire and I now asked Mr Fenton after his family. He informed me that he resided in Fishguard, a town in the county of Pembrokeshire with his dear wife Eliza and their three sons of which John is the eldest. Mr Fenton explained that it was through the investigation of the history of his native county of Pembrokeshire that he had the good fortune to become acquainted with Sir Richard Colt Hoare of Stourhead in Wiltshire. The two gentlemen had spent many pleasurable summer excursions together unravelling the mysteries that lay within the barrows and cromlechs of that place and had become firm friends. Sir Richard Colt Hoare's gaze was now drawn to the horizons of his own county of Wiltshire and in combination with the gentleman that I shall have the good fortune to meet tomorrow, Mr William Cunnington, a great deal of antiquarian investigation has already been undertaken here. The Baronet, for that is indeed the master of Stourhead's correct title, is now embarking on the most ambitious of projects, a great work entitled "The Ancient History of Wiltshire". In stentorian tones Mr Fenton gave full vent in support of this grand undertaking, raising his glass in a most theatrical and humorous manner.

"We shall speak from facts not theory and every barrow that raises its dome above the green sward and has not already been violated by the curious or the tomb robber, shall be cracked open like a hot egg and its contents spooned out, poured over and their meaning digested. It shall be nothing short of an antiquarian feast."

Mr Fenton then smiled at his own outburst but assured me it would be a pioneering work with new maps and surveys on a scale never before attempted and every article uncovered is to be illustrated in full by an expert employed to the task. I did not like to presume that one day I should dearly like to meet the Baronet and contented myself that tomorrow would bring its own opportunities with the elucidation of a subject in which Mr John Fenton and I were to be initiates.

Mr John Fenton then returned from his attendance to the travelling twins to stir the fire vigorously as if to relieve his frustrations. He then turned his attention to me and spoke in a very earnest fashion.

"Henry, there go two of the handsomest young women that I have ever had the good fortune to encounter, who are away to the city of Bath in the morning and where are we going, I ask? Answer, to visit a jumble of rocks in a barren wasteland. What say you to this?"

I had not before met with this kind of talk and I took the

younger Mr Fenton's stance very seriously and indeed began to defend Stonehenge confirming my own enthusiasm for the visit. Mr Richard Fenton smiled and said that I should have to become accustomed to his son's ways.

"He often speaks to witness the effects of his words on others. It is called raillery and it is an art in which he is already a master. I can assure you sir that he is as keen on this long awaited visit as yourself but wishes to suggest to you, as you are a young man with the same susceptible warm blood in your veins as he, that the city of Bath is now a worthy diversion and is soon to be doubly bolstered in its attractions although neither redeeming feature on this occasion are of an antiquarian or geological nature."

"Exactly father," confirmed Mr John Fenton.

Father and son made no indication that they were about to retire for the evening as they were content to refill their glasses and enjoy the fire. I expressed my pleasure and good fortune in making their acquaintance and bid them both a good night, conscious also of my duties with the pen. My wrist is now aching but it is a labour in which I feel a growing pleasure and satisfaction for without it my stumblings here in South Wiltshire would have little purpose. I thank you for your patience my dear uncle and wish you a good night also.

Your persistent Nephew

HENRY CHALK

Tuesday 13th October 1807

MY DEAR UNCLE,

Immediately upon meeting our guide for the day, Mr William Cunnington, I felt at ease in his company for he is a kindly man whose every effort is given over to ensuring to the needs and comfort of others. Some gentlemen are attentive only when listening to the tone of their own voice and can smother any conversation, our host and pilot could not be more at odds with this type as he is very thoughtful and considers deeply the words of others before responding. You may be certain, my dear uncle, that I am much taken with Mr Cunnington after but one day in his company and I have a great deal of sympathy also as he suffers from the most severe headaches that are both sudden in their onset and are greatly debilitating.

Once we had settled our business with the landlord of the Deptford Inn, I joined our host in combination with the two Mr Fentons and our carriage was soon to begin its long and slow ascent to Yarnbury Castle. On reaching this great plateau that marks the beginning proper of Salisbury Plain we found a vast earthen camp that is circular with deep ditches and great grass banks and there exists a large central expanse within the entrenchments. Mr Cunnington informed us, whilst we were still within his carriage, that a great sheep fair is held each year at this place on October 5th and indeed there are indications on the ground where sheep pens and compounds have lately been established and then abandoned. Today we had for company an icy wind that travelled without interruption from the north east across the open plain and only at the base of the deepest ditch was there any respite. Witnessing my discomfort and seeing that I had not sufficient clothing for this exposure Mr Cunnington kindly offered me a thick coat from under the seating within the coach. Mr John Fenton was similarly attired but believed his coat had a rank odour although he only expressed this view in hushed tones to myself. I reasoned that it was the strong animal residue from the recent sheep fair that filled our nostrils and the overcoats were not to be blamed and I assured my travelling companion of this fact. We now began a circuit of the place and it was soon apparent that it is a position that has been chosen with care for there is a good aspect in all directions. On the neighbouring ridge and across the valley lay Grovely wood and my thoughts again turned to Peter Winter and Tam and for the moment I envied their life amongst the shelter of the woodland for at the centre of their world was always a warming fire. Beyond the ridge I could again see the top of the tower that I had observed with Tam as we travelled by cart to the New Inn and it has occurred to me that it is an object that I had first sighted even before my arrival in Salisbury. From the roof of the London coach I had witnessed the distant spire yet beyond that existed a duplicate interruption to the horizon to which at the time I had paid little regard as I believed that my vision had been impaired by the terrific jolting that I had received. I fully intended to establish what structure it was that could possibly compete with Salisbury Cathedral yet as we walked along the crest of the outer battlements any words uttered were soon discarded by the wind. My thoughts turned to a dark and turbulent history that has determined such an undertaking here and also on the slopes across the valley on the Grovely ridge. To inhabit such places is to spurn the shelter of the valleys and a great fear has driven these ancient peoples to draw up the earth and chalk around them on such a grand scale. It is an enterprise requiring an enormous degree of labour that in the world today I can only compare to the creation of our new canals.

At the event of our completion of the circuit I quite forgot to resolve the puzzle of the mysterious tower as my thoughts were trained on the sanctuary of Mr Cunnington's carriage. Once inside our host clapped his hands together and expressed his pleasure at the invigorating effects of the clean and dry air of this place. Mr Richard Fenton, who is himself no stranger to Salisbury Plain, concurred wholeheartedly and produced a small flask from his pocket which he then passed amongst us. I had not before tasted strong liquor and it caused a sudden coughing and spluttering as it passed my throat which provided much merriment and laughter within the carriage. Once the fiery effects of the liquid had calmed sufficiently, I conceded that there was an eventual pleasant taste to the experience. Mr John Fenton was all for administering another dose to make me repeat the spectacle but Mr Cunnington kindly advised against this and then knocked on the carriage roof with the handle of his cane as a signal to the coachman to continue with our excursion.

As we made our way to the next point of antiquarian interest, I must have looked thoughtful in my silence as Mr Cunnington, who occupied the seat opposite to myself, then asked for my view of Yarnbury Castle. It was a request that caught me off my guard and after consideration I felt that as I was a stranger to this county and also to the study of the ancient peoples of this land I believed that I was therefore unqualified to offer an opinion and I informed our guide as such. As I had now become accustomed, Mr Cunnington paused before responding.

"Then I would judge that you are surprised and not a little disappointed that your guide cannot elucidate the matter of who, why and when regarding Yarnbury Castle, am I not correct?"

I felt myself redden and it was as if the gentleman sitting before me could read my very thoughts and I began to fluster. Mr Cunnington held up his hand to prevent any apology on my part and then continued.

"Beware of any man who talks with absolute certainty on a

subject as there will always be more to learn. I have listened to the great and the learned who from their study of ancient manuscripts and of the classics are wholly convinced of their correctness. I put it to you sir that Mr Henry Chalk is equally as capable as Mr William Cunnington or indeed as any rational man, in resolving the who, why and when conundrum. I would direct this also to Mr John Fenton. The answer lays out there in the soil amongst the banks and the ditches and with the broken pottery and the burials and not yet on the shelves of the greatest libraries. I am a wool merchant who is neglecting his business to play my small part in unravelling these mysteries, I fear though that I shall not live to see the day when there exists a clarity and understanding of the lives and struggles of our great ancestors. Mr John Fenton and yourself however are fortunate to have that future in store and to live in an era where I sense there are great opportunities ahead."

Mr Cunnington then paused to look at both aspiring antiquarians in turn as if to emphasize this statement before continuing.

"I would not bring you both to Yarnbury Castle and then desert without offering some scrap of an explanation, for it is indeed little more. There are some that would place it firmly with the Saxons and the Danes but it is my own view that it was a place of occupation and security of the British aboriginals before even the arrival of our Roman masters. There, I have said enough."

The rain now thrashed at the outside of our coach and Mr Fenton again circulated his flask, to which I politely declined. I then produced my pocketful of "panshards" that I had collected before departing from Grovely and Mr Cunnington looked on with curiosity.

"Well you have begun already, that was swift action indeed," he said.

He then studied the pieces, identifying some fine Roman work which has a bright red colouring and is exceedingly well made whilst the remainder is dull and crude in appearance. The coinage he described as that used by the Ancient Britons but offered caution as to whether there was at that time a general circulation of currency amongst the population. Mr Richard Fenton then looked sternly upon his son John and questioned his contribution to this research and, when the young man offered a blank expression in return, his father proclaimed loudly that he had brought shame on the family name and he should go forth on his hands and knees and retrieve some of the same without delay. I confess I find it difficult not to show my amusement when in Mr Fenton's company as so often he is intent on mockery and theatrics and would not be ill suited to the stage.

Our carriage halted at a crossroads where Mr Cunnington lamented that he had hoped to escort us to the most extraordinary array of ancient burial mounds which were so perfectly arranged that you can draw a straight line through their centres, once their positions are laid out in a plan. As the rain fell unabated our guide did not wish to subject us to a soaking before we reached our primary goal and he prayed that we should at least have an opportunity to inspect Stonehenge in some degree of comfort. Through the rain distorted glass of the carriage window I could observe one enormous mound of a considerable length to which Mr Cunnington referred, not without good reason, as a "long barrow". These, he stated, were once supposed to be battle barrows and they were necessarily large due to the heavy mortality of the combat, with the slain being buried at the site of the conflict. Our guide was now at odds with this view but confessed ignorance as to the reason for the great scale of these tombs although he could report that no metal goods had been unearthed in their investigation thus far from which we may draw our own conclusions. The remainder in this curious line were "bowl barrows", "bell barrows", "pond barrows" and "druid barrows" and as Mr Cunnington signalled to the coachman to proceed, he promised the present company a return excursion as it was a sight worthy of a detailed inspection. Mr Fenton, who had before visited the ancient cemetery, then stated that if you were a barrow purchaser planning in advance of your demise you could do no better than to view the array on offer at this location as the variety was unsurpassed in his estimation with a suitable tomb for every need and occasion. He then added with sincerity that a great many of the barrows in the vicinity of Stonehenge and indeed across the breadth of Salisbury Plain had undergone a thorough examination by our guide and it was a plague of the most severe case of modesty that prevented that same gentleman from giving a detailed account of their nature and content. Mr Fenton also recommended a future visit to view the produce of these investigations at the home of Mr Cunnington in Heytesbury where they are on display in an annexe called the "Moss House" and have caused great curiosity and fascination to those who have already signed the visitor book. The proprietor of that place acknowledged that nothing would please him more and he then made the curious suggestion that we should raise the window shutters and travel in darkness to our next destination.

Mr Cunnington's carriage finally came to a standstill and there was a pause before our guide broke the silence.

"Gentlemen, welcome to Stonehenge."

The weather had been kind for as the sodden coachman opened the door, we were greeted by the brilliance of the sun for the showers had temporarily abated yet the wind had not lost its icy thrust and we drew our coats tightly around us in preparation. From the dark confinement of the carriage we were forced now to shield our eyes as we climbed down onto the green sward and then cowered before these giant stones until we became accustomed to this exposure. It is one matter to view illustrations of Stonehenge in books but that reduction in scale gives no impression of the true experience of confronting this ancient structure. Mr Fenton then threw up his arms and called out above the wind.

"How Grand! How Wonderful! How Incomprehensible!"

A statement, I believe, that voiced all our thoughts. Mr Cunnington then summoned us together to explain his hidden purpose for arriving in darkness.

"To witness Stonehenge from afar is not the correct approach as it is dwarfed by its open surrounds and this insignificance then disappoints. To behold it as we have today, and so it has been proven to me on many occasions, is the only method. It is an inconvenience, for which I humbly apologise, but one that is wholly worthwhile in its effect."

Our party was unanimous in support of this action and we then commended our guide on his good reason and judgement.

As with all the illustrations of this place that I have viewed in the British Library there is always a flock of sheep and attendant shepherd in view as if by some ancient agreement and we were not to be disappointed today. In no time this wind weathered and toothless figure had presumed to avail himself on our party and furnish us with all the details as he perceived them and how he had felt the ground shake with the falling of "Thic gurt stone" some eight years ago, which narrowly missed him but took one of his master's flock. Mr Cunnington took out his purse and pressed a small coin onto the watcher over the stones, I believe on the understanding that the fellow should return to his drifting flock and then leave the narration of this place to the guide appointed to the task. The shepherd departed after marking his success with a gesture to the north east.

"Looks sauf 'twur gwain to rain snaw," he said, casting his eye about to register some reaction to this prophecy.

I was all for practising my local tongue but Mr Cunnington gently dissuaded me least I should encourage the man and he returned to impart more of his wisdom. Our guide apologised for demanding that our attention for a moment should be drawn to the two differing rocks on display. The larger inner pairings of stones with their capping lintels are named "trilithons" and are constructed of a rock local to Salisbury Plain termed "sarcen" and I am informed that this surface sandstone is plentiful in its natural state in the Marlborough area where it litters the valleys and hillsides. The outer circle is of the same material and before the ravishes of time would have formed a perfect ring, capped with lintels. The second type of rock, which makes up an inner ring of smaller uprights and also a horseshoe shape, or a broken oval, are a variety of granite and hornstone and perhaps originate from some part of Devonshire or Cornwall. We then entered the circle and our group dispersed to wander and weave between the ruin while the sun retreated behind a cloud that was darker than the very stone of this place. I sheltered for a brief interval, with my back against one of the pair of uprights that formed a colossal "trilithon" and then closed my eyes to listen to the song of the wind as it passed between the stones. Was it the sound of the wind or the sound of the stone for there could not be one without the other? With my palms flat on the rock behind me I sensed that my fingertips had traced slight depressions in the surface and I turned to inspect what may be designs or rough carvings although I could not easily make out their form. I left the sanctuary of the "trilithon" and wondered at the hollows created in the fallen lintels to enable their secure attachment when resting on the uprights, as there is a nodule that has been formed there to fit into these depressions. It brings to my mind the construction of heavy timber frames that I have observed in the repairs to the roof of the brewery in Southwark, for it is a similar form of jointing. On one of the smaller uprights I detected where a portion had been struck, perhaps by some tourists' hammer, and a remnant lay on the grass which I inspected and found it quite speckled in colour. When my tour is finally over my pockets shall be fairly laden with items of antiquarian and geological interest.

I cannot believe that I have made such a long account of the day's activities and I fear that there is still a little more to report. It is not an excursion that is made perhaps more than once in a lifetime by the majority and yet I feel certain that one day I shall return for there is so much more to observe. This evening I have forfeited my evening meal as my resources do not permit me to join the two Mr Fentons, here at the George Inn in Amesbury. I have made my excuses that I have an ailing stomach when in truth it is crying out to be fed. Mr Cunnington has suffered a severe headache and has returned at once to his home in Heytesbury and I have commented already on these bouts which so often afflict this poor gentleman.

I return once more, my dear uncle, to the events of the day and our small group gathered at the "Hele Stone", which is set on the periphery of Stonehenge. There is a significance of the alignment of this irregular stone as on the morning of the longest day of the year the sun will rise from above this stone and is witnessed by those situated within the main circle of Stonehenge. There is much talk of "Druids" and their ceremonies of which I know not what to make and certainly Mr William Stukeley is an advocate of this practice. This same alignment is also represented by a broad course that runs between two parallel banks and I could detect this route as it passed across the closely cropped grassland. Our guide informed us that this was the "avenue" and it was first recognised by the same Mr Stukeley and it forms the main approach to Stonehenge in the darkness of the midsummer morning before the ceremony commences. I sensed that our visit was concluding and I requested that I should be permitted to follow the "avenue" for a short distance along its descent from the stone circle. Had I realised that Mr Cunnington was ailing even at this stage I would not have wished to protract the visit but as there was already rain in the air, I promised to be as swift as my weak ankle would permit. As the party returned to the shelter of the carriage I departed in the opposite direction and I very soon found myself at the base of the shallow valley. With the rain beating down on me I turned to find Stonehenge now completely obscured by the slope with only the parallel banks of the "avenue" to guide me back to my destination. As the wind urged at my back, slowly the tops of the stones and their lintels came into my view until the whole of the form dominated the horizon in perfect orientation and it was as if the structure was once again complete. This was surely the correct and only approach to Stonehenge and yet if this way were made in darkness on midsummer morning then the effect would be lost. The sun rises in the east and sets in the west and I wonder that we are facing the wrong direction and at the wrong time of day for when you approach along the "avenue" with all its dramatic effect, this should be undertaken in daylight and observers would look not back to the east but directly ahead to the west. There must be some equidistance relating to the sunrise and sun set between the longest and shortest days in the calendar year and perhaps the end of the shortest day is the event that should be witnessed by looking to the west through the correct apertures of this giant stone arrangement. From this day grows the slow lengthening of the day light hour which must surely be a cause for celebration with the prospect of a new year and the seasons of growth and fertility ahead and we can emerge from our time of darkness. I rushed back to the carriage as quick as I was able to propose this fanciful notion to Mr Cunnington but I found him cradling his head in his hands and I was full of apology at delaying our departure and protracting our guide's agonies and torment. There is so much more that I would like to ask of this gentleman concerning Stonehenge and other matters and I dearly hope that one day we shall meet again.

One cannot visit this place without formulating some notion as to its purpose and it is then customary to write at length about it to convince the world of your own wisdom and the short-sightedness of others. There, I have now accomplished that tradition and I am afraid, my dear uncle, that you have been the unfortunate recipient.

*

I have received a visitor to my room. Mr John Fenton appeared as I was in the process of cleaning my own boots, an act to which I was surprised that he made no reference and instead he proceeded to ask after my health. He then produced a bottle of port wine and two glasses claiming it a remedy for my ailment, and he filled these glasses until they could take no more and then pressed one upon me, encouraging me to drink it as he was certain that it would do me some good. He then bemoaned the fact that Mr Cunnington had returned home and his father was attending to his journal. His eyes fell on my own account of the day and before I could prevent it, or make my protest, he gathered up the sheets of paper from the table and held them aloft.

"Henry, you have written this much? We have been in each other's company throughout this day and made the same visits yet your account has filled all this. With what, I ask you?"

He then began to leaf through the papers and then kept the pile from my grasp as I tried to retrieve them. His eyes fell on one passage and I feared that I had made some reference to this gentleman that would offend and embarrass.

"The "mysterious tower" to which you refer, I can assist you with that particular detail. It is the tower belonging to Mr William Beckford's great folly Fonthill Abbey. You have not heard of this most wealthy of gentlemen?"

When I informed Mr John Fenton that I only knew of him that he prevented the local huntsmen from gaining access to his grounds and that it was a sanctuary for foxes, he nodded and confirmed that this was indeed a view acknowledged by all who were aware of Mr

Beckford and his inclinations. He then thought for a moment and continued.

"Mr Henry Chalk, I wager you the sum of five guineas that you cannot ascend Mr Beckford's tower, we are soon to return to Stourhead and if you put up at the Stourhead Inn, we can there settle the issue. What say you to this?"

Wishing only for the return of my papers and this access was to be denied save only by the shaking of this young gentleman's hand, I did so, and the correspondence was returned. My glass was refilled and Mr John Fenton then proceeded to tell me that life can become dull without a wager here and a wager there and he rubbed his hands together as if life had of a sudden become more exciting now that this wager was set and hanging in the air. Having enlivened his evening Mr John Fenton then departed with his bottle and I confess my dear uncle that my hand is now at odds with my head after the intoxication of the port wine and I bid you goodnight.

HENRY C

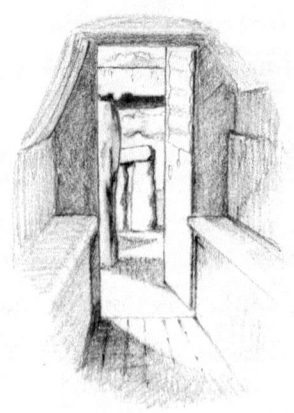

Thursday 15th October 1807

MY DEAR UNCLE,

I write now in a state of absolute confusion and fatigue and I am resigned to giving over the day here at the Stourhead Inn to commit to paper the details as best as I am able in the order that they occurred for it seems an age ago since the evening of my wager with the younger Mr Fenton. I have slept for two hours since my arrival here earlier this morning though I feel sure that I will be required to rest again before this day is through.

I left the George Inn at Amesbury before daybreak on Wednesday morning unable to take breakfast due to the effects of the port wine which I have vowed never to touch again in this lifetime and my head still throbs at its very mention. Unsettled by that evil tincture and with my thoughts spinning, I felt a heavy cloud of uncertainty hanging over me with the prospect of my fulfilment of the wager and I spent the night in a cold clam sweat. After settling with the landlord and paying the price of the postage for my correspondence I calculated that I had sufficient for one further nights lodging only. As you will recall my dear uncle I have already forfeited one evening meal although on the morning of my departure from Amesbury, food could not have been further from my thoughts.

Having seen so little of this county I found myself following in reverse the course of Monday's excursion and I passed by Stonehenge in the early morning gloom. I had forgotten the feelings of excitement from yesterday's visit for these shadowy stones now threatened my nerves and appeared as a mustering of darkly cloaked figures intent on conspiracy and I was glad to find that I had passed from their view.

There was some early traffic on the road and I met a flying eastbound stage at the burial cemetery crossroads. I am still in possession of my thumbstick, to which I have become greatly attached, although I have found it at times in my right hand so I gauge that it has become less of a necessary support for my left ankle and more a comfort and a reminder also of Peter Winter.

The small village of Winterbourne Stoke was coming to life yet I believe no one person noticed as this sallow figure slowly arrived and departed. The climb to Yarnbury Castle seemed to be without end and as I viewed its lumpy shape on the horizon, I appeared not to be making any distance towards it and so I flopped down under a roadside apple tree. The bulk of the fruit from the tree lay about the grass but I could not bring myself to taste it although I picked up a handful of the small rosy red apples to keep for my journey. I sipped at water from a bottle which was my salvation and I thank you again my dear uncle for the help and guidance that your small publication has assisted this simple and foolish traveller for without water I believe that I would die. In a vacant mood I read for a while from my book "A Sentimental Journey" by Lawrence Sterne, which has kept me in quiet amusement although I do not really know why.

In time I picked myself up and filled my head with all manner of nonsense to distract myself from the act of walking until I eventually drew level with Yarnbury Castle. I could now look across to the object of my wager, the very top of the tower of Fonthill Abbey and how my empty stomach sank more and I confess that I wretched again at this sight although my stomach could not have been more vacant. After descending to the village of Wylye I stopped at the river and watched the bright green weed snaking in the flow and then rinsed my face in its clear cold waters. I observed as a distant figure worked in the regular ditches and grass causeways that lay across the valley floor and I had seen before, when I had passed through this place on my way to the

Deptford Inn, the stone blocks and wooden hatches that must combine to control the flooding of this land. The corn mill nearby was all noise and motion with gushing water and grinding gears within that shook the very ground under my feet. Carts were hauling to and fro and it was altogether too busy and loud for my delicate condition but this is a fine river that supports life and industry here and, I imagine, in many other places along its entire course.

My spirits rose as the morning grew older and I did not now care whether my wager was won or lost for I was alive. The day was clear with small puffs of white cloud drifting slowly across a pale blue sky and it was as if summer had returned but the rustling of the leaves gave a clue to the advancement of the seasons and no warm trickery of the sun can halt this decay into autumn. My carefree notions took a sharp turn with my first full view of Fonthill Abbey. This colossal form is promoted to the full by its placement on a high ridge and its surrounds are a brooding forest of dark green and it appears a most forbidding place. When I reached Fonthill Bishop I was confronted with the great stone gateway to the estate that I believe spans the public road. Having passed only humble dwellings with mouldy thatch and crumbling walls this structure is bold and shouts aloud of wealth and prosperity. I passed as silently as I could beneath this giant arch thinking that at any time a great booming voice would question my purpose here but I met with no one. The land here has changed of a sudden from the gently rolling bulk of Salisbury Plain with which I am now more familiar to a lush parkland of majestic trees, strange shrubs and a long glistening lake. I found great curiosity in an activity taking place not far from the road which was all dust and destruction and at first I thought it a stone quarry from the amount of carts loaded with blocks of stone departing from the site. On taking a closer look I could see the foundations of a former building that once occupied this position and a portion had escaped intact from which I could gauge the design and immense scale of the original. I enquired whether a great fire had caused this extraordinary destruction but I was informed by a labourer that this was not the case and that it was simply "Master's orders, tis shame but there tis".

I continued to a crossroads where there is a busy inn with many post chaises and coaches lingering outside and I asked for directions to Fonthill Abbey of an old hunched maid who was transporting a great pile of dried branches on her back. She gestured that I should continue straight across and she hurried on her way shaking her old wrinkled nut brown head and taking her own council on the matter. In a short while I was following a road through woodland and I stopped some distance short of the gatehouse and lay on a grassy bank to observe the comings and goings. There is every sign that uninvited guests and intruders are not welcome here as the stone block wall of twelve feet or more is fortified with iron spikes. I was passed by a succession of tourists who pulled up at the entrance in their chaises and were then turned away by the gatekeeper and I pondered how my own challenge could be fulfilled. I began a sketch of the scene with the Abbey looming up high above the wood, its carcass and great neck clad in a blur of scaffolding as if some great arachnid had ensnared the beast. The sketch is incomplete but I forward it to you my dear uncle as I have committed myself to send you all that is engendered by my foolish travails. I was disturbed from my labour with the pencil by a short elderly gentleman who halted his single horse carriage alongside my position and then disembarked. I know not how to place these words politely as his purpose was to relieve himself of some liquid burden and he had begun this operation before noticing my presence. This gentleman did not appear overly concerned at my close proximity and even raised his hat and after bidding me a good afternoon he requested that he might observe my effort with the pencil. After completing his original task, he took my sketchbook and studied the drawing thoughtfully but I soon realised that it was the subject that had prompted his reverie and not my ability as an artist.

"I am late," the Gentleman reflected, before handing back my work without comment.

I enquired as to what hour he should have been in attendance as I sensed that he was destined for the Abbey itself and here perhaps lay my opportunity. His reply could not have surprised me more, as he climbed aboard his chaise.

"Young sir, it is not the o'clock that is the problem, it is the calendar month."

I hurriedly introduced myself and stated the terms of my foolish quest to which he responded with great charity.

"All I know sir is that you are a young artist and it is a singular breed that may be more welcome than most into the lair of the Caliph of Fonthill. Permit me to introduce myself, I am Mr James Wyatt the architect of that great folly on the hill."

He then indicated that I should show some haste if my intention was to join him in his chaise and I quickly gathered up my belongings and bundled myself aboard. Sitting next to this gentleman I could now sense a strong fruity odour and he looked very weary with dark shadows around his eyes and I believe sir that he was "in his cups". Our carriage halted before the entrance and from the expression of the gatekeeper he was obviously familiar with the gentleman by my side for he did not hesitate in opening the gate and he touched his hat as we passed by and called out.

"Mr Wyatt zur," and as an afterthought he then added, "n' the young gent'man zur?"

Mr Wyatt was not for pausing to discuss the matter of my identity with the gatekeeper and he ushered the horse to trot away at speed. The way was steep and the straps tightened on the flanks of the horse as it laboured under the encouragement given by the driver with his whip. There were many twists and turns with dense green foliage on our right and between the trees on our left I caught sight of a sheet of water which gave me some surprise as I did not expect to find a lake at this elevation and at some distance from the valley bottom. I took this opportunity to ask the architect of Fonthill Abbey about the destruction of the large house near the giant stone archway and he shook his head in some dismay before answering.

"Ahh, Splendens, a very grand building, indeed a perfectly adequate building, that stood for barely fifty years since its destruction by fire in 1755. In truth for all the past wealth of this accursed family, and it has been sir on an extraordinary scale, quite extraordinary, dear old Splendens has now fallen with the sugar market as Mr Beckford has not the money or materials for his project and so his father's house has now paid that price. Mr Beckford is not one who is prone to remorse or regret and cares not a brass farthing for what I or anybody else thinks. I have made my protest sir, but to no avail."

The architect then explained how at first cement had been utilised in combination with timber throughout the new property but this method was deemed inferior and all was now being removed and the reclaimed stone from the earlier house was being used in its stead.

At length we reached level ground and it is on this open and elevated plane that Mr William Beckford's giant new curiosity is at present undergoing its construction and I drew a gasp at the enormity of the sight before me.

"Now sir," said Mr Wyatt, as we drew to a halt, "my business takes me to the rear of the building. I suggest you take the main doors on the western side and there you can make an entrance. Good day young sir and pray be on your guard."

I had barely time to climb down and thank the gentleman before he had cracked his whip and trotted on.

I am now very tired and I must put down my pen and seek

sustenance and also rest a while. I can heartily recommend the Stourhead Inn as the service is excellent and the beds are soft, clean and dry.

*

My dear uncle, how my life has changed and I wish I could race to describe that moment and share it with you but my story must unfold as it occurred for you to make any sense of it. I have yet to make my approach to Fonthill Abbey and I must for the time being dispel all other thoughts and place myself on those closely cropped lawns and savour the resinous odours from the strange trees and plants that abound in Mr Beckford's estate. At first, I felt that the distance between myself and this immense structure was not in any way being reduced and that I was simply lifting my feet up and down to no effect. I viewed the industry amongst the scaffolding, the endless lengths of rope hauling up stone and timber, with tiny creatures massing in groups that I knew to be labourers and like cannon blasts from a great distant galleon there were puffs of dust and scatterings of fallen debris raining down. I reasoned that these small explosions were caused by the crumbling and spillage of the cement material as it was being removed to be then replaced with block stone. In accordance with Mr Wyatt's instructions I made a circuit to the western side and was straining my neck to view its every detail but I was disadvantaged by the sheer size of this building and as I drew ever closer, I found I could look up no more. Finally, I climbed the steps before the western entrance and I could only wonder at the dimension of the pair of doors that towered above me and laughed out loud as I recalled the words of the architect of this place; "There you can make an entrance". I rapped on the solid studded wood as if tapping on a great oak tree, such was the impression made by my poor knuckles. I tried again using all my force with the end of my walking stick yet, as with knocking on any door, one must wait for an answer although I was in full doubt that any inside could hear my efforts.

To my great surprise I could hear faint steps from within the building and I straightened my appearance and stood, and stood, and stood my dear uncle as the footsteps grew in volume and with this waiting my heart beat ever faster. Surely the ogre of Fonthill would not answer his own front door. At last there was a huge echoing clunk as a latch or a bolt was drawn and these great arched doors silently drifted apart. The aperture grew wider and I looked upwards at the effect of this opening yet there seemed no human agency involved in this operation. Indeed, I should have looked down as there stood between these giant slabs of wood a minute gentleman dressed in an embroidered gold costume. At this extraordinary vision and gross conflict of scale I could not utter a single syllable while this tiny servant screwed up his face and even picked at his nose as he observed me. It was then as if a thought had occurred to him, for he looked puzzled and after this odd succession of facial contortions he finally spoke.

"You have come from London? Is Franchi with you?"

His voice had a rasp to it and I judged that he was an English speaking foreigner. At last I found my voice and answered truthfully that I had indeed embarked from London and I was alone. The small man then stood aside for me to enter to which I obliged and with barely a touch of one finger he reunited these giant doors and seemed to take no small amount of pleasure from his control of their smooth and silent motion. The refastening of the latch echoed around a cavernous hall and I looked about the place in wonder; at the floor, the walls and the vaulted roof. The golden servant grunted an instruction for me to follow and I puzzled at my reception here and that my appearance was in some way expected and yet this could not be possible and I knew no person by the name of Franchi. The boots of the servant made a great clicking as he marched ahead of me and at first I thought there was a curious odour to this place yet I realised that it emanated from this little man as I trailed silently in his wake. Standing in a recess on the side wall was a statue of a man frozen in a position of animated speech and on the floor beneath this figure was a diminutive table and chair with paper, ink and pen at the ready. I gauged by the size of the furniture that the little servant had been at this position when he responded to my tapings on the great door for no other soul would have heard. We changed levels to a vast chamber and the little gentleman raised a hand as an indication that I should wait as he then disappeared behind a drapery of deep crimson that extended up beyond the height of most town houses. I realised that I was standing in an octagon and as there were a corresponding eight sides to the great tower then I must be directly at its base. I moved to the centre of this space and span slowly around. My dear uncle, it is as if the ink well of my own thoughts and imagination has run dry for I know not where to begin a description of this place. All is awe and I looked in vain for some familiar object to reassure and on which to rest my gaze but found none. Everywhere is light and darkness and I am bathed in yellow and purple sunshine as the coloured glass of these vast windows is projected upon the stone floor and this effect then floats across the enormous purple and crimson draperies that adorn these walls. Heavy black furniture forms a further contrast and indeed on studying these pieces I find that they are studded with a white ivory and so it seems that every detail here is attended to. I am of the conviction that these effects are designed to perplex the viewer and transport him from the known world to a place of fantasy. It is a building constructed for a tribe of giants and I could not believe that any normal being could make this his abode without soon descending into madness. I heard brisk footsteps approach and the creator of this vision appeared and then stopped abruptly in the doorway to observe me and even from across this great open chamber I was taken aback by his unblinking stare. For the second time in only a short period my words would not form. I know not how long we stood in silence before Mr William Beckford spoke out with his high voice echoing around the place like that of a choir boy in a cathedral.

"So, you have not travelled to Ireland?" he said, eventually.

I was much taken aback by this question and also further convinced that my presence here was confused with the expected arrival of another and I simply shook my head in response. Sympathetic to my obvious discomfort, although not suspecting its cause, in a sudden movement the owner of this place was now standing before me and stopped just short of holding onto my arm. He studied me closely.

"You seem .. more..," his observation remained unvoiced and his mood then relaxed, "dwarfish courtesy has not extended to offering you refreshment after your journey? No! no, of course he has not, it was never his strongest suit and you must I fear excuse him as he is excitable for today he presides at the head of the election dinner in my stead. It is a small matter of my return to parliament and it is a tiresome and costly business and a bacchanalian orgy of excess, all of which I cannot abide. The poor fellow has set up his table and chair at the feet of Alderman Beckford in the vain hope of drawing inspiration for his election address but he will be too drunk to read his own illiterate scrawl so it matters little."

Mr Beckford then clapped his hands together in a quick volley not as a summons to his domestic but out of irrepressible excitement which seemed to be brought about by my presence which puzzled and worried me in equal proportions. When the servant did appear, he was flicked away as an irritation although the young and callow domestic bravely persisted and informed his master that Mr Wyatt the architect had arrived. The messenger retreated and in the purple and yellow light Mr Beckford slowly encircled me.

"Yes, you are a deal older and more worldly than I recall from that night at the Circus Royal. In my imagination I have you as a child genius of the tightrope, yet now I see that it is all theatrical effect.. I have ropes aplenty here."

He let out a long sigh and informed me that he had business with his architect that could not be delayed and he insisted that I should eat and rest. I stammered that I should dearly like to ascend the tower, a request that clearly irritated my misguided host.

"The tower, the tower, is that all that is of interest to the entire world?" Of a sudden, he caught me by the hand and pulled me in his wake. "Come, come and see the wretched tower."

His voice then rang with instructions to summon the assistant to the clerk of works as he cast me adrift and flew to his outstanding appointment with Mr Wyatt.

My appointed escort duly arrived carrying a lantern and he was a large nervous gentleman who spoke little. We began the ascent of a seemingly incessant spiral of stone steps and the lantern was immediately warranted for without it we would be in complete darkness as there was not a single aperture. As shadows flickered and I followed the bulky form of my guide, I lost my count of how many times around we went until daylight was obtained once more and we emerged into a gallery. From this position I could overlook the axis of the entire building where I had awaited the arrival of Mr Beckford and I tried not to consider how I was going to exit this place without causing embarrassment and anger for I had already sensed a flash of his temper. The way ahead was a jumble of steps and ladders into unfinished rooms heaped with building debris and with glimpses through windows I had small previews of the eventual vista from the summit. We could hear the calling and the chattering of the workforce from the scaffolding beyond the walls as we climbed a final succession of ladders to the apex of this giant construction. My guide was breathing noisily and we could access no further than this eight-sided room and each wall had its corresponding open and unglazed window. I immediately went from one opening to next, around and around and at first my eyes were streaming with the effects of the air and wind at this altitude and I could see little more than a division between blue and green. As my vision cleared, I requested of my guide the names and whereabouts of distant features and I realised that the poor gentleman was reluctant to leave the centre of the room and was in some discomfort.

"Truth be told sur," he said, "I fears the heights and I reckons thas why he do send me to this task."

I could only apologise and was then very conscious of not protracting his discomfort during my indulgent excursion. I wish, my dear uncle that you could be with me at the very top of Mr Beckford's tower and I fear that I will not be able to relate faithfully this experience for I know not where to begin. The distant spire of Salisbury Cathedral appears amongst woodland although I know that not to be the case but there are many tree tops between these two landmarks. Salisbury Plain is conspicuous enough and where this chalk mass rises up, I could see many flocks of sheep grazing in small clusters and the gentle parched green folds of the Plain extend to a hazy horizon where clouds gathered. I continued my circuit of the octagonal room and enquired of my guide as to the location of a further tower and he replied without venturing to the window. "That would be King Alfred's tower at Stourhead sur".

Indeed, this conspicuous building aided my eventual approach to the Stourhead Inn and I intend to ascend that structure also, when time permits. Of a sudden I felt the desire to fall from this great height and as quickly as this strange feeling entered my thoughts and turned my stomach over it then departed. With the shock of this notion of self- murder I took a pace back from the window but I believe now that it is a trick of the mind when it makes for itself that unimaginable thought. I felt a deal more cautious for the remainder of my viewing from this position but was determined to overcome this foolishness. A movement caught my eye and I followed the course of a large brown bird as it sailed closely beneath me in the warm afternoon air with barely a twitch of its great ragged wings. I am certain that this most regal of species would have expended even less effort had it not been pursued by two smaller angry black birds that I believe to be crows. I took one last look below at the building itself, at the industry involved in its creation and at the grounds that display great variety with a determination to avoid any regularity or conspicuous plan. I have not yet visited the alpine regions but I believe that the author and artist of these surrounds has borrowed from his travels for it is not England that has been his inspiration. My guide shuffled politely in the centre of the room and I gestured that we should reunite with terra firma for both our sakes, to which he needed little encouragement. As we descended slowly and with caution, I realised that I had indeed fulfilled my wager although I had no proof other than my word. I revealed this matter to my guide who begged my pardon and informed me that it was his duty to escort me back to await Mr Beckford in his chambers. I regretted that this was not my intention and that I must depart for fear of causing more confusion than currently existed. The poor gentleman was all of a quiver in his dilemma as he dared not fail in his duty. At length he told me that it was more than his life was worth but he would report that I had fled from his company into the grounds and then suggested in hushed tones that a team of wagons were due to depart for Hindon very shortly. I apologised sincerely for making his situation troublesome and he led me to a much humbler exit than that of my entrance to this place and I made my hasty departure.

As my guide had indicated the wagons were mustering and I slipped aboard at the rear of one vehicle where the dusty workforce appeared to be in a condition of intoxicated oblivion and were altogether ignorant of my presence. I looked back as we made our slow retreat from that fantastic structure and I make no pretence that I was in some fear of reprisal and wished myself away from this place as swiftly as possible. I kept my vigil as the wagon rumbled on and this attention was fully justified as I spied a figure on horseback, who in a short while would intercept our course and I soon established that it was the diminutive servant on a toy white steed. As we passed between some lush greenery, I quietly slipped from the back of the lumbering wagon and pushed my way into the darkness of the evergreen woodland and crouched down from view. The rider hailed for the driver to halt and my pursuer rode around the open wagon inspecting each weary and grimy face in turn until I heard the course rasp of instruction to the driver to continue. The little man then turned his pony towards my position and skirted the edge of the woodland and I held up my hands before my face but could not resist to peak between my fingers as he passed close by. His face was screwed up in anger and he mouthed unprintable obscenities until he spied another wagon departing from the Abbey and he then dug in his heels and galloped to inspect its passengers. I lay back in my position of concealment and with my head resting on my pack I must have passed into sleep for when I looked next the light was failing and dusk had crept in as a grey smoke gently drifting across the parkland. On awaking I sensed my dreadful hunger and remembered the roadside apples that I had collected and I drank deeply from my water flask before continuing on my way. In time this track led to a gatehouse where I could hear hounds snarling and barking, a sound which sent my heart racing and as silently as I was able, I approached the closed gates. A light flickered in the window of the lodge and I gently drew up the heavy iron bar which fastened the gate as the first of the dogs appeared from the rear of the small house. The heat of panic was upon me and as I tried to squeeze through the narrow opening that I had made, the pack on my back then caught for a moment but before the snarling hounds were upon me I was able to pass between the gates and drop the bar back into place. I then rolled from view behind the stone gate pillar as the slavering dogs hit the slatted gate as one and, sensing my close proximity, they continued their noise and displayed their vicious teeth with wild eyed frustration. Having released these guard dogs the gatekeeper followed behind and mercifully, being unaware of my presence, he then set about them with a stick and snarled his own instruction for them to disperse into the parkland within the great wall. I stood with my back to the gatepost, breathing deeply and thankful that I had made my exit and that I was not still at large within the grounds of Fonthill Abbey.

My writing hand is near seized in its position around my pen and I must halt and rest. I shall also take some air for this is a place most worthy of exploration and unlike the lair of the Caliph of Fonthill, visitors are made welcome to the grounds and garden of Stourhead and also to the house itself.

My dear uncle, I include a letter to myself from Mr Richard Fenton that I received on my arrival at the Stourhead Inn which explains much. I fear that I have not the time or energy to transcribe it as I have more of my own adventure to relate but if you are able to read Mr Fenton's hand you will find that it confirms my status as a guest of Sir Richard Colt Hoare for the duration of my stay at this Inn. It is an act of generosity for which I am truly grateful and I am honoured that I shall be able to thank my host in person.

Wednesday 14th October

DEAR MR HENRY CHALK,

It was with great alarm that I learnt of the challenge and wager that was made between yourself and my son John at the George Inn on the evening of the 13th of October and I have scolded him for such a foolish action although he claims that it was made in jest after much libation. I suggest that you embarked upon a wager that you could not possibly afford to lose for my son has informed me that when he entered your room you were cleaning your own boots at a saving of perhaps 6d, which can only indicate a condition of severe impecuniosity. I regretted your absence at dinner and believed your ailment to be genuine and I sincerely hope that you are recovered yet I have a suspicion also that your lack of funds prompted an early retirement to your room when you were without question a guest at our table.

Sir Richard Colt Hoare shares my concern at your ill advised venture as any uninvited approach to the dark domain of Fonthill Abbey is certain to end in failure as Mr Beckford is not one to entertain the casual or the curious visitor and there are real dangers attached to such a mission. Sir Richard has made arrangements with the staff at the Stourhead Inn to welcome you as his guest for the duration of your stay and extends an invitation for you to make your acquaintance with the Baronet at Stourhead House.

Your presence will be anticipated at the house in due course and my son John will be on hand to make his apology to you in person.

Your anxious and faithful friend,

RICHARD FENTON

*

It is now evening and I have just eaten the best meal since my arrival in this county which I must neglect in offering an account. How can a traveller relate all his tales, as I am attempting, when an equal proportion of time appears necessary for both the experience and its committing to the page. Perhaps, my dear uncle, I have mistaken my worth as a correspondent and these letters are now received with a sense of dread. I know not how long I shall remain at this location for I should welcome any news of your own to redress this flow of correspondence as it floods from my pen.

It was too dark to consult my map and the Stourhead Inn was a distant goal that I had not the strength in my limbs to attempt for I felt hollow with hunger. I drained the remaining water from my flask and shuddered at the howls of the murderous pack as they patrolled that forbidden territory within the fortified walls of Fonthill Estate and I then followed the road downhill. I thought no further than spending the night in a barn or stable but encountered no such opportunity and in time I found myself entering a village where I thought I might find a simple inn and part with my few remaining pennies for the sake of a bed for the night. There were indeed many Inns in this place for it was a coaching station and I soon established that this busy village was called Hindon, which was the location for the parliamentary election that Mr Beckford had referred to. There was every sign of the bacchanalian excess that the prospective candidate so abhorred with fellows lurching about the high street calling and jeering and swilling from bottles and there were other poor souls at a more advanced stage of celebration who were simply laying still in the gutter. A fire had been lit in the centre of the road which prospered from all manner of election detritus with placards, rough benches and the election hustings tossed in to feed this haphazard conflagration. A small fire engine had been employed to squirt water at this blaze to ensure its containment yet even the operators of this device had been smitten by the pervading sickness of the election process as they lurched and stumbled wildly in the execution of their pumping duties. Somewhere amongst this bedlam of parliamentary procedure Mr Beckford's representative was at large and I clung to the shadows as best I could, for I did not relish a further encounter. I asked discreetly at a number of inns for a night's lodging but election fever had ensured that there was not a bed to be found in the place. I was drawn to a brazier and I purchased some hot chestnuts from a boy for twopence and I received them in a twist of old news and set about prizing open the blackened shells to gain access to the steaming treasure inside. This was welcome food indeed but I became aware that my actions were being observed by a stranger and as our eyes met across the wavering heat of the brazier, I felt a shiver pass through my body as I sensed a malevolent intent behind this man's unfaltering stare. I slowly withdrew from the fire's glow and began a retreat back into the shadows. I looked behind me and this short and stout character had left the brazier also and now followed me downhill at a distance. My dear uncle, the situation soon worsened for approaching me and coming up the street were three figures with one holding aloft a lantern and the person in the middle, who was wearing a tall hat, was half the size of those on each flank and I knew in an instant that it was Mr Beckford's diminutive servant. A course bark from that little fellow told me that recognition had been mutual and I felt too drained of my strength and my ankle not sufficiently healed to outrun any pursuer. Fortune was with me as I sensed that a narrow gap existed between two large stone built houses and I slipped off my pack and stepped sideways between the stonework, not knowing what lay ahead of me in the darkness. With my chest compressed in this limited space I was barely able to breathe as I pushed on and I could just find room to turn my head to look behind and for a moment the stout man from the brazier looked on before his form was replaced by the illumination of the lamp thrust in between the buildings. I could clearly see the snarl on the little servant's face as he observed me and he then growled to his henchmen.

"We must teach that boy a lesson."

The only person capable of pursuit was clearly attired for more important duties and both henchmen protested that they were unable to follow my route due to their size, although an attempt was made and one man was soon lodged firmly between the stonework and shrieked like a pig to be hauled free. This was surely no passageway but simply two buildings that did not touch and I squeezed out into a small yard. Returning to darkness, I climbed walls and fences with the fear that danger awaited me at every turn and I was determined that I should escape this hell on earth. However hard I tried, I could not find a way to open country and I was soon back in the yard of another inn and I heard again that course voice out in the street beyond the arch. My will was broken and I felt too weak to attempt a further blind stumbling amongst the rear of these properties and I was now fully prepared to meet my pursuers and accept any consequences that were due to me, however painful and unpleasant they may be. As I walked towards the street and in the shadows of the archway I met with a figure and begged their pardon as we had made contact in the darkness. I could smell a fresh flowery scent that was at odds with this dreadful place.

"Excuse me madam," I said.

I was taken aback by the response, for this young woman was clearly in distress.

"Sir, I fear for my safety in this place, please can you help me?"

I could hear Mr Beckford's servant approaching as he made further demands of his men to seek me out.

"Madam," I replied, "I will certainly help you but I too am in some danger and there is little time to explain."

"Sir, I hope and believe I can trust you, please act swiftly for both our sakes. Will you please take my arm."

The young lady's voice was filled with uncertainty but I assured her that I was to be trusted and that I would explain all, once it was safe to do so. I guided her to the yard where only moments before I had passed a stationary carriage and I ran my hand along its side until I found the door handle. I slipped off my pack and tossed it ahead of me with my stick and once inside I offered to lift up the young lady with both hands and she first handed me her own stick and also a paper parcel. I then ensured that she was sitting comfortably on the seat before quietly closing the carriage door. I heard the little man's boots on the cobbles as he approached the carriage and he then struck its wheel.

"And in here," he demanded.

"But I done 'im earlier Mister Pierro," protested the henchman.

"Again," growled the dwarf, "I go to take my place at the 'ead of the table, come find me when you get 'im."

The boots retreated and we listened to the underling grumbling to himself.

"Yous' jes a stinkin' dwarf, is all you is, n' Mistur Beckford kin rot in hell".

We heard the door to the inn open and close with a brief burst of the bacchanalian excess within and we then sat listening to our own breathing inside the darkness of the coach. How long we sat in silence I do not know but in time I whispered that I felt that we were safe to talk and I introduced myself and apologised for my clandestine behaviour. The young lady introduced herself as Miss Sarah Foster and indeed this was not a usual situation in finding ourselves alone together, but it was a circumstance that could not be anticipated. I asked whether I should now be allowed to escort Miss Foster back to her lodging but she responded that it appeared unsafe to venture from our current security and that we should wait a while longer. Miss Foster then asked quietly whether I was now at liberty to explain my own predicament as I had at first promised and I was relieved to notice that the distress had now left her voice. I answered truthfully that I knew not where to start and she advised me that as with any story I should start at the beginning and so, my dear uncle, I found myself again on the roof of the Exeter stage all those days ago. In the darkness I listened to my own voice as it trailed the route of my excursion and I found that I could not exclude the details of the loss of my purse or the warmth of my feelings for Peter Winter and the boy Tam. There was also no omission of the antics of Mr John Fenton although these were thoughts and feelings that I had not even voiced to myself. Miss Foster wanted to hear every detail of my uninvited excursion to Fonthill Abbey and she knew not that such places existed in this world. I related that Mr James Wyatt, the architect of that building, had referred to the sugar market and I believed that Mr Beckford's great wealth had been accrued in this way. Miss Foster spoke of her sadness about this cruel trade as slavery was at the heart of that business. I confessed to knowing little about the subject but I was assured that it was a matter about which her family held very strong views. There was a great sincerity to her voice as she spoke about this evil to mankind and that Mr Beckford was surely the worst kind of man and Fonthill Abbey a monument to inhumanity and she informed me that she was raised to always speak out about such an injustice. I felt myself recoil inside my own ignorance as this young lady then lectured me on our nation's history and as a pioneer of the trading in slaves, we have much to be ashamed of. The people of this country though have won the day and our Government has been made to follow with the passing this year into law of the Bill to abolish the entire British slave trade. Miss Foster then showed curiosity as to whether I indeed followed the affairs of the world at all? I confessed that I was not accustomed to reading newspapers and knew very little of interest other than perhaps a few dusty facts that were of no consequence to anyone. This young lady however appeared my antithesis and seemed quite at ease with the affairs of Government, war and reform and she also assured me that she had never read a single newspaper but instead enjoyed the learned company of her family where discussion on all matters was encouraged. Miss Foster then urged me not to consider her as one with only strong and serious views as she also held an appreciation for music and the theatre and above all she considered that laughter was the greatest panacea. For my part my dear uncle I did not know how to proceed with this dialogue for I have no experience of such encounters with the opposite sex and Miss Foster appeared so forthright in her manner. I recalled the book that I have read a portion of on my travels "A Sentimental Journey" and for want of any other subject I could bring to mind I asked of Miss Foster whether she had read this work. I at once knew it to be inappropriate but could not retract my question from the darkness and she at once demanded to hear of it. My voice stumbled and I apologised that I had mentioned it for I now considered that its content was improper.

"I am not so delicate that I may faint at the slightest indelicacy and I should like to hear of it," Miss Foster replied boldly.

I could find no exit from this situation and I suggested that I had a short candle in my pack and I could light it with which to read. The young lady was quick to oppose this action least the men should return and instead proposed that I should recall it as best I could for it must still be fresh in my mind. I cleared my throat and paused to gather the threads of this strange tale. I explained that the hero of this little volume was Yorrick and he travelled with no objective through France other than to cross paths with beautiful women and indeed from the narrative you would believe that little else existed in that country. There are many distractions along the way and I recalled how Yorrick requires guidance to the Opera Comique and passes a dozen shops until his eye settles upon someone he considers worthy of interruption from their business to supply these directions. In a glove shop he spies the "Beautiful Grisset" whom he engages in conversation and from the doorstep of her shop she patiently tells him which streets to take to find the Opera Comique. Yorrick then repeated his thanks as many times as her instructions and then reluctantly departs only to find that he has not gone ten paces before he fully forgets every word that the Beautiful Grisset has uttered. He then returns and with great boldness offers the excuse that "tis possible, replied I, when a man is thinking more of a woman than of her good advice". I advised Miss Foster that the situation grows worse for the shopkeeper invites Yorrick into her shop for she has a delivery boy soon to depart in our hero's intended direction, if the gentleman would like to wait. They enter the shop and I know not how he contrives it for in a moment Yorrick is sitting beside the Beautiful Grisset and has her delicate hand within his and he is feeling her pulse. I stopped the narrative at this point for I felt I had already related too much of this tale which appeared all the more full of scandal, now that I was hearing it in my own words. Miss Foster then demanded to know what happened next to the hero Yorrick and the beautiful Grisset and I had to inform her that the husband then appeared in the shop at that very moment, to which I heard a short gasp by the young lady. Her shock was short lived for she soon began to laugh and perhaps out of my own nervous condition I too began to laugh, at the narrative, at our situation as two strangers sitting within a stationary carriage and at the loss of my senses within this darkness. Miss Foster then calmed her laughter.

"And what would the hero of your tale make of my pulse?" she asked in earnest.

I knew not how to answer her request other than to say that I felt certain that it would be a situation to his liking for it had all the correct requirements; an implausible excuse, an intimacy with a young woman who is also a stranger and a scene set in a carriage that is going nowhere at all. I remembered the chestnuts that had grown cold in their newspaper wrapping and offered this suggestion to Miss Foster. At first she made no reply and in the black interior I could sense my own pulse beating at my wrist and bounding through my heart and at my temples. An eternity passed before she calmly revealed that in the package she was carrying were apples and some bread that she had intended to feed to the horses and indeed that was her purpose for straying from her room. I fumbled for the package on the seat where I had tossed it and then tore and ate the bread for it could not have been more welcome. Miss Foster then informed me of her own circumstances and that she was travelling with her brother Robert and they could only find one room on this the busiest of nights. Her brother had assured her that he would find somewhere to reside even if it was on a table and, despite her protests, he had left his sister to enable her to retire for the night on the understanding that she would under no circumstances stray from her room. Miss Foster felt ashamed that she had not heeded her brother's advice but she found that she could not sleep for the noise in this place and confessed to a great fondness for horses and felt a desire to feed that most worthy and friendly of animals. Whilst I ate she told me of her great admiration for her brother and then introduced me to her family life and her anticipation at being soon reunited after their visit to London. Miss Foster spoke of her pleasure and experiences of London life and in her short stay she knew more of the heart of the place than I and I confessed to being a cosseted resident. She then talked at length of this and that and in time she sighed and made a wish.

"I do not want this one night to end for daybreak will bring this ugly place back onto its knees and we have travelled in our carriage to a special destination that I have never before visited.."

I could not answer and in that pause Miss Foster bowed her head and made her own response.

"It has already happened, has it not?"

Pale and uninvited, the beginnings of the new day had crept into our carriage and my night was over and in this callow light I could see that Miss Foster was without sight. She was indeed more beautiful than I ever imagined throughout our passage in darkness and now the dawn had conspired to tell of her secret. She smiled and spoke softly.

"So, Mr Henry Chalk, you have the advantage of me and do you not consider that we have been on equal terms and should remain so until our journey is truly over and we leave this carriage?"

Miss Foster gently raised her hands before her and I positioned myself so that she could easily find her target. Tenderly she first ran her fingers around the outline of my face to gauge its shape and then explored the interior from the line of my hair to the eyes and cheekbones all the while reading with her fingertips these contours until she traced my nose downwards to my lips. There her hands fell away and she requested that I should escort her back to her room.

My dear uncle I am truly exhausted with the telling of the events of this day and night. Before my pen drops to the floor I would request that if you discard, neglect or light your fire with my scraps of correspondence I hope that you will safeguard these last few pages for this shall be a memory that I will endeavour to retain but that one day I might be reminded of its every detail. Before I have a second thought about dispatching this most intimate of accounts, I shall seal this letter and I pray you will not be offended by its content as there is surely a hope that honesty shall win the day over any suggestion of impropriety.

This pedestrian tourist, having returned Miss Sarah Foster to her room, took a long drink of water from the pump and then stepped over the squalid remnants of yesterday's parliamentary election; the bodies, the limp bunting and the smouldering benches and banners and I do not recall my feet making contact with terra firma again until I reached my destination, the Stourhead Inn, and neither do I recall a single detail along the way.

Goodnight or good morning, my dear uncle, for I know not which applies.

Your persistent Nephew,
HENRY CHALK.

Friday 16th October 1807

MY DEAR UNCLE,

This morning I found difficulty in raising myself from my fine bed and I shall not tell you of what hour I took my breakfast. I find I have still not awoken fully and I cannot break the cycle of lifting myself from the chair and going to the window, rubbing hard at my sore eyes with tight fists and then returning to my chair. I have a callous on my finger from its contact with the pen for which I have only myself to blame and my mind feels like the struggle of an injured pedestrian tourist as I cannot put one thought in front of the other. All the while I have in my grasp a piece of paper that has on it a name and address written in my own hand and it is the only proof I have that my encounter at Hindon was not a cruel but beautiful dream. I have an appointment to keep with Mr Richard Fenton and an invitation to make the acquaintance of Sir Richard Colt Hoare at Stourhead House and I wonder that I am not in a more healthy state of anticipation.

*

The day has now passed and I can report, my dear uncle, that although I did finally manage to escape the comfort of my room I am installed once again in my chair with pen and callous reunited.

After making myself as presentable as a walking tourist's wardrobe would permit, I made the short journey up the hill to Stourhead House. There is an attractive twin towered gatehouse through which you make your approach to the Baronet's home. Beyond this archway there stands an orderly line of fine sweet chestnut trees that I can recognise from the curious twisting of its bark as it spirals up the girth of the trunk and also by the littering of its produce on the lawn below, with the splits in these spiky green cases revealing the glinting darkness of its seed. The house has a grand façade and a neat symmetry, but what do I know of such places save to say that it is pleasing to the eye? There is a large expanse of parkland before the house and then level ground beyond which ceases with a range of hills and evidence of earthen banks or ancient fortifications at the summit of this abrupt ridge. It is indeed appropriate that the author of this county's ancient history should have this visible daily reminder of prehistoric occupation occurring on his doorstep. I judged that I could also see the tower of Fonthill Abbey and the strangeness of that place sends a chill down my back and it seems that it is a landmark that shall haunt me for eternity. There was a succession of tourists approaching and entering the house and I followed behind and then announced my presence to the footman. I was informed that Sir Richard and his guests were shooting today and I was for departing but it appeared that the public were quite at liberty to inspect the place and this was a fact confirmed by the footman and so I became myself a house tourist for the afternoon. In this fine and spacious entrance hall there is barely a section of wall that is not covered with a painting and I suspect that many of these faces that loom from their dark backgrounds are ancestors and members of the Baronet's family. I overheard a member of the staff addressing one small group of observers whilst pointing out a representation of Sir Richard Colt Hoare and his son. I waited for the party to continue before I took my position beneath this heavy gilt frame. Sir Richard has a gentle countenance and also a detectable sadness and while the son seems keen to explore beyond the confines of the painting the father is preoccupied with his portfolio of antiquarian studies and seems reluctant to leave his position. I found myself reflecting on my own father's refusal to submit to my childish whims as if it were a display of weakness to revisit those feelings of playfulness from one's youth. I heard a voice speaking aloud these very thoughts and I was taken aback to recognise it as my own.

"Go with your son and leave those encumbrances that build walls around yourself."

I quickly looked about me to ensure that this advice to the master of the house had passed unnoticed and I need not have concerned myself for I was soon overtaken by a very vocal lady and her entourage. I followed this group at a distance and it soon became apparent that very little here at Stourhead House met with her high expectations and a display of appreciation or condemnation was proclaimed most publicly. I wonder that the owners of these country houses admit such critical tourists for this lady was keen to list the many other large establishments to which she had gained admittance and how Wilton House was "Too grand, too gloomy" and even regarding the surrounds here at Stourhead; "I cannot think it equal to a situation in our own neighbourhood". As the party confronted each painting in turn the male escort would look to this lady arbiter of good taste before offering any hint as to his own views on the matter least it should be for when it should be against and vice versa. This prima critic even adopted the cunning means of hinting at her feelings and then would playfully change her course in the opposing direction once the unfortunate gentleman had mustered the courage to voice an observation.

"No, no, no, Mr James it may be well executed but it is most certainly NOT hung to its best advantage."

This poor fellow would then retreat to the rear of the party and keep his silence, I suspect, for the remainder of the excursion. The most curious object encountered was a heavily ornamented cabinet that once belonged to Pope Sixtus and I cannot say my dear uncle whether it is to be attributed to good taste or consigned to bad for at this stage of the proceedings I had thankfully parted company with the critical tourists. It is old and it is odd is all I know and I fear for the male entourage once they are obliged to pass judgement on this unique piece of furniture for whatever they propose will result in apoplexy and, I am certain, receive a withering response from their female Cicero. There are a number of small paintings here by John Robert Cozens that I favour if I have to show my preference which I am glad to say I am under no obligation to do. I then left the house and sought out the tower which is perhaps a distance of a mile or so and I found it strange to walk without Peter Winter's stick which I now fully associate with walking any distance at all and neither did I have my pack on my back to which I have become so accustomed. On this fine and clear afternoon, I instead carried a burden of a much weightier variety for there is only one subject to which my thoughts constantly return and I fear that I shall soon be driven to madness by this turmoil. I am perpetually required to gather my senses and return them to the task of observation but I may as well be in the streets of Southwark, Paris or Calcutta rather than the environs of Stourhead House. A human being is a curious thing for on the exterior of it we are all busy with some activity and even a crowd of this species can appear to have a single purpose yet we are all churning away at our own thoughts. Today, my dear uncle, I can report that I have successfully manufactured some fine Wiltshire butter where previously I had a rational mind.

King Alfred's Tower stands one hundred and sixty feet high and such was my preoccupation I very nearly stumbled into the sheer brick sides of the place. There could not be a better remedy for my pathetic ailment than ascending these one hundred and sixty feet in near darkness to then be exposed to the brilliance of the day at the summit and I believe that this is the calculated effect and purpose of such a structure. The body savours the conclusion of this endeavour and the reward is total for we are now united with the sky and all earthly matters are left two hundred and twenty two steps beneath our feet. I was content to gulp great volumes of fresh air to fill my lungs before unravelling the patchwork blanket of the countryside below. There are but three sides to this tower compared to the eight of Fonthill and although the elevation may not be as great at Stourhead the position of this structure commands a greater view to the west as the land falls away in that direction. Fonthill Abbey again demands the attention whilst I strained to establish the spire of Salisbury Cathedral as faint and distant landmark. Looking to the west there is a pimple rising from a flat plain with a building at its apex which I am informed is Glastonbury Tor, which lies in the heart of the county of Somerset.

There is a significance with the positioning of this tower which has everything to do with the activities of our ancient monarch King Alfred who fought and defeated the Danes in 879 AD and his march to battle passed this very spot and his deeds are rightfully remembered by this erection. It is indeed fortunate that our royal ancestor passed this way as I believe that there could not be a more suitable location for observing the manner in which this land changes. The great hub of chalk that forms the bulk of South Wiltshire finally comes to an end, at perhaps its most westerly point, and I have already referred to the signs of prehistoric occupation that perch on this final chalk crest and are evident from the front door of Stourhead House. At the foot of the termination of this chalk there lies a broad flat area that is largely under cultivation until a further ridge is met on which line King Alfred's Tower stands and there is a large tract of woodland where oak trees appear to flourish. With this further step down to the west which is coincident with the meeting of the adjacent counties of Somerset, Dorset and Wiltshire there could not be a more natural division for it is determined by the changing nature of the land itself. Somerset and the west is a place of small fields contained by thick hedges and there is a sense of lushness and I can detect water glistening in the afternoon sun where it has settled in the cart rutted trackways and drainage ditches. There is a parched dryness to the chalk hills to the east and I wonder that this holding of the water on the land has much to do with the nature of the soil itself and the earth below.

Having found a place of sanctuary for my troubled mind I spent a good hour on the roof of this elevation and in that time a number of visitors huffed and puffed and then departed. A boy of perhaps nine or ten ascended with his father and proceeded to furnish me with more details than I can now recall about the tower and indeed it was he that informed me of the height and the number of steps that we had to traverse to reach the summit. This youth was fairly effervescent with facts for he then numbered the amount of bricks required to build King Alfred's Tower as near on one million. I asked whether he had made a count of them all to which this resource of information finally dried up and the father who had been silently observing the enthusiasm of his offspring owned up to having read the eager child a pamphlet on the subject. This gentleman then continued to relate the remainder of the details regarding the structure itself and that these million red bricks were manufactured near to this very spot and we then discussed the changing nature of the ground hereabouts that yielded brick earth or clay suitable for the manufacture of such fine bricks. Before the father and son departed, we introduced ourselves and I can inform you that their names are Mr Charles Brown and Master James Brown and they reside in the town of Frome in Somerset and indeed Master Brown pointed to the cluster of distant buildings as proof of the existence of that place. With the roof again vacated I patrolled its three sides for a final inspection and observed for some minutes the progress of a team of horses drawing a plough across a field of stubble. There was surely some satisfaction to be gained from this procedure by the ploughman, this visible record of control and accuracy left in his wake after each passing with the dramatic change from dull weathered crust to dark freshly broken soil. A straggle of white birds followed this slow excavation to reap its immediate reward as they descended onto this disturbed ground directly after the plough had done its work, seeking which soil born creature I wonder other than the earth worm? By their actions I believe these to be sea birds and the simple worm must be a rich delicacy indeed to draw these feeders from the distant coast and all the fruits of the sea.

I then descended the two hundred and twenty two steps fearing that my mind would again resume its former turmoil once my feet made contact with the earth's surface but I am pleased to report that the prescription of elevation and fresh air has had its good effect. On a scrap of paper, I have made a drawing of the tower for it is an impressive monument and a conspicuous landmark. I then drifted back to my lodgings, not assiduously observing everything in my wake nor churning butter in my head but a pleasant nothingness existed between King Alfred's Tower and the Stourhead Inn. On my return I received a note from Mr Richard Fenton apologising for their absence today but tomorrow a barrow opening is arranged and I should be welcome to Stourhead House, after breakfast has been taken. I have sent a note of acceptance to this kind offer and now for a while I am content to enjoy a good coal fire in my room before I again put pen to paper and you will be relieved to learn my dear uncle that it is, for once, a correspondence that is not heading in your direction.

Your faithful and bewildered Nephew,
HENRY CHALK

Saturday 17th October 1807

MY DEAR UNCLE,

Another day has passed and how they pass! I am again sitting before the burning coals and I have a fug in my head which I hope will clear as I proceed. At breakfast I received a letter, the very sight of which sent my heart leaping yet the contents could not have had a more unsettling effect. This correspondence arrived from Hindon and it is in the hand of Miss Foster's brother, Mr Robert Foster. We have yet to make our acquaintance but Mr Robert Foster has been charged with the responsibility of committing to paper the warm and gentle thoughts of his dear sister, for it is a task that she will never be able to undertake. In addition, Mr Robert Foster has corresponded on his own behalf, in part to express his concern at his sister's foolish excursion from the safety of her room but also expressing the firm trust that he places in his dear sister's judgement, as to the character of the one whom came to her aid. The author then gives an account of the events of that same evening which explain much and have shocked me greatly. Indeed, there could not be a greater disparity on one page, with the former news all grace and beauty and the latter unsettling in its darkness and danger. Sir, it is sufficient for me to inform you that Mr Robert Foster could not fail to overhear a loud and drunken soliloquy from Mr William Beckford's diminutive servant, delivered whilst his head was resting on the election table. At the time Mr Robert Foster knew not of the characters or circumstance to which this little man referred until the next morning when brother and sister were again reunited. The small man's utterings made it clear that an intruder had entered the Fonthill Abbey grounds and at the great door to that place had been mistaken for another by this same servant and admitted to the building itself. Indeed, for his culpability in propagating this misunderstanding, the miniature domestic had then received a severe beating from his master. It is apparent that the intruder's visit coincided with the long anticipated arrival of another, not dissimilar in age or appearance to myself, for whom Mr William Beckford has "an unspeakable and fundamental interest". My dear uncle, I am not so sheltered in the ways of the world that I cannot understand to what Mr Robert Foster is referring.

I wished to banish the worst of these thoughts from my mind yet treasure the remainder and such was this mix of feelings that it spun my head around as I approached Stourhead House to meet its master, Sir Richard Colt Hoare. On my arrival Mr Richard Fenton took one look at my countenance and realised that all was not as it should have been and set me down, calling at once for a large brandy. I could not explain my turmoil nor did Mr Fenton attempt to establish the cause of my palpable suffering but was content to put me at my ease and offer his kind assurances which, in combination with the brandy, did indeed straighten my senses. I was soon able to present myself to the Baronet who could not have shown more sincerity in his welcome and I confirmed that I was in eager anticipation of the antiquarian activities in the day ahead. I thanked him also for his kind generosity in arranging my accommodation at the Stourhead Inn but it appeared a matter that he regarded as of little consequence and he shook his head gently. Mr Fenton was on hand to rescue this brief awkwardness and he assured me that his son was to appear shortly to make his apology for the incorrect and injudicious wager that was made at the George Inn at Amesbury. I was ordered to take my seat in this fine drawing room and I knew that I could not divulge any part of my tale without explanation of the whole and so I resolved to say nothing on the matter and I was content for the present company to judge that I had not been successful in my appointed task. Mr Richard Fenton stated that there was ever only going to be one outcome to such an impossible challenge and he expressed his delight at my safe return. At this point Mr John Fenton appeared and he greeted me warmly and appeared to show a genuine remorse as we shook hands and he offered me a comprehensive apology for the foolishness of his actions. I confirmed that I was determined to settle with him the full sum of our wager when circumstances permitted, as my financial situation and impecuniosity now appeared to be common knowledge within the present company. At this point Mr Richard Fenton leapt to his feet and interjected most forcibly as he addressed me.

"Sir, you will do no such thing. It is my son that is at fault and it is he who should fully compensate for his mischief and the suffering caused to yourself that we have indeed been witness to on this very morning. What say you John?"

The younger Mr Fenton then rose from his seat to say his piece. "I agree sir and offer again my unequivocal apology to Mr Chalk and so father, as you are the holder of my allowance and as a consequence are therefore my banker, I request sir that a sum of the full cost of the original wager is paid immediately to the unfortunate young gentleman, without delay."

Mr John Fenton then sat down and it was the turn of Mr Richard Fenton to twist and turn and pat at his pockets with some uncertainty until Sir Richard Colt Hoare, who looked on with a sign of mild amusement on his face, then gestured for Mr Fenton to sit down and cease his fluster. He then quietly assured all present that to see an end to this increasingly unseemly muddle he would see to it that wager was settled in my favour and that they could now turn their attentions to the important issues of the day which were purely of an antiquarian nature. I opened my mouth in protest as I did not see for one moment why Sir Richard should be inconvenienced in this way but I was silenced by a firm glance from the Baronet as if to say that really was the end of the matter. Later in the afternoon, on our return to Stourhead House, the steward presented me with a purse containing five guineas which I had no option but to gratefully receive. I resolved then to repay this kind gesture when time permits.

We then departed from Stourhead House and made our way in the carriage to the crest of the chalk downs. I was in eager anticipation of my activity with the pick and shovel as there was a damp chill in the air and I had determined that barrow excavation would be warming work indeed. I cannot pretend, my dear uncle, that I was disappointed to discover that this undertaking was well in advance as two labourers had already been employed to the task and it seems the timing of our arrival had been judged accordingly to witness their near completion. I was introduced to the two Mr Parkers, Stephen and John, who are a team of father and son and are Mr William Cunnington's men and I have been informed that they have "opened" many hundred of these sacred burial mounds, under the guidance of that same gentleman. To my mind no greater care seemed to be exercised as with the digging of any hole, ditch, well or indeed anywhere that there was a deal of soil to shift. The expected object, or "primary internment" can be predicted to exist at the original turf level where a "cist" or small hole has been dug into the native chalk. This would have occurred at the origin of the barrow and into this depression the body or the cremated remains of the occupant would be lain and perhaps, in the case of the latter, a crude pottery urn is often the preferred vessel. The mound itself would then be created above the burial as the surrounding ground was excavated and then heaped up into the centre leaving an outer ditch from whence this raised material had been borrowed. I believe at their initial creation these domes in the landscape would not form part of the green sward as they do today but would be white beacons of glistening chalk and from their prominent positions would present extraordinary landmarks. I thought back to yesterday and my hour

Alfred's Tower

Fonthill Abbey

Wihtesheet Hill

spent aloft at the top of King Alfred's Tower when I had wondered at the natural division of the land here where this great bulk of chalk in South Wiltshire finally plunges down before the boundary with the county of Somerset is met. In ancient times a traveller coming from the west would leave the wet lands behind him and witness the unfamiliar dryness of this elevated chalk country. A gleaming white barrow on the crest of the ridge would call out to this stranger from the west; "We are the chalk people and we live at the beginning and at the end of the chalk world". I wondered how this stranger would be met and what trade would he make with these occupants? The barrow that was currently undergoing the attentions of the pick and the shovel is perhaps not the earliest landmark on this ridge for it is positioned on the edge of a circle which Sir Richard Colt Hoare has determined, from the faintness of its vallum, as that of high antiquity. I walked the circumference of this ancient ring that would have at one time in the history of this place also have presented its bright whiteness to the west before the passage of time had subdued the virgin chalk and the grazing beast trampled its form. It is a circle of small proportions when compared to the gargantuan Yarnbury Castle or indeed to the fort that exists not a half a mile from this very spot on this same ridge with its bold banks and ditches where its defensive purpose is plain for all to see. What purpose then for a circle that is not a fortress yet commands the same aspect as its neighbour? I wished to confirm with the Baronet that the burial mound was indeed of a later date than this circle on which it had been so blatantly positioned yet on the near completion of my circuit I was urged to hurry by Mr Richard Fenton to rejoin our small group to witness an important stage in the antiquarian ceremony. The barrow from which the two Mr Parkers had ably disgorged such great volumes of this chalk now finally relinquished its content for our cursory inspection and a single skeleton was revealed with not an urn or single artefact to accompany this lonely occupant. A signal was given to the two perspiring labourers to reverse this operation and our party retired to the shelter of the carriage where refreshments were on hand and the circulation of the bottle kept a warm glow upon this high exposure. Indeed, the antics of the two Mr Fentons kept us in amusement also with John producing a flute on which he performed with no small amount of skill and his father then sang a song which demonstrated his Cambrian origins. In time we were interrupted by the tapping of Mr Stephen Parker on the carriage door who having heaved the spoil back into position on the initial barrow had now, as instructed, set to work upon one of the three smaller examples that lay on the very crest of Whitesheet Hill. We were informed that a skeleton had been unearthed and we then left the sanctuary of the carriage and made our way across to the barrow closest to the edge of the slope with Mr Richard Fenton approaching the heap of freshly spewed chalk on tippy toes in a most theatrical manner. On peering into the excavation and observing the skull he then gasped and threw up his hands.

"It grinned horribly a ghastly smile."

Our host, Sir Richard Colt Hoare smiled at the dramatics of his good friend but the visage of this unfortunate occupant, exposed from its chalky slumber, did indeed present a most unsettling sight.

I confess my dear uncle that after a large brandy in the morning and a turn or two of the circulating bottle, I felt very weary and it was suggested that I should rest a while in the carriage and indeed I fell fully asleep and only awoke on our return to Stourhead House. I apologised profusely to Sir Richard Colt Hoare and I found him to be most understanding. He then explained that he had not been expecting a great return from the barrows that had been opened today as they had already attracted the curiosity of an earlier excavator and any worthwhile content had been removed. It was important however to exercise great thoroughness throughout the entire operation and he would duly record the events of the day, in the absence of Mr William

Cunnington. The Baronet then kindly extended an invitation for me to visit him in the library on Monday at noon followed by dinner at five o clock, to which I gratefully accepted. He then bid me a good evening and as I was departing the steward presented me with the five guineas as determined by Sir Richard and I returned to the Stourhead Inn with the gold weighing heavily in my pocket.

I have another letter to compose, my dear uncle, and it is one that will raise to the fore those mixed and muddled feelings of this morning. I believe, however, that I shall procrastinate a little longer for I have a thought that requires being committed to the page lest it slips my mind. I shall place myself again on the lofty heights of Whitesheet Hill looking down upon that even plateau, witnessing again the steady passage of a ploughman with his team of four. I wonder at that same soil through which the plough has cut year upon year and the toil of the generations, throughout all the stages of cultivation. Where are the bones and the burials of these lost centuries of labour? I believe that to study the contents of the barrows of South Wiltshire and to build a history of the ancient peoples from this research is to mislead in the same manner as to take a foreigner on a tour of our grand country houses and estates and inform them that this is how all Englishmen live. Within these barrows are surely the ancient Kings and Queens, Dukes and Baronets and it is to these conspicuous tombs that all antiquaries are inexorably drawn. If I can succeed in but one thing that illuminates the lives of all our ancient ancestors from the Nobleman to the simple ploughman then I should dearly like to present these details to Sir Richard Colt Hoare, for he is currently embarking on his great work and it would be as some small repayment for his great generosity towards me.

Sir, I shall now bid you goodnight and I shall stir the fire before again taking up my pen and my head clouds over for I know not yet how I shall respond to Mr Robert Foster or how I shall couch my true feelings towards his dear sister, as they must first pass his lips before falling on her ears.

Your obedient servant and Nephew
HENRY CHALK

Sunday 18th October 1807

MY DEAR UNCLE,

The resounding bells from Stourhead church tell me that it is the Lord's Day and rather than make my way against the tide of arriving carriages, I left the Stourhead Inn from the rear and followed a steep path that soon enabled a view back upon that picturesque vale that is so much the making of the Hoare family, past and present. On reaching flat ground I thought I had left the pious behind me yet on a rough path that crossed fields and hedges I met with a steady succession of souls that were making their way to a different church. These were servants and their families who when questioned informed me that they were the congregation of nearby Bonham Church. They were altogether more sombre in their attire and at odds with the boldness and grandeur of the mustering of the great and the good in the street outside the church at Stourton and I believe that the establishment at Bonham must be a popish chapel. I confess my dear uncle that I did not feel drawn to either establishment but felt content in a quiet contemplation of my own, observing the comings and goings of small birds from hedge to hedge and the rustlings and furtive movement of harvest mice. Of all God's creatures it is only our own species that observe a day of worship whilst the remainder go about their business in the hedge, tree or stubble as if days were not labelled with names at all and the warmth of the sun and the distance between dusk and dawn is all. One larger bold and colourful bird caught my eye and impressed me greatly with browns and blues in its make and a stripy black and white bonnet. I observed the progress of this most singular bird from close quarters and compared her to a lady out in her finest clothes until she disgraced herself with a most unholy screeching that did not befit her appearance and a courser tongue in a lady I have yet to experience. In the naming of these creatures I feel largely ignorant but I experience great pleasure in their observation. Near the footpath that conveys the large Catholic population of this village to its place of worship is a field that has been lately cultivated and it has presented me with an opportunity to study the make up of this sandy soil that I believe extends throughout this entire plateau. There are brown stones of hardened sand amongst the sandy soil itself and also in places a peculiar dark and glassy substance that is more dull and coarser than flint and as I now recall the picturesque rock arch that straddles the road near the lake is constructed almost entirely of this material. It has a curious liverish complexion and perhaps has a similar relationship to the sandy rock in the same manner that flint appears wedded to the chalk. As I picked over the ground, to my surprise, I found a piece of flint glinting darkly in the furrows and I was soon to find many more. I believe that I am not being fanciful my dear uncle if I suggest that these exceedingly fresh and well preserved fractures of flint have been caused by the hand of ancient man. In the first instance they are alien to the natural state of the soil here and must therefore have been imported and to confirm my thoughts some have been manipulated to such a high degree and these designs are replicated and are surely no natural accident. I intend to make drawings of some of the finer examples and I feel certain sir that you will in an instant confirm my own feelings on this matter. There appears a propensity for long and slender slithers of flint that is of a remarkable quality, far exceeding that extracted from the pit on the boundaries of Grovely Wood by Peter Winter, and the edges of these pieces are as sharp as any good razor. The flint occurs here amongst the soil in clusters and as I move away from these concentrations the flint is altogether absent. I recall from observing Peter Winter at his flint work how the waste material lay and accumulated about his feet after a period of time of sitting unmoved in one position and the evidence is comparable here. I can hear your voice asking my dear uncle whether this material is not just the detritus from another gunflint industry in the manner of the one that I have described surrounding the pit at Grovely? I have a conviction sir that it is not and I shall hopefully convince you in my argument that here is not the source of the flint and this material has been brought from elsewhere and then minutely chipped on this spot to extract the desired pieces. I have already forwarded my drawings of the making of gunflints and you must agree that they bare no comparison in their method. In combination with these slender pieces are also the flint nodules from which they have been struck and on every face of these small fists of black stone are the scars of this gradual reduction. I have also retrieved pieces that bear such remarkable similarities to one another that they must themselves be tools and I can only believe that they are devices for scraping as they each have a distinctly hooked underside and the above surface has then received a great deal of attention and has been rounded to perfection to meet this curved end. Above all I confess that I am perplexed by the freshness of these pieces although there are a minority that have

grown cloudy as flint is wont to do and these appear to be the longest
and most slender fractures. I am wondering whether it is the nature of
the soil, in which these pieces have lain, that determines their decay or
this clouding of the surface. In the main I would gauge that they are
much in the condition that they once fell from the maker's hand to
the earth and from whence I have now retrieved them. Sir, it is a great
conundrum as to the period of time between these two events.

I then walked across this level plain of sandy soil, to the foot of the
chalk lands where Whitesheet Hill and its ancient earth works and burial
mounds are in constant view and I made my return, passing as I did, the
Red Lion Inn which stands on the crossroads of the London Road. I
found in turn, where areas of cultivated land permitted my inspection,
a uniformity in the nature of this brown sandy soil and indeed further
evidence of these small clusters of fashioned flint. I could not collect all
that I encountered but instead made a plan showing their position and
I have now, as I write these words, emptied my pockets of all their sand
covered content and I shall make a proper inspection. I intend to spend
the rest of the evening making studies of these flint pieces which I shall
then present to Sir Richard in his library at noon tomorrow.

*

No sooner had I embarked on the exercise of inspection and illustration
when I heard a familiar and welcome voice outside on the landing
and "boots" made a knocking upon my door and announced that
I had visitor. I was very pleased to receive Mr Richard Fenton and
I apologised for the disarray in my quarters as I had every possible
surface covered with unfinished correspondence and broken flint. Mr
Fenton made light of this issue and I invited him to settle before the
coal blaze and I called for a brandy to make as warm a welcome as
I was able. Mr Fenton then apologised for his intrusion at this late
hour but wished to confirm that I was in no way ailing as my presence
had been anticipated at Stourhead Church this morning and it was

thought that there must some malign reason for my absence. There then followed the most awkward of situations which still hangs in the air and it is entirely of my own making. At Mr Fenton's initial enquiry I felt myself redden visibly for I could not readily explain my absence at the morning service and I was indeed lost for words. My guest then clasped his hand to his mouth in a realisation that perhaps I had attended a church after all, but that it was one of an opposing faith.

"I..I..I see, you are a c..c..cath..? How most dreadfully impertinent of me..I..I..understand completely...we had no..idea.."

Mr Fenton then took a large tip of his brandy glass to rectify his composure whilst I was in a great state of anxiety not knowing which was considered the greater issue; to be of the catholic faith or to abstain from a church service of any denomination and instead to wander about the fields all the day with my hands in the soil. My dear uncle, I confess that I then said nothing, which I acknowledge is a poor tactic that I often employ in these the most awkward of situations. This silence appeared to suit Mr Fenton as he was quickly able to change the subject of conversation and fill the void with the first matter which entered his head, as he looked about the room.

"So, you collect stones Mr Chalk? Then you will have much to discuss with Mr William Cunnington, when you next meet for he is a great collector of the same and you are a writer of copious letters also?"

I informed Mr Fenton that I had been recording the events of my pedestrian excursion in a series of letters and that I had made use of more writing paper, bent more nibs and drained more bottles of ink that I thought possible. To this information Mr Fenton clapped his hands together with a crack and even rose from his chair in his display of enthusiasm.

"Sir, you are a man after my own heart," he said, demanding my hand so that he might shake it vigorously before continuing his enquiry.

"And this correspondence, what is to become of it? Is the recipient to publish and what has been your agreement?"

I confessed that there had been no agreement and I knew not what was to become of my letters. On hearing this news my guest then folded back into the chair and clasped his hand to his chin and then remained in that fixed position so that I dared not interrupt this reverie. Finally, and with a sudden movement that made me start, he demanded a pen and paper to which on taking receipt of he then thrust back into my hands as he again leapt to his feet and paced backwards and forwards on the hearth before the blazing fire. I knew not what task it was that I was set to record as I waited with my pen poised above the page.

"A tour.."

My guest gestured that I should commence in my written duty and he then ceased his circuit of the hearth to question why I had chosen to make my pedestrian tour here in Wiltshire and not in Gloucestershire, Devonshire or his own county of Pembrokeshire? I believe my answer was a cause of some surprise for he repeated it over and again, after I had explained briefly about my observations during the digging of the great well in the brewery yard at Southwark.

"Chalk...Chalk..Chalk? I see, well, chalk it is then," he said, returning to his original purpose, "a tour, in search of chalk, through parts of South Wiltshire, in the year 1807, written in a series of letters to..to whom are you corresponding sir?"

I then informed Mr Fenton that it was to you, my dear uncle that I had been directing the entire account of my experiences.

"I see," replied Mr Fenton, now in full flow, "to an uncle. Is he lost? ..lost is best, it lends to more drama..to a lost uncle..encountering on the way..let me recall..a charcoal burner, together with a visit to Stonehenge, Fonthill Abbey..it may be a false trail but it will sell.. and Stourhead, interspersed with various anecdotes and, I will wager

Mr Chalk some antiquarian observations, am I not correct?..and to conclude..it must be anonymous which is of course a false modesty as not only is the author's true identity woven into the title page, it will also be liberally sprinkled about between the covers of the book and it will gratify the reader in making him elucidate the ownership of the piece. So, by..by..whom? Why by A. Pedestrian of course. There must be every kind of typeface and bold lettering employed in this title page and it should be rushed to meet the printer's deadline and on the bookstands before the year is out. There, is that not sufficient?"

Mr Fenton then returned to his chair and drained his brandy with an expression of great satisfaction and I believe that he is at his happiest when he can explore a humorous avenue until he can reasonably go no further. On the inspection of my written account of his presentation he shook his head and made utterances before taking up the pen himself to make a better order of my work. My guest now assumed an air of great expectation and I now began to realise that he was indeed sincere in his proposals regarding the publication of my letters. I confessed that this never was my intention to which he appeared greatly disappointed and was at a loss to understand my apprehension.

"Sir, I can assure you that it is the only course, you travel, you correspond, you embellish and then you publish, the printing presses in Paternoster Row are a blur of ink and machinery and the bookstands in the capital are creaking under the very weight of such publications. I confess I know not where lies the problem?"

I called for another brandy for my guest to rescue him from this glumness but you can be certain that Mr Fenton will not remain downcast for any period of time for his character simply will not permit such behaviour and in no time an air of conviviality had returned to the room. Mr Fenton then asked after you, my dear uncle, for as the recipient of my correspondence you had featured in his design for the title page of the proposed publication of my scribbles. (You may rest assured sir, it is but one of Mr Fenton's more fanciful notions, for who would wish to read of the thoughts and deeds of one so immature?) I was able to give an account of my childhood memories when you then lived in the metropolis with your occasional visits to our family home and I can recall your patience in lining up my soldiers only for me to then carelessly destroy these opposing toy armies. I am saddened that distance, these last ten years, has dictated that we should only make our written communications and I believe that my father, your brother, showed little encouragement whenever I made a request that we should meet again. I believe that you will find me almost beyond recognition from that small boy that you once knew and I sincerely hope, my dear uncle, that there is now no obstacle to the arranging of this event and that we can again be reunited. I was able to relate to Mr Fenton the details of your own pedestrian adventure in North Wales and he informed me that it was a part of the world that inspired awe in all who had the good fortune to visit that wild and wonderful and most secretive of places. Indeed, our very discussion has resulted in an invitation from Mr Fenton to act as my guide in a future excursion to that same place, which excites me greatly. My hand trembles before the page as during my discussion with Mr Fenton he then asked after your business as I gauge that he found himself in accord with your adventurous spirit and wished to know more of you. I confess that I know not of your business but I recall in a conversation that perhaps was not intended for my ears between my father and a bank official that you had encountered some financial misfortune which then resulted in your move from London to a place called Fleet. My father would never elucidate when asked about the whereabouts of this town or perhaps even a village by this name and he commanded me to talk no more about it. At the mention of this place called Fleet, Mr Fenton at once drew a grave expression and leant forward to clasp my hands and by this display of consternation I knew it not be a good place at all. My dear uncle, why have you not approached your own family, my father when he was alive, with a request for help rather than face the incarceration of a debtors prison? I knew not that such places existed and I cannot imagine the despair that you must have endured. I would dearly like to put right a wrong that our family has caused and yet I cannot anticipate my own position as I have turned my own back on the future that my father had determined for me. I sincerely hope that your own circumstances are now more secure and I am ashamed at my own indulgence, with the daily succession of my trivial correspondence, all of which is of little consequence. Mr Fenton was distressed that he should be the one to make this dreadful situation known to me but he has assured me that sadly it is a common enough event in business and a full recovery is often accomplished. Mr Fenton has asked me to forward his fondest regards and he is of the firm belief that your situation must now be secure. As a former lawyer Mr Fenton states that he is able to make such an assertion, on the evidence that one who is without good resource would not embark upon and then publish an account of their own pedestrian tour as it speaks of some financial security. He added that it is also an endeavour that is to be commended and one that his nephew must surely have the good sense to follow.

I cannot stress enough the friendship I have found in Mr Fenton for although I felt great alarm to learn of your past circumstances, I believe in my friend's assertions that you have now made fully your recovery. I sincerely hope that this description of my conversation with Mr Fenton has not embarrassed in any way or awoken past memories that you must wish to forget. It has brought me closer still with my feelings towards you my dear uncle and confirmed my commitment that we should soon be reunited.

It is not the evening that I had planned upon yet it has given me much to think about and my sandy stones have been neglected until

another time for with Mr Fenton's departure and my completion of
this letter to you, I am now more than ready for slumber.

Your obedient and faithful Nephew,

HENRY CHALK.

Monday 19ᵗʰ October 1807

MY DEAR UNCLE,

Today I find myself in very noble surrounds as Sir Richard Colt
Hoare has kindly admitted me to his great library and here I
sit before a beautifully crafted desk where I now commit these lines
to you. I believe that the Baronet is suffering from an illness called
gout and is in some considerable pain as he has now retired for the
afternoon. I feel that I am writing in a whisper, such is the effect of
this place with its great looming tiers of leather-bound erudition and
knowledge crushing my very small notions that I have formed of late.
I felt myself redden at the collar when being addressed by Sir Richard
as he kindly explained the great project he has embarked upon that
is to be called "The Ancient History of Wiltshire". There are maps
of tracts of the south of this county drawn up by a gentleman called
Mr Philip Crocker who is the surveyor and draughtsman appointed
to this task. The content of each barrow has its own illustration and

there is a great beauty to both the maps and the plates of drawings. Indeed the organisation of this grand project is profound with Mr William Cunnington as co-adjutator with a responsibility for the opening of the barrows with the two barrow diggers themselves, Mr Stephen Parker and Mr John Parker, Mr Philip Crocker the surveyor and draughtsman and Sir Richard himself the commander and author who will commit to the page the facts and conclusions of this great exercise. I do not fully understand the role of Mr Richard Fenton in these proceedings except that he is perhaps an aide to the Baronet and there is surely a friend no more committed than is Mr Fenton to his noble host. Mr Fenton brings warmth to the place for he cannot resist a humorous view even in the most solemn of moments and as I have discovered today Sir Richard alone is not one to encourage dialogue but then I flatter myself that I have something to offer to such a well planned enquiry. I have a pocket full of flints and a head full of notions and I wished that I could again meet with Mr William Cunnington as I consider that he is a man who believes in what the eye can perceive rather than what is already written on the page. My dear uncle, if you were within reach of my ear I feel certain that you would box it and speak to me very firmly with a reminder that I am sitting in the best private library in the land and I should put down my pen and for once suspend my flow of nonsense.

*

Sir, I may have contrived your words and deeds but it was surely the very best of advice for which I am truly thankful. After a circuit of this room I knew not where to start with numismatics, the writings of Tacitus, Caesar and Pliny and the topographies of every possible county. I instead settled upon books already selected and laying open and available on Sir Richard's desk and one volume displayed plates of Stonehenge and a short article by Mr William Maton relating to the fall of one of the major sets of stones in 1797. I thought back to

my recent visit to that place and the description of this same ground
shaking event by the toothless shepherd who was swift to approach
our windswept party and engage our sympathy. The illustrations
depict a before and after view of the effects of this fall and in both were
present the same lady and gentleman, an artistic device to suggest the
scale of the structure to the viewer, but by their very persistent presence
and air of affected innocence I fancied that they must in some way be
culpable. I turned the pages of this same volume and my heart took a
great leap as before me were two plates that appeared to be illustrations
of a similar flint object that I had collected from outside the brickearth
pit in Salisbury and the circumstances for the provenance of these
crafted flint pieces were identical in every way. The author of this short
account is Mr John Frere and the location of this find is Hoxne in the
county of Suffolk in the year of 1797. Mr Frere describes these objects
as "Flint weapons" and that they lay in great numbers at a depth of
twelve feet amongst the strata of a brickearth pit and in combination
were found "Some extraordinary bones, particularly a jaw bone of
enormous size, of some unknown animal, with the teeth remaining
in it." On receiving this information, I fell back into Sir Richard
Colt Hoare's chair that was placed before his desk with these words
encircling my head. I asked out loud to a library empty of souls save
my own.

"Why and how can this information lay dormant and not be
considered a matter of extreme import and astonishment?"

I have not heard The Baronet or Mr William Cunnington
make any reference to this discovery that happened barely ten years
before. It is as if Mr Frere has been alone in his comprehension despite
his reporting of these events to the Society of Antiquaries and their
subsequent publication in this edition of their Proceedings which was
issued in 1800. I gathered up my senses and completed my reading of
this article and I submit this lengthy tract in Mr Frere's own words as

it only confirms my own thoughts, ideas and indeed strong instinct that has been haunting my mind and dreams since the first day of my pedestrian excursion here in this county;

"The situation in which these weapons were found may tempt us to refer them to a very remote period indeed; even beyond that of the present world; but, whatever our conjectures on that head may be, it will be difficult to account for the stratum in which they lie being covered with another stratum, which, on that supposition, may be conjectured to have been once the bottom, or at least the shore, of the sea. The manner in which they lie would lead to the persuasion that it was a place of their manufacture and not of their accidental deposit; and the numbers of them were so great that the man who carried on the brick-work told me that, before he was aware of their being objects of curiosity, he had emptied baskets full of them into the ruts of the adjoining road."

Sir, the earlier account of the twisting of my own ankle in the ruts in the road outside the Salisbury brickworks will tell you that the circumstances are identical in this respect and indeed in all respects to that of Hoxne in Suffolk. Mr John Frere's words have fully reinforced my own belief that the dark period of our ancient ancestors extends to a time when the land was not yet truly formed as we know it today and yet behind this veil of ignorance we now have a beacon of light. Is it not the common substance that we call flint that is the key to the continuity of life itself upon this earth and is not the instance of the very first discovery as to its remarkable fire giving properties and keenness of edge that has sent man on his remarkable journey? The flint fragments that litter the sandy fields beneath Whitesheet Hill are I believe the detritus of more modern and settled farming societies and I do not mock when I refer to man as "modern", before even the advent of the use of metal. Sir, I apologise for I am dealing in incomprehensible fact and would be branded a man not in his right senses if I were to

broadcast this view beyond these pages. I would welcome an audience
with Mr John Frere as I believe his frustration must be as great as any
man for his printed word collects dust and is ignored by those who do
not understand the importance of such a discovery. I must now depart
to my lodgings to then return for dinner at five o clock at Stourhead
House although I now draw strength from the knowledge that my
burden is not imaginary nor is it solitary.

*

My dear uncle, I have now acquired a compulsion to write even at this
late hour for it was almost midnight when I returned from Stourhead
House but I feel alive and some distance from making acquaintance
again with my pillow. I trust that you can imagine the grandeur of
dining with Sir Richard Colt Hoare and his selected guests. Dinner
is at the respectable hour of five o clock and I ensured that I at least
had a clean white shirt for the occasion. It is not clean now and I shall
reveal in time how this occurred and you will not be surprised to learn
that Mr John Fenton has a part to play in that tale. The guests were
few in number and of those whom I had not yet met were a young
lawyer by the name of Mr Edward Phelps and another young man
of fashion who had earlier arrived from London by the name of Mr
George Button, who was familiar with Mr John Fenton. Mr Philip
Crocker who is the surveyor and draughtsman to the Baronet was
also present and I wished for an opportunity to remark on the great
skill involved in his illustrations and plans for "Ancient Wiltshire".
Mr Crocker was seated across at an opposing end of the great table to
myself and then retired early to prepare for an excursion in the morning
and so that I was unable to make my compliment. There were no
ladies present which permitted an air of relaxed familiarity with much
humour and laughter. Mr Richard Fenton was, I am glad to be able
to report, sitting directly across the table from my position which was
a detail that offered me great reassurance. It was this same gentleman

that proposed the first toast of the evening in an acknowledgement of the privilege of dining in such a superior room.

"And although our number may be few, we recognise the great honour that our host has bestowed upon us this evening and I propose a toast of thanks to our noble host, Sir Richard Colt Hoare."

This was an expression to which we all heartily concurred and we then raised our glasses in unison. Indeed the saloon is as grand a surroundings as I ever imagined and is quite the distraction for the partaking of food as I gauge that it is fully fifty feet in length with the ceiling rich in its ornamentation and with large painted panels on each wall and the whole is furnished throughout with style and magnificence. Before me on the table lay an array of silver cutlery that I approached with great caution and I sincerely hope that I did not broadcast my attempted discretion as I followed the example of the other guests as they greeted each of the many courses. As I negotiated my way through the earlier passage of dinner, in amongst such a display of social confidence, I felt increasingly that my presence here was a gross error. What did I know about events in the English Channel or of the siege of Copenhagen although I dutifully raised my glass? Mr Richard Fenton, perhaps sensing my discomfort, then drew attention to my presence and demanded that a toast was drunk to "Mr Henry Chalk, our pedestrian tourist and adventurer", and I felt myself redden as I am so often wont to do in any such situation. The company were most warm and generous in making this toast and Mr Richard Fenton then flattered me greatly by his suggestion that I was an "Antiquary in the making" at which point more wine was imbibed and I felt helpless to resist. The young gentleman of fashion, Mr Button, then proclaimed that there was already plenty enough of that species who were only too ready to make acquaintance with the dust of their ancestors and "..surely young Mr Chalk was not to be encouraged". Mr Button then proposed that I should be directed to more useful and becoming pursuits, after all it is well known that "what antiquaries do not know they make up anyway". Being seated at the table of Sir Richard Colt Hoare, the man of fashion was soon shouted down and his comments that I can now comfortably identify as raillery were all taken in good humour. Mr Richard Fenton then rose to his feet and speaking in those rich theatrical tones, to which I have now become accustomed, he made a firm rebuttal to this onslaught.

"We speak from facts not theory and it is our duty as fellow antiquarians to cast aside the shrouds of darkness and mystery and reveal to all the history and lives of these ancient inhabitors of our land, for we must not forget that they were real people like ourselves. Our fashionable friend would have us believe that the sole purpose and industry of our ancestors was to cast artefacts and broken urns across the green sward that is Salisbury Plain to keep us in employ and far from mischief in their reverential and not inexpensive recovery."

These words induced cheers and support from around the table and Mr Richard Fenton appeared well satisfied with his stout defence of the antiquarian battlements, yet I felt that the comedy of his delivery had disguised the gravity of his observation. I found myself bolstered by the flowing wine and I brought my hand down on the table and startled the host and guests alike as I discharged a piece of cutlery from the table to the floor. Having now attracted the attention of the entire company I felt that I must continue with my support for Mr Richard Fenton.

"Sir, you have put into words my own feelings and thoughts and as always with great wit and eloquence that I cannot hope to emulate. It is indeed the relics of our ancestors that are retrieved by the persevering antiquary and I concur wholeheartedly with Mr Fenton that they once belonged to real people."

I bent down to retrieve the knife from the carpet before the footman could round the table and undertake the task and I then held it aloft.

"Gentlemen, this is a knife but I would not be buried with it today.."

"It is one of a set, Mr Chalk," remarked Mr John Fenton, "and it would not do for it would then make it an odd set."

Amidst more laughter I continued steadfastly on my course to I knew not where.

"It is but a tool and our ancient ancestors, before a time of metal, would have knives also for how else would they cut up their meat as we are cutting up ours this evening? I suggest that every man had his knife and not just the kings, queens and warriors that have now had their slumber disturbed. I propose that these common tools were fashioned from the flint that abounds in the south of this county and these discarded tools still lay about the fields where they once fell all those generations ago. Indeed, I have examples about my person.."

At this point Sir Richard Colt Hoare slowly rose from his chair and with a pained expression excused himself from the table and naturally we, the present company, pushed back our chairs and rose as one as the Baronet then left the room. There was a great deal of sympathy expressed for the obvious suffering of our host and once the diners were reunited with their chairs then the subject took a different course and I believed that my observations on the widespread use of flint tools had been lost amongst the fields of idle conversation. In due course Mr Philip Crocker excused himself to attend to his work and Mr Richard Fenton then declared that he had duties to perform and in turn excused himself also. I was for returning to my accommodation as a hand of cards was suggested, to which I felt no inclination. I warmed myself at the great fireplace before departing and I was looking up at the chimney piece carved from the finest white marble as Mr John Fenton approached. He then retrieved the subject of my observation that I thought had fallen upon deaf ears and suggested that if antiquarians were to be taken seriously then they should be able to prove their theories. I then declared that I had the evidence on my person and I first produced my flint tool from the Salisbury brickearth pit and stated that I had intended to show it to Sir Richard earlier today in combination with a number of pieces fashioned by human hand. I explained its provenance and it was then passed to Mr Phelps and even the man of fashion, Mr Button, tested its edge. I then displayed the tool that had recently been manufactured by Peter Winter and this was also passed between the remaining company and its freshly prepared edge was acknowledged as being keen and sharp to the touch. Mr John Fenton then suggested that he had a notion of how my theory could be put to the test which must surely be the correct course, if we are a breed to be taken seriously and he then indicated that we should all follow after him. We were taken to an outbuilding across the courtyard where the game larder was situated, the night was cold and our breath made great clouds in the lamplight. We were presented with the sight of various species of bird and game all dangling from hooks with their shadows wavering in false animation on the back wall. I gathered that some form of demonstration was required to back up my words and suggested that a large rabbit, that Mr Fenton informed me was called a "hare", would suffice for our purposes but he stated that if we were going to take this matter seriously then it demanded a larger beast.

"There is your meat," said Mr John Fenton, gesturing with a spilling wine glass towards a large deer that hung from a hook in the ceiling, "Henry Chalk, please can you now demonstrate that you are indeed, the ancestor of all butchers."

As you will be aware my dear uncle, I had observed the clandestine butchery of a deer in the stable of the New Inn some days ago and I had now drunk sufficient wine to believe that I could replicate this task in the name of science. I am not sickened by the sight of such things and agreed to prove my case but I required help lowering the beast onto the large wooden chopping board and for the light to then be positioned in my favour. The carcass had been previously cleaned with the head and lower limbs removed. I then parted with my coat and rolled up my sleeves and chose the tool replicated by Peter Winter, as it presented the sharpest edge. I recalled how I had observed its maker, when he had turned it about in his hand and found favour with holding the piece between thumb and forefinger. At the first incision, the man of fashion produced a handkerchief from his pocket and buried his long nose in it, exclaiming his disgust at the sight and smell of the operation. Mr John Fenton returned to the house for wine to assist with the viewing and returned also with another lamp. I experimented with my crude butchery skills and favoured tugging at the skin with my free hand and making it taut and then presenting it to the cutting edge. I could then roll the tool between thumb and forefinger along this tightness which would in turn easily part the skin from the flesh. I found a cloth to clear the collected fat from the flint and fully forgot my audience as I made good progress. I employed the same method to the jointing of the meat but found difficulty in dealing with the bone itself but I had successfully removed several parcels of the meat and was now attacking the haunches. It was at this moment that the young lawyer, Mr Phelps, made a suggestion that shocked me greatly.

"Was this not the beast that Sir Richard himself shot last week and was intended as a gift for Mr Matthew Fortesque and was to be transported in the morning to London?"

"I do believe that you are correct Mr Phelps," said Mr John Fenton with feigned surprise.

"By the time young Mr Chalk has finished with it," concluded Mr George Button from behind his handkerchief, "you'd be lucky to make a peasant stew."

I was aghast as the three young men then burst out into uncontrollable laughter.

"Good night master butcher," called back Mr John Fenton, as

the three disingenuous young men withdrew noisily from the game larder, taking with them one of the lamps.

"Perhaps your stone wedge can be put to good use, to prop open the door when you leave," suggested the man of fashion, with a wave of the hand.

I have been made a fool of by Mr John Fenton whose appetite for such things is I fear insatiable and I believed them sincere in their interest. At first the tears streamed down my cheeks as I thought of my betrayal of the kind Baronet's hospitality and I could not comprehend the purpose of Mr John Fenton's cruel humour any more than I could excuse my own foolishness. As best I could I completed my task and stacked up the crude joints on the wooden board with the skin, bones and remnants to one side. I found a pump and bucket in the yard and drew water to wash the mess from my hands as I heard the clock strike one quarter to midnight. I did not wish to reach the inn after midnight as I would be required to raise the staff and make an inconvenience and so I determined to make good time back to the Stourhead Inn. I found my way around the side of the house and then extinguishing the lantern I left it in a small porch that must be the access to the domestic quarters. The night was clear enough to see before me the broad drive with the dark and grotesque shapes of the twisted chestnut trees and I felt a shiver pass over me as if I were again a young child who feared the unknown terrors of the night. I began to walk and then run faster and in turn faster still until I could feel the cold night air forcing into my face and I believed that I could keep abreast with the fastest racehorse. My ankle felt strong and I know that all the paths on the Baronet's estate are kept in the best order possible and as my feet pounded, I felt no fear of stumbling and falling. I could sense the stone gateway looming ahead of me and I slowed my pace least the gatekeeper should be startled by a person fleeing through the night but once I met the road I again flew down the hill through the darkness to the Stourhead

Inn, with my footfalls resounding between the steep embankments on either side. I slipped quietly through the back door and once inside my room I soon heard the clock strike midnight.

I do not know how I shall explain myself to Sir Richard Colt Hoare yet I feel in some way justified in my actions for I did fulfil the challenge that those disingenuous young men had concocted for me. I consider that they mock me for my too serious nature in one so young for I do not truly believe that Mr John Fenton dislikes me but I care the less for what people think of me and I will follow my own trail. There is one for whom I care greatly and I hope with all my heart that this feeling is reciprocated. Even at this late hour I must send a note to Miss Foster's brother to ensure that he should suspend any further correspondence to myself at the Stourhead Inn. Tomorrow, my dear uncle, I shall leave this place and again become a simple pedestrian tourist for my ankle is now fully repaired and I shall make a resolution to not be drawn so readily into the lives of all whom I meet, for it seems only to lead to complication.

Your serious yet still foolish nephew,
HENRY CHALK

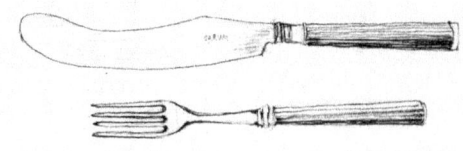

Tuesday 20th October 1807

MY DEAR UNCLE,

Sir, it is my grave responsibility to report that tragedy has struck and under the most unfortunate circumstances for which I can only attach the blame to myself and my own selfish and foolish actions. I believe that it is best to recount the events of the morning in the order that they occurred and yet I fear, my dear and faithful uncle, that in whichever arrangement these facts are presented they will cause you great distress. At breakfast I was approached by the landlord and informed that the parish constable wished to interview me, an event for which I quickly prepared myself and descended to the front of the building as instructed. At first, I believed that the butchery of the deer had in some manner been drawn to the attention of the parish official yet I was soon to discover that there was a far more serious purpose to his enquiry. I was led to an outhouse by the landlord and the parish constable where on a large rough table the body of a man was laid out and I felt that their eyes were upon me as I was presented with this tragic sight. I could not at first place where I had seen this unfortunate gentleman but I felt the stirrings of some recognition and the parish constable was made to repeat his initial question as his words became lost to me, as if I were embattled in some malevolent dream.

"Mr Chalk? You arrived late back at the inn, did you not sir?"

I explained that I had indeed returned just before midnight. The parish constable revealed that the deceased had been found lying in the middle of the road by a milkmaid early this morning at a point halfway between the Stourhead Inn and the stone gateway to the house. I informed them that the lane was dark and overhung with trees and I felt certain that I would have stumbled upon the body had it been there when I passed that way, for I surely would not have seen it. I now believed that I was under some suspicion for the enquiry then turned to the bloody gash on the forehead of the dead man and, in turn, to my white shirt of yesterday that I had earlier submitted to the maid for washing but was now produced before me and I was asked to explain its condition. I assured the two gentlemen that the now dried dark brown bloodstains were most certainly animal and not human and it was a circumstance that would be difficult to explain here but could easily be proven if required. The parish constable then produced a folded letter from his coat pocket and with the same grim and unaltered expression requested that I should read it and then explain its content. It was addressed to a Mr Joseph Barklay of Exeter with a request that he should; "Advance to Hindon at once and put up at the Lamb Inn until I can establish the movement of our subject Mr Henry Chalk." The note was dated 12th of October and signed "J Chalk". I had no sooner digested the content of one short letter when I was presented with another, which also displayed your signature my dear uncle and had been posted on 15th October; "Our subject will be staying at the Stourhead Inn. Put up at the Red Lion Inn, Kilmington. Ask no questions and do not draw the attention of anyone. Once you have delivered your message return to Exeter and I shall honour the second instalment of your fee."

The parish official then held up further property that had been retrieved from Mr Joseph Barklay, for it was discovered that on his person was a cloth purse containing a little short of ten guineas. I must have appeared in a state of weakness for the landlord guided me to a place where I could sit as the true meaning of all these events now formed in my mind. My gaze was drawn to the profile of the dead man, his staring but unseeing eyes and the grey lifelessness of his skin and no more would his broad chest rise and fall with the drawing of breath. I recalled aloud the circumstances that had proceeded this

fateful situation, the details of which you are only too painfully aware
my dear uncle. I informed them also of my regular correspondence to
you containing my deeds and whereabouts that had alerted you to my
predicament and prompted the execution of your plan to come to
my aid. From my seated position on an old beer barrel I then stood
before the table and studied the visage of the corpse in more detail
and I then realised where I had before seen Mr Joseph Barklay and
I felt a sudden chill at this recollection. It was on the occasion of my
visit to the village of Hindon when by the light of a chestnut brazier
I had felt his unsettling gaze upon me and he had also pursued me
for a little way. I thought him then to be a man in Mr William
Beckford's employ and feared the attention that he had paid me but
I now realise sir that he was engaged to execute your own plan. I
informed of this fact and lamented deeply that if only I had let him
approach me on that election night, he would have carried out his
duty and returned to his family in Exeter some days ago. The parish
constable thanked me earnestly for my cooperation in elucidating
the necessary facts and that he was sorry for the obvious discomfort
that his enquiry had caused me. I was informed that by good fortune
there was a guest staying at the Inn who was a doctor of medicine
by profession and he had agreed to give a cursory examination of
the body in due course. I then returned to my room and sat for an
age in a blank daze not knowing what course to take. It is plain my
dear uncle that my foolish exploits have cost the life of your poor
associate for knowing my state of impecuniosity you dispatched a
letter immediately to Mr Joseph Barklay for him to then come to
my aid and whilst he awaited instruction at Hindon by chance he
observed a young pedestrian tourist who then unfortunately eluded
him. In time you received the further accounts of my progress which
you then relayed to the long suffering Mr Barklay and so he was
able to locate me at Stourhead and there he remained faithful to your

instructions by behaving with the utmost discretion. Rather than make a direct approach to my place of lodging he waited to intercept me, perhaps at a far later hour than he first imagined but he remained the model of patience in executing his duty.

*

The parish official has again sought me out and I have been informed that the medic has viewed the body of Mr Barklay and he is of the opinion that the unfortunate man died of a heart seizure and the blow to the head was consistent with the subsequent fall to the ground on his collapse. As I flew through the night at that late hour from Stourhead House, I unknowingly passed your associate who was perhaps ailing then for he surely could not have caught up with me and common sense suggests that he would have called out my name had he been able. An open knife has also been found on the road that must have fallen from the pocket of the late Mr Barklay and the parish constable considers that it provided him with the protection necessary when burdened with the task of carrying a purse containing that not inconsiderable sum. The official then instructed me that Mr William Whitmarsh, the coroner, has been summoned from Salisbury for it is his official duty to preside over and register the cause of all deaths in his district before any burial can take place. He then shook his head and said that it was indeed a sorry end to a plan that had been undertaken with the very best of intentions and I informed him that I would contact you at once to report these dreadful events. I found the parish constable to be a stern but also a and kindly man and altogether a different breed from his equal that I encountered some days ago at the New Inn, who appeared devoid of all manners and any semblance of integrity. The steward at Stourhead house is to be informed of these tragic events and is then to be entrusted with the body of Mr Joseph Barklay and his property until the arrival of the Coroner in due course.

I have another onerous duty to perform for I must now write to Sir Richard Colt Hoare to humbly apologise for destroying the deer carcass that he intended as a gift to a gentleman in London. I hold my head in my hands when I consider the trouble I have caused at my every turn. For what it is worth, I shall endeavour to explain my misguided action which I undertook in the name of a practical scientific experiment but I feel certain that it will not meet with his approval. I shall also include my thoughts on the everyday use of flint by ancient man in the Baronet's own neighbourhood of Stourton. I have a conviction of their correctness and I shall accompany this description with the drawings of the flint pieces that I have undertaken thus far. I will submit also an illustration of the flint tool from the Salisbury brickearth pit and a sketch of the overlying strata with a reference to the printed account of Mr John Frere and his most remarkable discovery in Hoxne, in Suffolk, that resides in the pages of a book within the Baronet's own library. Sir Richard Colt Hoare has far exceeded the bounds of common generosity towards this troublesome pedestrian tourist and I fear that he will not accept a financial settlement of the debt that I feel that I have incurred as a result of his hospitality. The author of the Ancient History of Wiltshire can assess the small worth of my own contribution and do with it what he will, as he shapes his own account of this dark and remote period.

I know not what else to relate my dear uncle and I dispatch this final correspondence to you with the heaviest of hearts. When I am able, I fully intend to reimburse you for the expense that you have incurred on my behalf and I shall do likewise to the family of the late Mr Joseph Barklay.

*

Before sealing this letter to you my dear uncle, I have been visited by my good friend Mr Richard Fenton. He has been informed of the sudden death of your associate by the steward at Stourhead House and wished to convey his own sympathies and those of our host, Sir Richard Colt Hoare, who has also now learned of this tragedy. Both gentlemen have expressed their desire to commend you on your own actions in attempting to come to my aid, knowing as you did my precarious situation. Mr Fenton has informed me that once the coroner has carried out his official duty, then the Baronet will arrange and make provision for the burial of poor Mr Barklay.

My visitor then remarked on the incident of the previous night for he had overheard Mr Button making laughter at breakfast and naturally enquired as to its cause. There appeared a reticence between the three young men present to divulge any information until Mr Richard Fenton insisted that his son Mr John Fenton should explain this behaviour. The account of the visit to the game larder was then related and as with the occasion of the wager that was struck between Mr John Fenton and myself at the George Inn in Amesbury, an excess of wine and high spirits was given as its cause. Mr Richard Fenton then asked whether I should ever get used to his son's propensity for raillery and mischief making and he cautioned me to never entertain any idea or proposal from that same gentleman, for there will surely only ever be one outcome. I asked what was to become of the intended gift from Sir Richard to the gentleman in London and I was assured that the matter had been swiftly dealt with and no harm has been done. The Baronet has been informed that the carcass was already maggot blown and he will be required to again pick up his gun which is a pursuit that will only result in pleasure and the encounter with fresh air will serve to raise his spirits. Mr Fenton then asked of my future plans and I explained that the tragedy here had made me reflect deeply on the consequences of my actions and the effect of those actions upon others. I informed him that I fully intended to depart for London in the morning to fulfil my father's wishes and accept my family responsibility. Mr Fenton then surprised me greatly by speaking with great sincerity about love and I shall try to recall his every word as they touched me greatly.

"You will have noticed a sadness in Sir Richard's eye and it is a melancholy that has been with him since before I was fortunate enough to make his acquaintance, indeed you can detect it in the portrait of father and son in the reception hall. It is not a matter that he will speak of even to his closest friends and I am indeed flattered to class myself as such. In 1785 Sir Richard lost his beloved wife in childbirth. He was heartbroken then and he is heartbroken now, as the heart is the most difficult of devices to mend, but he lives and he smiles and sometimes he will laugh. Above all our noble friend needs distraction which he seeks in the task of recording the antiquities of Wiltshire and it is indeed a very worthy cause but it will never replace the loss he has suffered. A coldness has settled on his heart which can affect how you treat even your own family. One day he will be reunited with his beloved Hestor and only when his heart ceases to beat will it also cease to ache. You are young but you will learn that love can be a force of great power and its loss can defeat even the greatest and strongest of men and if you find love Mr Henry Chalk you may forever regret the losing of that love. Young men sometimes think that they love when all is confusion and some speak of love knowing that it is a powerful word that can unlock the heart and passion of a woman, but love is more than words uttered at an opportune moment."

I do not know why Mr Fenton chose to tell me of Sir Richard's most intimate of circumstances or how he thought that it would affect my situation yet after his departure from my room I sat with these words resounding in my head. I believe that my good friend has spoken in a very wise and paternal way to help guide my decisions as he must sense that my ramble here is a diversion from my duties elsewhere, and indeed he is correct. I have reflected now about my own father, your brother, and how he may also have suffered a broken heart at the death of my mother for I was too young to understand his pain but I grew up knowing his coldness and perhaps a heart can become so cold that it is no longer capable of warmth. Love must be a fundamental thing that binds people as one and to lose love is to become cast adrift alone on a cold sea.

I cannot now forward my letter to Sir Richard Colt Hoare as he is not aware of the incident with the deer to which I allude and then apologise for wholeheartedly. I feel that these matters are only mere distractions and I flatter myself greatly that I can help to contribute to his pioneering work. I have therefore posted the letter into the fireplace where it meets with the conflagrations of the Radstock coal and with it perish my own foolish antiquarian aspirations.

Mr Richard Fenton I sincerely hope that I shall meet again for his wisdom has guided me towards a reconciliation where I feel I should now embrace my father's wishes. I believe that he has been able to look into my very soul and as I write these words, I can also hear his mellifluous voice.

"If you find love Mr Henry Chalk you may forever regret the losing of that love."

Sir, you will be glad to learn that my stock of writing paper is now exhausted, my nibs blunt and my ink well dry. I shall give the callous on my finger a much required rest as I believe that I have initiated and then documented quite enough disruption in the south of this quiet county of Wiltshire and I feel certain that the population here shall be glad to witness my departure.

On my adventure I have now met with a division in the path ahead and Mr John Cary cannot on this occasion assist for neither destination on this handpost are recorded on his map of Wiltshire. Indeed, there exists no map that can offer this confused and love tormented traveller the guidance he requires, for despite the best of advice he knows not whether he should now follow his head or his heart. Bless you my dear uncle, for if the former shall be my guide then you will know where to locate your troublesome relation yet if I should choose "the peaks and troughs of adventure", I know not what fate awaits this pedestrian tourist.

I am forever your faithful nephew,
HENRY CHALK.

PART TWO

A

TOUR

IN SEARCH OF

FLINT

THROUGH PARTS OF

SOUTH WILTSHIRE

IN

1808

WRITTEN IN

𝕬 𝖘𝖊𝖗𝖎𝖊𝖘 𝖔𝖋 𝕷𝖊𝖙𝖙𝖊𝖗𝖘

IN WHICH ARE DESCRIBED; THE ACQUIRING OF A
SNAKECATCHER'S HAT, THE RESURRECTION OF DON
QUIXOTE OF LA MANCHA, A TRANSACTION WITH
MR. HENRY SHORTO, ESTEEMED CUTLER OF SALISBURY,
A SINGLE STICK CONTEST INVOLVING THE EXTRAORDINARY
MR. WILLIAM HAZLITT AT THE WINTERSLOW HUT,
AND A SOURCE FOUND OF THE HIGHEST QUALITY *FLINT* AND
EVIDENCE OF ITS EXTRACTION BY ANCIENT MAN.

BY

A PEDESTRIAN.

LETTER TO THE EDITOR

The earlier publication of my nephew's letters to myself entitled "A Tour in Search of Chalk" has not engendered the expected response from its author Mr Henry Chalk and, as a consequence, I have been unable to establish his whereabouts and thereby ensure his wellbeing to my satisfaction. South Wiltshire does indeed appear to hold some fascination for my young and naive relative and provides fertility to his imagination for it is only when he is at large in that place that the ink flows from his pen. I know of no other means to provoke a response and ensure contact other than to replicate the earlier method and publish a further flood of these letters from the same itinerant source. The noblemen and gentlemen who have deemed it their responsibility to befriend my nephew have thus far been ungraciously reticent to my direct pleas to encourage our reunion and I believe that they are stifling my requests for contact to the extent of withholding my correspondence.

His responsibilities in life are clear and simple and as his sole surviving relative it is my avuncular duty to provide the correct guidance. Chalk's Brewery in Southwark, London is thriving with its new source of water and yet the trustees are desperate for its young heir to take up his position at the helm as is only proper and correct.

As a plea to the general reading public I shall offer, through my publisher, a reward of TWENTY GUINEAS to whosoever can provide information that leads directly to the location of HENRY CHALK- PEDESTRIAN TOURIST.

Yours faithfully
J. CHALK
July 1808

Friday May 6th 1808

MY DEAR UNCLE,

With my crossing again into the county of Wiltshire I am back with pen in hand. There is a palpable eruption of the earth's goodness through every unfurling and trembling shoot and indeed the birds and mammals need no convincing of these issues for there is both a bold and furtive activity on land, air and water.

I write these words beside the River Nadder, whose sandy waters contain the secrets of the steep and wooded slopes of this vale. There is a tree that appears to thrive on its proximity to the river here, it has a dark waxy green leaf and its roots cling to these soft banks in knotted desperation. Under just such a tree I have sought some welcome shade for today is exceedingly warm and having removed my pack I sense the wetness of my labours thus far upon my back and I feel justified in stripping down to my shirt.

How can I apologise to you sir, not only for the great trouble I have caused you but also for the neglect in not communicating my whereabouts these last few months? You will surmise that I have not yet returned to my duties in London and I still struggle to find the words to make good and explain my behaviour but I hold no doubt that the business of beer can still prosper in my absence. The chief clerk, Mr Hooper, and the head brewer Mr Gerrity at Chalk's Brewery are both honourable men though they may be as perplexed as you, my dear uncle, as to the antics of the son and heir to that place, since the death of my father last year.

On departing from Wiltshire last October, I retreated to the coast of Pembrokeshire in South Wales at the invitation of Mr Richard Fenton and was made most welcome at his family home in the town of Fishguard. I have spent some weeks employed in the task of making orderly the affairs of Mr Fenton where he has fishing boats and also property in the harbour. My host has some business but he is no businessman and it is a failing to which he readily admits. I have been able to set in motion some improvements to the maintenance of the properties that were suffering from neglect. I can hear you suggest, my dear uncle, that if I am happy to labour behind a desk in Fishguard then surely I can assume my responsibilities at Chalk's brewery in Southwark? In my heart I know that once I return, I shall never leave and as a consequence I am not yet fit to do so.

Mr Fenton has spent a deal of time in London as a companion to his good friend Sir Richard Colt Hoare but family life at Glynamel, Mr Fenton's home, has been a succour to me and I have been able to straighten my senses a little. I still have two major preoccupations. The first is of a romantic nature and you will not be surprised to learn that Miss Sarah Foster has a firm hold on my heart and by necessity all our correspondence is directed through her brother Robert. Without Robert we would be lost for he commits to the page his sister's thoughts and from his lips my words are transmitted in return. Whilst I am unable or unwilling to settle, I cannot be introduced to the Foster household yet Robert deems me trustworthy and honourable in my intentions towards his sister for our communications to continue. When Robert is absent, as he is presently, then our intimate thoughts remain unwritten and unread so I have chosen to embark again on a short pedestrian tour of South Wiltshire to occupy my mind. Indeed, I have arranged to meet with Robert Foster in seven days time at the Winterslow Hut which is situated on the London road some miles to the east of Salisbury. Robert is returning from London on his way back to the family home in North Somerset and it has been agreed that we should make our first acquaintance with one another, a meeting to which I am greatly looking forward.

I list two preoccupations my dear uncle and the latter will also fail to surprise. The former I have explained and the second could not offer more opposing properties for it is the hard and cold flint that abounds in this county. Sir, you have been the recipient of the accounts of my earlier rummaging through the soils of Stourhead to retrieve examples of fashioned flint and it is a subject on which I have puzzled at great length. I carry some of the finer pieces around with me along with the flint weapon from the Fisherton brickearth. Whilst I dwell on geological matters, I also have a fragment from one of the smaller upright stones that I found detached upon the ground on my visit to Stonehenge. It is however the pursuit of flint of the richest quality that has brought me back to Wiltshire and Mr Richard Fenton would suggest in all seriousness that I had embarked upon "A Tour in Search of Flint..etc..etc". My aims are modest and I am reticent even to impose them upon your patient self and not, as my good friend would recommend, to broadcast them to the whole world.

I shall now continue my pedestrianism and I will take my time for what would there be to report if, after a hearty breakfast at dawn and with head down and elbows out to the sides, I should be beyond the county boundary by dusk? I prefer to sit and stare, to circle a hill before ascending it, to stand without boots and stockings in a clear stream and to creep up and ensnare a view with my pencil. It is ponderous but it is all at a pace that permits observation. For now sir, I wish you the very best of good afternoons for there is no untruth, that I can detect, in that statement.

*

I have tarried again on my journey and I realise my dear uncle that I do not even possess a watch, so I can only judge the time by the positioning of the sun. I have placed myself before an old ruin with pencil in hand and in that duration the shadows here have lengthened and I would gauge that it is now perhaps five o clock. I have yet to truly complete any drawing in my life and I make no exception here but this scene of crumbling strength, now crowned with a neglect of ivy, is a model of the picturesque which even Mr Gilpin's critical eye may approve. There is a wondrous stillness here broken only by a stark cawing on my arrival of a large black bird that dwells in the upper reaches of this place. As I settled to my task the only movement and sound became the passing of lead from pencil to paper and I have been lost under the spell of great concentration.

Forgive me sir for I am a distracted traveller and I have neglected to describe my route thus far. Mr John Cary's map is still in my possession and I have flattened it out before me upon the grass. I see that this place is called Wardour and there is a grand new property not a mile away with its fresh white stone shining in the evening sun. Sadly, Mr Cary's map can only inform of villages and their connecting roads and does not contain sufficient detail to negotiate the web of paths and feint trails that thread across this most mysterious quarter of Wiltshire. This is not chalk country but heavy land that holds water with small fields and flourishing hedges with many marshy places. On leaving the hilltop town of Shaftesbury I met again with the green sands that I first encountered in Stourhead, on the estate of Sir Richard Colt Hoare. Indeed, there is a ridge at a place called Windcombe where on its steep northern slopes great excavations have been made that must surely have provided a great deal of the large green blockstone for that nearby town. Today these giant scars have been healed over by a cloak of trees and low tangled growth but I wonder at the immense scale of this operation and at man's tireless ability to plunder any useful resource. I then descended a dank and dark stony way with many plants of a lush greenness upon each bank. They prosper well in this shade and must feed upon the many water seepages here on these slopes and I noted the appearance of a deep yellow ochre clay on my boots. Upon reaching the base of the valley I crossed a stream

Old Wardour Castle

where both man and beast have left their mark in the bankside mud; a bootprint and a cloven hoof side by side. A street or a cobbled road does not spark this deep reminder that we share this earth with our silent partners, yet today my own buried senses have been stirred by this close proximity to nature. I have followed paths not created solely by the padding of human feet for they are also coincident with the passing of smaller creatures; a gathering of fur upon a bramble, a rank scent in the air, a dark stool deposited in a shallow scraping and signs of burrowing and homebuilding nearby.

At the crossing of field boundaries there are wooden rails set across these footpaths and the sighting of which aids one's progress as to the way ahead. The top bar of these structures are made smooth by use, oiled by the palms of country hands and then buffed to a gloss by the seats of many pairs of Wiltshire breeches. I observed the human users of these paths from a distance as I am uncertain of my own entitlement to follow. I have greeted oncoming walkers with politeness by raising my hat but I understand by the curious expressions on these faces that they know that I am a stranger who passes this way but once. In the farmyards and the fields there is much activity. Cows are led to feed upon the bright grass by calling boys with whipsticks whilst gangs of men are digging at the steaming dung in the cattle pens in the yards, heaping it up and throwing it aboard open carts with long forks and it is then hauled away. In a cultivated field I have seen rows of men and women upon their knees picking at the small weeds. In another field a plough is drawn by a team of two set one before the other turning a narrow ridge of soil with unerring straightness.

Today the River Nadder has been my faithful companion from its infancy near Shaftesbury and it has led me in turn through the villages of Donhead st Mary and Donhead st Andrew. I have observed its opaque waters gushing at two old greenstone mills whilst I myself have been observed by two suspicious millers. I finally abandoned my friend the river at the first sight of the Wardour ruin and by skulking across open parkland and around small lakes in my quest to reach this place, I have splashes of mud and clay up to my knees which will not endear me to any respectable innkeeper.

Not only does Mr John Cary's map accompany me to Wiltshire but also the charcoal burner's azel stick has made its return after a dormant winter. I thought it dry and lifeless in the hallway in Pembrokeshire but now I believe it would sprout fresh growth if it were able, such is the keenness it displays probing and tapping the ground and flicking at thorn wands that threaten to snag at my stockings. I have thought much about Peter Winter and the boy Tam but I shall resist disturbing their business in Grovely for I am determined not to become entangled in the lives of others but shall keep my own company. The arrival of evening at my ruin has brought a succession of visitors in their carriages and I believe that it is time for me to depart although I may enquire of a nearby inn that would welcome a mud splashed pedestrian tourist.

*

Sir, how a mood can change in a day. On my arrival at the Glove Inn, which is situated on the turnpike at the foot of a steep escarpment and not two miles from the Wardour ruin, I was greeted with indifference by the landlord. I have a small room to myself and have now eaten a moderate supper and there should be little out of the ordinary to report. It has not been so. I had not even been escorted to my room when in a passageway I was confronted by Mr William Beckford's diminutive servant who recognised me in an instant and then barred my way with feet apart and hands on hips. His voice chilled me for it is a rasping growl and it brought back the horrors of my foolish venture to Fonthill and the resulting pursuit in the village of Hindon.

"Well, well, well, look and see it is the trespass boy."

He then turned and beckoned with a stumpy finger for me to

follow and I felt helpless to do otherwise. He showed me to a side room and gestured for me to enter and he then repeated his initial greeting for the benefit of the occupants inside. Seated in two padded chairs on either side of the window were Mr William Beckford and another gentleman whom I did not recognise and I was ushered further into the room by the little servant as he pushed the door closed behind him. Mr William Beckford viewed me in silence for a moment before addressing the other seated gentleman.

"Franchi, please permit me to introduce to you a young man whose identity has never been established. Trespass is a serious matter and our nameless friend here, on October last, entered my property under a cloud of misunderstanding which he made no attempt to dispel. Instead he scampered up the tower like a town rat and then fled the building and Mr Dwarf suffered at my own hand as a consequence."

The second gentleman did not address me directly and with a strong foreign flavour to his voice he enquired of Mr Beckford what was to become of this intruder. The owner of Fonthill Abbey considered the matter for a moment and drummed his fingers together under his chin as if fidgeting whilst at prayer.

"I believe it calls for official proceedings, this instant and in this very room."

He then issued highly pitched and sharp commands to his scowling servant to rearrange the dining chairs so that three were placed behind the table with one remaining on the opposing side. I was then instructed to put down my pack and stick and take my position upon the single chair whilst the other three gentlemen aligned themselves before me across the table with Mr Beckford in the centre.

"Mr Dwarf, will you gather the pen and paper from that worm-eaten writing desk? Franchi you shall make a record of the proceedings...and so, in this filthy place that is but a rustic brothel, let us commence."

Mr Beckford rapped upon the table with his knuckle and pronounced that the court was now in session and then turned his penetrating gaze upon me before requesting my name and address to which I dutifully responded. "Mr Henry Chalk you stand accused of trespassing in the grounds and property of Mr William Beckford of Fonthill, how do you plead?"

I tried to gather my thoughts. From outside in the courtyard the regular beat of a blacksmith's hammer upon his anvil grew louder in my mind..tink ..tink..tink..tink..tink.. tink..until it became the mechanism of some great ticking clock and in my confusion time flew, ebbed and then stopped still altogether as the blacksmith ceased in his labours.

"Is he dead?" asked the gentleman called Franchi.

"I do not believe so," advised Mr Beckford.

"Ee is stupeed?" suggested the dwarf.

Finally, the words gushed forth and I was able to explain the circumstances that led to my unauthorised entry and the making against my will of the wager with Mr John Fenton. It was established that I had profited to the sum of five guineas, by which time I sat with my head bowed at the unravelling of this foolishness.

"Are these somewhat pathetic excuses now duly recorded Franchi?" said Mr Beckford.

"Yes, your worshipful majesty and lordship."

The judge in this mock courtroom then requested that I take my chair with me and sit out in the passageway whilst a verdict is reached and my guilt established, to which I tamely obeyed.

How long I sat with my back to the wall in a listless torpor I know not. I heard a coach clatter into the yard and a hubbub of activity ensued and I was soon required to tuck in my feet as the passengers then trailed passed my position in the hallway, noisy and impatient and with the odour of having been confined in close proximity on a hot day. There appeared to be a collective anxiety about what lay ahead in the dining room and would there be a meal prepared in readiness? Would there then be sufficient time to eat this undoubtedly costly meal and still return to the carriage to retain a favoured seat? Age or sex presented no barriers to the ambitiously hungry for there was a great amount of jostling on the way to the table. The call of "All ready" by the coachman was greeted by cries of distress by the only partially fed as they stole away with anything that could be carried from the plate with the landlord in pursuit.

"Oi, you brings that back!"

My feet received another trampling in the race back to the coach and with more jeering and calling their journey continued and in a short while all was silent again.

A service maid passed me and before I was able to state that the gentlemen within did not wish to be disturbed, she proceeded to open the door to the side room. The maid gave me a curious look and demonstrated that the room was now empty and sure enough on my inspection the furniture had been restored to its original position and it contained no persons at all. The maid retrieved my chair from the hall and placed it before the table, she then departed through another door that I had not noticed in a panelled wall that led through to the parlour, leaving me alone to collect my pack and my stick. So, Mr William Beckford and his men have had their fun with me and I cannot say that I did not deserve it. Whilst I sat forlornly in the passageway they silently departed through another exit, no doubt with much amusement. The landlord later informed me that their purpose at the inn was unusual and was caused only by Mr Beckford's horse throwing two shoes as they descended White Sheet Hill and the farrier was required. My timely appearance it seems has supplied the three gentlemen with some idle amusement whilst the son of Vulcan carried out his work at the forge.

I believe that my supper was first served up late to the agitated passengers of the evening stage, who had not the time to enjoy it and I derived little pleasure at my turn with it. I have ended the day with my spirit crushed when previously, before my arrival at this place, it had been soaring with the sights and sounds of my return to Wiltshire. My thoughts shall now retreat to a place that always brings me hope and courage and I bid you goodnight.

Your errant nephew
HENRY CHALK

Saturday May 7th 1808

MY DEAR UNCLE,

I am now aware of the punishment that Mr Beckford and his men have inflicted upon me after their holding of a mock court at the Glove Inn. On leaving that place with a desire to reunite myself with the chalk and ascend the steep ridge that rises up above the Glove Inn, I found that my azel stick had been fractured in the middle. I had not noticed last night as I was downcast and still smarting from the humiliation of my unwelcome encounter with the owner of Fonthill

Abbey, but as soon as it struck the turnpike this morning my stick buckled beneath me. Whilst I had been banished to the passageway, I did not hear the crack of the stick across the little servant's knee for it was surely he that executed the punishment. It is only a stick and there are plenty more to be had in the thickets and hedgerows but it is a spiteful thing to inflict upon a pedestrian tourist and I hope that is now the end of the matter.

There is a tollgate at the foot of the downs and the road from Salisbury now avoids the perilous descent down this spine of chalk that bears the name of White Sheet Hill. The old trackway forms a conspicuous chalk scar and has a rocky water worn surface and it is here last evening that Mr Beckford's horse lost two of its shoes. I believe that this cleft in the chalk was not so naturally formed as it first appeared to me for it bears the signs of its construction as a highway. Upon the banks in the field on the lower side there are great spoil heaps now grassed over and also there are cuts through this lower bank to discharge the rain water. Considerable excavation has taken place here in a battle against the natural form of the land in order to make this way passable and less precipitous, but the creaking wheels have now abandoned this road and it is left in neglect for the more adventurous traveller. I write these words at the very crest of White Sheet Hill for I have not yet travelled any distance at all on this hot morning before placing myself down upon an ancient burial mound that Mr Cunnington, a man whom I respect greatly for his judgement and reason in these matters, would term a "long barrow". It is yet another display of man's desire to make their mark upon the chalklands but in this instance it is the work of our ancient ancestors and its purpose is I believe sacred and not a matter of utility. I hold no doubt that beneath my seated position at the higher eastern end of this mound lie the bones of a people who lived in an age before the advent of metal. Mr Cunnington has informed me that no metal objects have ever been retrieved in their examination and I therefore surmise that these are indeed the most ancient of all the tombs that abound in the south of this county. It is a life wholly dependent upon the utility of flint that draws me to the creators of these fine and elegant long barrows. I can only wonder where these mysterious people obtained the stone that was essential to their every need. The natural and weathered flint that lays in abundance amongst the plough soil is not to be compared with the rich and dark material of which their early tools are manufactured.

I shall make a simple plan of this long mound for you, my dear uncle, as its form is so perfectly preserved and it has indeed been fortunate in avoiding the attentions of the plough.

I can see a distant tree clump upon the horizon that shall be my next goal and it is a landmark that has already gained my attention for I viewed it yesterday from the Donhead villages. My spirit has been restored and I shall cast my eye about for a suitable replacement for Peter Winter's stick. I have been loath to part with it this morning but what use is a broken stick to a pedestrian tourist?

*

With my landmark before me I then set out across the closely cropped grass and I determined that I would not fill my head with noble thoughts but instead crave a greater lightness of spirit. Sarah does tease me in her letters that I have the gravitas of one who is at the end of life's journey and not one who is just setting out and so I began to sing aloud a song of nonsense to help me along. I was not overheard in my foolishness or silenced by some brooding thought but by the twinkling sounds of an invisible flock whose magical song descended from the heavens like the faint chiming of tiny bells. I stopped and guarded my eyes against the morning's brightness and studied the clear blue sky but still could not detect the originators of this mysterious birdsong that accompanied me to the foot of the chalk slope. Here I again met with the sandy green soils that appear to exist beneath the chalk and I traversed around the grounds of a large house that barred my progress. Towering trees were alive with spurting bright green leaf and as I walked in their flickering shade, I spied a piece of paper lying on the wayside amongst the fresh grass. I retrieved the folded page and I was drawn to read, with mounting guilt, the most intimate of letters between two young people in love and estranged by distance to which I had an immediate empathy. This final sheet of correspondence was signed "Percy Bysshe" and the eloquence of these most sensitive words and verse made me halt. I read the page again with no more pangs of guilt but just wonderment, and I believe envy, that these were not my own words. A fat pigeon clopped its wings together as it left a perch above my head and I am now very thankful to that bird for it broke my reverie and got my feet in motion again for at that moment a young woman appeared on the path ahead of me. Here surely was the recipient of the letter and I have not at all been a gentleman in spying upon their love. I could not now cast the page back onto the verge for we were too close and this action would have been conspicuous. Instead I folded it in two and pretended to stoop to retrieve it from the ground and I would be seen to carry out this movement, without the time to be aware of its content. I cannot pretend, my dear uncle, for this deception has left me feeling that I am the worst kind of person and I flush with some embarrassment at my own actions as I write these words. As we drew close, I removed my hat and bid the young lady good morning whilst I also held out the folded page. Before I could enquire as to whether she may have suffered the loss of a scrap of paper the young lady instantly recovered it from my grasp with a snap of her wrist and she then held it tightly to her breast.

"Thank you, it is private correspondence and I did not realise that I had mislaid it."

I introduced myself and declared my purpose as a pedestrian tourist. The young lady did not reciprocate but instead looked at me askance.

"So, you are not a vagabond then? I should like to continue with my business and your business appears to be that of taking a liberty by walking on my father's property, that of Mr Thomas Grove of Ferne, and we should be gratified if you do not pass this way again. Good morning Mr Chalk."

I assured the young lady that I would pass this way but once when in truth I had doubly trespassed for I had entered upon the intimate affairs of her heart and to tread upon such sensitive ground is surely the more unforgivable. As we parted the young lady then paused and called back.

"Pedestrians would not be welcome upon the Chase either as you seem to be venturing in that direction. Should Lord Rivers' men catch up with you then you can expect no quarter."

I made the long and hot ascent to my goal not thinking of warnings or admonishments or even the wretchedness of prying upon the intimate lives of others but instead of the rich poetry and incendiary language of one who signed himself "Percy Bysshe".

It seems that I have made more use of my pen than my boots on this morning but I believe that it is not unreasonable to seek shelter from the ferocity of this sun. My clump of trees smells strongly of the residue of the shepherd's flock but it is a vantage point that demands time of the viewer and indeed the landscape can be made some sense of now that I have looked up from my writing. I can see my trail thus far this morning and I can also detect the glinting of some shiny object upon the distant long barrow.

*

I am now installed at the Woodyates Inn. Night comes with some relief from the relentless sun for today it has surely scorched my skin. It is not as cool as night should be for my window is wide open and it is a warm breeze that plays with the candle. I shall sleep with a single sheet when I reach my bed but there is still much to recount and I hope sir that you will forgive my indulgence.

I must begin with the telling of a woeful tale about my own carelessness and the loss of something very precious. On the advent of my eighteenth birthday, I was presented with a portable eyeglass by Mr Richard Fenton. It was indeed an unexpected and handsome gift contained within its own black shark skin case. It has seven draw tubes and alongside the makers name there is inscribed "Mr Henry Chalk-pedestrian tourist". With this instrument I have scoured the wild ocean from the Pembrokeshire cliffs in search of sea tossed ships and it has also accompanied me to the barren mountains of Prescilli. I used it yesterday to view my tree clump from the Donhead villages and this morning, from the long barrow, I spied upon the progress of the building of the tower of Fonthill Abbey before turning my back on that place. I wished to use it to establish the origin of the glinting object that caught my attention but I could find only the black carry case in my pack. The cause of this shining was none other than the lens of my own spyglass flashing in the sunlight yet it was not dancing about on its own upon the long barrow for it is now in the hands of another. Upon this realisation I felt giddy with distress and paced about awaiting further flashes as a confirmation of my loss. I resolved to retrace my steps as swiftly as I was able and I stowed my pack and even my coat amidst dense cover and taking only my water bottle I scrambled back down the steep and grassy slopes. You will gather from my frustrations that all my haste and exertions were in vain for as the long barrow eventually came into view, I could see no figure upon its summit and on my arrival I found neither my spyglass nor indeed even my broken thumbstick. I then returned to the Glove Inn to report this loss and also to ask of the landlord to be vigilant should he see or hear of anything that might lead to the recovery of such a precious object. A silver coin affected I believe only a temporary interest in my plight and

I left after informing him that I should be at the Winterslow Hut on the London road in five days time. I drank deeply from the well in the yard and refilled my water flask before a slow and weary return to my belongings upon the hill. I was gratified that the daughter of Ferne did not reappear before me for I had boldly promised to pass through the grounds of that place only once and not thrice as misfortune had now dictated.

I resolved to continue my journey in an easterly direction along the grand and undulating chalk ridge for I did not wish to again relinquish the advantage of this hard won elevation. To the south of my position I could see across great portions of the county of Dorsetshire until land and sky met on hazy and indistinct terms which it seems is a general accompaniment to a blazing sun. In time I absently deviated from my course and began a slow descent amidst a large tract of woodland with all the while a distracted mind for company and a growing unease that I was somehow being observed. For want of any other possibility my imagination had now contrived that Mr Beckford's men were in possession of my spyglass and that even here in the forest my treasured gift was being used upon me. My dear uncle, I had good reason to start when of a sudden a large deer erupted from the undergrowth beside me and then crashed away between branches only to stop and then turn to watch my own movements with the utmost caution. My heart made a giant leap at this outburst but I felt some assurance that there must be no other human form nearby or I would not have startled the creature so. I then looked down to see that it was a mother's concern that had prevented a full flight, for her new offspring, of perhaps only minutes into this world, lay wet and helpless beside me. I continued on my way, walking backwards to gain confirmation that the mother would make a swift return and not now neglect her new born for I would then be culpable in some fatal disruption of nature. My slow backwards progress and preoccupation prepared me not one jot for what happened next. A heavy hand was clamped onto my pack and the force of this arrest caused the expulsion of every piece of air from within my chest. This shock and suspension of breath ended with my choking and gasping for air which then caused my assailant to hiss and to shake me violently until I was again silent. Fearing for my life should I make even the smallest of sounds, I slowly turned my head to find that I was being held at arms length by a man whose intent lay not upon me for his gaze was directed at the forest floor. His appearance shocked me as much as the manner of our encounter for his clothing and hat were draped in dead snakes and I could not at first comprehend what kind of wicked magic I had stumbled upon. With my silence now established the man relinquished his iron grip upon me but hissed again to deter any further interruption to his business. He slowly crept a short distance along the path before leaping with an agility that belied his age, holding before him a thumbstick and with the cleft to the fore he then stabbed hard at the ground. A loud curse and a glare in my direction made it known that I was to be blamed for this opportunity lost and I believe that my puzzled countenance then provoked this strange fellow to demonstrate his purpose upon me. After creeping up close enough for me to smell this man's very snakeness and with two clawed fingers poised before him he made a sharp hawking noise from his throat before stabbing his hand upon my calf with such a jerk that I jumped up into the air. He roared aloud with a burst of cackling laughter at my distress and in doing so displayed one fang fewer than might be found in a snake's head. The man was keen to parade the many dead snakes that hung from his belt and before I had a chance to express a view on the matter, we exchanged hats. With my initiation over, our curious partnership then continued along the path, he determining our slow pace and soft tread and me wearing this strange man's hot and fetid hat and without even a stick to defend myself against the deadly serpent. In a pool of sunlight we soon detected our quarry and I awaited its attack by placing myself well behind this expert in snake combat. The creature did not rear up and confront us but instead it sought a fringe of longer grass to conceal itself and I detected a shyness in its manner and I believe that we had disturbed its sunny slumber. The snakecatcher demonstrated both stealth and swiftness of movement in pinning the creature to the ground with his forked stick and he then smeared its head with the heal of his boot. Before adding this lifeless form to his collection, he dangled it before my face and I was taken by the rare beauty of its bold markings and the pale blueness across its underbelly. I removed the man's hat from my head and informed him that I was going to continue on my way for I had no desire to participate in his activity and indeed I felt some sadness at the manner of this creature's death. Our brief partnership was now at an end and I was, of a sudden, viewed with great suspicion as if my purpose here within this snake infested wood was being questioned for the first time. His tongue flickered and in an instant, the snakecatcher raised his stick and made to strike me upon the head and it was only my own fleetness of foot that prevented the blow. Many more swipes were directed at my poll as this venomous fiend pursued me along the path until youth prevailed and I left the snakecatcher behind me, bent double and breathless. The legacy of this misadventure is that I am now in possession of an old and stinking felt hat with a desiccated snake for a hat band. My own hat now resides in a place called Cranbourn Chace, if Mr John Cary's map of Wiltshire is to be relied upon, and I make a sincere wish that I never see it again. Upon fleeing from the swinging blows of that woodland devil, whose mind had surely become poisoned by his occupation, I then became hopelessly lost. I hastily cut myself a thumbstick from an azel bush and although it is misshapen and crude and displays no barley twist this pedestrian tourist now feels complete again. It was with no small relief that I eventually left the large and brooding forest behind me and

I found a single tree upon a hill and in its shade I succumbed to grateful sleep. I did not wake until shadows began to lengthen and if it had not been for the buzzing flies around my head I may be there still. In a hot daze I stumbled across open downland until I met with the turnpike and there I took directions to the Woodyates Inn.

It has indeed been a very strange day for I have suffered the important loss of my spyglass, lost and also gained a hat, retrieved a love letter and also met with an interesting acquaintance at the Woodyates Inn. Perhaps it was the day's exposure to a violent sun but as I made my weary way towards the inn, there before me in the shimmering heat, I believed I saw "The Sorrowful Knight" and his "Squire" approaching upon their trusty steeds. You will know that these are characters from Cervantes' great novel Don Quixote and they exist only upon the page where they wander the Spanish Plains and should not at all be here at the Wiltshire and Dorset border.

Sir, my candle gutters and will very soon expire along with your patience and so I must bid you goodnight. I shall now continue the account of my arrival at the Woodyates Inn before breakfast.

Your tired and tiresome nephew
HENRY CHALK

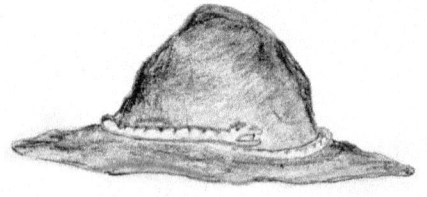

Sunday 8th May 1808

MY DEAR UNCLE,

I am sitting before the open window of my room at the mustering of the day and I can report that a doctor has been summoned for a guest has been taken ill in the night. I make a sincere wish that all will be well yet I hold a palpable fear in the pit of my stomach. There is little that I can do as I await the arrival of the medic, for I cannot sleep, but I may at least recount to you the events of yesterday evening and my arrival at this place. I must also remind myself that it is now early upon Sunday morning for I am much confused by all this disruption. We are, in normal circumstances, still deep in our slumbers at this hour and indeed it is a secret time that only exists in these early summer months. The cockerel has stirred but he has for competition a growing chorus of birdsong that I have not before witnessed and indeed I shall hold still my pen for a moment for when again will this opportunity present itself? My stillness shall be a prayer to my ailing neighbour and I shall close my senses to all but the glorious tribute that heralds the new day.

*

On my approach to the Woodyates Inn, I gauged that my arrival would be coincident with that of two figures on horseback and I had time to muse over the appearance of these characters. I have indicated that I was reminded of those two great inventions of Cervantes: Don Quixote and Sancho Panza and in the early evening sun my fancy exchanged these two unknown travellers for the Noble Knight of the Sorrowful face and his faithful Squire. As the distance between us lessened I could detect that one was of a fuller, rounder shape on a larger horse and the other a taller rider in the saddle but his steed was squat and encumbered with plenty of baggage. Here was surely a reversal of the original arrangement and I afforded myself some simple amusement over this observation. This was after all no parched Spanish plain and I could see no evidence of lance, shield, sword or armour to confirm my idle dreaming and I expected no chivalrous deed. Our arrival at the gateway to the inn was indeed as I predicted and I raised the snakecatcher's hat, for in the beating sun it was better than no hat at all, and I wished the two gentlemen the very best of evenings. I could detect no Iberian flavour in a response yet the greeting was both warm and sincere. I introduced myself and the red faced gentleman on the tall horse smiled under a large moustache.

"Ah, a fellow adventurer, is not ours the only means of travel? To be enclosed in a wheeled box is to admit to time wasted between destinations, yet we have discovered that all is destination. Let it be our secret, Mr Boyle at your service, my valet Thomas."

Thomas had already found his way to the mounting block and was soon leading the baggage laden animal to the trough where it was left to drink its fill. Mr Boyle then took some prising from his mount by his valet and was even assisted on his descent from the block, demonstrating great stiffness after his time in the saddle.

"Do not get old Mr Chalk... or corpulent," called out Mr Boyle across the courtyard, "for to be both is misery indeed."

I drank deeply from the bucket at the well and a stable hand then appeared to attend to the horses and as the master was led into the inn, he loudly voiced his concerns to the valet.

"Keep an eye on him Thomas....and see he treats the cavalry well."

"I shall return shortly sir, but I will see you rested first," his faithful servant calmly replied.

I followed behind the weary knight and his squire but my way was barred by the landlady who stood with her arms folded for she had evidently witnessed my arrival.

"No gent'mun arrives 'pon foot," she stated bluntly, "on yer way."

I had experienced a prejudice before against the pedestrian tourist and with a coating of dust, a hot face and a battered snakecatcher's hat, my appearance did little to endear me to this bony faced woman. I returned to the well to fill my flask and to splash water upon my face and I sat for a while and wondered where I would now pass the night. The valet Thomas returned to observe the stabling of the horses and as I bid him a good evening in passing, he then queried my departure. I explained that pedestrian tourists were a breed that were unwelcome at many establishments and that I had been turned away by the landlady. He remained inscrutable at this news and nodded in return as I again bid him a good evening and then made my way from the courtyard. I had not travelled two hundred yards along the turnpike when I heard a scampering behind me and a calling for me to halt. Boots had been dispatched to explain that there had been a misunderstanding and I was after all to be welcomed at the Woodyates Inn. This was indeed a puzzling turnabout of circumstances and on my return, I was greeted warmly by the landlord who then cursed his wife's poor manners and I was referred to as "Sir" when often my age and young looks determine that I am addressed as "Master". A comfortable room awaited me and a jug of hot water was soon to arrive and was "Sir available to discuss my requirements for the evening meal?" On descending for dinner, I was shown to a decent table where nearby Mr Boyle was already in advance of me and was being waited upon by his own manservant, Thomas.

"Ah good news Thomas, good news, we have splendid company tonight in young Mr Henry Chalk, our pedestrian tourist."

I bid Mr Boyle a good appetite and the inscrutable Thomas raised an eyebrow in acknowledgement before quarter filling his Master's glass with claret. Mr Boyle then held up his vessel in protest.

"We are at war with France but I do not believe that wine is in short supply, fill it up man, fill it up."

Despite the heat of the evening I began a hearty meal and mused that I should be now settling down for the night under a tree with no food at all if it were not for the intervention of the landlord.

"Are you faring any better Mr Chalk for I am enjoying sharp wine and short measures?" said Mr Boyle.

My fellow diner then turned to observe that I was not drinking wine at all with my meal and he questioned whether I was ailing.

"Thomas, a glass for Mr Chalk."

Upon the conclusion of my meal I was ordered to pull up a chair and join Mr Boyle as he sniffed suspiciously at half a glass of port.

"I believe that Thomas would have me die of thirst, so Mr Chalk shall we talk of the weather, which is excruciating by the by, or have you an adventure or two that you might share with an old man?"

I then described my journey thus far and Mr Boyle appeared interested in my ramblings and as I have not spoken but a few words since leaving Pembrokeshire I was glad to find my voice again. In turn Mr Boyle informed me of his route of which I can but recall a few towns visited; Winchester, Romsey, Ringwood, Wareham, Dorchester and next Salisbury, before a return to London. It is a journey that this same gentleman first undertook in 1782 and many parts of the British Isles have been visited between times. That he had once been a military man I had little doubt and indeed Thomas the valet had earlier confirmed this fact by suggesting that I should raise my voice "for the Colonel has spent a deal of time beside the field guns in battle". Mr Boyle later asked me whether I had at all considered serving my country and I confessed that I had little knowledge of warfare above the playing of lead soldiers and neither had my family any association with army or naval matters. My dear uncle, I think back to the weeks spent in Pembrokeshire and with my late lamented spyglass how I observed distant ships before they slipped beyond the horizon. I have even held childish thoughts about a life at sea and now hold a great admiration for any who cast themselves upon the wild ocean for before my time on that rugged coast I had only before witnessed the activities in the Port of London. I believed then that all was the loading and unloading of ships with sailors brawling in taverns and I had not perceived what went on beyond the sanctuary of the brown sliding waters of the River Thames. I now hold a vision of two unwieldy warships engaged in battle upon a harsh and boiling sea and I believe that it is akin to two bugs fighting upon a bear's back, for at any moment he might scratch this irritation with one gigantic paw. It is a visit in my seventh year to the port of London that provokes this comparison for there I witnessed a dancing bear upon the quayside and I will forever make this curious association. Perhaps bugs have more sense than to fight amongst themselves. I did not share these thoughts with the Colonel but I believe that you know me well enough sir, to tolerate such idle nonsense.

"Danger will put wit into any man Mr Chalk and will be the making of many a timid fellow."

The Colonel then advised me against joining the navy. "Their ships are but old and leaky tubs, yet an admiral will be greatly adored by the people of this island. Sir, I can inform you that I commanded the defence of Frederick of Prussia's rear but you shall not hear of me when I die. Mr Chalk, I do not wish to become maudlin for I will drink of too much brandy but let me now propose a toast; The travelling life and to Colonel Boyle on his last ride and to young Mr Henry Chalk on his second pedestrian excursion."

We duly raised our glasses and Mr Boyle then produced and fuelled his pipe and between whiff and whiff he surprised me by expressing his admiration for that race of eternal travellers referred to as Gypsies.

"They know their horses sir and I shall judge any man by how he regards his horse, be he any creed..excepting of course the Spanish."

The Colonel then stated that although their existence and conditions were often pitiful, the Egyptians are a proud race with their own language but are much maligned for they are blamed for any thieving in the district where they make their camp. I informed Mr Boyle that I had not yet met with such people and I was then urged to do so, should the opportunity present itself. "They have grimy faces Mr Chalk but their children grow strong out of doors and do not wither in infancy like our own and they understand the horse like no other. Do you ride sir?"

I confessed that I did not and I was now reticent to describe my distrust of horses and so I promoted you, my dear uncle, to the Colonel for I know that you have been a keen horseman in your time. I believe that you once sat me upon your horse outside my home in Southwark when I was but a small child and my mother then rescued me, for I disgraced myself by crying pitifully to be let down.

In time Mr Boyle viewed me with watery eyed disapproval through a vale of smoke of his own making. "You are not drinking sir, and are slowing me down by example."

Despite my own temperance and avoidance of port wine altogether, the Colonel drained enough for both our thirsts and instead of retiring to comfortable chairs to continue our conversation, he soon began to snort and snore aloud at the table. Mr Boyle's valet, with the assistance of the landlord, was soon on hand to escort the Colonel to his bed and as a parting gesture this seasoned traveller then waved an arm in the vague direction of our capital city and proclaimed loudly;

"I ride to London in the morning."

I retired to my room to begin this account and in time then tossed and turned in my bed as sleep evaded me in the discomfort of a warm night. I know not at what hour but I heard voices out in the corridor and movement in the neighbouring room. I entered the landing where I found Mr Boyle's valet, Thomas, in a state of some agitation and he was making a request to the landlord that a doctor should be called for immediately. Once the landlord had departed the valet then informed me that what he had feared had come to pass for the Colonel had been taken gravely ill in the night. Thomas retreated to his master's room and there was little I could do other than return to own my room and I soon heard the stable boy upon his mount clatter from the yard to summon the doctor.

I believe that I have slept a while in my chair for the sun is now clear of the horizon. I left the snakecatcher's hat upon the window ledge overnight and I have just been startled by a large black and white bird that was intent on picking at the dead snake hat band. I flapped at the assailant and the mischievous creature then tugged the hat from the sill and caused it to fall. These are quick and intelligent birds that would, I believe, not resist any morsel of carrion or indeed any defenceless living creature. They have a malign rattle for a song like some witch's chatter and I have observed their predatory nature before and I sincerely hope that this bird's presence is not an ill omen for the ailing Colonel. I am thankful that I can hear horses approaching on the turnpike and I believe that it must be the doctor arriving, for some hours have now passed and I have heard little movement from the next room. I shall now retrieve my hat from the yard and wish you good morning.

*

Another exceedingly warm day has now passed and I am again before my open window at the Woodyates Inn for I have not yet continued with my pedestrian excursion. I have opened wide the door to my room to encourage a draught and I am inclined to remove some clothing in an attempt to cool myself and yet that might cause alarm to any who cross the landing.

I must resume my account of this morning for the doctor had duly arrived to attend to Colonel Boyle. Whilst at my breakfast the medic then appeared and any concern for his patient was well concealed for he was able to gulp down as much as could be mustered by the landlord. I asked about the condition of the Colonel to which he shrugged.

"I have bled him a pint. He will revive or he will not..more cream?"

On returning to my room I received a knock at the door and upon opening it I found the stern faced valet and at first I feared the worst possible news. I still had not become accustomed to this servant's lack of expression for instead he requested that I might attend to the Colonel as he had expressed a desire to talk to me. Mr Boyle lay pale and clammy in a large bed and turned meekly as I entered the room.

"Ah, the pedestrian tourist, not yet on your travels?"

I then stated my concern for his wellbeing and wished for a swift recovery and that he might also sit aboard his horse and enjoy the day.

"I fear not. Not today Mr Chalk, or perhaps any other day. This was to be my swan song for I have not been well."

He then patted the sheet above the girth of his stomach.

The valet departed at a nod from his master and I was then gestured to sit upon the edge of the bed.

"I believe that Thomas has made a vow to Mrs Boyle to ensure my safe return to London. He waters the brandy and thinks that I do not notice for as I get older my brandy gets weaker and the port he thins with inferior wine. He ensures me good company of an evening to prevent the melancholy descending and the seeking of comfort in a bottle. He is a fine valet, the best I ever had.."

The Colonel then winced after some internal pain and in a whisper began to relate a song or poem;

"Hey nonny no,
Men are fools that wish to die

Ist not fine to dance and sing
When the bells of death do ring?
Ist not fine to swim in wine
And turn upon the toe
And sing hey nonny no
When the winds blow and the seas flow
Hey nonny no.

"Our relationship has been brief Mr Chalk and that saddens me, yet I would offer you this, be both brave and bold in life, for otherwise how will a man know his true worth? Have you a passion sir?"

I informed the Colonel of my curiosity for flint and its import to our ancient ancestors, to which he made a weak demonstration of disapproval.

"Puh, flint is that cold hard stuff that litters the ground and plagues the hoof, have you not yet found love Mr Chalk for you have much to learn?"

I then spoke of Miss Sarah Foster and our meeting at Hindon but refrained from describing her blindness. Mr Boyle sank back onto his pillow in palpable relief at this news.

I explained that I wished that I could compose beautiful poetry and I thought back to the daughter of Ferne House and her letter from one "Percy Bysshe".

"Poetry is worthy," replied the Colonel, "but is there not a gift that might adorn your loved one, a locket perhaps? There should be no timidity in the scale of the purchase for there is not a price to be placed upon love. Do it on the advice of an old man and I should then die happy in the knowledge that somewhere love does flourish."

With that instruction Mr Boyle patted my hand and closed his eyes. I did not believe him to have expired but I then summoned Thomas who continued his bedside vigil.

I could not depart this place and continue on my way with death in the air and so I resolved to stay another night as necessary. I determined that I should at least see part of the day and so I stepped out into the fierce sun with my snakecatcher's hat to wander the neighbourhood.

There is a confusion of earthworks scattered about the Woodyates Inn and if I can believe my judgement, the inn itself is positioned upon a Roman road. This is most appropriate for an old building that serves the need of travellers yet I doubt if its longevity can be extended to the time of our Roman masters. It is likely that the use of these superior roads continued well beyond that time and indeed the Roman surveyors and engineers have determined today's route for the road to Blandford appears to run straight for as far as the eye can see. These are uncharted territories upon Mr John Cary's map of Wiltshire and I shall have to invest in a map of the neighbouring county of Dorset if I were to extend my excursion into that county. In the opposing direction the raised form of the Roman road can be clearly seen as it departs from the turnpike and strikes off across the down. I then met with a large ditch that crossed at right angles the Roman road and conflicted with all Roman principals for it meandered for some distance across the down before climbing to meet the horizon. With the huge vallum upon its southern side it spoke of gargantuan defence against an approach from the north. I lay back upon its grassy bank to ponder the origin of these monuments to organised labour. The construction of Roman roads can somehow be imagined for upon the small world of a simple village the great machine of the Roman empire imposed its thoroughfare that was to change forever the lands that were so familiar to its inhabitants. Every able person was demanded to participate in achieving this statement and now through this small world the traffic and trade of the empire would pass and indeed history had truly arrived for Tacitus documents these years where previously no written record survives. The great wandering ditch has more

mystery attached to it for I have not been able to determine whether
the ditch interrupts the course of the Roman road or whether the road
carves through the ditch, for it is a confusing junction. That the ditch
was dug in desperate defence there can be no doubt and this was no
simple delineation of boundaries for it is indeed a great wall of earth.

In time I resumed my excursion and found more confusion
in a plethora of mounds, long barrows and parallel banks that made
my hot head spin with the unravelling of all this ancient activity, for
I could make little sense of it. I wished for some inhabitant who had
miraculously survived the many millennia, from that day to this, to
appear and explain their intent and circumstance. Yet the raising of
mounds and banks and the etching of lines upon the landscape are
an accumulation across many centuries and I am certain that these
mysteries are not solely our preserve. My ancient guide may describe
proudly his own contribution but confess that he was at a loss to know
what all those long banks and ditches were about.

Upon a shelf this morning at the Woodyates Inn I spied an ancient
broken urn and on enquiring of the landlord I established that those
indefatigable antiquarians Sir Richard Colt Hoare and Mr William
Cunnington have in the past made their excursions from that place. The
broken urn was a gift to their host after excavations at Oakley Down. I
informed the landlord that I had accompanied the Baronet in the opening
of barrows upon the hills of his own estate at Stourhead. The landlord
appeared unsurprised by my lofty associations and was as courteous
as any host that I have met with on my travels and he requested that
I might extend his best wishes to Sir Richard Colt Hoare, to which I
happily consented. I feel perhaps treacherous when I confess that I am
now at odds with the belief that the opening of each and every barrow
that exists upon the chalk hills of South Wiltshire and North Dorset
also, will indeed illuminate the lives of our ancient ancestors. Are not
these recovered treasures but the crown jewels of the kings and queens of

ancient times? I propose that the answer to many a grand puzzle lays not in the conspicuous but in the inconspicuous; the fragments of fashioned flint lying where they fell from the tool makers lap, the interruptions in the natural soils and chalk that betray past activity, the broken shards of pottery, a soil encrusted coin or a rusty belt buckle. These are not the riches of the past but the comings and goings of ordinary people, of villages long extinct, of forgotten battles and lost generations. The story of life and death is scattered all about the place if one but knew where to start.

My dear uncle, I sensed that I would receive the worst possible news upon my return to the Woodyates Inn and I thus dragged my feet and craved distraction at every turn. As I at last arrived at the front door to that place a great commotion ensued from within and I was forced back out into the yard by none other than Colonel Boyle, as large as life itself and remonstrating loudly with the landlord.

"No sir, indeed I shall not pay for laying-a-bed this morning. Thomas, muster the cavalry."

Upon seeing me, and before I could express my delight at his recovery, Mr Boyle slapped a large hand upon each of my shoulders and roared in my face.

"Mr Chalk, it was but a bad bout of the wind and a royal wind it was too. I feared for the window panes at the grand expulsion but all is now well, all is well."

The Colonel then shook my hand vigorously and whilst Thomas the valet was ready to assist his master at the mounting block, I shook his hand also and even detected a faint smile as he wished me a good afternoon.

"Hey nonny no, Mr Chalk, hey nonny no," boomed out Colonel Bolye, as they clip-clopped from the yard and in my fancy, the man from La Mancha and his squire departed for the Sierra Morena.

There have been no more comings and goings or commotions that I can report and all is now quiet. I sincerely hope that I shall sleep well tonight for it has truly been a long day. I have been directing my thoughts towards poetry and yet I have a gulf of ignorance to cross before I shall commit my true feelings to the page. In Cervantes great book there is a playful style, referred to by Mr Richard Fenton as; "versos de cabo rato" and I have, this evening, constructed my own:

To walk and walk is point
You may as well in darkness wan
If flowing water we cannot sav
Or find a spreading oak to clam

Our silence will detect a rust
And a view seek our atten
A wind will escort us with its whist
There is too much to see and men

Tomorrow I shall follow the Roman road to Salisbury for there can be no route more straight or direct than a Roman road. Once there, I shall purchase an expression of my love for Miss Sarah Foster and for now I shall spare her my poetic blushes.

Your apoetical Nephew
HENRY CHALK

Monday 9th May 1808

My dear Uncle,

I have now departed the Woodyates Inn and am set fair upon the Roman road. I cannot keep a smile from my face and I must hastily relate my conversation with the landlord of that place. I thanked him for his welcoming me back to the inn after being denied entry in the first instance to which he replied that they should never turn away a young Earl in any guise. I then dispelled any idea of a noble birth and that I was indeed as I appeared, a pedestrian tourist, yet I have paid and tipped as well as any titled traveller. The man grew pale with confusion and questioned again whether I was not Henry Earl of Euston to which I gave my name and stated that I could not account for this misunderstanding. I then bid the landlord a good morning whilst his bony faced wife scowled behind his back as if she were now vindicated in her original action. For a good few hundred paces I could not fathom these curious circumstances until I again considered the characters of Don Quixote and Sancho Panza. Was not the knight of the sorrowful face always under some misapprehension about even his own identity and certainly that of any imaginary foe that he encountered? Yet I do not believe that it was Don Quixote who has committed a chivalrous deed on my behalf by inventing my nobility, but that it was his faithful squire, the valet Thomas. It was Thomas that witnessed my departure after being turned away from the inn and I now believe it was he that informed the landlord of my erroneous nobility. The valet had made a vow to Mr Boyle's wife to return her husband safe to London and essential to this plan was good company at dinner and a distraction from the bottle. On seeing his master's evening companion fast disappearing along the turnpike, he took swift and ingenious steps to reverse the situation. I am honoured that he considered me a worthy distraction and I shall long remember his blank expression and forever regard him as the resourceful valet with the sorrowful face. I must now gather up my belongings and make swift progress to Salisbury for I believe Mr Boyle's advice to be valid and born of some experience in affairs of the heart.

*

I am currently paddling my feet in the chill waters of a river that flows through the little village of Tony Stratford and my earlier Roman determination has now faltered in the withering sun. One can but admire the vision of our Roman master's in the construction of such a highway. Rabbit burrows and spoil heaps have enabled a view of the layers of chalk and rounded flint pebbles that have been utilised in its upper layers. The chalk can be won from adjacent ditches but I do not believe the rounded gravel to be a local material. The heavy clay cap that often sits upon the crest of the chalk downs only comprises of angular fractured flint and has not the water worn appearance of these pebbles. Therefore, the quarrying and transportation of substantial quantities of this bulky gravel has been undertaken by the road builders and I wonder at a possible source and also the distances covered in its haulage. At the very base of the raised causeway is a seam of very large irregular flint nodules packed tightly together and it is altogether a construction that would accommodate the heaviest of today's traffic yet it is largely neglected by all travellers. I wonder that it has not become the main turnpike to Salisbury for the work is already done yet there is but a worn thread of human and animal passage that wanders all about the elevation and into the ditches as bushes and burrows are avoided.

The sheep flock with their fattening lambs nuzzle upon the downs and shift as slowly as the puffs of white cloud in a windless blue sky. I wish for more cloud for it would break the sun's present unseasonable conspiracy of burning my skin these last few days and I can now believe why shepherds and ploughmen have nut brown faces.

Hedgerows offer occasional relief and now display a cloak of white blossom whilst the verges are thick with a creamy flower and it is as if a master confectioner has been at large in the country with his sweet white icing, drizzling it over wayside bushes and whipping it into the banks and verges to produce a bubbling froth.

On descending into the valley, I completed a circuit of the village church of Tony Stratford and I can inform you, my dear uncle, that it has almost every South Wiltshire stone in its design. There is a pleasing chequer of flint and freestone upon the tower and a combination of red brick and halved nodules of flint about the walls. A round door arch has been constructed from greensand stone amongst which are small fossil shells and it is altogether a jumble that would please the geologist if not the church antiquarian. To further offend this latter breed I did not enter the building and can therefore offer no critical description of aisle, nave, chancel, plate or rood. The church is placed precariously upon a bank above the river and there has been some considerable buttressing upon the northern walls to prevent the whole from joining the valley floor.

The range of local materials has been ably demonstrated by the creeping church yet two items are missing and one has been rectified by a neighbouring cottage that appears to have solid chalk blocks incorporated into its walls. There must be a seam of chalk hereabouts that can withstand the weather and not crumble at the first visit of Jack Frost and I hope that I shall be able to record further examples. The church has also spurned the use of mud, yet it is surely the most available of all materials and I can record that I have witnessed its use here in Tony Stratford with the building of a small house. I believe that it is a simple and ancient ingenuity where a dwelling can be constructed from its immediate surrounds without recourse to the costly excavation and carriage of materials and I shall attempt to describe this process. Upon a tall base of flint nodules, a sloppy mix of soil and chalk has been cast by the bucketful, yet to give form to this operation long

planking has been shored up at the horizontal to create the eventual
thickness of the walls. These are temporary sides that prevent the
immediate seepage of this material until it dries and I gauge that the
planks are then raised and trussed up against the next level and the
process begins anew. This blazing sun causes ideal conditions for the
drying to occur and perhaps within only a single day the mix is firm
and in this fashion, piece by piece, the solid walls of a simple house will
in time be created. Door frames and windows are but simple wooden
poles introduced to form the necessary apertures and I suspect that the
whole will conclude with a roof of straw. To the side of the building
the various components of valley soil, chalk and also small flints have
been gathered and thrown together into a congealed wet mess. A small
horse led by a boy has been assigned to trample about this heap as pails
of river water are splashed before the hooves of the animal and even the
beast's own droppings flop into this unruly mix. My close interest in
this whole process has caused some entertainment to the four men and
a boy employed to the task. I believe that from my appearance they
perceive me to be an itinerant snakecatcher and so, in the passing of but
two hours, I have fallen in my standing from Earl to a lowly hunter
of vermin and an object of amusement to a gang of mud splattered
labourers. One of these men first pointed to the feet of another, under
the pretence that there was a serpent about to strike to which the fool
would jump about and cry out in mock alarm. They would then all
join in with this mirth and begin drawing imaginary snakes from their
pockets and from beneath their hats. One poor fellow took fright that
such a game would conjure up a living peril so great was his fear of
these creatures. With this weakness now displayed he was then fiercely
pursued by another and on having a muddy hand thrust down the
back of his shirt, he took off in a flapping panic. He then abruptly
ceased his flight and shook violently his clothing until he was able to
confirm with an expression of simple satisfaction that there was no

viper present after all and his life could now continue. I slipped away
during this commotion to paddle my feet and eat a crust of bread taken
from the table of the Woodyates Inn and also to expend some ink.

*

My dear uncle, I sincerely hope that my pack and thumbstick are still
concealed under a thorn bush where I left them at the outskirts of the
city of Salisbury and for ink, paper, pen, nightshirt, supper and a bed I
have again the generosity of strangers to thank.

It is another exceedingly warm night and the sounds and odours
of this place float up to my open window for I occupy a room at the very
top of Mr and Mrs Shorto's house in Rollestone Street. Mr Shorto is
an esteemed cutler of the city of Salisbury and metal is at the heart of his
business and yet it is the discourse upon the provenance of flint at our
initial meeting that has brokered this friendship. I fear, however, that I
make a disruptive presence within the home of a kind and respectable
family and I shall endeavour to explain this matter in due course. At
first light I shall depart and leave behind a cowardly note of apology
and I wish that I should heed my own advice in not becoming involved
in the lives of others for it always leads to complication.

I must now retrace my steps and turn back the clock to before
noon where on a ridge above the city it was finally necessary to depart
from the Roman road for to continue on its course would lead me to
Sorviodunum, or Old Sarum, when my quest required the services of
its young sibling, New Sarum. The turnpike brought me in turn to
the south of the city with a view of Salisbury Cathedral that must
surely demand a halt by even the most weary of travellers. Yet I am
reminded of Mr Boyle and his detestation of wheeled traffic for I was
near run over by a flying stage as it hurtled by in a downhill fury
with unstoppable anxiety to appease the clock and to rush its hot and
bothered cargo betwixt destinations. As the spire beckons and guides
the traveller toward the city, it is first necessary to cross a broad river

and to this end a fine stone bridge has been constructed with multiple arches and its antiquity must surely challenge its lofty rival. Upon entering the Close itself and approaching the Cathedral, it is only your own tiresome nephew that would become animated by the presence of flint in the exterior wall of the cloister upon the southern side. It is a rear view that I am certain is not presented for general inspection for it has a rough appearance comprising of irregular stone and successive courses of flint. It is a feature that most tourists to Salisbury would not notice far less comment upon even as an unsightly comparison to the grandeur of the stonework and carvings upon the western end. I, however, felt gratified that the simple utility of flint has found a place in surely one of the finest buildings in the whole world. I believe that I have promised before to offer a full account of Salisbury Cathedral but I fear that it shall not be today. Upon leaving the Close and entering the tangle of humanity that occupies the streets of Salisbury, I was made to question the wisdom of my excursion to the city for my nose soon longed for a gust of fresh air but encountered none. I later questioned my host, Mr Henry Shorto, about the plethora of rivulets and gutters that accompany each and every street in this place. As a visitor I did not wish to quickly find fault but there is a stench where certain of these drains accumulate filth and where men with long poles and rakes are employed to assist the passage of this detritus and yet there are other sections that flow with more certainty. There is a daily cleansing of the accumulations of the nightly chamber pot, caused by the opening of up stream hatches where fresh water is diverted from the River Avon through this street system and the foul is flushed back downstream into the parent river. Mr Shorto informed me with a laugh that Salisbury has been referred to as the "English Venice" with its streams and little culverts and bridges and yet it is with a serious tone that he then warned of this open system through the hotter months and its association with flies and a mortal sickness that has claimed a great many residents. This clawing at the back of my throat hastened my purpose for I have lived away from the city long enough to forget its pernicious flavours and quickly I scoured the shop fronts for some meaningful gift yet I knew not what I was searching for. I soon found myself in the market square which today was not gathered but tomorrow is I believe market day and this place will become busier still.

I am a poor reporter of topography and even less so of civic affairs yet there is a new Council House built in one corner of the square that is very grand and shouts of pride and prosperity should there be any doubt on that score. There are also a great many streets at right angles to each other in the city which suggest an orderly plan yet the buildings themselves are too haphazard and irregular in form for the eye to consider it a place of real beauty. But what do I know my dear uncle, for there are many better qualified to pass such a judgement rather than this simple pedestrian tourist?

It was whilst I stood pondering my purpose in this place that I believe I witnessed one of my own species pass by, for a pedestrian tourist in a busy city street is a conspicuous creature indeed. I have, for the sake of anonymity, temporarily shed my own accoutrements as I did not wish to become prey to any rogue or pickpocket as happened on my first visit to Salisbury. This fellow had a full pack and sturdy boots and tapped at the city streets with his thumbstick with all the while an expression of bemused curiosity upon his face. He holds our secret in his breast for he knows that once he leaves behind the people of Salisbury to their prosaic tasks, then adventure and the unknown lie just around the corner. There must be a map about his person and perhaps a book that has inspired this excursion and I wonder also if there is somewhere an exasperated recipient for the prolific correspondence engendered by each fresh experience. I wished to approach and have my questions answered yet I believe that we are not a breed that would naturally flock together but are a more solitary animal. To gather in a swarm would be to amplify the tread upon a path and alert every bird and beast of our presence and these treasured encounters may therefore be lost. I had stalked my prey along two sides of the market square before I realised that I was doing so until, in Queen Street, I ceased my pursuit and let this furtive gentleman slip from my view for he then turned a corner and was gone. I then felt a great urge to depart from the city and return to my own adventure and yet I had still my quest to fulfil. Across the street, having been led to this spot by my quarry, my attention was then drawn to a curious sign above a shop for it was a large folding knife that on a much smaller scale would be intended for the pocket and yet this object would ably serve a giant. I investigated further and found this to be a cutler's shop and the proprietor was one Mr Henry Shorto. The window displayed a fine and overwhelming range of goods with silverware and jewellery also promoted and yet it was the wording upon a small card that arrested my eye for it stated simply; "Gunflints". This was encouragement enough and I entered the shop but soon found myself in near total darkness for my eyes could not easily adjust to the gloomy interior, by contrast to the sun's brilliance out in the street. After blinking and rubbing my eyes I soon regained my vision and found before me a young couple who were obviously much in love and I dared to imagine Sarah and myself one day being so bold together in a public place. That they were married I held no doubt for the lady had selected a silver locket and the husband then took great care in fastening the chain clasp from behind, as the lady held up her hair to enable access for this delicate operation. I wished to observe the success of this possible purchase but with discretion and so I feigned to study some nearby silver gravy boats and indeed my interest was perceived as genuine by one of the shop assistants. He then described in detail the merits of one gravy boat upon another and I now know all that is to be known regarding silver gravy boats and narrowly resisted embarking upon a final transaction to alleviate the awkwardness of the situation. That my poor Sarah should become the bewildered recipient

of such a curious gift was unthinkable and I only had to imagine Mr
Boyle's exasperation at such foolishness.

"A gravy boat Mr Chalk? You travelled to Salisbury with your
love in mind and purchased... a gravy boat?"

I left the gravy boats and lamented that I had been unsuccessful
in my observation of the trial of the silver locket and I instead retreated
to the rear of the shop. The same assistant came in polite pursuit of his
customer who was evidently hard to please and had now drifted from
silver gravy boats to powder flasks and dog whistles. I then expressed
my interest in gunflints to the tireless employee.

"What sort of gun does sir possess?" asked the young man.

I responded that I had no kind of firearm but wished to observe
gunflints nevertheless, if it was not too much trouble. The man obliged
and set out a number of different sized gunflints upon a counter and
politely left me for a more reasonable customer. These flints were
neatly trimmed and of a dark and fine quality stone for there were no
flaws, flecks or any irregularities and it was of a superior quality to that
from Peter Winter's pit in Grovely Wood, where I had last year joined
him in his work. Of a sudden a voice stirred me from my concentration
upon these dark flint nuggets.

"I have been informed that you wish to view gunflints and yet
do not possess a gun. They are indeed the least expensive items in the
shop and I am intrigued that you find them the most interesting."

I looked up to find a gentleman of perhaps thirty years, dressed
smartly but with the sobriety of a businessman. He introduced himself
as the owner of the establishment.

"Mr Henry Shorto, at your service and if you will pardon my
impertinence, that is a very curious hat that you are wearing sir, for I have
not before witnessed an adder upon the premises, albeit a dead one."

I in turn introduced myself and yet I did not at first accept
Mr Shorto's interest as sincere but I was soon to realise my failing. I

explained that my hat was acquired whilst going about my business as a pedestrian tourist and such things were to be expected. Mr Shorto had a kindly face and was not to be easily dissuaded from engaging in conversation, despite my awkwardness.

"Indeed? I sometimes crave adventure and yet I have a business and family to attend to."

Mr Shorto then picked up the largest of the gunflints and turned it around thoughtfully in the grip of finger and thumb.

"I am told that they rarely fail but then I do not possess a gun. I believe that I would gain little pleasure from fowling and would sooner study Mr Bewick's illustrations than put to death a woodcock or a shoveller duck. So, what is it Mr Chalk, this mysterious substance we call flint for I can admit to some degree of fascination myself regarding its provenance although I have never, before today, confided in another upon the matter? Do you hold a view?"

I soon found something endearing in Mr Shorto's manner and I informed him of the progress of my own interest and understanding and the good fortune of my encounters with those tireless antiquarians Sir Richard Colt Hoare of Stourhead and Mr William Cunnington of Heytesbury. Indeed, it was the latter Gentleman that recently wrote to me on this self-same matter and I was able to quote verbatim his ever sensible and balanced views to Mr Shorto. The natural provenance of flint has long been a subject of speculation and there are three schools that vie for the trophy of breaking this mystery. It is the glassiness of flint that first promoted the idea that it must be formed by heat and a state of fusion, in the manner that glass is so formed and it was therefore an igneous business. Another way is that flint was once soluble and has solidified from an aqueous mass and this may account for the curious bulbous shaping of the nodules and so the chemists might win with this notion. The third way belongs to the biologists and that flint is in someway due to the marine animals and indeed they have left their clue as fossils within the chalk.

A boy of perhaps twelve years wearing a long apron appeared from a room at the rear of the shop and waited politely until he had gained the proprietor's attention but remained unnoticed as Mr Shorto thought at length about these three possibilities.

"So, which is it to be Mr Chalk; igneous, chemical or biological for I should dearly like to know?"

The boy looked up at me as if he also wished for clarification to a problem that had so apparently vexed his master. I confessed that it required a scientific mind to resolve these issues and ignorance on the subject prevented me from throwing my hat into the ring. Mr Shorto smiled and then stooped to attend to the needs of the young employee who having now gained his instruction, departed quickly from whence he came. I felt that I could take this gentleman into my confidence regarding my true purpose in his shop and Mr Shorto listened attentively before making his own suggestions. He then guided me to the jewellery cases and demonstrated great patience as we handled the finest silver and gold items and discussed the merits of each and every one. Despite this good progress we strayed again to the mystery of flint for we both found it an easy diversion and instead of fine filigree and Welsh gold our subjects became fossils and fashioned flint. Mr Shorto then drew out his watch and stated that he must now cross the street to the workshop and requested that I might like to join him and that we could continue our discussion on the way, with a promise that we should soon return to fulfil my quest. I readily agreed and was introduced to the business of cutlery from the sulphurous odours, immense heat and ear splitting noise of the forge to the busy fingers of the improvers in the workshop. I had not before considered the business of iron and steel, for they are so bound up in modern enterprise and industry that I have shied away from such matters. I confessed my ignorance to Mr Shorto, who suggested that the creation of metal from rock was of an equal significance to mankind as perhaps the creation of fire from flint and the fashioning of flint tools. I observed the bladesmith at his work with new interest, as if he now of a sudden represented the many ancient metalworkers that have over centuries crafted daggers, swords and other weaponry before a blinding heat. My eyes were drawn inexorably to this small but fiercely white hot fire within the hearth that provided the means to treat and form the metal, whilst a man at the bellows kept a steady breath of oxygen to feed and regulate this conflagration. Another man was on hand to grip with iron tongs these brilliant bands of red metal, drawing them swiftly from the hearth before slamming them upon the anvil and striking down mightily with a bouncing hammer blow to shed sparks and make my ears ring, for this operation is repeated many times over. There were others hearths around which more workers concentrated their efforts and these glowing strips were then quenched in a water butt to hiss and steam for a very short while before examination and further plunging. In one dark corner a worker at a treadle grinding wheel then screamed a shower of sparks against the wall of the forge as a blade was shaped and Mr Shorto tugged at my sleeve to indicate that we should depart and by our returning to the street, conversation again became a possibility. His was not the only forge for there were others nearby and the chimes of this anvil music could be heard resounding around this quarter to which my guide referred to as the Coal Market. I questioned Mr Shorto on the stage of blade production that I had witnessed and it appears as though a piece of steel could be placed between two sections of wrought iron and then be fiercely heated and hammered until it became a single piece of metal. This is a process called "Mooding" and ensures the sharpness and longevity of the cutting edge. The quenching of hot strips in a butt of water is a means to "Temper" or harden the metal and the time in the water is critical for the cooling metal can display a veritable rainbow of colours each indicating a differing eventual property to the blade. Mr

Shorto confirmed that this judgement by the quencher was born from long experience and upon this great skill the reputation of the Salisbury cutlery trade depended more than any other. A knife may appear fine with its handle ornamented in gold but it would only ever be as good as its blade.

We then ducked into a doorway in the Butcher Row which by contrast appeared a world away from the hellish forge and yet it was here that the various blades were introduced to handles, hinges and springs and all the various components that made up the finished articles. The sunlight through broad windows ensured that a half dozen quick fingered craftsmen standing before benches could locate rivets and punches and pearlers could file and embellish their fine work, whilst each had a small vice to hold steady their task. In this way folding knives and scissors, carving knives and cutlery for the table, all of the finest quality are made, and upon each is present the stamp of SHORTO SARUM.

My dear uncle, my wrist is cramped by the task of writing and I have no other to blame but myself. I wish to complete my account and yet I must put down this pen, I do not believe that I shall disturb the bed that has been made available to me and I shall instead study a while Mr Bewick's book of birds that belongs to my kind host.

*

I know not what hour it is but I do not yet sense a lightening of the sky beyond the open curtains. I have been contemplating why I should feel obliged to commit so much to the page and not to just let events pass by without record. I fear that it might be that I only exist upon the page and ink is therefore my life blood. I have not again met with Sarah from the time of our first chance encounter at Hindon and as a consequence all has since been conducted through the pen. If I ceased to write to my love then I should then cease to be, for the more alive I feel the more I shall write and I do feel alive whilst at large in South

Wiltshire and therefore I shall write. Until Robert Foster returns home I cannot communicate with his sister but I fear sir that I must live through my correspondence to you. I do sincerely apologise for the size of my handwriting and I am certain that it must cause you great exercise for the eye but as the cost of postage increases by the page it is indeed a matter of economy. I believe that you will say "Spare the cost, my persistent Nephew, spare your wrist and therefore spare my eyes."

As you will know by now, I am a guest at the home of Mr and Mrs Shorto, for a swift invitation transpired when I suggested to my host in his shop, once we had established the nature of my gift to Sarah, that I must now depart from the city and continue my journey. Mr Shorto was most insistent that I should do no such thing and that I must spend the night under his roof for we still had much to discuss. I was introduced to Mrs Eliza Shorto and their very young family and indeed Mrs Shorto has not long been out of confinement and I heard from the nursery Master Edward Shorto exercising his lungs to great effect. Mrs Shorto was very welcoming and interested to hear of my family and circumstances and as dinner progressed, she then established that both my parents were deceased and that I had no other relation other than you sir, my uncle. Mr Shorto attempted to guide the conversation to other territories and yet Mrs Shorto wished to establish why I was not then in Southwark at Chalk's brewery to attend to my duties there and to oversee my father's business. Her husband had indeed found himself in the self-same position after the tragic loss of first his mother Ann, who died in childbirth, and then six years later his stepmother Elizabeth also lost in childbirth followed by his father Henry, who died of a broken heart the very next day. I offered my surprise and sincere commiserations at this news but I had not yet heard the concluding moral to this tale for the cutlery business was then carried on by Mr Henry Shorto, at the age of eighteen, "For the sake of the family."

Her husband cleared his throat and offered a toast at this disclosure.

The height of its steeple,
The pride of its people,
It's scissors and knives,
And diligent wives.

At the conclusion of our meal Mrs Shorto, although pale in countenance, had sufficient energy to demonstrate her skill upon an instrument called a guitar. It was apparently made in Salisbury by one Benjamin Banks who was largely renowned for the construction of violins and they are indeed favoured by the best musicians in England and I was instructed that Salisbury had not only to be justly proud of its cutlers but of its musical instruments also. The nine strings of the guitar were gently plucked to accompany a delicate voice as her husband and I sat attentively in the drawing room whilst Mrs Shorto treated us to her full repertoire. Fatigue, I believe, curtailed the performance to a premature end to which she apologised whilst we applauded and as Mrs Shorto retired, we then rose to bid her a goodnight and retreated to Mr Shorto's study. The business of flint was quick to surface and I explained that whilst my current quest was to locate a source of quality flint, I had also a fanciful notion to one day publish a short volume entitled;

"Manufactured flint tools and their essential use in everyday life before the advent of metal by the ancient people of South Wiltshire."

Mr Shorto thought this an excellent idea and then suggested that he might prosecute his own investigation into the origin of flint and would read every known fact on the matter and to explore himself any available outcrop of native flint to assist in solving this conundrum. We then made a toast to seal this pledge and Mr Shorto proposed that my work should perhaps be entitled; "Life before the knife and fork", whereupon I raised a glass to my host and to his investigations into "Undergroundology". Once we had mocked each other's venture, I made an earnest enquiry to establish the source of iron and steel that was so crucial to the business of cutlery for one day I should like to witness the creation of crude iron from rock. Mr Shorto stated that he believed his early predecessors had long depended upon a supply of bar iron from the New Forest in Hampshire and indeed foundries and the smelting of iron continues there to this day and they largely fulfil a naval requirement. A variety of domestic sources now supply Salisbury's cutlery production and even the raw material, iron ore itself, is shipped about the place as from a variety regions they offer differing properties and their utility is quite specific. As an example Mr Shorto cited grey ore as being very suitable for the production of gun metal and the craft of barrelmaking is long established within the city. In addition the mechanised, and as a consequence "inferior", Sheffield cutlery industries imported a large proportion of bar iron from Sweden. My host explained that Salisbury had suffered very recently in its ability to import and export goods by canal, which is a system that so ably supports the northern cutlery industries. The Salisbury canal is now bankrupt and falling into neglect and Mr Shorto considered it a tragedy for it was never concluded at its approach to Salisbury and the city had still to depend on wheeled transport to supply its every need. I enquired as to the location of the canal, for I may now inspect this fated project as it will guide me to a quarter of the county of Wiltshire that I have not yet visited. Mr Shorto lamented that he should dearly wish to accompany me but his duties would not permit this, yet it was hoped that perhaps in the future the business of cutlery may excuse his absence for a short while and he might himself become a pedestrian tourist. Mr Shorto also signalled that he held a perpetual dread as to the health of his wife and young family and I have already described the open channels to which my host addresses the cause of the exceptional mortality in this city, especially in the warmer months. I was greatly shocked to learn that Mr Shorto lost five brothers and sisters in infancy and I wonder that there should be a cure sought to expunge Salisbury's fatal epithet of "Little Venice". I understood fully why my host was reluctant to leave his home and family for any period beyond his working hours.

Mr Shorto has promised to forward my gift for Sarah to the Winterslow Hut where, you will recall, I have arranged to meet with her brother Robert Foster. My host then kindly provided the means to make this correspondence and he escorted me to my room. I thanked him warmly and revealed that I now considered him a true friend to which he responded that he owed me much for making a fire under the question of the origin of flint where only a spark had existed before. "We shall resume over breakfast, Goodnight Henry." That I have blown into the lives of these good people, like some strange and disorientated foreign bird, can surely only disturb and raise a dormant curiosity of life beyond the city boundary. In my heart I knew that as my friend greeted the new day, then I would have already departed Salisbury's choking confines and shall again be reunited with all the accoutrements of the pedestrian tourist.

Your irresponsible nephew

HENRY CHALK.

Tuesday 10th May 1808

MY DEAR UNCLE,

I cannot pretend sir for I feel weary and lacking in sleep these last few days and today has already signalled its intent, for it is still early and I can already sense a building heat. I have again found a river beside which to rest a while and there is much to observe as it slips by. A fly presses down its long legs upon the water skin whilst a shadowy predator below noses up against the surface and it is as if this tense barrier between these two worlds can never be broken. With a muscular flop, the water is shattered, the fly eaten and the fish returns to its lair to digest its prey. Perfect rings grow and fade toward the bank and the sky's reflection is once more restored and another fly settles. I believe that I could sit and watch this sequence over and again and the poor fly can find no sanctuary either whilst in lazy flight for a small brown fan tailed bird will dart from a bush upon the bank to snap up this morsel in one blink of my eye. This fly has been dealt a poor hand and must question its purpose upon this earth between snap and snap if it has the time, or more crucially, the wit to do so.

Mr Boyle determined that I should be brave and bold in life and yet I quietly slipped the latch at Mr and Mrs Shorto's house at the first cock crow leaving behind me a cowardly note. I believe that my spirit of adventure has had an unsettling effect upon that household for responsibility is graded above gratuitous wandering by Mrs Shorto and this is a sentiment, my dear uncle, to which you may wholly concur. I will, in time, correspond with Mr Shorto for he has confided in me that whilst cutlery is his trade it is not his passion and that place shall be reserved for his future study into the origin of flint.

My being on the streets in the early morning enabled me to again experience the accumulations within the drainage channels for the hatches had not yet been opened to flush away these human and animal suppurations. Today is market day in Salisbury and upon the approaching streets I met with the mustering of beasts with their attendant masters. A dairy cart clattered by to join the growing throng and I bought a penny loaf from a baker boy's basket. I thought to fill my flask from a pump but shied from the Salisbury water least it should be privy tainted and chose instead to wait until I reached a neighbouring village. Beside the Close wall I saw a family of small water birds dipping and diving under these still and opaque waters and even the young and paler offspring were practising this dipping for food. At my approach the family squeaked in alarm and found sanctuary under the bridge before the eastern gate to the Cathedral grounds and I believe that the channel emanating from these Holy quarters held no less a stench from that of the remainder of the city.

My belongings remained undisturbed beneath their thorny lodging and once reunited I then followed a drover's road to the village of Britford. At that place I took directions to the ferry for it was a route proposed by my host, Mr Henry Shorto and I was required to cross broad and lush meadow land and was there able to witness a system of ditches and raised channels controlled by wooden hatches. I believe that it is a complex means by which to irrigate the grass that I do not fully understand but that sheep have been grazing freely here I hold no doubt. Across the river there is a small boat moored and a ferryman's cottage where I have observed a woman at her washing but she has not yet spied me. She is indeed the ferrywoman for two women with baskets brimming with posies now require passage across this broad river and I shall hastily collect myself and make an opposing journey.

*

I have earned my crust as a diligent pedestrian tourist for I have endured the direct sun in prosecuting a drawing of the canal. Mr Shorto informed that it was now abandoned and laid to waste and yet I have witnessed activity of sufficient interest to find employment for my pencil. A great volume of chalk has been extracted from pits adjacent to the canal and deposited in a barge for transportation to a farm some ten miles east of this village of East Grimstead. The small church in the drawing now offers me some sanctuary from the rays of the sun and if I may intrude upon your time once more, I shall relate my progress thus far for it is not without interest. At the ferry, once the two market bound passengers with their baskets of fresh posies were deposited upon the bank, I was fully prepared to step aboard the craft and make my crossing. The ferrywoman however held a different view and instead, with a few stiff pushes upon the pole, returned immediately to the opposite mooring and despite my protestations stepped ashore without so much as a glance in my direction. It was as if I did not exist and perhaps in her world, of the passing and the repassing of familiar faces, I did not. I had no option but to pull off my boots and string them around my neck, remove my stockings, lift up my coat-tails and step into the oozy bankside mud. The passage underfoot was stony and I prodded ahead of me with my thumbstick. At its deepest the water rose to cover my breeches and I fancied that the river was tainted with the smell of the Salisbury drainage channels for it is indeed the receptacle for this filth. After hauling myself from the river I wished to glower at the ferrywoman to show that my progress had not been affected by her obstructive nature yet she was nowhere to be seen. I soon encountered more passengers who viewed me with great circumspection as it was obvious by my dripping condition that I had passed through the river and not over it. I raised the snakecatcher's hat and wished an elderly couple a good morning and trusted that they would be met with more civility than I had just been dealt with by the ferrywoman. The couple chose not to respond and instead scuttled by as if I were some blackguard and I felt certain that their tongues would soon be engaged in exchanging suspicions with the ferrywoman. I continued on my way whistling as loudly as I was able to demonstrate

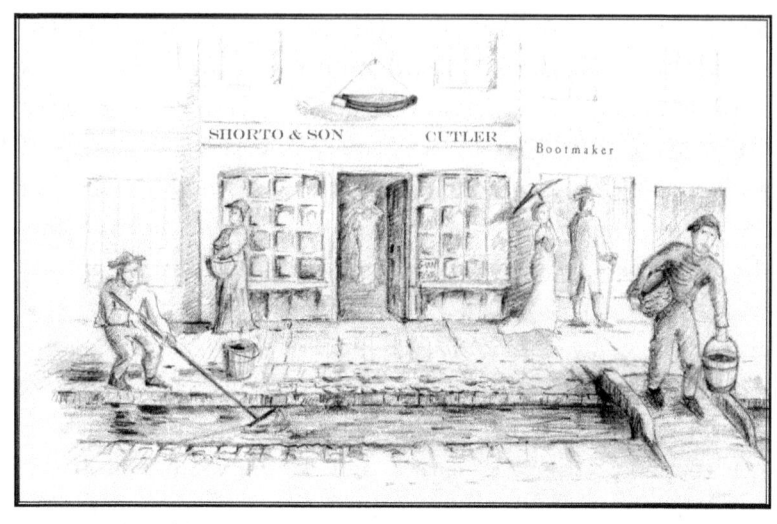

Mr Henry Shorto's Cutlery Shop, Queen Street, Salisbury

The Doomed Salisbury Canal

to this closed corner of Wiltshire that I cared not one jot for their
welcome. In time I replaced my stockings and boots and made steady
uphill progress away from the broad and flat plain of grass meadows
and mused that the river was now pushed up tight against this valley
cliff. In distant times the entire valley, some miles wide, must have
been scoured by a vast and swollen mass of destructive water and yet
today it was a mere trickle by this comparison. I should like to see
the ferrywoman navigate the ancient course of this river for she would
require a pole of perhaps one hundred feet in length.

The land about soon displayed signs of a change in the soil, with
orange sand spilling out of rabbit burrows and with a concentration of
the oak tree, which does not seem to prosper so well upon the chalk.
As the road continued its upward curve I noticed where gravel pits had
been recently dug on a broad verge and I believe their purpose is to
service the road itself. That gravel existed here was of interest enough to
one who is so easily pleased by even the mildest geological occurrence
and yet as the road straightened a most peculiar and unsettling sight
unfolded before me. Huddled amongst a continuation of these pits
were clusters of men in grimy yellow uniforms with red waistcoats and
they had evidently spent the night here for the smoke from dampened
fires hung heavily in the air. Standing in groups upon the road were
militiamen with muskets and with a further number preparing to
mount their horses, I had little doubt that the men amongst the gravel
pits were prisoners and the whole party was about to depart from this
makeshift camp. I drew close enough to hear a drift of conversation
amongst the seated men to establish that these were indeed French
prisoners of war in transit. I could see now that these were not English
faces and yet they were unhealthily pale with too much of the shape
of the skull showing through stretched skin and, as I passed, I was
made to feel greatly ill at ease by their hollow eyes as they followed
my progress. One prisoner hissed to gain my attention and the nearest

militiaman, of perhaps my own age, waved the barrel of his musket up to the horizontal to indicate for the Frenchman to remain silent. The prisoner however persisted and revealed a small white figure, perhaps carved from bone, and then rubbed his thumb and forefinger together and whispered hoarsely.

"Moneys, moneys."

The young militiaman advanced and gave the man a firm prod with the barrel of his gun and called for silence. "Else I'll send you back to the stinkin' 'ulks, see if I wont".

I asked the soldier what was to be the destination for these men to which he looked first at my battered snakecatcher's hat and then at the shiny wetness of my breeches before stating that it was no concern of mine and indicated with a jerk of his head for me to be on my way. The whole party was evidently waiting on the arrival of the captain and as I left behind me the prisoners and their escort, the mounted captain and two officers appeared from their nights lodging at the Green Dragon Inn. In France I judge that there must be a reversal of this situation with English prisoners of war held captive and how many hundreds, thousands or indeed perhaps many thousands of men? I have been sheltered from the bare facts of war as English life continues; dairymaids are abroad in the early morn, beasts are herded to market, cutlery is produced, barrows are dug by noblemen and yet war goes on beyond the horizon. My ears cannot hear the crack and shriek of battle and yet today my eyes have surveyed the emaciated ghosts of free men and as I ambled through the village of Alderbury it was if I were troubled by an unsettling dream. Dreams must turn to vapour with the reassurance of the morning sun and yet inside I feel a scratch upon my soul for this very morning I have witnessed another's nightmare.

*

My soul has received a greater laceration and my conscience is greatly troubled. I wish for guidance but I am alone. I do not feel that I have the spirit to continue with my account and yet I must somehow unburden myself. Would that you were here beside me, my dear uncle, for you remain the last attachment to my family and I have foolishly closed my eyes to summon your presence. Sir, I have drunk brandy with no evening meal and the candles waver so.

My stomach is now truly empty and I have revived my sorry condition by placing my head under the courtyard pump of this place and it is a place that I do not even know the name of, other than it is an inn upon the road to Romsey. My biliousness will pass and I should screw up this nonsensical page and start anew for it smells of bile.

Please forgive me.

I have a sorry tale of my own treachery to tell and if the fug in my head will permit it, I shall begin and yet I cannot even recall where I left myself without casting my eye back over the page. Indeed, it was the small church beside the canal where I hid from the cruel sun to take up my pen and write to you and then slept a while. I could not readily awaken from this slumber amongst the graves and for a time I wobbled along the canal tow path rubbing my eyes and yawning at the bankside creatures as they fled my heavy footfall. At the next lock I met with the cargo of chalk that had since departed from the bridge and I wondered whether the levels of water in the canal were sufficient to float this heavily laden vessel. The four hauling men were already perspiring from their labour upon the rope and were now required to begin again as they aligned themselves on the towpath. From my earlier enquiry I had established that the two men upon the barge were the barge owner, who had brought the vessel up from Lockerley and the farmer who had purchased the chalk as a manure to enrich his fields. The barge haulers from West Dean had been engaged to dig and load the chalk from the pit and must be grateful for this employment for as Mr Henry Shorto had indicated the canal was now bankrupt and with no prospect of a future. Upon the still surface of the canal a bright green carpet of small leafed weed has been able to accumulate on these undisturbed waters and I wondered at the effects of future neglect. To enable passage, even for local requirements, water levels must be managed correctly and locks maintained and I reflected that I had perhaps witnessed one of the last voyages upon this doomed canal. I bid the company farewell and slow pedestrianism soon left the barge and its gleaming cargo far behind.

Before the village of West Dean an inconvenient spur of land has presented a great obstacle to the steady progress of the canal and a deep cutting has been made. I wonder that the planned route did not deviate to avoid this undertaking and follow instead the course of its living ancestor that naturally makes it own easy passage around the hill. Water will find its own route but to engineer its course, a succession of locks must be constructed to assist with this artifice whilst here a whole hillside has been gouged out and piled high upon steep banks. I scrambled to the summit of the grassy slope and was gratified to discover the necessity for this great excavation as the façade of a large and very grand house soon revealed itself with its many windows having a southern aspect. The owner has therefore not welcomed the view of the canal with its passage of chalk, coal, timber or any other commodity nor witness the honest toil and language of the barge haulers.

After this polite and enormously costly diversion the canal and river converge at West Dean and surely it is a village that believed that it should prosper from this bold enterprise with its broad wharf, warehouse and inn. It is as if the cast of this busy drama had deserted the stage to leave behind the set and scenery and indeed the theatre had been abandoned save for myself in the open auditorium and one soul who had made his bed upon a heap of horse dung in one corner of the yard beside the inn. His contribution in this production is to snore loudly and he embraces his part with gusto. Lo! Enter stage left a phaeton drawn by a single horse, imagine the clip clop if you will, and aboard is I believe a parson. The horse is led to drink on this hot day and the parson surveys the scene and spies the man asleep upon the dung heap. He calls across.

"You there, you there."

There is no response from the dung heap except perhaps that the snoring gets louder. The parson repeats his lines.

"You there, you there."

The horse is left to drink its fill and the parson climbs down from the phaeton and strides across the yard and stops before the dung heap.

"You there..."

My dear uncle, you will by now have gauged that this is not Shakespeare, Sheridan nor even Kelly, but the work of an undiscovered talent, Henry Chalk, and I believe that it is the brandy that has skewed my senses but continue I must. Back at the dung heap the parson's wrath at this dissolute behaviour has caused him to poke the snoring man with his stick to which, in response, there is a change of pitch but not of volume. The parson steps gingerly upon the foothills of the dung heap and then grips the coat of this resolute sleeper and tugs with all his Christian might. The snores are replaced by a puzzled grunting and this disturbance is resolved by the shrugging free of the troublesome coat by the disturbed fellow who then crawls back to the comfortable summit of the dung heap. The parson meanwhile is dusting off his breeches for he flew off in the opposing direction along with the empty garment. The coat is then cast to ground and an assault made upon the steaming mound, the soundly sleeping man is dragged by the ankles and he drowsily tries to gain purchase with outstretched arms to arrest this downward motion and succeeds only in removing two handfuls of dung from the pile. Having now achieved his primary goal the parson hauls the man to the vertical and embarks upon a sermon on the pernicious evils of drink. The sleeper sways gently for a moment before pressing a handful of dung into the face of his assailant and then turns and clambers back upon the soft and odorous pile and the snoring resumes.

At this juncture I came to the aid of the clergyman for he was blinded temporarily and he rubbed at his eyes and spat to clear his mouth between loudly excoriating the dung flinger.

"Pah...you are a drinking bad fellow..pah."

I led the parson down to the canal to cleanse his face and with my handkerchief I then removed any remaining material from the corner of his eye. A small audience had finally mustered in response to this commotion with one or two extending their interest to inspect the occupant of the dung heap. The clergyman had by now recovered his composure and he stood to address the villagers of West Dean with a censure that they should tolerate such drunkenness and human degeneracy. In response to this admonishment four geese waddled across the yard and with extended necks then hissed at the parson, whilst the onlookers soon dispersed and the snoring continued. The parson thanked me for my assistance and stated that he must be on his way for he still had some distance to travel and yet make his return journey at a respectable hour. He then explained that he hoped to meet with a family of itinerants upon Whiteparish Common as he had made this same journey on this date, with the exception of it falling upon a Sunday, for the last ten years and on only one occasion had he failed to locate his wandering congregation. I questioned whether these might be gypsies or "Egyptians" as they have been termed, and the clergyman declared that this was indeed the case and he informed me that the Staveley family had accepted the Holy Bible and were receptive to prayer. Of a sudden I found myself making a request that

I might accompany the parson to which he readily granted his consent and we then hastily made our introductions and I can inform you my dear uncle that I was now in the company of the Reverend Mr Dickson. There was a sense of urgency in his every action, from the retrieval of his horse to the clambering aboard the phaeton and I had no sooner stowed my pack and found my seat then we were clattering over a small bridge and I fancied that, in our wake, the curtain then closed upon the farce of the bankrupt canal.

You will recall that it was Colonel Boyle at the Woodyates Inn who had so had impressed upon me the notion of meeting with gypsies when the opportunity arose and I now found myself in the company of one who was bent on their salvation. I was soon to learn that each and every one of us are sinners and are due to perish and face an eternity in hell, if gracious salvation is not immediately sought. I reasoned that the parson would soon question my own spiritual dearth and so at the crest of a long chalk ridge I remarked upon the fine views available to the south before us and also, at our rear, a great forest extended for as far as my eye could tell. The parson's eyes were still smarting from his encounter at the dung heap but his gaze was fixed firmly upon the road ahead and he confessed to little interest of distant views on either horizon.

"Mr Chalk, I do not travel to seek the picturesque in crags, vales and cataracts and yet I am aware there are many who hold an identical position to my own in our church and who care but little for their own flock and would eagerly seek distraction in such matters."

As the clergyman urged on his hot and labouring horse it was clear that the Reverend Dickson ventured forth with only one purpose in mind and that was the saving of souls from eternal damnation.

We forged ahead at reckless speeds along narrow lanes banked high with flourishing hedges, spared only from disaster at each twist in the road I believe by the divine purpose of our mission. We crossed the Romsey turnpike on the outskirts of a village called Whiteparish and then followed a poor road across the common. This was indeed a curious place for it was neither a wood nor an open field and where single trees flourished with their many pole branches emerging in a cluster at a tall man's height from the ground. The trunks are made smooth by the interests and rubbing of animals and I saw geese, cows and horses scouring about this hard, hoof pocked soil for a morsel to feed upon. Amongst these pole trees with their spring browning of flower and unfurling leaf are the dark rich green crowns of the spiky leafed holly, a tree that I can readily identify. A whiff of woodsmoke soon betrayed the presence of a cluster of simple canvas tents beside the road where perhaps three or more generations of one family of gypsies had made their settlement. Our clattering arrival caused little surprise to the occupants of this sprawling encampment save for the barking of a number of lean dogs and indeed there were also cats, chickens with their chicks in tow and horses roaming about the place. All around lay evidence of the simple trades of the gypsy with scattered chips of wood from the manufacture of carved spoons and pegs and also a hearth constructed of raised earth for metalwork with beside it a pair of hand bellows and a small stone anvil. A central fire smouldered with a timber tripod erected above it from which was suspended a large black pot. Amongst this haphazard industry children scampered about like kittens whilst mothers carried their very young tight to their hip in a band of cloth. From their various positions and activities, the Staveley tribe slowly gathered together in silent anticipation, standing or squatting and a dog's growl was stifled by a single gruff command. The parson swooped down from the phaeton and wasted no time upon introductions or explaining my presence to the reticent family and instead demanded the bible that he had bestowed upon them at an earlier visit. I remained beside the carriage as the bible was retrieved and presented to the visitor who with book in hand then visibly trembled as

if the tome was a source of violent electricity. Whilst this conspicuous
veneration was taking place one small boy found instead the plight of a
thirsty horse an irresistible distraction and slipped away to return with
a splash of water and presented this to the harnessed animal. Whilst
the horse gratefully sucked at the pail the boy then laid a flat palm
upon its stooped neck before looking up to study the stranger in the
camp. I smiled at the boy but this had not the desired effect for he
started and with a look of great consternation he then hastily returned
to the family and hid amongst the legs of the elders. He then began
whispering to others and pointing in my direction whilst also patting
at his head. At first, I could not comprehend this concern until another
member of the tribe touched at his own hat and I then believed that
the snake hatband must be the cause of this alarm and so I removed the
snakecatcher's hat to prevent further disturbance. I wondered whether
the desiccated snake had presented some form of bad omen for I knew
not the lore or superstitions of the gypsies and yet I believe that they
had been truly unsettled by this occurrence. With the snakecatcher's
hat placed upon the seat of the phaeton, the attention of the tribe was
restored to the actions of the parson who was now displaying the full
force of his convictions before the apprehensive congregation. I had
now the opportunity of studying the appearance of this burgeoning
family and Colonel Boyle had warned of a grimy countenance upon
the weathered faces of these out-of-doors dwellers and the darkness
of their skin could not be truly determined as the soot and dust had
created its own patina. The children stood shoeless and even a young
woman displayed bare arms and feet and indeed the younger men and
women were strong and handsome. There was no Englishness about
these striking faces and common to all was the blackness of the hair
and their eyes were as dark and mysterious as freshly broken flint. An
elderly woman, who by virtue of her age must be the grandmother of
the tribe, could not have displayed more wrinkles as she squinted into

the sun at the clergyman whilst sucking upon the stump of her pipe. The continued silence of the family as they stood before the parson was a measure of their guarded nature, and I could not begin to perceive what thoughts they held about the clergyman's drama or the references to the Old Testament for their faces betrayed no opinion. Despite this voluble expounding there was a great calmness about this church in the open air with birdsong abounding and these loud words, uncontained by any cavernous stone building, soon drifted away into the half wood. I wondered that it might indeed be I, the visitor, who was being shown a way, or a path through life for these travelling people had lived long enough on the periphery of our civilisation to follow the example of a sedentary life if they should wish it. I wondered how these wandering tribes would survive in a world empty of villages, towns, cities and of all constraints and boundaries. I believe that they might drift with the changing seasons, to gather and hunt and this ease of movement eschews the accumulation and encumbrance of belongings and also the requirement of the owning by deed the land under your feet. On our jolting journey to this place the parson had spoken of "The unhappy plight of these itinerants and indeed if they might cease their eternal wandering and embrace the word of God then they may yet be free of their heathen customs and vices." As I studied closely the Staveley family, I saw the grime upon their clothes and faces but I believe that there is a surety about their posture and also the knotted strength of a large family that will ensure their survival. I sense also that our presence creates a tension that will not abate until our departure.

The clergyman then looked across at me as if unaware that I had not yet joined the congregation and he gestured with some impatience for me to leave my position and stand alongside the family. He then began the Lord's Prayer to which I was the only one who gave vocal support until the end when a low "Amen" was prised from the onlookers with a deal of encouragement. At the conclusion of the service the parson stood and swayed in the bright sunshine with his head bowed whilst the itinerants shuffled and murmured amongst themselves. The pipe smoking grandmother then approached me and held flat her calloused palms and I did not comprehend her purpose until another woman gripped my wrists and I was made to show my own hands. I had thus far heard little of the language of these people but as they now gathered close around me, I could hear the strange and rapid exchange of the most mysterious words. I knew not the purpose of this close inspection of my hand, called by the Staveley tribe a "dukering", but evidently the old woman took offence by what my palms revealed as her eyes widened and she uttered strange sounds that caused gasps and whispers amongst our audience. At this moment the parson intervened and he forced his way through the tribe that had now encircled me.

"MR CHALK, MR CHALK..CEASE THIS AT ONCE."

I was then pulled from the ring of Gypsies by the clergyman and severely reprimanded for participating in a heathen act when I should be still in quiet contemplation.

"Mr Chalk you have done me a disservice and I now regret your presence here today."

I sincerely apologised to the Reverend Dickson and by explanation I informed him that I had no notion of what had occurred and knew not that it was a bad thing. The clergyman's storm was quick to subside and he then explained that it was an old Gypsy tradition to read a stranger's fortune by the inspection of the lines and creases upon their palms and for this dubious service a coin is demanded in return. It was indeed this type of superstitious nonsense, explained the parson, that good Christian teaching should soon dispel. He then declared that we must now depart for he had a good many miles to travel back to his own parish. As the parson returned the bible to the elder of the family, I inspected again my own palm to see if I could establish what had caused such alarm to the old pipe smoking woman to whom I was now in financial debt.

My dear uncle my candle has just exploded which will explain the wax across the page and if I had not more to write then I would now gladly take to my bed but instead I have fumbled with flint, steel and tinder to enable me to resume my account for there is a grave conclusion to my meeting with the family of itinerants.

Before our departure from the encampment the parson took a small package from the carriage and gave it to the grandmother for which she thanked him profusely. As the clergyman took his seat beside me, he explained that each year he brought a gift of tea for the family and at the first visit he had made the mistake of participating in the drinking of it. He described how they would boil it all up and then pass this heavy stew of tea around in large tin bowls and he then made a face and shuddered at the memory of this experience.

"Mr Chalk, it is another aspect of civilised life for which they require guidance."

With the sun at our backs we then lurched our way across the common for there was to be no respite in the haste that the parson required of his horse. I was soon shaken from my thoughts by the appearance of four horsemen approaching who arrested their charges and demanded that we also halted. These were militiamen and their captain enquired as to the whereabouts of a tribe of gypsies upon the common to which the parson explained that we had just now departed from their encampment, for they were a family aspiring to be good Christians. The captain laughed at this notion and declared that in his opinion they were all thieving blackguards and as the mounted militia then galloped on, he called back.

"We shall soon see if they are good English Christians." The clergyman sat for a moment in silence and then rubbed at his chin before speaking.

"In my experience, Mr Chalk, four horsemen shall never be the bearers of glad tidings. We must return at once." As fast as we were able, the Reverend Dickson reversed our course and began our race back along the rough and undulating track, in rapid pursuit of the militia. I too now feared what might become of the family and as we neared the encampment, we could hear a great commotion with many raised voices. The tribe were mustered as before when in anticipation of the parson's open air service and yet it was the barrel of a pistol that had now caused this herding together and not the promise of a packet of tea. Another dismounted militiaman was slashing at the canvas tents with his sword and complaining loudly.

"God, they stink Sir, it would be a blessing to burn this filth. There's no Frenchie in 'ere."

The captain remained mounted as he observed the destruction of the gypsy's few belongings and as a barking dog was kicked and a tethered ass released and thumped on the rump with the flat of a sword, this was too much for one young gypsy and he flew at the uniformed assailant. The pair wrestled in the dust until another soldier brought the butt of his rifle down upon the head of the itinerant to which he fell motionless upon the ground.

"ENOUGH, ENOUGH," roared the clergyman as he rose up in the phaeton with the reins trembling in his hands. "EXPLAIN THIS BARBARITY SIR."

The Captain of the militia drew level with the wide-eyed parson.

"Calm your fury sir, for we are at war least you forget it and these..good Christians of yours are known to harbour Frenchmen on the run. A prisoner has slipped our convoy this morning and I intend to track him down, take what may. Line up the men sergeant, surely you can tell apart a Frenchman from a gypsy?"

As the women, children and older men huddled together, the younger male gypsies were made to speak out their names to the sergeant. The one who suffered the blow upon the head was forced to stand also and swayed unsteadily, unable to comprehend this new ordeal. Before further damage was inflicted upon this unfortunate man the parson leapt down from his position and stood before the impatient sergeant.

"If you are to deal out more blows then you must strike me down first and you shall then have God to answer to. Captain I have known this family for ten years and observed these boys grow to be men and I will swear before you upon the Holy Bible that there is no Frenchman here, so help me."

I looked down upon the fear shown in the faces of the children and hoped that the parson's interjection would end this ordeal. One small girl fumbled with an object and let it fall to the ground at her feet before quickly stooping to retrieve it and then concealed this piece within her garments. I knew at once that I had seen this self-same object only hours before, as it had been offered to me by a desperate man in exchange for money as I had passed the convoy of French prisoners of war. It was a white carving of a figure, perhaps of bone and its presence here could mean only one thing. I was not alone in witnessing the falling of this object for the grandfather of the tribe now had his dark flinty eyes fixed upon my face and our gaze became locked and I was unable to look away until this eternity was broken by the call of the captain to remount.

"We have wasted enough time here," he called back as he moved on, "and you, parson, should keep better company in future."

As the thundering hooves departed, I could not look up for I felt those same cold dark eyes still burning into my very soul and yet I was wholly aware of the treachery to my nation that I had caused by not speaking out. I knew not what to do. The Frenchman had gone yet he had passed this way today leaving behind him the bone figure, perhaps his sole possession in a trade for food or clothing. What benefit to make captives of all these people for their brief harbouring of a desperate and helpless man. The gypsies' nationality is obscure and it is as if they are foreigners in their own country and I had not the cold courage or conviction to bring further misery and mistreatment to these people. Should this lone Frenchman return to France and English lives become lost as a consequence, then that blood would be forever on my hands.

I spoke of none of this to the clergyman who I believe demonstrated the unstinting proof of his own conviction and acted with great bravery to spare further bloodshed. I hold nothing but admiration for his deed today and I believe that he contains within his body not one ounce of doubt regarding his purpose upon this earth.

I only wished to be released from the unblinking stare of the old gypsy for he knew that I held their future in my hands and perhaps this was indeed the vision witnessed by the gypsy grandmother after the sermon as she read with horror the lines upon my cupped palms. The parson wished to stay and assist with the reparations to the camp and yet the Staveley family urged him to depart, not with anger but so that they could repair themselves for I believe I have witnessed that strength today, of a family long used to facing adversity together.

At the turnpike, I requested that I might be let down to find my own way. I then sincerely apologised to the parson for he had good cause to admonish me and that I should never have requested to accompany him when my motive was but idle curiosity. This stern faced clergyman then surprised me greatly for he smiled as he took my hand.

"Mr Chalk, if you have learnt something today then that is sufficient. We are all sinners after all but it is only those that forever seek salvation that may yet be saved. Go with God in your heart and you shall never be found wanting."

As the parson turned a corner and disappeared from view, I strode out upon the turnpike with much to dwell upon and walked in my lengthening shadow until I met with an inn that I believe lies in the neighbouring county of Hampshire. I know not what tomorrow holds for tonight I am but a hollow shell and weak of spirit.

Goodnight my dear uncle, I pray that you will not judge me too harshly for I have openly confessed to you of my treachery. I hope and trust that you will understand when I tell you that I do not consider myself a traitor to the circumstances as they presented themselves and indeed how would you have acted in my stead?

I wonder that I shall ever understand my own purpose upon this earth save for the abiding love that I hold for another.

Your confused nephew
HENRY CHALK

Wednesday 11th May 1808

MY DEAR UNCLE,

I have just climbed from my bed and I can report that pedestrianism and sleeping exhaust in equal measure. I awoke in a tangle of hot and twisted sheets believing that I had already made some reparations for my treacherous silence before the militia at the gypsy encampment by now enlisting for the army. In my tormented dream I had been packed tight amongst a thousand men aboard a ship and then endured a stormy voyage before rowing ashore to face a wild eyed foe. Our force was ill equipped against thunderous guns and long slashing swords for we each had only a knife and a fork to make our defence. I recall my protestations to a most senior commander that the inferior quality of Sheffield goods would not do and we must in its stead utilise the best steel cutlery from the workshops of Mr Henry Shorto in Salisbury. I was swiftly cast in irons for my insubordination for I had no notion that the general was a proud native of Sheffield and a stout defender of its modern industry.

There is much early activity at this inn, of which I still do not know the name and I would rest further but a weary gentleman traveller has just entered the room and upon eyeing my vacant bed has swiftly claimed it for himself. The blankets and hot damp sheets are hauled in vain across his head and this bed thief now makes a weak groan against the cruel probing of the morning sun.

The day has begun without a purpose and I can think of no destination that hurries me to my breakfast and yet I have been spared further torment for I am no longer that clammy and writhing lump aboard the creaky bed.

I have thrown open the window to attract a fresh draught of air into this small room for the malign gusts within have greatly increased with the arrival of my uninvited guest.

The ink is flowing freely from the pen at this early hour and once the nib is charged above the page and thoughts are already formed in that glob of black liquid then there is but little labour required in the task of writing. I believe that I must avail myself of this opportunity for I have some explaining to do if I may impose further upon your time.

I have promoted to you my dear uncle that the purpose of my return to this mysterious county of Wiltshire has been the search for flint of a fine quality that would satisfy the needs of our ancient ancestors. I have not been disingenuous for that is indeed the case and in addition I have the great pleasure of a first meeting with Robert Foster at the Winterslow Hutt. I have indicated that whilst brother and sister are estranged then no longer can I communicate directly with Sarah Foster and this hiatus has also presented an opportunity to continue with my pedestrianism and the spilling of yet more ink upon the page. Sir, I have given you two good reasons but I fear that I have been reticent upon the manner of my leaving the home of Mr Richard Fenton in the county of Pembrokeshire. There is indeed a third reason for my being abroad in Wiltshire and I feel bound to present to you the facts that hastened my departure from that place near two weeks ago. Mr John Fenton, as you will recall, is a young master in the art of raillery and I have before suffered for the sake of his own idle amusement. I truly believe that he expects reciprocation in equal measure and yet I am not built that way and would gain little pleasure in such combat. Defeat for John Fenton exists in my indifference to these pitfalls and mantraps that he lays out before me for they are now to be expected at any moment of timely distraction. I am forever on my guard in his company and yet we may walk and talk and become an amicable pair to the casual observer for there is much that is of mutual interest. There was a mustering of friends at Glynamel, the home of Mr and Mrs Fenton, but Mr Richard Fenton was not present for he had returned again to London. Mrs Eliza Fenton had arranged an admirable table in the gardens as the weather had just become fair and there was much amusement with singing and games. I was chosen to become blind man's buff and then spun around relentlessly until dizziness near overcame me and the tight scarf across my eyes let in not even the smallest portion of light. I did not rove about with my hands before me but stood inanimate for a good while longer than any previous participant on that afternoon. I at first tried to tell my direction from the faint wind upon my cheek until the slamming of the front door betrayed the position of the house and my orientation was then established. The distant chiming of bells informed me that it was three o'clock and I began to believe that our eyes make very short work of the world around us. Before the blindfold had been attached I had only thoughts of preparing the garden and with the arrival of guests, as one is wont to do, I began the study of unfamiliar faces. In the blackness I now distinguished between voices that were known to me and also the tones of strangers who possessed the lilting singsong richness of the Cambrian accent. Amongst this chattering and a clattering of cups upon saucers there existed also a furious industry of insects and birds in the garden and this rich orchestra of sounds soared about my head. The children then goaded me into moving slowly forward and yet I was not seeking to catch the nearest and boldest of the players for I was thinking all the while of Sarah and her perpetual blindfold. It was through all these sensations that I then heard the voice of Mr John Fenton, not in a loud and mischievous manner but a portion of whispered conversation that was assuredly not meant for my ears.

"He has but a bankrupt and untrustworthy uncle for a family and the poor lamb cherishes the love of a blind girl. We must therefore be charitable towards our young pedestrian."

I know not to whom he was talking and it matters little for it was the earnest manner and attempt at discretion that made the effect of his words one thousand times worse than any taunt or intended cruelty.

The birds ceased their singing and the crockery and children's laughter became silent also for the thundering inside my head replaced all these things. The younger Mr Fenton did not witness the removal of the blindfold for he had become distracted by the arrival of a mother and daughter into the garden and it was the latter that was receiving his full attention. The children were quickly drawn towards chasing a playful puppy into the shrubbery and I stood alone upon the lawn shielding my blinking and watery eyes against the bright afternoon. I soon retired to the house and sat upon my bed without knowing what to do with myself and yet I could not remove John Fenton's whispered words from my thoughts. I cannot believe that discussions have taken place between Mr Richard Fenton and his son John regarding my most private affairs. I have entrusted the details of my meeting with Miss Sarah Foster to no one other than her brother Robert and can only gauge that John Fenton has spied upon my correspondence and secretly availed himself of the nature of her affliction. Such behaviour is surely despicable but not I fear beyond the capabilities of this young man, for he has before taken my unsealed letters and read them in my presence when I could not prevent it. I know not also what he means by branding you sir as untrustworthy! What an affront on your good character by one who has proved himself not to be trustworthy himself. I wished now that I were bold and brave and had challenged John Fenton in his garden to demand an explanation. I wonder that I shall ever boil over in anger and let my actions speak out for themselves as to be timid all one's life will gain respect from no quarter. Indeed, if Mr Richard Fenton had been present then I may still be at Glynamel for he would surely get to the bottom of these most serious of issues and then admonish strongly

his son's indiscretion. Instead I packed my bag, leaving behind all
that I could not comfortably carry on my back and also retrieved my
thumbstick from the hallway before departing. I was but a few paces
from the house when I realised that I could not leave without speaking
first with Mrs Eliza Fenton, for I had become a very welcome guest
in her household these last few months and she was indeed deserving
of some explanation. The afternoon visitors had long departed and I
found the mistress of the house busy at her writing desk and as I did
not wish to disturb Mrs Fenton, I quietly made my retreat but she
paused to ask who was there. I entered the room fully and yet I found
that I could not state my true purpose and instead I commended Mrs
Fenton upon the success of the day to which she concurred that the
weather had again been favourable to the event and they were indeed
most fortunate. There was then a moment of silence before I thanked
Mrs Eliza Fenton sincerely although I do not believe that she knew
for what purpose my gesture was intended and I hastily departed to
enable her to continue unhindered in her writing. I fully intend to write
to both Mr and Mrs Fenton to give some account of my actions and
whereabouts for I believe that there must be some concern as to the
abruptness of my departure and its cause.

     From Fishguard I took the evening coach to Milford for I
had already constructed a feeble plan that I soon failed to execute. I
recalled that Mr Richard Fenton had once made a sea voyage across
to Minehead upon the Somersetshire coast departing from Milford
aboard a small packet ship. Once at the home of Miss Sarah Foster I
would announce myself boldly at the front door and all would be very
well indeed. I have already advised you sir that it was a feeble plan,
burgeoning with desperation and short on discretion and therefore
doomed to failure. On arriving at Milford, I found lodging at the Lord
Nelson Hotel which is a large and newly built establishment. Milford
is altogether a new town constructed to the design of the Hon Mr

Charles Greville and there is a great deal more to observe here than at lowly Fishguard, for the harbour is alive with small vessels. In the dockyards below the town great naval ships are under construction with these infant vessels resting in their giant cradles, the progeny of our war with France and they attract the interest of all who visit Milford. I was most surprised to learn that it is a Frenchman, Monsieur Barralier, who is assisting with the building of these English warships for he is a nobleman that fled "Le Terror" and is now an architect in thwarting the grand schemes of the little Corsican. My dear uncle, I did not bring you to Milford for any other purpose but to explain my progress from the Fenton household. It was indeed my intention to depart for Somersetshire as soon as possible for in my troubled mind I was able to consider no other course of action and it was as well that upon my arrival at Milford I hastily put pen to paper and wrote to Robert Foster in London explaining all that had passed. That I should still be in Milford to receive his reply I have the simple oyster to thank. I can report that good fortune and extreme discomfort were contained within the shell of this little creature for one dose kept me in and out of my bed for three days and nights. Upon the fourth day I was able to shuffle meekly to the window and observe through my telescope the Waterford Packet arrive and then slowly depart for all wind had ceased and the sails upon the bay were as limp as my own constitution. The arrival of a letter from Mr Robert Foster in London then provided the best tonic of all for it contained sweet hope and plans and there is nothing more essential to raise the spirit than hope and plans. It was Robert Foster's suggestion that I should again prosecute a pedestrian excursion to my favoured county of Wiltshire. Some five years ago the Foster family found sanctuary from a snow blizzard at the Wintersow Hut whilst on a journey from London and as this establishment was known to Robert Foster, he believed that we should make our first acquaintance there for he was soon to return again from the capital city. I could not reply swiftly enough to commend him on this suggestion and was able to pack my belongings and depart from unfinished Milford leaving behind a measurable degree of my own substance for my clothes were now made loose by the effects of that blessed oyster. I suffered uncomfortable and halting progress before gaining a crossing of the River Severn at the New Passage and thereon my journey became hot and cramped to Bristol, Bath and Shaftesbury. Upon entering into Wiltshire I felt my old self again and had no longer the scent of rotten low tide in my nostrils and I shall consign oysters to a list of undesirables that already contains port wine.

The bed thief here in this little room has woken from his sketchy slumber and after clawing back the sheets from around his head has now the impudence to scowl that the scratching and scraping of my pen is playing with his nerves. He seeks the chamber pot, a prospect that prompts my own swift vacation.

*

I have this afternoon arrived at the Winterslow Hut that is perched beside the busy London road and it is the desire to hear news of my beloved Sarah from her trusted brother that has guided me to this place. At the sound of each approaching stage I survey the yard below for a passenger that I know will not arrive for two more days and I curse again this absurd expectation. My journey is ill planned for Robert is not expected until Friday 13th and it is surely better to be busy with pedestrianism than laying idle in a coaching house. I shall at least receive some grateful shelter from the pounding sun and escape from the curious and alarming circumstances that have plagued this troublesome correspondent whilst he is abroad in the open country. I sincerely hope that to settle a while at the Winterslow Hut will keep the hounds of adventure from snapping at my heels for this appears a very ordinary place.

So, what of my day? Curiosity demanded that I first retraced my steps of yesterday and I found myself again crossing Whiteparish Common and passing between the scant concealment of the trees until I could gain a vantage point. I lamented again the loss of my looking glass for it was an occasion well suited to this surreptitious behaviour. My anticipation was in vain for the encampment was no more and gone were the ripped open tents, the animals and also the great strangeness brought to this place by the itinerant Staveley family. I felt no mystery still lingering upon this spot for that exists with the tribe and will inhabit the next verge or glade where tents are raised and where animals feely graze. A warm hearth and a scattering of woodchips were all that remained behind and I did not care to investigate further over the detritus of these perpetual wanderers. I wondered whether they would ever return to Whiteparish Common and again produce the bible upon the arrival of the stern faced Reverend Dickson. In truth I believe that it was the prospect of encountering the yellow clad Frenchman that drew me back to this now vacated encampment, as if he might be sitting pondering upon a stump and awaiting my arrival to escort him back to his place of detention. I can report that he was nowhere to be seen and I was therefore unable to make amends for my treachery. Indeed, the prospect of a flash of yellow in the corner of my eye kept me in a state of great vigilance as I continued on my way until I then stumbled upon some fashioned flint in the grounds of Breach House, whereupon my distraction was easily won and complete. The earth here is sandy with flint pebbles but it is also patchy with evidence of a heavy clay that is now dried and cracked. Hidden amongst trees and thick undergrowth a river has once gouged its deep course but today I found a mere rusty trickle between small shingle banks that enabled me to hop along the revealed bed in perfect concealment from the fields on either side. I clambered from this secret watery passage with caution for I knew not upon whose private land I was freely wandering. I then spied a barren field and amongst this exposed soil I scraped and probed with my thumbstick, turning over smooth pebbles and prising out promising lumps for inspection. The flint here is stained a honey brown and yet these rounded pebbles retain a freshness despite this attractive opacity. That they have been stained, rolled and rounded by their longevity amongst water there can be little doubt, but I believed that this ready supply of flint in the river bed and upon its fringe must have been freely exploited by our early ancestors. I wished to prove this theory to myself and the longer I scoured the ground for evidence to support this fact the more determined I became in my search. I could hear a boy calling and hurling his rattle about to keep the birds from the nearby crop and yet I was not to be deterred from my quest. I at last retrieved a broken slither of flint and felt a tremble at this reassurance as my close inspection revealed its sharpness and slender regularity. There is also a feature of any piece of flint that has been purposefully struck from the parent block for it displays a small pimple on its underside at the exact point of this impact and it is a record left upon the stone itself of this moment of detachment. I pushed my thumbstick into the soil to mark the spot where I had found the flint slither and began a closer scouring of the ground. I thought back to Peter Winter beside the flint pit in Grovely as he worked at his gunflints and the fast accumulating mass of waste flint detritus that lay about his feet. The great passage of time, the earthworm and the disruption of the plough will bury and disperse these working clusters and yet a proportion will remain, if sought closely enough. I was rewarded for my perseverance for I spied a pebble that displayed the equal and parallel scars of these purposeful fractures. It was once the shape of a large egg and indeed its dark outer rind is no thicker than that of an egg shell. The flint inside is now as cloudy and grey as a sky upon a stormy day but I wager that when this piece was last held and struck open the revealed flint was bright and uniform. I then collected a complete pebble from the soil and another larger broken piece to act as a blacksmith's anvil. A third pebble was required for a hammer and with three blows I had shattered the complete pebble and was able to confirm the fresh regularity of the flint within. My concentration upon the soil beneath my feet had drawn me across two fields and I found myself conducting my noisy experiment within full view of a very large red brick house with only an ornamental lake between my position and the grand façade of the building. The chinking of the flint had attracted the attention of the gardener who was busy shaping a large hedge and he called out to me across the water. More heads popped up from amongst this hedge and there was evidently a team of workers employed to the task. His exact words were not apparent but by his gesticulations I gathered that I should not be roaming about the master's field and so I quickly pocketed my prized flints and politely waved before continuing on my way. The white shirted man was soon intent upon my pursuit and once he began to round the lake and was lost from my view behind some greenery, I then changed my direction to return from whence I came. My devious turnabout was loudly reported to the white shirt by his team of lookouts aboard the hedge but in that time, I was able to retreat to the secret passage of the sunken river bed and retrace my steps without fear of having to break out again into open ground. I thought this the end of the matter until I heard dogs barking with men calling loudly and my stomach turned with the realisation that there was now a genuine intent upon my capture. I hastened my pace splashing on through deeper pools, pressing farther up this narrow and twisting gorge all the while cursing how preciously these county gentlemen guarded their property. A large tree had fallen to lay slumped from bank to bank and I was required to duck down low to pass beneath it but forgetting my pack I then became ensnared amongst the stubs of its broken branches. In a wild panic I struggled the pack from my shoulder and heaved it beyond this obstacle to hear it splash heavily upon the other side. As I emerged from under this spiky and resinous tree my heart gave a great leap for my eyes set upon a pair of old and broken shoes, ragged breaches and then as I raised my head further an old patched shirt. To complete this picture of wretchedness a man with a bony face and sunken fearful eyes stood swaying and gasping before me. Of a sudden he became overcome with weakness and fell to his knees in a pool of rusty water and shook his head in desperation. I knew in an instant that I had encountered the emaciated form of the escaped Frenchman that had only yesterday offered me a carved bone figure in Alderbury. His hours of freedom had now come to an end for he had not the strength to walk another step. From my pack I quickly extracted a half loaf of dry bread that I had secreted from the breakfast table and also a handful of coins from my purse and I thrust these things with some urgency towards the man. He nodded slowly in acknowledgement and with a realisation that I was also by some manner a fugitive he whispered hoarsely "Allee, Allee" and indicated that I should depart with haste. He then rolled back against the bank and tore weakly at the crumbling bread and with the barking dogs splashing ever closer I clambered up the bank and darted away between the trees. I did not turn to witness the apprehension of the French prisoner of war but I could hear well enough the great crescendo of barking and the raised excited calls of the pursuers that heralded their victorious discovery. I lessened my pace and in a short while rested up against a tree to draw breath and to wipe the coating of sweat from my face. That the triumphant hunting party would return immediately to Breach House I held no doubt and none would question how their quarry might have altered from a pedestrian tourist to become a fugitive Frenchman. I now believe that the roaming militia would have informed widely of the presence of the escaped prisoner of war and therefore any stranger at large would have been viewed with great suspicion. By the clashing together of flint pebbles I have caused the capture of this man and as a consequence I have played my unwitting part in his apprehension. Any blight on my conscience could therefore be expunged forthwith and yet all was not so settled in my own mind. When confronted with the plight of such a pathetic and desperate soul is not the human and indeed the Christian instinct to provide help and succour? I believe that the Staveley family supplied clothes to the fugitive and perhaps such sustenance that they were able to give. I sincerely hope that the captors at Breach House gave food and drink to strengthen the nameless Frenchman for I consider that he would surely die without it.

At a safe distance from Breach House I left the rusty river behind me and in time crossed the Southampton turnpike. I then found myself walking the same narrow lanes along which I had rattled only yesterday with such urgent fervour beside the Reverend Dickson. I know not at what stage I took the decision to proceed to the Winterslow Hut or indeed whether I made any such decision at all for in the heat my head had become a vacant shell. Upon John Cary's heavily folded map I have travelled not one little finger's length from the inn upon the Romsey road and yet it has been a hard day's toil. I longed that a great cloud might appear to cast a roving shadow across the land and I could then chase that shade all the day to keep my skin from the burning sun. No such cloud arrived and my face is now dry and nut brown and I do not believe you would know me from a shepherd or indeed a gypsy, if we had the good fortune to meet upon the road. There is everywhere a preoccupation with the weather for it is either "Unreasonably hot" or "Nation warm snaw" depending on whether the commentator might be fanning a flushed face at the breakfast table or leaning upon a farm gate. The beasts in the field are presumably similarly engaged across fences and hedges upon the subjects of irritating flies and a shortage of mud to roll about in.

My weary legs drew me to the sensible shade of the fringes of any wood that I had the good fortune to encounter and I paused to slumber a while in a thick and busy hedge amongst the rustlings and flutterings of the creatures there.

On approaching the Winterslow Hut, I dusted myself down and prepared for an indifferent reception but on crossing the threshold I could detect raised voices and it proved to be a suitable distraction for the landlady was in the throws of an altercation with a disgruntled gentleman.

"Madam, you are most disobliging. It is after all a simple matter."

"Loike I say, I aint n'thas that."

The troubled gentleman stood with his back towards me and shuffled uncomfortably before the intransigent and purse lipped landlady.

"I shall write to the Salisbury Postmaster in the strongest terms," said the troubled gentleman.

It appeared that no amount of sighing, shuffling and remonstration was about to persuade the landlady from concluding the delivery of this gentleman's correspondence and it was to stubbornly remain at the inn for his collection. At this juncture I surprised myself by stepping from the shadows to promote a bold suggestion.

"Madam, sir. May I offer albeit a temporary solution, for the short duration of my stay here at the Winterslow Hut, I should be willing to deliver any correspondence to this gentleman personally. Indeed, I should welcome the task for I have little to occupy me until the anticipated arrival of a dear friend from London on the thirteenth day of this month."

In the silence that followed I hastily pressed on with my ingratiation towards the landlady and removed the snakecatcher's hat.

"Madam, Henry Chalk of Southwark at your service."

I then turned to the dark haired and furrow browed gentleman who consistently refused to meet my eye and he offered eventually the limpest of hands that could not satisfactorily be shaken. After scowling once more at the landlady and recovering his flaccid hand, this abrupt and unhappy gentleman then turned upon his heal and swiftly attempted his departure only to find the latch upon the front door equally uncooperative and he cursed that also. I then pursued the landlady to play upon the tentative understanding that my offer to conclude the delivery of the gentleman's mail had in some way now become a silent acceptance and as to my own right of accommodation.

"Madam, I did not catch the gentleman's name..if I am to..?"

The landlady spun about to face me with arms still tightly folded.

"'Is name is Asslit. Newly weds 'pon the 'ill, n' I ain't deliverin' no mail n' thas a fact. Landlord be round presently."

Muttering to herself, the landlady then shuffled away beyond the public domain and in time a slender and taciturn landlord appeared and found little fault in accommodating a dusty pedestrian tourist. Indeed, by his weary demeanour I believe that he has witnessed all that there is to witness beside the busy London road.

*

So, my dear uncle, here I am at the Winterslow Hut and I have just heard some late arrivals enter the building and could not resist a casual inspection and there are none that would match a description of Robert Foster for they are all older travellers. Their eventual destination is Powderham Castle near the city of Exeter yet one of their party has swollen legs and they have been forced to spend the night here and not continue on to Salisbury. It is one of the few pleasures of such establishments, to observe others who are all thrown together in the haphazard business of travel. There are those who are sociable and enjoy this tumult and revel in the opportunity to make merry with their fellow men and then there are those that perceive the whole as a necessary evil that is to be endured and are curt in their dealings with staff and guests alike. The new arrivals were four in number yet the one with "legs swelled like capstans" had already taken to his bed and the three remaining gentlemen were left to enjoy a late supper.

"He would be better dealt with in Salisbury. Better lodging and better company and I should require a fire," said the first gentleman.

"A fire sir! Look at you. I believe that I could boil a kettle on your pate if you would only oblige by first removing that cosy that passes for a wig. A fire indeed."

"Mr Curtis is a great friend of the fire and he thinks it purifies the air and that his fine constitution is living proof."

"Is it also true Mr Curtis that you wear six waistcoats in both summer and winter?"

"If you believe gentlemen that you can gain your entertainment by the mocking of my sensible habits then I suggest that you have neither enough wit nor brain between you to contrive even a rudimentary conversation."

"Ha, we shall see about that. I suggest then that poetry is superior to painting. What say you Mr Pilkington?"

"Indeed Mr Snape? Then how so the poet Wordsworth has not made more than one hundred and sixty pounds by all his labours when any mediocre portrait painter can appease the vanity of his subject for that much alone?"

"It is not simply a question of money Mr Pilkington, I wager that Wordsworth is driven to write and would do so if there were not a soul to read it."

"Hmm, I maintain Mr Snape that a painting will sit quietly upon the wall and behave itself. Poets are an unsettling breed and poetry forces one to smile in a sickly way as you are obliged to pretend that you understand it."

"I grant Mr Pilkington that poetry can never be wholly understood by anyone but can it not express love better than any daubing? Our mind will deal in words and they shall haunt and surface again when by contrast we need to be forever placed before even the very best of paintings to be reminded of their worth."

" Gentlemen, gentlemen, as you have concocted your laborious dialogue for my benefit then I shall determine that Mr Reynolds was a great painter and Mr Coleridge a wind bag and now I shall seek a fire, even if I have to break the furniture into little pieces and place it in the grate myself. Goodnight Sirs, I wish I could express my pleasure by your company but it is like the revolting hard water of this cursed place, to be endured."

The bewigged gentleman then retired for the night, leaving the two remaining guests looking about them for some means of entertainment, at which I discreetly slipped away from my vantage point.

Sir, I realise that I have parted company with my thumbstick and yet I do not believe that I shall return to the grounds of Breach House to continue with my investigations nor to retrieve my stick from the soil for I may easily cut another. Let it be a simple monument to the capture of the French fugitive for without my clashing together of flint pieces at that very spot then he may still be at large. I shall not forget the very sobering events of these last two days for it has given me much to ponder upon. I now have these sandy examples of fashioned flint set before me and I intend to give exercise to the pencil and make a careful study of them. I consider that ancient man gathered flint where need arose and opportunity occurred and would perhaps return over and again to the rusty river and other such fruitful places. My "tour in search of flint" continues but I have been thrown a gobbet of encouragement by my simple finds amongst the soils of Breach House.

I shall now exchange the pen for the pencil and I wish you goodnight.

Your faithful nephew

HENRY CHALK

Thursday 12th May 1808

MY DEAR UNCLE,

This morning I have received a letter of apology from Robert Foster to inform me that he has suffered a delay in his plans. He shall not now appear until Sunday 15th of May and all is frustration. This news has further exposed the folly of my early arrival at the Winterslow Hut. I have little to occupy me save for the task of transporting fresh correspondence to the home of the ungrateful and irascible gentleman who lives upon the hill in Middle Winterslow. It is a Wiltshire custom of speech to remove the "H" at any opportunity to satisfy the lust for an "Aaah" or an "Eee", so despite the landlady's taut lipped insistence that the gentleman's name is Asslit, I see from the letters before me that it is indeed Mr William Hazlitt. With this understanding I now believe that my thumbstick is cut from the hazel bush and is not spelt "azel", as I first thought.

On my return I must write to Mr and Mrs Fenton for a letter of explanation, however difficult that may be to compose, is long overdue.

I rapped upon the door of the small cottage in Middle Winterslow and was swiftly confronted by a portion of Mr William Hazlitt who then fidgeted impatiently with the door ajar as if he had been rudely disturbed. Presented with this awkwardness and his strangely averted gaze, I did not at first declare my purpose and instead bid the gentleman a fine morning. At this juncture a lady's voice could be heard enquiring from within.

"Who is it William?"

Mr Hazlitt paused to study my boots before answering.

"I do not know. He proposes that it is a fine morning when it is patently not so for the air is too heavy."

"What does he want?"

I then thrust the two carried letters towards the aperture between frame and door and reminded Mr Hazlitt that I had only yesterday afternoon promised to deliver his correspondence for the short duration of my stay at the inn.

The heavy brow puckered in confusion.

"He brings my letters from the Hut."

"Then give him a coin. Do you have a coin?"

At this point Mr Hazlitt was pushed to one side and replaced at the now fully opened door by Mrs Hazlitt, who with long fingers then delved into a soft pouch in search of a coin. I removed the snakecatcher's hat and hastily introduced myself, explaining my offer of yesterday which halted her probing for the elusive gratuity.

"Then that is most kind. William, Mr Chalk is himself a guest at the Hut. William?"

Mr Hazlitt had since lost interest in the events at the front door and could be heard thumping and bumping elsewhere in the small house. His wife sighed in resignation as if this misunderstanding could have been easily averted.

"You must wonder at Mr Hazlitt's strangeness. I am drinking tea, would you care for some tea Mr Chalk? Please do at least come in and drink some tea. William? We have a young guest."

I followed Mrs Hazlitt into the parlour where crates brimming with books were strewn about and a pleasant smell of turpentine hung in the air. Upon the bare floor a number of small canvasses stretched upon frames were turned to face the wall and I took these to be paintings although I could not gauge their subject nor their stage of completeness. A cup was found and books were then removed from a chair and also a space cleared at the table to enable me to join Mrs Hazlitt in drinking tea.

My hostess must have then caught my eye looking about the

place for she laughed as tea was poured and in truth I had not before witnessed such domestic turmoil and neither could I judge the standing of Mr and Mrs Hazlitt in their small cottage.

"We have been married barely a week Mr Chalk and there is much to do so please forgive our disarray but it is largely of my husband's making for there was some order to this place before his arrival."

I then stood and offered my warm congratulations to the news of their recent marriage much to the amusement of Mr Hazlitt who had just reappeared.

"It is a husband's duty to disrupt," he said, "it is what we do best."

"Do you think him rude Henry? Mr Hazlitt is not at all a model husband."

In referring to me as Henry and to her husband as Mr Hazlitt, Mrs Hazlitt had created for me a place of curious intimacy in their relationship, as if I were now in some manner a confidant. I returned to my seat and found some simple reassurance in cradling a warm cup.

Mrs Hazlitt explained that her husband was an author and also a painter and sometimes he could not decide which.

"Today I do not know which course he will take but he will soon declare that he must go out and traverse the countryside with only his thoughts for company and leave me to his unholy mess."

Indeed, as if to confirm this un-husbandly behaviour, Mr Hazlitt passed by the table with boots in hand and a black notebook under his arm.

As there had been no enquiry forthcoming as to my own occupation or purpose here in Winterslow, I then informed Mrs Hazlitt that I was a pedestrian tourist and that there was no finer county than Wiltshire in which to make such excursions.

"Why then sir..." enquired Mr Hazlitt as he completed the

lacing up of his boots, "..are you clucking and drinking tea in our parlour when the fine county awaits?"

This curious Gentleman then placed his hat and rattled open the cottage door before pausing for a brief moment to suggest that he wished that Mrs Hazlitt would let her hair grow long. The door was then firmly slammed behind him and his quickly departing paces could be heard in the silence that settled upon the parlour.

I slowly drained my cup as Mrs Hazlitt then sighed and shook her head wearily.

"Always thinking and walking, walking and thinking. I believe that he is also married to the barren wastes and woods of Winterslow."

I did not wholly believe that Mr Hazlitt's remark, made whilst lacing his boots, had been a formal invitation for me to accompany him and yet it may have been construed as such from any other reasonable mortal. It was however a situation of grave impropriety to be left alone in the company of Mrs Hazlitt and therefore any reason for a swift departure was to be sorely welcomed. Salvation came in the unlikely form of the snakecatcher's hat that I placed upon the cluttered table and Mrs Hazlitt's gaze settled upon this curious object and her eyes then grew wide in consternation.

"Your hat..?"

I apologised for my ill mannered behaviour and quickly retrieved the battered and shapeless hat from the table.

"You..you have a snake upon your hat.. and ..there.. beneath it lay Mr Hazlitt's pencils. He will be in a rage once he requires his pencils."

"Madam, I must make amends and transport Mr Hazlitt's pencils immediately for I am at fault. Please excuse me."

With this heaven sent opportunity, I pushed back my chair and snatched up the pencils in their cloth wrap whilst Mrs Hazlitt pursued me to the door.

"Follow him Mr Chalk, follow and see where he goes. He has a fine pair of legs and you will do well to keep pace."

I had no genuine obligation to continue for I could sensibly return the pencils tomorrow and yet the fast disappearing form of Mr William Hazlitt soon caused me to skip along and lengthen my usual ponderous stride in order to keep sight of him. I had not my pack to slow me down nor duties that would suffer by further procrastination and indeed I had now become invigorated by tea and curiosity.

From a tree crowded church atop a hill to a church resting comfortably on the valley floor, we marched a good mile with Mr Hazlitt looking neither left nor right and most certainly not behind him. In the neighbouring village to Winterslow, ancient observers at the doors of simple mud and chalk houses slowly turned their heads as not one but two strange fellows passed them by with some unaccountable distance set between them. We crossed a road and began our ascent once more upon a worn trail that led I knew not where. In the deep chequered shade of trees and bushes the dark striding figure ahead tugged me from the distraction of rounded flint pebbles in the soil and the study of curious flora upon the verges. The path dipped again as we passed a labourer's cottage, deathly quiet in its sequestered vale where a rabbit and a pedestrian startled one another in near collision. In time my legs told of gradients achieved and signalled the reaching of a plateau within the wood for muscles eased and breathing was again regular. The vegetation soon became green and lush with oak trees abounding and I gauged that the settled clay upon this chalk ridge was now of a good depth with moisture retained in the heavy bright ochre soil. I wished to deviate and search about for pits and other secrets concealed within this wood and yet I had become enslaved in this preposterous and unrelenting pursuit.

A bank rose up upon the northern fringe of this woodland plateau and in the brightness beyond the thinning trees lay the promise of distant views.

The figure ahead then deviated from his course to enter an open and curiously undulating place where buildings with solid walls had once stood but there now remained amongst the short grass only the crumbling stumps of their foundation. Upon every rabbit throw lay broken red brick and tile fragments and you may well imagine my great curiosity at this discovery. Standing defiantly amidst this decay a single segment of wall, perhaps an end wall, constructed of densely packed flint and greensand stone had survived the years. As I approached to inspect this impressive remnant all was quiet save for the soft jangling of sheep bells in the distance and I had become quite distracted from my pursuit of Mr Hazlitt and indeed knew not what had become of him. Whilst rounding this monolith I did not show due attention to my footing and then stumbled over part of the fallen debris of the wall and ended sprawled upon my knees before the seated Mr Hazlitt who then justly sprang up in exclamation.

"WHAT ..WHAT.. WHO.. what in goodness name are you about?"

I had not the breath to utter a word for a moment and Mr Hazlitt continued his protest, whilst pacing back and forth.

"Are you..are you mad? You deliver my letters and then.. and then..creep about for how many miles to make me jump from my skin. Explain yourself sir."

I returned to my feet and then dusted the small embedded stones from my grazed palms.

"I have your pencils sir," I stated meekly.

"What do you mean you have my pencils? I have my pencils. What tomfoolery is this?"

"I placed my hat upon your table.."

"What has your hat to do with it?"

"And concealed your pencils beneath it. I have your pencils."

We then both went to our pockets where I soon retrieved the

cloth wrap of pencils and held them out before me whilst Mr Hazlitt patted and pulled out pocket linings in his prolonged and fruitless search.

"You have my pencils," conceded Mr Hazlitt.

With this resolution we then sat down upon the grass and for an age not another word was spoken. This was not an awkward silence or one of embarrassment but a silence acceptable to both. I have indeed spent long enough at walking and pondering to recognise a moment when the body is content to be idle after exertion and the mind shall drift happily enough on its own. The spirit of a place may at such times waft into the mind's ether and perhaps, of such fine gossamer, poetry is spun. A poet may gather and fashion this delicate fabric but it will not survive my clumsy grasp and by the first thrust of a pen becomes torn and lays in ruin upon the page. You will recall, my dear uncle, the letter mislaid by the young lady of Ferne House that contained poetry of such precious beauty? Indeed, I cannot now return to my lumpish prose when I again write to my beloved Sarah after the example set by one "Percy Bysshe". I have conducted a hapless search for any such latent gift but must concede that poets are born and cannot simply learn their craft as might a cobbler, cutler or brewer's clerk. Mr William Hazlitt has I believe the measure of me and was the first to break our pact of silence.

"As you are a tourist Mr Chalk then you will require information and explanation, for is that not what all tourists seek? I take it that you are not acquainted with this place? Nor I, but I have passed it by on my walk to Salisbury when I first visited Winterslow."

Mr Hazlitt went on to explain that it was a place where the Norman kings enjoyed their regal privilege; to hunt and feast and to plot against those who defied them.

"Thomas Becket died in Canterbury Cathedral but he was surely murdered the instant that King Henry the Second uttered his fatal instruction," Mr Hazlitt leapt up and then manoeuvred himself centrally before the remaining wall of the ruined palace, "perhaps.. here, Mr Chalk, for where else would a king be placed but at the end of the great hall, seated upon his royal dias? You have Mr John Britton's Beauties of Wiltshire to thank for these bare bones and I have added the dramatic flesh, for the benefit of the tourist and pencil bearer."

As I continued to observe this gentleman, he then muttered crossly about how antiquarians will trample over the bones of a place and sift through the dust of their ancestors, but to what end? People will be people and will have behaved like all people do. The scenery and props will alter around them whilst fashion and invention cast a changing hue, but it is all just patina, settled dust, a rusting over, a mist that conceals no mystery at all.

Mr Hazlitt removed himself from the remains of the great hall and strolled about for views and angles from which to make future paintings and concluded that it was not picturesque and a more Gothic ruin would suit better with perhaps a blasted tree.

Having dismissed Clarendon as an unsuitable subject, my unwitting guide then declared that he must now depart and with no invitation forthcoming for me to continue in his company, I was content to find my own way back to the Winterslow Hut. As I took one final look about the place a bright flash upon the horizon then caught my eye and I called out aloud.

"Look there."

Mr Hazlitt stopped to observe me and then his silent gaze followed the direction of my outstretched arm.

"There it is again," I stated, "it is my spyglass, I am certain of it."

"Firstly, it is pencils, then hats on tables and now spyglasses' upon distant hills, you are indeed a curious fellow Mr Chalk."

I had already embarked upon my direct course towards the

glinting object and called back.

"I have not the time to explain."

It was now Mr Hazlitt's turn to pursue me, for I did not at first realise that curiosity had overwhelmed his desire for solitude. I had reached the floor of the valley when I had cause to start as Mr Hazlitt drew along side me. Between breathless pauses I then recounted the details of the gift of the spyglass and the witnessing of the same bright flash upon the distant long barrow, that preceded the realisation of its loss. Mr Hazlitt appeared to enjoy this mystery and also the prospect of its resolution and he assisted in guiding our course, for we no longer had sight of our distant goal. I was not prepared for such exertions and neither did we have between us a single drop of water and it was I that was soon perspiring greatly and lessening my pace as Mr William Hazlitt forged ahead. I was not to be left behind and determination soon brought us together again stride for stride. As we climbed the final ascent, I could now see that our destination was an earthen encampment upon the crest of the hill and it was these distinct lines that had formed the crisp horizon visible from the ruined palace. The raised form of a Roman road crossed our path, dormant under its blanket of turf and in a hundred more paces we bisected the dusty London road, all the while with an eye upon the fortification ahead. I can inform you sir that when we mounted the steep vallum of Figsbury Ring, for that is its name, there was no other person to be seen and twice now the pursuit of my phantom spyglass has been in vain. As I slumped down upon the grassy bank Mr William Hazlitt was unperturbed at my disappointment and suggested that the thrill of the chase was justification enough. Neither was I permitted to dwell over this further frustration as my companion was insistent that we made a circuit of the place.

"Come Mr Chalk, nature does not commiserate for the lark sings heartily in the heavens and neither is the small blue butterfly grief stricken by your loss. Let us walk some more."

There was not the width to walk two abreast upon the raised outer ring of the fortification and so I trailed behind my tireless companion and was soon to shed my disappointment for indeed there was beauty all around us to behold. Across the central expanse within the earthwork a carpet of yellow flowers dazzled in the sun and the once creamy blossom of the thorn bush was now bleeding pink in maturity. As we progressed on our circular course, Salisbury Cathedral was soon to reveal itself with its spire barely able to pierce the pale ridge beyond and Old Sarum could also be detected crouching below the horizon, such was the extent of our own elevation. Indeed, Figsbury Ring had suffered no accident of placement by its ancient constructors for it commanded distant views in every direction. With Mr Hazlitt perhaps thirty paces ahead of me I was soon to notice that the path between us was a straight line and not the gentle curving arc that is associated with a circle. Now alert to this curiosity and five more paces on, Mr Hazlitt's direction altered perceptibly and it was as if the ring was not after all a true circle but instead comprised of many facets to make a round. Each facet of this narrow ridge was a straight line of perhaps thirty paces or more, a ditch dug straight, a straight bank also and how many of these sections were required to complete the whole? With this pleasing observation I then engaged in imagining the digging of this great entrenchment, not as a continuous and daunting endeavour but instead apportioned in short and manageable straight sections. I caught up with Mr Hazlitt to describe the part that he has played in assisting with the unravelling of this antiquarian conundrum. Without lessening his pace or turning his head, Mr Hazlitt then gave no encouragement to my discovery.

"I am not a practical man Mr Chalk and this is surely a practical matter and whether it be done yesterday or many centuries ago I shall not consider it. Tell me it was done in the spirit of revolution and I shall be all ears but I propose that fear alone made this place."

With this rebuff I could only smile to myself and puzzle on what Mr Hazlitt meant by the "spirit of revolution".

At our first meeting Mr Hazlitt would not meet my eye and I thought him rude, yet today I have found a strange attraction to his company. He is not I believe a wealthy man and yet he has the luxury of a great mind in which to reside with all its many rooms. I do not understand all of what he says yet there is a certainty to each word for it has a precision and a sharpness that has been honed by long and private consideration. Mrs Hazlitt had informed me earlier of her husband's dual occupation as an author and also a painter and yet I felt that the subject of poetry may also be embraced by this curious and most able minded gentleman. I had received short shrift upon my antiquarian observation and yet now as I trailed at the back of Mr William Hazlitt and had not his dark scowl to contend with, I found myself enquiring whether the making of poetry was also a "practical matter". I was quite prepared for a further haughty rebuff to this impertinence and continued with some trepidation.

"No," came the eventual reply and I at first thought this the end of the matter, "no, Mr Chalk, composing poetry is not ..a practical matter ..and thank you for the kind return of my words ..like books, they suffer at the hands of the borrower with bindings scuffed and page corners turned over. I am not a poet but I have some association with that breed. They are assuredly not practical men."

Mr Hazlitt chuckled to himself as if reminded of some demonstration of great impracticality that confirmed this notion and then paused before reflecting that the poet Wordsworth would find this circuit ideal for the composition of poetry.

"I see him now, going around and around and the continuity of his verse should suffer no interruption. The same arrangement would not do at all for Mr Coleridge, for he is a very different animal."

I then asked my companion what would be Mr Coleridge's preference, for I considered that these were indeed cast aside treasures on how great men conjured their work from thin air and I was determined to retain them.

"Oh..give him instead a piece of uneven ground to tumble about on or a dense thicket through which to struggle and that would serve him well enough."

Mr Hazlitt then enquired as to my age and I informed him that I was now eighteen years old.

"I do not envy your intellect Mr Chalk but I would exchange our years for as we taste the pleasures of life the spirit evaporates. In youth our ideas are clothed and fed and pampered with these good and abundant spirits and we breathe thick and thoughtless happiness. I had the good fortune to make the acquaintance of poets whilst still enveloped in youth's slow waking dream and for that I shall always be thankful and yet it did not shape me to be a poet. You are ripe for poetry and the company of poets, question them about their..trade, do not ask me."

With three or more furious circuits of Figsbury Ring already to our name I wondered in desperation how many more Mr Hazlitt would now contemplate. With my lips cracking in the sun and a throat as dry as chalk, I wished for all the world to throw myself down upon the grassy slopes of this place and rest. In calm reflection, as I write these words and sip cool water, I still do not know why I continued to compete so in this physical manner. Mr Hazlitt is perhaps ten or more years my senior and measure for measure I cannot match his brain but I had determined that I would not be defeated by this extraordinary gentleman's legs. I resented more and more his shape striding ahead of me, as I stumbled meekly behind until I felt that I had not the strength to walk another step in pursuit. In my parched and deluded condition, I wished to strike him down or leap upon his back to cease these endless revolutions and then I near walked into him for he had stopped to face me upon the narrow ridge.

"Walking alone is the path to all good thoughts Mr Chalk whether you be a poet, painter or pedestrian. I crave company in the city and solitude in the country and I am not for criticising hedgerows and black cattle, I simply wish to see my vague notions float like the down of thistle before the breeze. Once I begin, I am elsewhere in the grateful motion of walking with the blood doing what blood does around the body. I sense the beauty that envelops; the gate now an entrance to my thoughts; the bridge adjoins two estranged notions and the bramble tears at the skin but shall not disturb me from my meditations. Solvitur ambulando, Mr Chalk."

Our encircling of this ancient ring was now at an end for Mr Hazlitt trotted down the raised bank of the fortification and took a new direction towards the north where I was not required to follow. I slumped to the ground and watched his disappearing form and observed that he cast no shadow under a vertical sun. With his departure all possibilities turned to vapour and I then became lost upon the path to lucid understanding.

How long I sat, crumpled amongst the folds of Figsbury Ring I do not know. In time I sought the shade of a thorn bush and observed the rabbits in their slow dismantling of the ancient embankment.

There exists within the centre of this fortification a large inner ditch and with no great accompanying bank, I then wondered that the spoil from this ditch was utilised to raise further the outer vallum? Mr Hazlitt is correct in referring to the construction of this place as a "practical matter" and I make no apology for my interest in such prosaic issues.

Rabbits have been at work here also upon this inner ring and I retrieved a bright white nodule of chalk and immediately sensed the dryness of it in my mouth as if this property had penetrated through my finger tips. This nodule bore all the marks of its extraction with deep scratches and claw marks where it had been ripped from beneath the turf by the industrious rabbit. As man builds, so will nature undo.

With no prospect of even a splash of water to quench my slating thirst I made my weary way back to the Winterslow Hut. The busy London Road was too dusty to contemplate and I chose instead its quiet ancestor, the Roman road, to return me to Winterslow. I encountered, upon the final ascent to the village, a modern deviation from the unerring straightness of the old road and a little sunken lane wound its way up between steep and chalky banks with tall trees providing welcome shade for toiling horses and parched pedestrians. Before descending again to the London road from the elevation of the village, I sat for a while to look out upon the great expanse of open Plain that extended for as far as the eye could see beyond the Winterslow Hut. I had thus far only considered activities at the front of this place with the frustration of hopeful arrivals but I shall tomorrow explore this open tract of land.

Upon my desperate and leaden footed return to the Winterslow Hut, I sought out the well and drank greedily from the pail before retiring to my room to cast myself upon the bed and I did not arise until dinner. As I complete these pages the light fades at the window and it is a golden glow that promises no interruption to this unseasonable heat.

You will gauge, my dear uncle, that the curious Mr William Hazlitt has left his deep impression upon me. He has indeed provoked a great mixture of sensations of which awe and anger are most ably demonstrated as I read again my account of our strange excursion. Whilst in his company I believe that my mind is excited by a proximity that enables the transaction of a strange electricity. My thoughts then crackle with all these possibilities and yet upon his departure I was left a desiccated husk for this inspiration soon drained to the parched earth. There exists also an infuriation whilst in his company for his character does not bear this tremendous gift easily and his manner is barbed and ungenerous. I have not before felt the desire to strike any person however wronged I have been or how deserving the circumstance and yet today this sensation near overwhelmed me. I can make no excuse for this except that it may be a delusion caused by my exposure to the severity of the sun.

I wish you a good night my dear uncle and I can inform you that I shall have not the slightest problem in sleeping soundly in my bed. Indeed, it is those waking and waiting hours by which I suffer for I am not then deeply cosseted within my sweetest dream.

Your weary nephew
HENRY CHALK

Friday 13th May 1808

MY DEAR UNCLE,

It is Old May Day today and I have learned that there is to be a single stick contest here at the Winterslow Hut. The winner shall receive a hat and three guineas and I have been informed by an excitable chambermaid that there shall be great crowds here this afternoon. At breakfast the tables are all taken and more visitors are expected upon the diligence from Salisbury. I know not what this single stick contest entails but I welcome the distraction. Mr Hazlitt has today one letter from London and so I must make my journey up the hill to Middle Winterslow.

It was with some dread that I knocked upon the Hazlitt's cottage door and I wished only to fulfil my self imposed duty and to then hastily depart. I was greeted by a wan faced Mrs Hazlitt dressed only in her night gown who then dashed to the parlour to make fearful retching noises, leaving me at the threshold with Mr Hazlitt's correspondence in hand. I looked up and down the street to judge whether there were any witnesses to this unseemly behaviour. In time I could detect Mrs Hazlitt's weak voice straining to make herself heard from the parlour.

"Mr Chalk... Henry..please excuse me..it is but a morningtime occurrence. I am not ailing."

A cart trundled by and the driver offered only a sly glance in return to the raising of my hat.

The breathless voice from within explained that Mr Hazlitt was painting in the woods and in return I called out that there was to be a single stick contest at the Hut this afternoon, for I could think of little else to say.

Mrs Hazlitt then slowly emerged and excused herself for not making me more welcome and accepted Mr Hazlitt's letter. I raised my hat and was about to bid the pale faced Mrs Hazlitt a good morning when she reflected upon attending the same event at the Hut with her brother, Mr John Stoddart, perhaps five years before. There was then an awkward silence whilst I shuffled on the doorstep and Mrs Hazlitt shivered in the warm morning sun before sighing deeply.

"We would do well to participate in village life. They already think my husband a strange fellow, pacing about the place or nailing his canvas to a tree. I shall see to it that we attend..please excuse me.."

Mrs Hazlitt then rushed back into the cottage whilst I took the opportunity to depart and wondered how such a sickness is to be arrived at if one is not indeed ailing. At the garden party in Pembrokeshire, before my departure, I overheard Mrs Eliza Fenton in conversation with their good neighbour, Mrs Gough, whose daughter married Mr Edwards. In hushed tones Mrs Gough expressed her concerns; "Mrs Fenton, woman do suffer overly, for is not the labour itself trial enough without the early morning sickness?"

If you will excuse my tittle-tattle, how can this same circumstance be possible for Mr and Mrs Hazlitt? They have been married for barely one week and nature surely dictates that such a situation cannot be arrived at in so short a time. You are correct sir, if I may anticipate your frown, for it is indeed none of my business.

I have prompted myself to direct my attention towards Pembrokeshire, and I should now write my long overdue letter of apology to Mr and Mrs Fenton.

*

I am again at my small table before the open window but the harsh sun has slipped to a warm and hazy dusk and after the festivities of the afternoon, I can report that all is now quiet. I see that I had promised to write to Mr and Mrs Fenton but distraction and procrastination have again conspired to ruin this plan. I must first give you my account of the Old May Day celebrations for there ensued the most unexpected event and I know not, my dear uncle, what you shall make of it. Bruised and bloodied I then explored the tract of land to the rear of Winterslow Hut and I can barely contain a great excitement at my discoveries there. I fear though that I must first suffer your disapproval at the description of my unseemly public display beside the London Road, outside the Winterslow Hut.

A finer day could not have been chosen for the Old May Day festivities for it was surely a welcome rest from the daily toil in the parlours, workshops, dairies and the fields about Winterslow. Ladies with baskets of ribbons and straw dolls sold their wares amongst the growing assembly whilst the tempting odour of freshly baked gingerbread wafted about the place. I purchased a pot of cider from a stall and at first sniffed at its acrid sharpness. After a sip I believed that I could not continue and then only by perseverance did it become tolerable. There was pleasure on the faces of these country people and as the cider crept about me in its warm embrace I soon felt as though I were a part of these proceedings and not just a stranger looking on. There were young men of my own age alive with expectation as pretty girls blushed at their mother's arm. The working elders mustered in twos and threes and had a word or two for the occasion as they sucked upon their long pipes.

"A proper druck o' volk Zimon."

"Ahh, n' Lanlard a wust var beer I zees."

Labourers seeking work remained stern faced and aloof amidst the frivolity, standing in silence with crook, pail or whip in hand to display their trade to each passing farmer or his steward. The landlord, who had previously demonstrated a weary indifference to all that the busy London road could offer, now appeared full of good cheer at the success of the afternoon and slapped a large hand upon my back to make the cider leap from my pot. "Mr Chalk. Mr Chalk," said the landlord chuckling to himself.

Other guests and acquaintances received similar irreverential treatment with a litany of surnames and spilt ale or cider left in his wake as he made his way through the crowd. Having replenished my pot, I then witnessed the most astonishing spectacle for I encountered two men each standing upon a chair and taking turns in making the most grotesque faces through a horse collar. The prize of a pound of tobacco was to be awarded to the creator of the most fearsome countenance or indeed the visage devoid of all sense and understanding. The most versatile performers could achieve both these extremes and even extended their range to form subjects as diverse as a baboon or the elusive great bustard that I have yet to encounter upon the southern plains of Wiltshire. The next contender had barely formed his features into "the spout of a jug" when he was jeered at by the assembled crowd for his efforts and this performance then ended abruptly as an egg hit him square in the face. It was at this moment of chaotic revelry that I spied Mr and Mrs Hazlitt and I made my way around the crowd to greet them. As they stood arm in arm viewing the curious spectacle of the "grinning match", as it is so called, they may have formed the perfect picture of newly weds enjoying their first excursion if it were not for Mr Hazlitt scowling and looking so ill at ease. Mrs Hazlitt had evidently recovered from her bout of sickness of this morning and Mr Hazlitt had a smudge of green paint upon his right ear. I heartily recommended the cider barrel for I had now fully overcome the initial strangeness of this drink. Mrs Hazlitt encouraged her husband to indulge whilst she spied an acquaintance and excused herself to leave me with Mr Hazlitt. He then muttered upon how there is a single character that is formed by the components of any crowd. As the next contorted face appeared through the horse collar, Mr Hazlitt made a decree that we should all be awarded a prize to observe this exercise in deformity.

To assuage his unwillingness to enjoy the afternoon I fetched my companion a pot of cider at which he sniffed suspiciously whilst children ran about his feet attempting to capture a greased piglet.

There was a distinction between the local revellers and those who had travelled some distance with only the main event in mind. At first, I believed that any fool could wield a club in the single stick contest but these are fellows who know their sport and are accompanied by a throng of supporters. At the announcement of the first stick battle the thrust of interest was palpable with the well dressed pushing to the fore whilst the countrymen were made to give way. Raised voices shouted the odds with wagers struck and of a sudden wide eyed expectation had replaced the rustic hilarity of the afternoon. I followed Mr Hazlitt into the thick of the circle for he was as keen as any to witness the first crunching blows. The stick is a yard of heavy ash-wood with an enclosed basket hilt around the handle giving the appearance of a brutish sword. The combatants are placed near together and all strikes are delivered with a whipping motion from a high guard. The left hand must grip a scarf tied loosely around the thigh and this barely enables the forearm to protect the face with elbow raised. Blows are confined to the head and upper body and none may strike to the back of the head. A winner is determined by the drawing of a bead of blood from the opponent's head that must measure greater than one inch in length, as declared by the judge of the competition. These are indeed the rules as best I can comprehend them and I confess that I have not before witnessed anything so harmful and yet so strangely compelling. The crowd roars in unison as blows are struck and I found myself adjoining this single voice under a sweltering sun. The bout appears endless as sticks clash, flesh is welted and bruises grow to a slippery redness under a sheen of sweat. Of a sudden the knowing crowd sensed blood and roared their man to victory, although I could discern no advantage to either party but one fellow was soon sprawling in the dust and we surged forward to gain a view of the gashed forehead to determine that the contest was over. No measurement was required of the judge for the white shirt of the vanquished contestant was soon blood soaked as he was escorted away by his men. The victor was hailed with his arm raised in triumph to which he looked bemused as if unaware of his contribution to the proceedings. Wagers were settled and cider pots were laced with strong rum in celebration. Mr Hazlitt rubbed his hands together in anticipation of the next bout and upon the London road a party of volunteers were cheered as they passed by on their way to Salisbury. The perspiring marchers to the rear of the group gestured to the onlookers for drinks and hung out their tongues as they observed the festivities at the Winterslow Hut. Cider was quickly slopped into pots and conveyed by eager boys and girls to quench the thirst of these local protectors of our sovereignty. Those to the fore of the marching party faltered at this unfairness until the captain rode back to call a halt to this unscheduled provision. We established that these were the Avon and Bourne and Blacklands volunteers returning from a fortnight's duty at Winchester and their unbending captain was Sir Richard Malet. Amongst the throng more pots were raised and toasts proposed "To King and Country" and "The brave men of England". The despicable tyrant Napoleon Bonaparte was then called any number of names and in this tumult of English loving and French hating, I found myself boasting of my own part in the apprehension of a dangerous Frenchman only two days previously. As you will know, my dear uncle, from my own account that this is an untruth, indeed a lie and yet in this fervour I puffed out my chest and praise for my actions was swiftly forthcoming from those hot and swaying men around me and was soon broadcast loudly for all to hear. In no time I was tossed aloft to cries of "Hip, Hip, Hurrah" and so of a sudden from my idle falsehood I had become at once a hero and more toasts were proposed. Upon the instant that my feet returned to the ground

I was met by a look of fury and spitting hostility from Mr William Hazlitt. "You are no better than these red faced fools, indeed much worse. I cannot abide such displays of ignorant pride."

In the lurching crowd Mr Hazlitt was forced hard up against me and continued his hissing tirade.

"Hard words and hard blows are all that an Englishman can understand and his brain is no more than soft-boiled meat."

I then stumbled back in the shifting tide of the swelling crowd and this motion was construed as a push by one nearby who had witnessed Mr Hazlitt's venomous intent towards me. Mr Hazlitt was then confronted and told that if there was a grievance between ourselves then it should be fairly resolved. This opportunity then spread about the crowd like a summer heath fire and our hats and jackets were quickly stripped away and the sticks that were soon to be employed in the next bout were thrust into our hands. Scarves were sought and hastily applied to tether our left wrists in the correct manner. A deal of pushing back and calling out soon formed space enough for this impromptu combat, a judge was self appointed and in the blink of an opportunity odds were taken. These sudden and alarming circumstances had not served to temper Mr William Hazlitt's fury and the cries of "Hero" were still ringing loudly in my ears and I had consumed enough of the cider barrel to wallow in this unfounded praise. Mr Hazlitt was goaded into making the first thrust forward and our sticks cracked together as I made a successful defence of my skull. The high forehead of my opponent made an ample target and yet each lunge forward was repelled by nimble stick work and the crowd offered their own solution to this impasse. "Break 'is arm. Get 'im in the ribs."

I think back now to the blur of this horror, as the crowd snarled about us and that we were both fully intent on causing untold damage to one another when only moments before I had considered Mr Hazlitt my companion. I still do not know the true cause of his anger towards me save for my shameful boasting for which I fully deserved any sound beating. I can only judge that Mr Hazlitt holds a sympathy for England's greatest foe as I recall yesterday the encircling of Figsbury Ring and Mr Hazlitt's dismissal of my proposal as to how such a place was constructed. He then made a remark which I did not at that time comprehend; "Tell me it was done in the spirit of Revolution and I shall be all ears."

Does he indeed believe that "Le Terror" was a just solution to the tradition of order and aristocracy for I have heard that such Englishmen exist and would perhaps wish the guillotine to be erected upon Hyde Park Corner?

As our sticks reigned down upon one another, in my opponent's mind, perhaps it was I that represented the ignorance of the British people? Was I not the face, forehead and single character of a crowd of misguided Englishmen who did not grasp the glorious purpose of the revolution or the actions of its child, Napoleon Bonaparte? Mr William Hazlitt was an older, stronger and angrier man than I and was to eventually gain the upper hand and drive me back for all the stout defence that I could muster. Blows struck my forearm and shoulder and, in this miniature battle, our great nation was about to suffer the ultimate assault and all freedom would soon be lost if it were not for the timely intervention of Mrs Hazlitt.

"WILLIAM!"

Mrs Sarah Hazlitt forced her way between the human wall that surrounded us and entering the ring grasped the stick from her husband's hand.

"William, what on earth..and Mr Chalk?"

The crowd protested as one at this interruption but the severity of Mrs Hazlitt's ejection of her husband from the proceedings caused sufficient mocking laughter and ribald comment to temporarily quell the lust for blood. Attention quickly turned to the real competition and I was left a forgotten hero to collect my hat and coat from amongst the dust before quietly retreating with shirt torn and an arm that has become a throbbing reminder of my stupidity. What a fool I have been to be caught up and carried along in the frenzy of a drunken crowd with all good sense abandoned. What do you think of me now my dear uncle?

The great exertion and the blows of the single stick contest had somehow dispelled the effects of the cider but a raging thirst required a quart or more of water at the well. To rid myself of the roars, cheers and mirth of the Old May Day festivities, I then stumbled along without aim upon the barren plain to the rear of the Winterslow Hut. I was at first drawn to a great barrow that would surely be worthy of the attentions of Mr William Cunnington's men for it appeared complete and unviolated by the tomb robber. Indeed, there were a number of the same clustered about and I fancied that I should seek a pick and a spade and become barrow mad in the conduct of my own investigation. As I form these words upon the page in calm contemplation before an unwavering flame, I wonder at the creation of these barrow clusters for they are to be encountered at every turn across the open plains of Wiltshire. The setting about Stonehenge is indeed a place for a conspicuous burial in the manner that Westminster Abbey is a place for a fine tomb and worthy neighbours. We cannot all be housed in Westminster Abbey nor our ancient ancestors within the shadow of Stonehenge and so there must be modest churches and empty plains in which to reside upon our demise. It is a mistake to think on empty plains for were there not planted fields, tended herds, villages, paths, festivities and a place where the earth is heaped upon the passing generations? In the neighbourhood about the Winterslow Hut, before the construction of a Hut, the building of a road or even the thought of a capital city, a grand barrow of white chalk was once raised to shine brightly in the sun. The deceased was surely a wealthy chief and had possessions, of which a portion accompanied him to his chalky eternity, but is it not the barrow itself that speaks loudly of possession? To the ancient stranger who once traversed these plains this vast beacon of whiteness warned of occupation and a people now prospering in life and death with more tombs on the way.

I do not believe that I had any such thoughts in my head as I sat upon the largest of these barrows for I could still hear the distant drifting cheers of a drunken crowd and so set off further into the plain until these sounds no longer troubled my senses.

It is a plain with a plethora of dark stunted bushes and a grass carpet already pale and parched by the drying sun but it is by no means a plain plain for it is enamelled by the prettiest of small flowers. There is a shifting decoration also in the brightness of the day as butterflies alight and depart upon a silent whim whilst the open sky is filled with sparkling song. The originator of this ethereal music is I believe the lark and it has accompanied me throughout my short journey in South Wiltshire. Under my feet I found areas where the steady green sward was interrupted by a rash of bumps or small hillocks and on closer inspection, I established that these are caused by the industrious ant. I hopped about from hump to hump as I recalled Mr Hazlitt's observations on how Mr Coleridge preferred uneven ground upon which to compose his verse. Alas, no poetry was forthcoming and instead I soon found myself sprawling amongst the ants. I chose instead a dusty track to follow and passed by flocks of the ubiquitous Wiltshire sheep whose appetite for grass appears insatiable and I willed that they might break with this tradition to perform a jig or muster into lines and curves to spell giant words and thereby astound mankind. Try as I might, I could detect no such behaviour and trod carefully least I wakened a shepherd who lay peacefully in the shade of a small bush with his cider flask laying uncorked and empty by his side. After a lifetime of tending to these predicable creatures it is indeed fortunate that he has not missed such theatrics through daylight slumber.

With no water to satiate my thirst, I curtailed my progress towards the centre of this plain and instead took a track that enabled me to walk with the sun at my back and in time turned again to direct me back towards the London road. My mind was vacant and I kept it so least I should dwell upon my folly with Mr William Hazlitt and I believe that I should have missed altogether a most remarkable discovery, if it were not for the interruption of a stranger.

I had paused to observe a small herd of deer that were in turn observing my progress when of a sudden the quietness of this plain exploded and sent me headlong into the shelter of a grassy hollow. With my ears still numb from this assault I peered out from this sanctuary to establish the cause of such thunder and spied a tall gentleman with a large and smouldering gun in the crook of his arm standing not ten paces away. His face was screwed up with the effort of peering into the distance, as if confronted by a thick fog and he then ambled forward to squint at who was to blame for the disturbance of his prey and an opportunity lost.

"A p.p.p..pox on you sir... now the b.b.b..bustards have f.f.. flown to who knows where. A p.p.p..pox I say."

I stood up in my hole to confront this hunter who appeared keen to apportion his faltering blame upon me and I informed him that I had witnessed nothing in that same direction but a herd of deer.

"F.f.f..fiddle f.f.f..faddle sir, there were a half d..d..d..dozen or more at my m..mercy, d..d..damn your eyes."

I felt a great temptation to correct this grumbling gentleman that it was his own eyes that were beyond salvation and that I would indeed take my pleasure in disturbing his intentions if it would spare the elusive great bustard from its fate. I believe however that the deer were no more in danger than the bustard from the effects of this inept hunter's murderous tube and with his departure I was left in my hollow to poke at two deaf ears.

I now thank this Herne of the Plains, for without my near perforation by a charge of swan shot I should have passed on my vacant way and returned in near walking slumber to the Winterslow Hut. Indeed, our encounter was most fortuitous for once I had stepped from my grassy hollow, I then spied that the ground all about was littered with flint pieces formed in the manner that occurs only by human intervention. I have before described, my dear uncle, the signs of such manipulation and they were plain to see on every piece and yet these fragments were broad and often very long. I sat back down to wonder upon this occurrence and picked up two large pieces that had been made white by their long exposure to the elements and upon tapping them together they chimed like the best porcelain. I then shattered another segment by pounding it with a large nodule and revealed within the rich darkness of the most perfect flint. Such profligacy could only occur at an abundant source of this material and I looked again at my grassy hollow and nearby there were similar depressions. Amongst this pock marked ground I found also nests of blue-grey gunflint waste. There is no question of the longevity of the older industry for the whiteness of the larger flint pieces is absolute whilst the recent gunflint detritus is barely clouded over by comparison.

My thirst and lethargy in the hot sun melted with the notion that perhaps these hollows were once holes in the ground from which this excellent flint was extracted and I leapt up and ran from one to the next until I lost count of their number. At the base of one such hollow I picked up a bar of white flint that I gauge measures perhaps a foot in length and is roughly hewn but I hold no doubt that its maker had every intention of forming a large axe for one end is bevelled to make a cutting edge. I have it upon the table before me and it is a crude and unfinished tool and was perhaps discarded for a more perfect piece of flint but I care not about its imperfections for it speaks loudly of an ancient industry that once existed upon this plain.

I shall now hasten to my bed as all theory must be proven by examination and I will rise at first light to request the loan of a pick and a spade from the blacksmith. Sir, before my discovery here behind the Winterslow Hut, I can admit to vain hope above firm belief. I am bruised but my faith in "A Tour in Search of Flint" has been restored.

Your impetuous nephew
HENRY CHALK

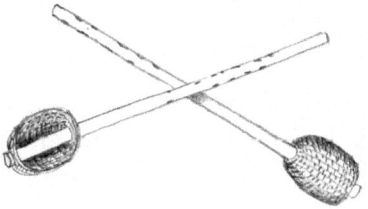

Saturday 14ᵗʰ May 1808

MY DEAR UNCLE,

I can now understand well enough from the blisters upon my hands the stoic role played by Mr William Cunnington's two barrow diggers, Stephen and John Parker. To arrive at noon to view the progress of a morning's toil is the way of the gentleman antiquary. To mix with the soil and impart one's own blood to the venture is heroic but foolhardy.

You will be impatient to learn of my progress thus far and I now realise that this is no short exploration beneath the turf. I began in a fury by hacking away at the grass and soil and then spread it about this way and that with no order. I have since exhausted myself and by necessity I dig and rest a while and drink greedily from my water pail. There has been some encouragement in the copious shards of white

flint that I have uncovered and I have learnt to inspect each spadeful
and ensure some order to the growing spoil heap.

I must retrace my steps as to my choice of grassy hollow for as
I have indicated this ground is pock-marked by these depressions and I
cannot examine them all. I found again the position where I retrieved
the long rough flint axe, for I believe it to be a good omen as to what
may lie beneath the soil. These hollows vary also in their breadth and
my chosen pit is perhaps smaller than many and therefore easier for a
sole excavator who has smooth hands and muscles that are unused to
hard labour. It has been sheltered from the sun to some small degree by
a clump of these stunted bushes which also makes a screen to prying
eyes for I am uncertain of the consequences of my making a large hole
upon this ground. In this heat the ink dries quickly upon the page for
the sun has now climbed above the stunted bushes to blaze upon the
fresh white chalk. You will see how my hand shakes with the effects of
this labour but continue I must.

*

Toil frees the mind and the mind can drift to strange places whilst the
body is left behind to work like a machine upon the earth.

I have considered Mr William Hazlitt at length for my bruised
and aching shoulder is a persistent reminder of that gentleman but I
shall not bear him any ill will. I believe that I have learned much in
his presence and also by the folly of our single stick encounter. You
will recall that Colonel Boyle, some days ago at the Woodyates Inn,
urged me to be both brave and bold in life. Being brave is not just
pretending to be brave or being seen to be brave in the eyes of others.
Bravery is I believe a boldness in one's convictions and being brave
enough to defend them. For all that I do not understand Mr Hazlitt's
convictions, he does not for one moment consider the consequences of
these convictions nor does he stint in their defence. I do not believe
that he would permit our friendship, such as it was, to prosper further

for I sense that his nature is unforgiving and without compromise. After all that has passed then perhaps I should also cast him adrift as a companion and yet I feel a great reluctance to do so for I shall treasure the moments that I spent in his company. Whilst striding in his wake there was much to stimulate the mind and I sensed that a greater understanding was waiting just beyond the brow of the next hill if only I could keep pace with this extraordinary gentleman. I can now recall a fraction of our one sided conversations and Mr Hazlitt's well considered thoughts were akin to pouring out a rich cream to quench a raging thirst and I could consume but very little. Consider if you will, my dear uncle, this savoured moment of consolation from Mr William Hazlitt; "One truth discovered, one pang of regret at not being able to discuss it, is better than all the fluency and flippancy in the world".

*

I am learning as I go and I believe that I must devise some means to make a record of my progress. I require a length of string along which a number of measured knots may be tied. I must again visit the blacksmith for I shall also require another pail to haul the spoil from the deepening excavation. The blacksmith is a man of few words and I know not what he thinks of each new request.

*

Sir, I now hold a fear within me that this was indeed not a pit for the abstraction of flint. What if it were a pit dwelling and, by their close proximity, a village of similar dwellings? There is no question that flint abounds here but is not this fashioned flint a mere residue of ancient occupation? I have become of a sudden made weary by this notion and so laid down my tools in despair.

This is a circumstance where I must consider what Mr William Cunnington would advise if he were here. I believe that he would inform me kindly that my yearning for a source of the best quality flint will not change one jot the result of my excavation. I cannot make a silk purse from a sow's ear. Will not the discovery of so many pit dwellings cast a great light upon the habits of our ancient ancestors? We have not before learnt where the carpenter, the ploughman, or the cow-herd lived in an age when metal was unknown. I also take solace in Mr Richard Fenton's bold statement that "We speak from facts not theory", for I believe that it is the gathering of small facts that will one day elevate a gentleman's pastime to a noble science. Who is to say that each spadeful of these tiny snail shells that lay buried amidst this soil is not worthy of record, for I have today cast a great many upon the spoil heap with little thought until now?

*

I have just retrieved a fine flint celt of perhaps six inches in length and also a number of worn sections of deer antler. The chalk rubble is packed tight toward the edges of the pit but I have found it easier to disturb toward the middle. I have now reached a depth of four feet by my estimation and do not know whether to be encouraged or discouraged by the discovery of a seam of inferior flint. It appears that the ancient excavators have taken little heed of it for I can see no signs of it being prized out from the original side of the pit. It is however a confirmation that flint, in its natural condition, exists in these horizontal seams.

The snakecatcher's hat is sodden but I dare not remove it for it is my only defence against the burning sun. My dear uncle I am exhausted. There is a small bird that occupies these dark stunted bushes and it has a call like the chinking together of two flint pieces. I have made it hop closer to investigate as I tap the flint celt upon another nodule and it now perches upon my water pail. Chink, chink, chink.

A curious event has just occurred. Whilst I struggled to keep my eyes from closing, I have seen figures shimmering in the sun with their skin a ghostly white. These spectres gathered around the chalk spoil and I could smell their odour. An old man squatted down at the edge of the pit and I could hear voices straining, singing, coughing and the chink, chink, chink of flint upon flint. I strained to view again this ethereal scene but the white ghosts are turned to sheep and the old man is now a shepherd leant upon his crook as he observes my excavation. We did not speak and the shepherd and his flock have now drifted beyond the stunted bushes. I believe that I am soon to be driven mad by this accursed sun.

*

It was all I could do to drag these aching bones from a comfortable bed to resume this penance to my own curiosity. I must also record that the day is Sunday. These hands are no longer my own for they will not do as I request and have suffered greatly by this labour but I dearly wish to conclude my excavation before the arrival of Mr Robert Foster tomorrow. Last evening, I stowed the pick and spade beneath a bush and today I have slopped across the plain with two pails of water reasoning that a great deal would spill forth. Water is a heavy burden to transport but I now have one full pail for two halves make a whole and indeed I am now curious as to how the ancient peoples who once occupied this plain availed themselves of water. Is not the digging of wells the preserve of our more recent ancestors? In the heart of winter, I understand that there are fresh springs that emerge from the ground near the Hut and rainwater may also be caught and preserved. In the dry barren months then water must be transported across some distance, perhaps from the river valley to the north of this plain. I cannot believe that an ancient water carrier would be so profligate as to lose half of what they started out with and so some sealed vessel would be preferable to an open pail.

*

I have obtained a depth of six feet but I realise that I must now remove a larger volume of material to create a working platform. Without this reorganisation my tapered shaft is not sufficiently wide enough to swing the pick and as I am not some chalk burrowing animal that can penetrate the earth with its claws, I must therefore broaden the aperture of this hole. This is demoralising work for the already excavated sections soon fill with this fresh spoil to create the antithesis of progress.

*

I have been spared further torment for the blacksmith has unexpectedly arrived at my excavation and demanded the return of the pick and spade.

"Tis Zundee."

I obediently handed back the tools and then watched his retreating figure whilst standing upon my freshly constructed ledge of chalk with my head just able to peer out from the hole. I felt too exhausted to resist or even question this blunt request. Hitherto I have found the blacksmith silently obliging and yet today his conviction has demanded that he should cause a cessation to my labours. So be it.

*

I am now returned to the Winterslow Hut and I shall not now complete my exploration before the arrival of Robert Foster tomorrow. I believe that I have wrecked my body and covered myself with chalkdust, all to no purpose. The chambermaid has just departed and I now know all that is to be known about the other guests and how the doctor who arrived last evening was taken ill but did not wish to cause any trouble by his condition. Neither did he wish to summon a doctor for he is a doctor and he insists that the drapes are kept drawn at all times to keep out the sun. The doctor is a very polite gentleman and he wished to know who was presently residing at the inn for any duration. As the chambermaid disturbed the fine white dust that has settled upon the contents of my room and then pulled my bed about, she continued with her chatter and I believe that by her speech she is not a Wiltshire girl.

"And I told 'im that there was you, young Master Chalk, and Mr and Mrs Saunders who have bin 'ere since I don't know when and

Winterslow Hut

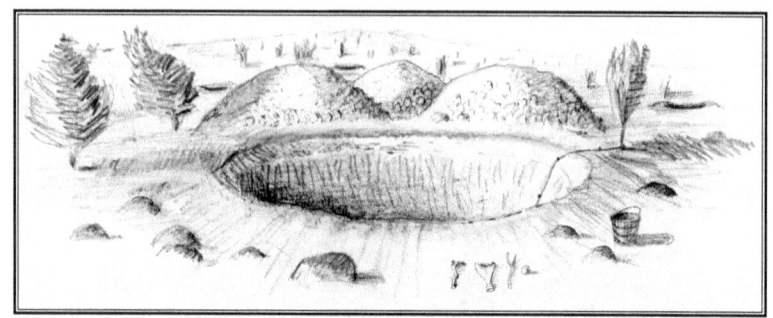

The Flint Pit

Floorstone (from the base of the flint pit)

Mr James who is moving to London now that 'is mother has passed away God rest 'er soul. Then the doctor says, if it i'nt too much trouble, could 'ee be moved to a quiet room cos the noise from the kitchen below disturbs 'is sleep and 'e gives me a shillin' to talk to the landlord. 'Ee's now across the 'all from you Master Chalk and 'e wishes to keep the door open fer the air but 'e dun't look well, no 'e dun't look well at all Master Chalk."

To be listed amongst the residents of the Winterslow Hut has only served to increase my gloom and I must now flee this place for the remainder of the day. I shall further explore this plain and perhaps encounter a subject suitable for the pencil.

*

The day has passed well enough but upon my return to the Winterslow Hut I then stopped to again observe my excavation. I embarked upon a further drawing and in that time an ever deepening shadow settled upon the pit. It is as if by the digging of this pit I have disturbed something that lay buried deep within me and from this white hole in the ground a black and restless spirit has emerged to haunt my thoughts and unsettle my senses. I cannot now dispel the memory of my father's fury upon witnessing me at play amongst the chalk spoil during the digging of the great well in the yard at Chalk's brewery in Southwark. Sir, I have written before of this occasion and the many long months of excavation endured by the well diggers employed to the task. With each passing week my father would stare down into the yard whilst wringing his hands and he then would curse me for suggesting the venture in the first place. Even the eventual success of the well did little to alleviate his mood and I was to dread each evening as we sat down at the table to eat our dinner in silence. I came to believe that my presence was a constant reminder of everything bad that had passed his way. My mother had suffered greatly at my birth and yet she did in time recover only to succumb at the birth of my sister. I stood at her bedside and watched as she grew so very pale until all life faded from her beautiful face. My sister Elizabeth lived but two weeks when she also passed from this world. I could not understand how first the loss of my mother could occur and then that of my most delicate sister Elizabeth. My father would not speak of it and for many years I believed that they had both died of a paleness to the skin. Should I ever encounter a person with a pale face then I would stand and stare to wonder if they to would soon also pass away. You will recall sir, my conversation last autumn with Mr Richard Fenton on the subject of the losing of love and the affliction of a broken heart. Mr Fenton's good friend Sir Richard Colt Hoare lost his own wife Hester in childbirth some twenty years before and he now seeks distraction in the recording of the antiquities of Wiltshire. In the words of Mr Fenton; "Sir Richard lives and he smiles and sometimes he will laugh but only when his heart ceases to beat will it also cease to ache."

I now believe that my father was so deeply in love with my mother that he could never recover from her passing. In my growing years I missed her dearly but could not comprehend this unseen world of love and loss until I met Miss Sarah Foster and sensed the stirring within my own heart. As I write these words and suffer these thoughts, my tears mix with the all pervading chalk dust and dry quickly upon the cheek. There is much that has been extracted from this hole in the plain for it appears that I have also encountered a rich seam of despair. I must now finally commit the circumstances of my father's death to the page. Sir, you did not attend your own brother's funeral and I can only believe that the cause of your absence was the belief held by some that his death was caused by self-murder. The Coroner ruled that a tragic accident had occurred for a verdict of self murder would demand that lunacy was recorded as the cause. I could not bring myself to believe such a thing. How could I think that my own father would chose to leave me alone in this world? It is only now that I am grown a little and have been shown that love is all conquering and how it can break the heart of even the strongest of men that I am thrown into doubt. In truth I do not know what occurred that evening and can only churn over again my own account of it which brings little solace. I do not believe that anything new may be gathered from a further trampling of these few facts that have become the threadbare carpet of my own soul, such has been the pacing up and down upon it. I shall nevertheless continue even as my spirit sinks lower with each written word. There was a caller at the door before dinner with a note delivered to my father. I then heard a loud and pained exclamation from the study and so presumed that the note had contained ill and unwelcome news. I had been reading before dinner in the drawing room with only a wall to divide us and so could not fail to hear my father's raised voice. I have tried so often to recall the exact words uttered but I was so truly engrossed in the tale of Robinson Crusoe that my attention was late in arriving. I then listened intently to the ensuing silence and even wondered whether anything had actually occurred at all. The note was never retrieved and it may have contributed nothing to his silence at dinner or the sudden pushing back of the chair to leave his plate untouched. Indeed, the outburst from the study was the last sound that I ever heard from my father's lips for he left the table, the dining room and the house with no excuse or explanation.

I am ashamed to think that I cared little for his departure only that a heavy cloud had been lifted from the house. I even retrieved my book from the drawing room and continued to read through the remainder of the meal whilst defiantly flicking over each fresh page. Sir, I had retired to my bed by the time that I received the dreadful news of my father's death and a chill runs through me now as I recall being shaken from my slumber. As I rubbed at my eyes, I could not comprehend the great anxiety in the voice of our housekeeper Mrs Harrison and her insistence that I should accompany her to the drawing room. I even became angered at her reticence in not explaining why my sleep should be disturbed. The solemn faces that greeted me in the drawing room were sufficient to quell my anger and soon made me sober from the effects of interrupted sleep.

I was requested to sit down before a standing Mr Hooper and Mr Gerrity from the brewery and also a large constable. Mr Hooper spoke first and I recall observing his ashen face but I do not recall what was said until I heard the words; "Master Chalk, your father is dead."

My gaze became locked upon the actions of the constable as he held onto his hat and rotated it between large and nervous fingers. The statement was then repeated and I could hear the sobbing of the housekeeper out in the hallway. Finally, I believe I said "Yes", least they repeated the statement over and over again. This grim visitation then slowly divulged the circumstances of my father's death and how he was crushed beneath a carriage on Fleet Street. The coroner's books must be filled with the details of such needless deaths. Fallen from carriages, fallen from horses, trampled by horses, crushed by the wheels of carriages. It is indeed a prosaic litany and a waste of life. Stifled by the awkwardness of these three late visitors I began to pace the room and then asked whether I could offer them a glass of something to which they all declined. Having delivered their news, I then wondered how long they intended to stay for I could find no words or display any expected emotion.

Finally, after clearing his throat the constable asked whether I had any notion of why my father would be abroad late into the evening. I recalled the delivery of a note before dinner and also my father's outburst and I then described his sudden departure from the house. The three men then glanced at one another before the constable continued.

"We believes Master Chalk, sir, that your good father wus robbed as he expired in the street."

This announcement became the blow to cut me down, to make me sink to the floor, for with these words came the image of the final moments of my father's life. The three grim faced men were finally able to assist me in my grief, moving swiftly to see me to a chair with a relief upon their faces as they spoke generous words of consolation and deep sympathy.

It transpires that before the driver of the carriage could halt and return to attend to my father, a figure was observed crouching over his crushed body. This wretched thief then departed for no money nor his old fob watch was found upon my father. Indeed, there was no means by which to place a name upon this poor soul until the body was carried to the Bolt in Tun Inn nearby. By chance the old landlord did recognise my father for they had conducted business together when my father was a young collecting clerk who visited regularly to dip the barrels. I think again of my father's last moments and that act of cold robbery as he drew his final breath upon this earth. With my pen now faltering above the page the evening stage has just clattered into the yard below to disturb my painful reverie. The night is warm with the candle's flame so perfectly preserved before an open window and yet the door to my room has now opened of its own accord as if by a sudden draught of frozen air. My neck prickles and I must investigate further this strange and inopportune occurrence.

*

I do not know how to describe what happened next but I must, and in good order to, for it is a short tale with a fine surprise at the end of it. Upon creeping to the open door, I then held aloft my candle to look up and down the hallway and found no persons to east nor west. The door to the room across the hall had earlier in the evening been left ajar as instructed by the ailing doctor but it was now fully opened. I moved across the hall to stand in this doorway and strained my ears but could hear nothing but the beating of my own heart. I now feared for the life of the poorly doctor but I was held in stasis by some unknown force and could not proceed. At that same moment the candle then spat and puffed itself out to leave me in complete darkness. Sir, I then became gripped by a certainty that there was indeed something familiar within that room, a stirring of a memory or a sense from my childhood. Of a sudden my orientation is lost and I am returned to a time when our house in Southwark was not a place of sadness or secrets but instead held my mother's presence and her laughter. It was a time when you, my dear uncle, would arrive and demand that I fetch my toy soldiers so that we might make a battle upon the floor. What could possibly be the connection between these two places so far apart in years and distance other than by the electricity of my own thoughts? Upon writing these words I now recall the terror of my childhood encounter with a dark and beckoning room upon the top floor of our house. I believed that I had heard noises from within and knew not where my mother was. As I wavered timidly upon the threshold it was you my dear uncle that emerged from the darkness to make me start so and caused me to flee back down the stairs. You then located me amongst the skirts of kindly Mrs West in the kitchen and suggested that we should at once visit the port of London and so we departed soon after. To a boy of seven years the sight of such giant ships teaming with sailors and a great dancing bear upon the dock became at once a romantic world of which to dream. Indeed, this was to be my last association with you sir for I cannot recall that you again visited our house.

To return to the curious and unsettling instance that has just occurred here at the Winterslow hut, I then heard a voice in the darkness and recognised it as my own.

"Sir, are you ailing? Has your condition worsened?"

I could hear no response and yet by the merest draught that betrays slow movement, I felt a presence so close that I might reach out and touch another person. Into this black void of mystery and the stirring of recognition came other voices and a flickering light from along the hallway. Boots appeared with a lamp to illuminate the scene and I could now witness my frozen position at the door to the doctor's room.

"Mr Chalk, zur...?" enquired boots.

The person accompanying boots now stepped into the light and we studied one another before this gentleman then held out his hand.

"Mr Robert Foster at your service, I am delighted to finally make your acquaintance Mr Chalk."

All dark thoughts were dispelled by these words and by the warm and smiling countenance of Mr Robert Foster. Before I could alert boots to my concerns regarding the ailing doctor, the door to the doctor's room then slammed shut as if by some petulant hand. I know not what occurred before the arrival of boots and Robert Foster other than my black thoughts had summoned up some strange association that I cannot comprehend. I shall not dwell upon it for across the room from me sits Robert Foster, now attending to his own correspondence, and I cannot keep a smile from my face by his presence here at the Winterslow Hut. By good fortune Robert was able to depart from London sooner than expected and his sudden arrival has caused me great excitement. We have talked much already like two dear childhood friends or indeed brothers that have been estranged by distance and are now reunited. I am so deeply overwhelmed for I have not before known such close and familiar friendship. I have no secrets from Robert Foster for he has read aloud my correspondence to his beloved sister Sarah and by his own hand has committed to ink her every word in reply.

I believe that Robert has now completed his own correspondence and so I shall now bid you a goodnight my dear uncle for there is much more that I wish to hear and to then hear again.

Your faithful nephew
HENRY CHALK

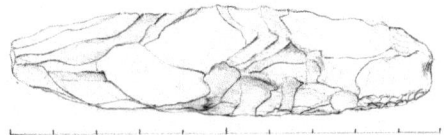

Monday 16th May 1808

MY DEAR UNCLE,

Mr Robert Foster and I both awoke in our chairs this morning such was the confabulation that went on long into the night. Robert opened his eyes to find me studying his face in the early morning light as I sought for a duplication of Sarah's features. He then obliged by displaying his profile.

"I am a Foster and have the pretty Foster nose. Pray Henry please can you explain why this room and indeed your own face is coated with white powder. Sir, you have been embalmed, observe yourself in the mirror. I thought you a spectral figure upon the landing last evening and worthy of a turn at Hamlet's Ghost."

Upon inspection my face was as described but the scouring by last evening's tears had spoiled this stage paint. I ensured Robert that I was indeed very much alive and was obliged to explain the circumstances of my quest for a source of the best quality flint. Robert listened patiently and then sighed deeply.

"Henry Chalk, why am I not very much surprised by this news? I require breakfast."

Hot water was sought and upon the completion of our repast I then asked Mr Robert Foster of his plans for the day.

"Plans, Mr Chalk? Plans? Am I to be excluded from your antiquarian investigation?"

I explained that I did not consider for one instant that he should sully his clothes in this way but meant rather that I may join him in a trip to Salisbury as befits a visiting tourist.

Robert pondered upon this proposition for a moment and then stated that all the talk in London had been of the famous and magnificent "White hole of Winterslow" and he was determined to see it for himself.

I now recognise raillery as a consequence of spending time in the company of Mr John Fenton and so was able to feign surprise.

"I have attempted great discretion by my excavation Mr Foster.. but sadly..the blacksmith has informed the shepherd and now..well.. you know how it is?"

"Exactly Henry," concluded Robert "and now ..all London knows about it."

I then asked in all sincerity whether Robert wished to assist with the digging of the pit to which he concurred wholeheartedly. He has also volunteered to approach the blacksmith on my behalf to request the further use of the pick and the spade, once we depart the Winterslow Hut. Today there is a heaviness in the air and I fear that work in the pit will be hard toil indeed.

With Robert soon to return home to North Somerset, it is with a glad heart that I am able to recommence my correspondence to Miss Sarah Foster and so the dreadful hiatus shall come to an end. Indeed, I have not forgotten the glimpse of that mislaid letter from one "Percy Bysshe" to the young lady of Ferne House for it has displayed how notions of love must be addressed. There must exist a dangerous fervour and a world in upheaval for thoughts of love cannot thrive in a safe and cosseted place. There shall be tumult and dreadful images as if we are clinging to flotsam upon a dark and boiling ocean or fleeing the burning wrath of a volcano. I believe that it makes my own past rhetoric to Sarah a calm and placid sea with not a wisp of wind and no prospect of a tempest upon the horizon.

*

Even with all our good organisation the morning was well in advance before we finally set out upon the plain. We could hear the distant toll of a solitary bell as Robert went in search of the blacksmith, whilst I filled the two pails at the well. My antiquarian aspirant soon returned with the pick and the spade but reported no sign of the blacksmith himself and all was strangely silent in the forge with the tools left at the door.

As we made our way upon the soft turf Robert declared a fascination for the "pleasing embreastment of this plain" by the many rounded barrows and then demanded that the great bustard should appear before us, as I had earlier informed him of the existence of this bird. Any hope of sighting this elusive creature was surely in vain by the amount of chatter and laughter that follows Mr Robert Foster wherever he goes. My companion has also demanded explanation as to why I have a dead snake upon my battered hat. The recounting of this tale also unravelled the tangle of misadventure that has befallen this pedestrian tourist whilst at large in South Wiltshire and Robert was keen to avail himself of every detail.

"I believe that you would cause less disruption Henry behind a desk at Chalk's brewery in Southwark. We may then all sleep safely in our beds."

Robert and I are both clinging to the shadow of one dark stunted bush with our pens scratching away in unison. The excavation proceeds at a furious pace as we each take our turn with the blacksmith's tools whilst the other empties the brimming pails of chalk upon the ever-growing spoil heap. Indeed, the blocks of chalk have now increased in size as we delve further into this plain and these larger pieces can barely fit the pail and must be handled on their own. There is great encouragement also by the discovery of large nodules of dark flint that have been returned to the pit by those early excavators and it is perhaps an indication of what may lie at a greater depth. To my great surprise Robert then related the tale of a piece of common flint and its journey from undisturbed slumber beneath a blanket of chalk to a life of turmoil as gravel upon the river bed or indeed sand upon the beach.

"It is only by some great cataclysm that this disruption occurs Henry and indeed is it not hard to imagine upon such a fine day?"

By the look upon my face Robert then stated with mock surprise that he was not an automaton that simply read aloud my letters to his dear sister. When put in these terms I then blushed beneath my mask of white chalk and upon hearing again my own words and thoughts I resolved privately to never engage upon such stony matters to Miss Sarah Foster.

*

We have dug perhaps for another hour and a further rest is required. Robert's hands have already become raw by the unfamiliarity of using such tools but his good humour appears boundless.

"Shall I make a fine antiquarian Mr Chalk? Is my swing just so with the pick and my push upon the spade without equal? To whom should I subscribe to join your most mysterious Order?"

I explained that true antiquarians did not appear until noon and that we were but simple labourers. I then recalled my curious dream of two days ago that had occurred as I rested beside the pit and I now spoke of it to Robert. Into my slumber had crept the originators of this pit for I could hear the very sounds of their excavation; their chatter and coughing and even a sonorous voice in lilting song. I could smell the sweat of their labour for they worked close beside me and all the while an old man struck upon large pieces of flint with some heavy stone tool. Chink, chink, chink. To Robert's great disappointment I then described the opening of my eyes to find that these ancient miners had become a flock of grazing sheep and the old man a shepherd with a look of disapproval upon his face. As Robert wished to hear more, I explained that at night in my bed whilst my bones and muscles ached, I have thought or dreamt a great deal about these holes in this plain. I had one persistent vision that it was not a plain at all but a forest and that the dormant flint that lay undisturbed beneath its white chalk counterpane was the means to turn a forest into a plain.

"How so Henry?" asked Robert in some confusion.

From my mouth then issued a verse or poem and I know not from whence it came;

Once a forest, now a plain
Felled by man, to open remain
By what means this action taken?
The source lay beneath the root
So long in slumber
This richness beyond all the world's treasure
A black jewel to spark and hew
This union of cold stone and warm blood
To fell a tree
And split asunder
To burn and bake
Toward a new horizon.

I have written down this strange arrangement before it slips away. Perhaps it is after all dreams that cause poetry to occur for there has been no waking thought or chasing about the page. Please forgive this new indulgence my dear uncle.

*

After enjoying our nuncheon of hard boiled egg with cheese and bread, I believe that Robert Foster has fallen asleep beside me. It is hard work indeed and the heavy air in combination with a ferocious sun condemns the labourer to suffer greatly in these conditions. By his knowledge of anatomy, Robert has been able to identify the most curious object that has yet been extracted from our pit. It is perhaps sixteen inches in length and is a broad and tapering flange of bone with a naturally occurring attachment of bone at the narrow end that forms the perfect handle. It is the scapula from a large beast of burden and this broad shoulder bone has been adapted to form the most perfect shovel. There is also a small pile of flint axes that lay beside a number of worn deer antlers and I shall make a drawing to record all these objects. One deer antler is assuredly a damaged pick that has been discarded and I have located a number of round holes in the walls of this pit where a bone pick has been punched into the chalk. This is of great interest for it displays the manner in which this pit was dug by such primitive tools. These three holes are aligned and they follow a flaw in the native chalk. We are digging a pit where the matrix of this ground has already been broken into and so are removing loose material. The ancient miners were confronted by a solid geology and have utilised every little help that nature may provide. I wonder how deep we shall be required to dig to establish the base of this pit?

I also believe that with the absence of pottery and other signals of domestic habitation I may now exclude the notion of pit dwellings as a purpose for these many depressions in the ground.

Whilst Robert Foster sleeps I may risk the recording of a conversation that has just taken place between us. He has explained that whilst he has been away from the family home his dear sister has been venturing out upon her own. Concern has been raised by their father, Mr Gerald Foster in correspondence to Robert. Sarah has described her excursions in detail to her father and is determined to continue. I can only cast my mind back to that night in Hindon when I first met Sarah and she had then defied the will of her brother by not staying in her room. Upon that occasion it was the horses in the stables that she had sought to feed but had then become alarmed by the many drunken men on that election night. It was indeed my good fortune that I was able to assist but I can now share in the Foster family's concern by this new display of wilful independence.

Sarah Foster has taken to walking upon her own the steep

gradient from the house to the quay. There is an unevenness to this steep street but in that unevenness, she has devised in her mind a map that she may read with her feet. The gaps between the buildings are felt by the currents of air upon her cheek and a change also in the sound of the tapping of her stick. She holds herself erect and tries to imagine how she looks to others. Sarah talks to the occupants and visitors upon the street and recognises their scents and coughs, their whistles and clicking heels and even the laboured breathing as they ascend the steep hill. She speaks "Good morning" to the shop keepers as they stand at their doorways but suspects that they are now waiting for her and so changes the time of her walk. In this way different people are met with and life is more haphazard and it is a quiet mischief as she senses this disruption.

Robert Foster has informed me that the purpose of his excursion from the family home is to seek medical advice and expertise into the treatment of blindness. He has travelled to Edinburgh and Liverpool and spent a deal of time in London. Robert informs me that if travel abroad was not so fraught with danger then he would visit every capital city in Europe if he thought that he might gain some knowledge there. I now consider my own churlish frustrations caused by Robert Foster's delay in not arriving at the Winterslow Hut until last evening when I did not understand the purpose of his journey. Whilst Robert has sought high and low for the best medical advice in an attempt to cure his dear sister's affliction (and believes it a fault of science that this cannot be achieved) Sarah is quietly finding her own way in the world.

*

We could achieve no more today and Robert Foster has been unstinting in his labour and interest in my investigation of this pit. He is a true friend and I believe that it shall be a friendship that will endure and prosper. Whilst my face and skin have become seasoned by my exposure to the ferocious sun so Robert's fair skin has suffered and is made bright red. His hands also are torn and bleeding but neither of these things have dampened his spirit and he states that; "Progress has been made my dear Henry. Progress has been made."

Upon our weary return to the Winterslow Hut, it transpires that there has been the discovery of some thefts. The landlord has advised that all guests must be diligent in the locking of their rooms for a fob watch has vanished and also a small quantity of money. Robert has suggested helpfully that as I was found creeping about the landing upon his arrival then I should be cast in irons without further ado and the landlord has accepted this proposal with a wry smile. The landlord also informs us that the ailing doctor is insistent that his door must still be left ajar and, as he struggles to sleep fitfully, he should soon witness any intruder no matter what the hour. Robert has indeed entered the doctor's room and offered his services, but has been informed kindly that it is a reoccurrence of an affliction that will only abate with rest and darkness.

After a necessary encounter with hot water before dinner, Robert has again returned to my room where he has picked up your slim volume of "A Pedestrian Tour of North Wales, 1805". I explained that it was the reading of this publication that prompted my flight from Southwark in October last, to conduct my own pedestrian adventure. I have read it over and again but more often will read the fond dedication that you yourself have written at the front. To hear it again read by Robert Foster renews the warmth and inspiration that I have gained from your kind words.

"To my nephew Henry, may you think of me not as your absent uncle but instead as a true friend. Distance and circumstance have conspired against us but you will see from this small publication that I am very much alive in mind and body. To the few that choose to turn these pages I shall be Anonymous but to you, my dear Henry,

I shall be forever your faithful uncle, James Chalk."

I confirmed that it was to you sir that my flow of correspondence is directed when I am embarked upon my pedestrian excursions, in the vain hope that you will enjoy these twists and turns. Robert then asked whether you had indeed reciprocated in the knowledge that your nephew was residing here at the Winterslow Hut these last few days? I confessed that I had not received word since the arrival of your book in Southwark over two years ago but would not be discouraged. I stated that I sincerely hoped that you are well and in good health but that you are too busily employed and perhaps engaged upon more adventures of your own. It is I who am at fault for my erratic and irresponsible behaviour and so I do not deserve your interest or sanction.

Tiredness has prompted an early night and out in the hallway Robert has confirmed his unerring support for our excavation by stating loudly that the "White hole of Winterslow" would finally relinquish its secrets and that tomorrow would bring great excitement. I then had to ensure that he bridled his enthusiasm, least he awoke the guests already in slumber and I also reminded him to lock his door to the prowling thief.

It is now as hot by night as it is by day and the perspiring landlord exclaimed that what was needed was a good "rattle-round" by which I understand that a storm is required to clear the air. Indeed, the pen slips between my fingers as I write and my body is infested by these little black bugs that makes the skin itch so.

Before I attempt the discomfort of sleep in this heat, I shall continue with my letter to Sarah for I believe that Robert Foster is anxious to return home despite his enthusiasm for my venture. Once my good friend departs, I shall not linger here beside the busy London road and must form a plan of my own. I believe that it is time for us to meet again my dear uncle for too much ink has been spilled in the recounting of my exploits and I know nothing of your own circumstances. Pray send word post-haste, if you are agreeable to this meeting after so many years.

Your faithful nephew
HENRY CHALK

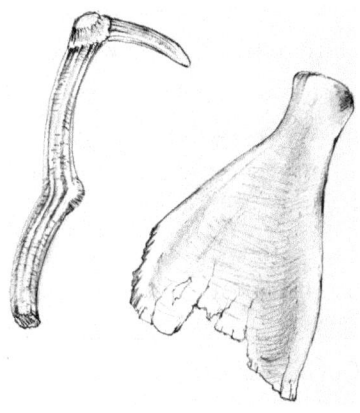

Tuesday 17th May 1808

MY DEAR UNCLE,

Even in the early morn the heat is intolerable and I pray that the "rattle-round" will come soon. The sky is heavy and the milk at breakfast is turned sour by this atmosphere and everybody complains at this helpless situation. Even Robert Foster appears weary this morning and admits to lethargy. It is as I feared, for Robert has informed me that he intends to depart for North Somerset this afternoon. He has been estranged from his family for too long and Sarah has not been made aware of the true purpose of his absence. I have urged Robert to depart sooner but he is insistent that the day shall be spent at the excavation for he does not wish me to work on my own for fear that the walls of chalk may collapse and I should be buried alive. We both sense that we are very close to reaching the base of this pit when its secrets shall be revealed and so Robert has now appeared at my door and we must depart.

*

We are now sheltering from the sun beside the pit but it is no longer the sun that is the enemy for it is the heat and the closeness of the air that is most oppressive. Whilst I filled the two pails, at our departure from the Hut, Robert sought the blacksmith to retrieve the tools but then returned with the saddest news for he has spoken with the blacksmith's eldest daughter. She has informed him that the family had attended the funeral at Winterslow church of her brother Edward who died upon the advent of his first birthday. Indeed, we heard the tolling of the distant bell and I now reflect upon the picture of the smallest and plainest of coffins carried by the father to the grave. Mr Rogers, the blacksmith, has been the most taciturn of men and I think back to Sunday and of his visit to the excavation to ensure that I ceased my labours upon the Lord's day. I now regret deeply my causing the blacksmith to be troubled by this disregard and yet I hope and trust that his faith will serve him well for it is a loss that cannot be easily accepted by a rational mind alone. There are many deep memories that may be stirred by such solemn and tragic news.

*

Robert has been strangely reticent this morning and we have gone about our work both deep in thought. We are now nine feet below the turf by my estimation and the original sides of this pit are no longer vertical for there is an undercutting or even a tunnelling into the native chalk. The steps and platforms that we have created to enable access to this depth require some contortion but this once disturbed chalk appears to hold its form sufficiently. There have been some minor falls of chalk upon the excavator but Robert is concerned regarding the overhang of chalk and questions the certainty of its stability but I can detect no fissures or cracks that might cause this to fall.

*

Robert has now broken his silence. He has announced his future plans
and it is as if he has also extracted more from this hole in the plain than
just chalk and flint.

"Henry, I have informed you of my purpose in being away from
home but I have since made a further resolution. You must promise me
Henry that you will never communicate to my sister the purpose of
my absence nor what I am about to tell you."

I ceased my digging at the base of the pit as if to emphasize this
pledge. I may now reveal these facts to you my dear uncle for I have
entrusted you with my every detail thus far and I believe that it shall in
no manner compromise my pledge to Mr Robert Foster.

Neither did I remind Robert that the communication between
Sarah Foster and my self is wholly dependent on his intervention.
Robert then reiterated the nature of his visits thus far to the eye
hospitals in the north of this country and also to those in our capital
city where he has questioned surgeons and medics upon the subject of
diseases to the eye.

"I know not on what scale I may contribute to a cure or to
the relief of those afflicted by blindness, but I intend to pursue a
career in medicine. I can no longer stand by, my dear Henry, when
I am convinced by all that I have heard and read on this subject that
science may achieve a great deal more than a dose of mercury and the
application of leeches to the back of the head. I shall do whatever is
required of me to achieve this goal and yet I believe that the most
difficult of these tasks is to keep this news from my dear sister as her
senses are the sharper for the loss of one."

I resumed for a moment the scraping at the bottom of the pit
but my preoccupation with the past and all that is long dead has of a
sudden become shallow and worthless by this news. Is it not obvious?
It is the living that require our best endeavour for we can no longer help

the dead by the discovery of their intentions.

I then climbed from the pit to shake Mr Robert Foster violently by the hand and declared my wholehearted support for this new ambition. If Robert Foster is to dedicate his life to medicine then I must commit myself to assist in this most worthy and noble aim. My thoughts are akin to a man running that cannot keep up with the speed that he wishes to achieve and his legs then slither about with furious instability. There can be only one solution to the assistance that I am able to give. By necessity Robert shall be estranged from his sister in the pursuit of his studies therefore would Sarah Foster consider me even as a poor substitute for the brother that she loves so much? My current circumstances would not permit any such approach least I return to my London obligations and cease my irresponsible ramblings. It is a course of action my dear uncle that I believe would gain your wholehearted support. Am I not too young to request of Mr Gerald Foster, the hand of his daughter Sarah in marriage?

*

Robert Foster is soon to depart for Salisbury and then via Bridgwater to Minehead. Our minds are racing with the possibilities of these new plans and I have returned to my room with the spade and the pick such is my disorientation. My heart is beating so fast that I believe that it will burst from my chest and I know not how to control myself. I must soon compose myself for I shall now write a brief letter to Sarah Foster. I have torn into many pieces my first letter for all has now changed. Gone forever is the grand poem and tumultuous prose for Robert has described how his sister receives my correspondence.

"Sarah does not crave for metaphysics Henry and is happiest when you have your hands in the soil. Indeed, earth and earthly matters will suit very well."

I am so very much relieved by this news for my cup of ordinariness doth overflow.

I am to be defeated by the pit for it has retained its secrets.
Once Robert disclosed his plan, I then escorted him at once back to
the Winterslow Hut to prepare for his departure and all thoughts of
excavation were abandoned. See how my hand still trembles but I
cannot delay further my dear Uncle and must now write to my beloved
Sarah.

*

The sky has grown so very dark and Robert has just this minute
departed upon the Salisbury coach. The air is thick with the brew of
the storm and it growls close by but has not yet begun to rain. I know
not what to do with myself and am pacing all about the place. I have
a great temptation to return to the pit with the pick and spade for I
am certain that there is but a small scraping to be made to reveal the
base of the pit. A great flash has illuminated the room and the boom of
thunder is fast upon its heels. I can hear the horses fearful in the stables
below and the dogs have begun to bark and howl. There is a great
excitement and an electricity in the air and I cannot remain cowering
here whilst the sky is at war with the earth.

ROBERT'S LETTER

Thursday 19th May 1808

My dear Sir,

It is my unfortunate duty, as a loyal friend to your young nephew Mr Henry Chalk, to correspond regarding an incident that has lately occurred. You will, I trust, forgive me if I delay my own introduction by assuring you that your nephew is alive but has not yet fully awakened these last two nights. His signs are indeed encouraging and yet your nephew has received a blow to the skull from which unforeseen complications may arise. I have witnessed before the results of cranial fracture and also the swelling of the brain cavity through the pressure of bleeding from within. Young Henry has also sustained at least two broken ribs but I do not consider that his lungs have been affected for his breathing is regular.

I am aware, through earlier conversation with your nephew and as his trusted friend, that he has kept you very well informed of his every movement whilst at large in South Wiltshire as a pedestrian tourist. I must also surmise that Henry has made mention of me, for his diligence would not permit otherwise, but I shall now introduce myself. My name is Mr Robert Foster and I hail from the town of Minehead in Somersetshire. My father is Mr Gerald Foster and my mother Mrs Anne Foster. I have also a younger sister, Miss Sarah Foster. I have of late travelled to the north of England and also to London but I am soon to return home. I am much gratified that Henry should agree to our initial union here at the Winterslow Hut beside the London Road upon my homeward journey. Indeed, exceptional circumstances have permitted a close friendship to prosper through the pen alone and we were both anxious to meet in person.

I can anticipate your alarm at the sudden cessation of correspondence from your devoted nephew and I sincerely believe that he will resume this duty as soon as he is fit to do so. It therefore falls to me to describe, as best I can, the events that have caused the peculiarity of my intervention in your nephew's affairs. I fear that you must also suffer the rhetoric of one who aspires to a career in medicine rather than that of bold adventurer and antiquary.

It is my intention to be brief although I have often been reminded of my perpetual failing in this regard. I hold little doubt that Henry will have furnished you with ALL the circumstances that have led to an excavation upon the plain behind the Winterslow Hut. (Indeed, how could he ever resist imparting the extent of his enthusiasm for such a venture?) I too have succumbed to the infection of antiquarianism for I joined with Henry in the digging of this hole. It is my great regret that I did not remain to complete the task, for I should not be writing to you now and Henry would not be laying abed with a bandage upon his head.

After many days, indeed weeks, of fine weather with not a drop of rain to be had, the dark storm clouds finally gathered above Winterslow. I said farewell to Henry Chalk as I departed for North Somerset and to this end, I was first required to make the short journey to Salisbury riding on the outside of the already crowded coach. I had not travelled one mile before the heavens collided and a great fork of lightning struck a large roadside tree causing a huge bough to crash down before us upon the turnpike. The team of four reared up as one at this terror and despite the great skill of the coachman in attempting to control the horses, the carriage then mounted the steep verge to be thrashed by the hedgerow before toppling over upon its side. All aboard the roof were thrown out with the luggage and those passengers who moments earlier were nestled contentedly on the inside were now very badly tumbled about. Two horses remained mortally wounded upon the road whilst two broke free of their harnesses and fled back to the Winterslow Hut, thus raising the alarm. You can well imagine the scene for there ensued a great deal of panic amongst these unfortunate travellers and whilst limbs were broken and heads were dashed, thankfully none were mortally wounded by this calamitous event. The coachman stamped about upon the turnpike and was much aggrieved at the damage to his carriage and the loss of his impeccable record after thirty years of service on the London Road. The passengers upon the inside were extracted and I was able to come to aid of those most in distress as makeshift splints were applied. The most severe cuts were bound by a torn petticoat that had become caught upon the hedge from the strewn luggage to which no lady laid claim. The returning pair of wild eyed horses surely signalled that a disaster had occurred to the lately departed Salisbury bound coach. A team of carts duly arrived to escort the damaged party back down the hill to the Winterslow Hut just as the first splashes of rain turned to a deluge and I have never before witnessed rain of such biblical proportions. As the sodden passengers either limped or were carried to shelter, the carts then turned swiftly about for there was a great deal to remove from the turnpike before night fall. I then requested of the landlord that beds should be made available for the needy and hot water was required aplenty to bathe wounds. A number of guests already in residence were made to double up and the ailing doctor who had been ensconced for some days in a room across the landing from your nephew had now inexplicably vanished without paying his considerable bill. I cared not for the landlord's defamatory remarks concerning this gentleman, only that his bed was now vacated. I recommended that a doctor should be summoned but the landlord said that I was "doin' a main good job Maaster Voster Sir,n' doctors be costly."

I had not given one thought to your young nephew until I sent the chambermaid to summon Henry so that he might assist with the care of the injured. She soon returned to inform me that his room was locked and that try as she might he could not be raised. The landlord then provided a key but of Henry there was no sign. As you know your nephew well sir, you will not be surprised to learn that he had returned to the excavation at my departure. That he was in peril I held no doubt and good fortune saw the arrival in the yard of the blacksmith who had returned from the upturned coach for a second block and tackle. I hurriedly explained my intention and the blacksmith took no convincing to hasten to the excavation aboard his cart. The blacksmith knew his ground and we were soon at the opening to the excavation. I leapt down upon the sodden turf to see the worst of my fears now realised for a fresh fall of chalk had detached itself from the wall of the pit to cover the base of the excavation. The steps and platforms within the pit that had previously offered help to descend the hole were now so slippery underfoot that I required a rope to cling upon that was then lashed to the cart. I called out "Henry, Henry" over and again to which I received no response. At first, with my bare hands, I scrabbled at the fresh chalk throwing it behind me only for it to return to the base of the pit and so the bucket was again utilised. Another rope was then applied to the handle of the bucket to enable the swift ejection of the now slippery wet fill by the blacksmith. The heavy rain continued unabated and I confess that I held little hope that we should find your nephew alive. I now employed a spade to the task and in time I struck metal and indeed I found one of the original tools utilised by Henry and myself. With the removal of more spoil I could determine that the pick and the spade had been crossed and wedged above the base of the pit and I believe they had formed a fortuitous brace to arrest the fall of the mass of chalk. Beneath these blessed tools I first found a pale and cold hand and in this small cavity that had been so formed I then encountered the poor crumpled body of your nephew and my dear friend, Henry Chalk. It was the bracing by these tools that had preserved the life of young Henry for without them he would surely have been crushed and submerged in chalk. A small gap had also been preserved at the under cut of the excavation which permitted the air to pass the collapsed spoil. Henry did not stir as I hauled him upright and he was a dead weight but not yet dead. I then placed the rope around him and with the blacksmith hauling and me pushing at the limp form, and so he was retrieved from the pit. No sooner had I also gripped the rope to be pulled to the surface then another collapse to the side of the pit occurred to send a fresh smothering of chalk to fill the base of the excavation.

With Henry in my arms aboard the cart we fought the driving rain until we reached the sanctuary of the Hut. You cannot imagine the appearance of your nephew as he was laid upon the kitchen table and indeed the chambermaid fainted as she looked upon this limp soul all soiled with blood and chalk. His pulse was very weak and he so cold that I called for a bath of hot water to raise his temperature into which he was plunged fully clothed. The landlady protested at my action saying that it was well known that a bath of cold water was best in these circumstances to which I replied that I wished my friend to live and not to perish from an old wive's remedy. I was then able to bathe and examine the wounds upon his head, still fearful that he may yet expire. His pulse became a little stronger whereupon we quickly stripped and dried him and then wrapped a great bundle of blankets about him. I then bled him only a half a pint as I could not gauge the volume of blood already lost. I wrapped his head and he was then put to bed and I kept a constant vigil upon his living signs. I knew that if he survived the night then he may yet live and I can inform you sir that it was the longest night of my life.

There were other patients to provide a distraction with window glass to be extracted from cuts and nerves to settle. By the morning a little colour had returned to Henry's cheek and his breathing had become more certain. Indeed, there was a flock of maids and female guests at the door who wished to confirm, to their own satisfaction, that Henry Chalk was still alive.

Two nights have now passed since the turmoil of the storm and Henry Chalk is most certainly alive. At first, he stirred and upon my examination of his ribs he then moaned in protest. His eyes have opened and a weak smile has been offered to please the chambermaid.

Sir, it is now late and I shall resume briefly in the morning before the post departs.

*

It is Thursday morning and Henry is awake and demanding to be fed. In fact, all the patients are on the mend and many have now departed but one gentleman with a broken leg requires very careful transportation and must therefore be a patient patient.

Henry should remain rested for a good many days and I have arranged for his good friend Mr Richard Fenton to ensure the continued care and convalescence at the home of Sir Richard Colt Hoare in Stourhead. Mr Fenton will arrive tomorrow when I must again attempt to depart for West Somerset.

I believe sir, if you will accept the meddling of a stranger, that your devoted nephew would dearly welcome a letter from his uncle for it would cheer him greatly and thereby aid his recovery. I believe that two years or more have passed since Henry last received word from you whilst the weight of correspondence has assuredly been flowing in the opposing direction to keep the post-chaises busy and the postmasters in full employ.

I sincerely hope that we shall meet one day and pray forgive my forwardness.

Your humble servant
ROBERT FOSTER

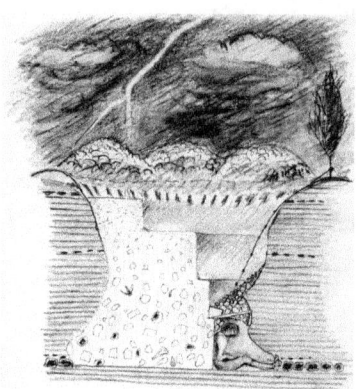

Something bad has occurred for the chambermaid shows great concern and even the landlord has appeared at my bedside to ask if I am now recovered. I have a dull pain in my head and more so when I attempt to move. There is also a great discomfort upon one side of my chest. Robert Foster is to return shortly and he has promised to explain why I am laying abed with a bandage upon my head and why he is here at the Winterslow Hut at all. I awoke with a compunction to write and so before departing Robert has reluctantly placed the pen, ink and paper at my bedside.

*

I have just opened my eyes to see a large wavering shadow upon the wall. This creature has a long neck and a large beak and it is a most proud and regal bird. The giant head turns warily back and forth but all the while it keeps its haughty pose.

I heard my voice croak a hoarse whisper.

"The great bustard."

In an instant this giant bird took flight as Robert Foster untwisted his hands before the candle. Robert informs me that he spied this giant bird yesterday as it bathed in the dust upon the plain.

He has now gone to request some broth for he says that I must eat.

*

It is morning and I cannot recall writing of bustards or eating broth and so it goes. At some moments I feel a charlatan for laying in my bed and then I find that I cannot remember what occurred the previous night.

Robert has now encouraged me to write if I am able, for he says that it will assist with my recovery. A blow to the head may scatter the memory and the act of writing will help to retrieve these lost pieces.

*

I believe that I understand a little now of what has befallen me as Robert has again told me the whole woeful tale.

Shall it ever be so? Henry Chalk has caused a deal of trouble. I have kept Robert from a reunion with his family by my foolishness. My dear uncle, I have found my letter that I began on Tuesday 17th and it has remained unfinished and unsent. Upon reading it again I sense and savour the great upheaval in my heart and yet this can by no manner excuse what then occurred.

Robert has informed me that he has corresponded with you and told of how he found your troublesome nephew laying buried in a grave of his own making. Were it not for the bolt of lightning and the accident to the coach then I would be buried still. Robert Foster has indeed saved my life and how can that debt ever be repaid? He has made light of it and the landlord has spoken of how he also treated and tended the injured passengers from the upturned coach. We are all fortunate for the presence here of Mr Robert Foster.

*

I have questioned Robert upon the bustard for after the storm there must be no dust upon the plain in which to bathe. He informs me that my excavation has been filled in by two labourers employed to the task before another injury is caused. At the base of the spoil heap lays soil that was not dampened by the rain and so this in turn formed the top crust of the freshly filled pit.

"It was here that I spied the bustard Henry, dancing and dusting itself upon your pit. It took offence long before my arrival and erupted into flight."

I now had two subjects to think upon. The bustard at the very place where I had spent so much time with the blacksmith's tools and the pit itself, now filled in.

*

I awoke in the night and it was not at first the returning memory of what occurred in the pit that stirred me but the recollection of a strange odour. It was the scent of freshly broken flint. I cannot describe it plainly other than it being a faintly malodorous gas. This was indeed a returning memory. From this essence I have been able to reform the puzzle that has so far eluded me. Each time it grows with more pieces attached. As the candle has been kept lit in my room, I was able to write down this strange tale. I then delved and burrowed like an ancient miner in search of flint and although the page of night thoughts appeared a mess I have now some notion of what took place.

Upon reaching the excavation I spied the shepherd nearby and he kept a constant vigil upon the heavens for the sky had darkened terribly with thunder and lightning close by. I quickly descended the shaft and then extracted a few pails of chalk to reveal the floor of the pit. If you can imagine, my dear uncle, I believe that the original pit was bell shaped for it is broader at the base than it is at the top. I then cleared the undercut which required climbing from the pit to empty yet more pails of chalk upon the heap. The shepherd again gestured to the sky and waved his arm as if to sweep me from this plain. He then drifted on with his flock and of a sudden it was as if the great swollen belly of the storm had been slashed open, for I felt a weight of water upon me. I hastened back to the shelter of the excavation but the chalk steps soon turned to a treacherous white paste beneath my feet and I slipped and slithered my way to the bottom.

I then made progress horizontally and in the subterranean half light, feeling with my hands, I found my goal. The miners had removed the thick tablet of flint at the base of the pit and here now was the abandoned face of their excavation. They had dared to go no further as they chased their treasure under the chalk overhang. The seam of flint was perhaps six inches in depth and with the pick I prised and twisted and shattered my way until I had a sufficiently large nodule to inspect. I hauled it back into the pale daylight at the base of the pit and I then sensed the faint sulphurous odour of flint. A thick white outer rind remained on one side but the meat of the piece was fresh and dark and was the cause of this, and the many other excavations here, all those years ago. In that watery gloom I recall staring at my own bloody prints left upon the chalky white crust of the broken nodule. I put down the flint to study my hands that soon became awash with falling blood.

Robert has informed me that the pick and the spade were found above my head, thus forming a brace to shield me from the collapsed chalk. Try as I might I cannot remember placing them there nor what happened next.

*

I have now informed Robert of this recollection and he has listened with one eyebrow raised and has resisted interruption. Finally, he announced that there was one fact that now puzzled him greatly and to date he had discovered no solution. Not only had the chalk wall collapsed upon me but the rough flint axes, that we had extracted earlier, had also found their way back into the shaft and were found resting upon the blacksmith's tools. Robert said that he had not considered this at the time but after hearing my own account he was reminded of it. "It was as if through the vortex of the storm these fashioned pieces and indeed the larger chalk blocks had been sucked back into the pit from whence they came, before the great fall of chalk. The pit has reclaimed its own."

I must count myself lucky and now shiver at the thought of my incarceration in the chalk. I have indeed offended the spirits of this plain.

My door is now kept unlocked and I questioned Robert about this fact. He tells me that the threat of the sneaking thief has now passed with the departure of the ailing doctor. Not only did he depart without settlement but fled upon another man's stabled horse during the tempest. I felt pity for those at the Hut who had lost their precious goods at the hands of this sly man for a repeater watch was stolen and now a horse and saddle whilst all hands were assisting with the upturned carriage upon the turnpike.

*

I have this early evening walked slowly to the window and that is adventure enough for this pedestrian tourist. The air is sweet and the sky has become alive with the flickering passage of birds that in my ignorance I cannot name. They twist and turn at a rate that is beyond my comprehension when compared to our own laborious trundling about the place. If the human race could travel at this speed then we would be arriving before we had even considered departing and the world would very soon spin from its axis of that I am certain. These sleek and darting birds live under the eaves of the roof here at the

Winterslow Hut for they have constructed nests of mud in which to rear their young.

The land has prospered from the rain and has become green when before this same view was straw coloured. I am pleased also that the bustards are able to dust themselves upon my pit.

Robert has again changed the bandage upon my head and informs me that he is to depart for West Somerset tomorrow. The thought that brother and sister will soon be reunited warms me greatly. I had not given any thought as to what I should do next and it appears that Robert has resolved this matter also. Mr Richard Fenton is to arrive tomorrow at the Winterslow Hut and whilst I deplore the great inconvenience that I have caused I shall be very pleased to see Mr Fenton once again.

Saturday 21ˢᵗ May 1808

MY DEAR UNCLE,

I have enclosed my undated pages for there is some news concealed there amongst a deal of confusion, if you should care to pick over these ramblings.

It is now raining again but it is a fresh and steady rain and not at all the same tainted and pent up water that fell to earth upon the night of the tempest.

I took delivery this morning of a small parcel from Salisbury and I could not guess at its content. Upon opening it I am now ashamed by my condition for contained within were two flint hearts that I had ordered from Mr Shorto. They are both set in silver and attached to each is a fine silver chain. One is intended for Sarah and I shall entrust it to Robert to deliver in person whilst I shall keep a duplicate for myself. Mr Shorto has also inserted a note to apologise for the delay and hopes that I shall still be at the Winterslow Hut to take receipt of this order. He explains that "..due to the unavailability of ancient flint workers the task has proved a challenge to even his best craftsmen."

The dark flint hearts appear rippled across their surface and are not polished or smooth like a precious stone. They are indeed perfect and I shall send a note at once to Mr Shorto to thank him warmly and also to wish Mrs Shorto and their young family well. I shall communicate to Mr Henry Shorto, in due course, regarding the nature of my excavation for I believe that it will interest him greatly but I sincerely do not wish to steer him from his responsibilities.

The arrival of this package has prompted the recollection of my pedestrian excursion of late for recent events have become estranged from me since awaking with a bandage upon my head. In my thoughts I followed the progress of my ramble and found either pain or pleasure as the story unfolded. I then turned cold with the realisation that I had mislaid the inscribed spyglass given to me by Mr Richard Fenton. That same gentleman is due to arrive here at the Winterslow Hut at any moment and I know not how to describe the loss of such a precious and thoughtful gift.

*

Robert Foster has now departed and I trust that his journey home will be swift and uneventful. I watched and waved from my window as he secured his berth within the coach and indeed the landlord and landlady were in attendance to bid their farewells. I believe that Mr Robert Foster will always be warmly welcomed here should he ever return. We discussed little at our parting for enough has already been said and it shall not be so very long before we meet again. I believe that we now have a bond that exceeds the need for platitudes or overt displays of civility and indeed one look between us is sufficient to indicate our true thoughts and feelings. As Mr Robert Foster departs so Mr Richard Fenton appears and of a sudden I am now a bed-ridden player in a farce fit for the stage. My friend has already whisked up a flurry of activity with the chambermaid required to plump up my pillows and boots to shave the paltry growth upon my chin. An inspection of my wardrobe has revealed a dearth of respectable clothes and more action is required of the staff here to stitch and sew and make good before my departure to Stourhead. My companion then lifted up the snakecatcher's hat and was about to question its origin but then thought better of it and tossed it to one side before inspecting his hands with some suspicion.

I requested that Mr Fenton should seat himself and rest for one moment from attending to my every need for I dearly wished to inform him of the discoveries made here upon the plain behind the Winterslow Hut. I have in preparation for this moment made a crude plan of the flint pit to illustrate my excavation. As you will recall my dear uncle, Mr Richard Fenton is an antiquarian of some considerable association and I was anxious to contribute to the understanding of how our ancient ancestors found and procured the best quality flint for their tools and fire making. I was also keen to steer the course of our conversation to a remote destination and far away from the subject of spyglasses.

At the outset Mr Fenton gave every impression of one who was listening but I gauged that he was in truth distracted for he was quick to resume his pacing about the room. The subject of my quest for a source of quality flint was soon to be replaced by how the curtains appeared threadbare and the furniture worn.

To my great astonishment Mr Fenton then picked up my telescope to survey the view from my window and soon described the appearance of a gentleman who was fast approaching the Hut from the village of Winterslow.

"He walks at a fierce pace Henry and indeed he has a ferocious visage to compliment this gait."

I could not at all comprehend the return of the spyglass but was overjoyed to see it in the hands of Mr Fenton.

Mr Fenton would not permit me to leave my bed and indeed it was to inspect the spyglass and not the subject at the end of it that was my intention. I then sank back into my pillow with some relief and yet a deal of confusion. A smile played across the face of my friend Mr Richard Fenton as he continued in his observation of the approaching stranger. Some mischief was indeed in the air but I did not yet show my surprise or pleasure at the reappearance of my spyglass.

I then suggested that the gentleman who was the subject of Mr Fenton's examination could only be Mr William Hazlitt. I remembered the service that I had provided in the transporting of his letters to the small house upon the hill in the village of Winterslow and explained this circumstance to Mr Fenton. I informed my friend that Mr Hazlitt was an artist and also a writer and that I had spent some interesting and instructive time whilst walking in his company. I added that he is also a fierce and uncompromising thinker and I recommended to Mr Fenton that he might make his acquaintance for I should like to witness their exchanges.

Mr Fenton suggested that it was convenient to study him from afar as too much thinking was to be avoided in his experience.

My companion then felt in his pocket and retrieved a note
that he had been given by a gentleman who had scrambled from the
London bound coach at the change of horse.

"I believe that he was one of your own breed Henry. A pedestrian
tourist returning to the metropolis to prepare and concoct the account
of his recent excursion for the press. No doubt it will contain the cream
gleaned from all the former tourists and a new syllabub whipped up
afresh."

I took this note from Mr Fenton and read it to myself as he then
continued to scour the fields, hills and hedgerows.

I enclose it for your inspection my dear uncle to see if you can
make some sense of it for indeed I cannot. I am grateful for the return
of my spyglass but I am concerned that the author of this short note
appears to know my every move and it is a circumstance that I find
most unsettling.

DEAR MR HENRY CHALK,

I hereby return your spyglass, you really should take more care
of it but I have profited by your carelessness for it has served me
well on my Pedestrian Tour of South Wiltshire. I have of late visited
Shaftesbury and also the Glove Inn where I enquired of the landlord
whether a loss nearby of a spyglass had earlier been reported. Indeed
he informed me that this was so and also of your intention to stay at
the Winterslow Hut. The landlord demanded a half crown from me
for the imparting of this information with the promise that you should
then reimburse the finder of this precious object to the same degree.

My route has been somewhat haphazard. I attempted to ascend
the summit of Fonthill Abbey, a place that you know well, but got
turned away at the gate. I should like to know whether Mr William
Beckford has green eyes for I have read somewhere that this is so?
I shall of course embellish my tale with a successful entrance to the

Caliph's lair and the mounting of his tower.

I have visited Stonehenge and have parted with a trophy of that place that I shall add to my splinter from Shakespear's chair, that I collected on a visit to the great Bard's cottage last summer. I have been treated very badly at the reprehensible New Inn that nestles beneath Grovely Wood. I met with no charcoal burners or deer stealers there, only incivility. I have also made visits to Salisbury Cathedral, Figsbury Ring and Old Sarum, to Wilton House, Longford Castle, Stourhead House etc..etc..

I shall now away to our Capital City where my tale shall grow before it is submitted to the press. The coachman beckons and so we must depart. I trust and pray, Mr Henry Chalk, that you will make a swift recovery and soon return to your pedestrian adventures.

Gratefully yours,

Mr Pedestres.

Mr Fenton smiled and then collapsed the seven tubes of the spyglass before presenting it back to me.

"I have paid the exorbitant tax imposed by the landlord of the Glove Inn to the bearer of the spyglass."

I then looked about hastily for my purse so that I might instantly reimburse my companion the sum of one half crown whilst Mr Fenton, with great theatrics waved away this requirement. I had not the strength to persist but made a private vow to repay this debt. I recalled to my friend the misery of losing the spyglass and the torment of twice seeing it flashing in the sunlight upon the distant horizon and confirmed my great relief at its safe return.

Having amused himself greatly, Mr Fenton then departed to secure some lunch.

And so my time here at the Winterslow Hut is near come to an end. My excavation is now no more than a dusty patch amongst the turf and yet it is to the satisfaction of the great bustard. The trophies gleaned from the pit now languish back from whence the came with only the roughest of drawings made to record their existence. I will now forward my plan of the flint pit to you sir, for it has escaped the attention of Mr Fenton who has not the correct pince-nez upon his person to view it thoroughly. I now await the return of Mr Fenton and before that I am to settle with the landlord.

There is one person whose warm presence in my heart has not diminished one jot when all else has become unhinged, indeed I long to be reunited with Miss Sarah Foster once again. I have good intentions and great expectations after my discourse with her faithful brother, Mr Robert Foster, that all may yet be resolved.

*

I am to finish this correspondence my dear uncle and post it directly. I cannot continue under the escort of Mr Fenton and I must leave quietly upon my own. Mr Fenton duly returned and looked the more distracted and then muttered of Mr William Cunnington who has been in London of late and has reluctantly sat for the artist Mr Woodruff on the say of Sir Richard Colt Hoare, but is not at all at ease with his new wig and the excruciating posture and wished to retreat back to Wiltshire to find sanctuary upon Salisbury Plain. Mr Cunnington's portrait is to appear as the frontispiece of the Baronet's great work in the making; "Ancient Wiltshire". Mr Fenton then looked aghast and stated that I was sworn to secrecy on this matter for it is to be a surprise and he should never have mentioned it. He then wrung his hands and stated that there was a subject of a personal nature regarding my affairs upon which he must delay no longer in discussing with me. I knew not what was coming next and it has surprised me greatly. Mr Fenton, under council from Sir Richard Colt Hoare, has made contact on my behalf with the trustees and bankers for Chalk's brewery in Southwark. An arrangement has been made where I am to receive a regular income until the hopefully imminent resumption of my responsibilities at Chalk's brewery. Indeed, whilst I resided at the home of Mr Fenton in Pembrokeshire in the winter months and put his affairs in order, it was an arrangement for which I received payment from the brewery alone. Mr Fenton hoped that my constitution was sufficiently recovered to withstand this news and he regretted deeply this deception but it was essential to acknowledge my whereabouts to the trustees and to ensure my safekeeping. It was felt that I would not give my sanction to this arrangement and so it was a decision taken without my knowledge but with my best interests in mind, as my sudden departure from Fishguard not a month ago had caused a deal of consternation to all concerned. It was then, with no small relief, that the Baronet received recent word from Mr Robert Foster as to my whereabouts.

"I have promised Sir Richard that I would inform you of this..arrangement and I do so now..somewhat belatedly..but quite essentially..before your arrival at Stourhead."

My dear uncle, I am perhaps too young and vulnerable in the eyes of certain friends and yet I believe that I must be wholly in control of my own affairs.

I have one responsibility before I quietly leave the Winterslow Hut for I must visit Mr Rogers, the blacksmith. He is a man of few words and I respect him greatly for his faith and resolution. I wish to apologise for the trouble that I have caused for he has lowered his own child into the grave upon the hill in Winterslow whilst I have been fool enough to bury myself upon the plain.

I must now hurry and gather together my belongings before Mr Fenton returns. Those half-forgotten events that occurred upon the night of the tempest will I fear plague me for ever and a day. As I lay helpless upon the floor of the pit with blood flowing from my head I believe now that I saw you there standing above me. Lightning glared upon the wetness of the chalk walls and I had not the strength or inclination to move. I looked up to the top of the shaft at the circle of violent sky and as a drowning man will gather the pictures of his life before him in that brief and fatal moment and so I saw your face illuminated by the storm. This vision had allowed for the passing of years to corrupt your features but indeed are we not both older now? Enough tragedy has kept us apart and we must repair these wounds whatever their cause. It is my intention that we should be reunited, indeed the omens and spirits of the pit have ordained that this should be so. I trust and pray that you will receive me, my dear uncle, for I am soon to arrive at your door.

Your faithful nephew
HENRY CHALK.

PART THREE

A

TOUR

IN SEARCH OF

THROUGH PARTS OF

WILTSHIRE

IN

1808

WRITTEN IN

𝔄 𝔖𝔢𝔯𝔦𝔢𝔰 𝔬𝔣 𝔏𝔢𝔱𝔱𝔢𝔯𝔰

IN WHICH ARE DESCRIBED; A WALK WITH AN *EXECUTIONER,*
A CHANCE ENCOUNTER WITH *REVD. JOSEPH TOWNSEND*
RECTOR OF PEWSEY. AND ALSO *MR. HENRY HUNT* OF UPAVON.
A WITNESS TO THE CONQUERING OF *BUSH BARROW.*
THE PARTICIPATION IN A *CRICKET MATCH* UPON STONEHENGE
DOWN, A DRAMA IN THE SALISBURY *COURT.* A SHORT EXCURSION
WITH *MR. HENRY SHORTO,* ESTEEMED CUTLER OF
SALISBURY, AN ENCOUNTER IN *SALISBURY CATHEDRAL* AND
THE *CONSEQUENCES* THEREOF.

BY

A PEDESTRIAN.

LETTER TO THE EDITOR

I f it is not entirely with the blessing of Mr Henry Chalk that the following pages should now be made available to the expectant public then it is with his indifference for he cannot imagine why any should wish to read of the events that have occurred since the earlier flood of this young Pedestrian Tourist's letters were inadvertently presented as "A Tour in Search of Chalk" and "A Tour in Search of Flint".

I can plainly recall our evening sitting before the blazing Radstock coals in the commodious Stourhead Inn where I first promoted the custom of travel, correspondence, embellishment and publication to which my young friend recoiled at the idea of such brazen self-importance.

Neither he nor I could foresee the travails and danger that lay in wait for our Pedestrian Tourist and it is only now that a grave tragedy may be laid to rest.

This final volume shall therefore conclude Mr Henry Chalk's pedestrian excursions and as the young author cares not one way or the other then it shall be my own small conceit to dub this work; "A Tour in Search of Gold etc etc.."

I wish only happiness for my dear young friend and if he never again sets foot upon a country path then let it be through contentment in domestic life for upon this course a destination surely beckons.

Your humble servant
RICHARD FENTON
November 1809

Thursday 1ˢᵗ September 1808

MY DEAR UNCLE,

If you have not yet disowned your errant nephew then I am indeed
the most fortunate and undeserving of relatives. You will perhaps
warm to my plea of forgiveness when I inform you that I write these
words at my father's desk in the house at Southwark for I have, at
long last, returned home to face my responsibilities. In truth I cannot
convey fully the degree of warmth expressed by all at Chalk's Brewery
after my lengthy absence. I had hoped that I might pass unnoticed to
my old clerk's desk and continue as if nothing at all had occurred but
I have now to occupy my father's office with my own name inscribed
upon the door. As it is my nature to disrupt, I then caused great
consternation by the cancellation of an order for three vast porter vats
from the Cooper's Company. Mr Gerrity, the brewery manager, was
soon at my door to protest at this action for he believes that we must
keep up with our competitors in this fashion. Not one week had passed
before I was fully vindicated in my decision for an identical giant porter
barrel at Meux's Horse Shoe Brewery had, of a sudden, burst its hoops
and three workers in the brewhouse were dashed against the walls and
killed outright. This is sickening news indeed but it has silenced the
clamour for greater volumes of porter than we are safely capable of
producing.

You will also recall my account of the digging of the great well
in the brewery yard and the hand-wringing that it caused my father,
your brother, whilst he was alive. Chalk's Brewery now has the purest
water in all London but it is also the hardest water for it is born from
the chalk deep beneath the city and as such is not so suitable for the
brewing of porter. I have instead, this last month, visited Burton upon

Trent where pale ales are now successfully brewed and for which our harder water is ideally suited. We are but a small concern when compared to our gargantuan neighbours at the Anchor Brewery in old Deadman's Place which now occupies a full nine acres with stabling for 100 horses. From our lowly beginnings as a vinegar factory in Dirty Lane we are spread to three acres with stabling for 30 horses but I proclaim that Chalk's Pale Ale will soon be the talk of all London and indeed I shall eat my snakecatcher's hat if I am to be proved wrong.

Today the bells have rung out in Southwark and all across London in celebration of a victory in Portugal after the defeat of General Junot. I do not understand the complexities of this engagement in the Peninsular but if it assists to end this raging war then there is just cause for such resounding celebration.

I am sir, unable to with-hold the news that I am to meet with Miss Sarah Foster and her brother Robert Foster in Salisbury upon the tenth day of September. I am first to spend some days in the company of Mr William Cunnington for he has invited me to a barrow opening upon the plains near Stonehenge and so Wiltshire is again to be my destination. Mr Gerrity has stated with good humour that he will be glad to see the back of me before I cause yet more disruption here at Southwark. The Chief Clerk, Mr Hooper, who is a kindly man, has I believe been entrusted by my dear friend Mr Richard Fenton to watch over me since my return to Southwark. I am to be cosseted lest my impetuous nature guides me towards some fresh and unforeseen danger for I am then to be passed into the care of Mr William Cunnington and in turn, like some delicate vase, to be received by Mr Robert Foster. Perhaps I am deserving of this watchfulness after my near burial in the flint pit upon the plains of Wiltshire. I should perhaps be more grateful for the concern displayed by my friends and associates as they weave their conspiratorial web but I do feel that I have grown up also as a consequence of my adventures.

I am doubly aware that I have neglected you my dear uncle these past few months and once I have all my affairs in good order then it is time that we should again meet in person after all these passing years.

So, it is with the scent of more adventure and excitement in my nostrils that I am compelled to pick up my pen to write to you for I believe that you understand your nephew better than my poor father ever understood his own son. Here upon my father's desk in a small heart shaped box I have found a gold ring that does not fit even my little finger and it is my mother's wedding ring. Also contained within the box is a golden curl of my mother's hair that mirrors in shape and colour the gold ring when I place them both upon my palm. I am saddened by the sight of the empty box for what is the heart but a box of love?

I will sir, keep you informed of my progress and I sincerely hope that my correspondence will not impose too much upon your time and patience.

Your tiresome nephew,
HENRY CHALK.

POSTSCRIPT,

A most curious event has just occurred that shall now cause me to bring forward my plans and to leave London before sunrise. It is as if by the mention of my father that he has now revealed himself before me and I am perhaps able to glimpse his true character for the first time in my life. Before this moment I only ever witnessed his anxiety in business and his buried grief at the death of my mother when I was but seven years old and since that time his anger would cloud the air and pervade the house whilst I long believed that I was the cause.

Upon the completion of my short note to you a butterfly passed silently through the open window of my father's study and in time settled upon the top shelf of the bookcase. Mrs Harrison the housekeeper, having found the door ajar, entered the study at this same instant and expressed great surprise upon seeing me at my father's desk for I had not before dared to venture into this room since my return to Southwark. Mrs Harrison is a goodly soul and over the last few months has ended our every encounter with the words; "And thanks be to God for your safe return Master Henry". Her flusterings were then directed at the butterfly and she was all for summoning a feather duster to expel the intruder.

I climbed the bookcase step to gain a closer view of the butterfly which had now settled upon the yellowed curl of a piece of paper that protruded from the pages of a book. I carefully lifted the volume from its place with the creature poised and with its colours concealed between closed wings. Mrs Harrison stood with her arms raised in a condition of great anxiety as I slowly descended from the step and she then gasped as the butterfly burst into haphazard flight to display its crisp scarlet and white markings imprinted upon black velvet. Our silent visitor then made a circuit of the room before sensing a draught of air upon which it quickly disappeared leaving me with book in hand and Mrs Harrison rushing to close the window lest it should immediately return.

At Mrs Harrison's departure I reopened the window and studied the spine of the book that I still clutched in my hand and I found it to be Gulliver's Travels by Jonathon Swift. Indeed, it is a book that I had long meant to read and only early last year I asked of my father whether he possessed a copy to which he answered that he did not and added that I was not of a sufficient age to understand its irreverence and it would only offend and corrupt. Each and every transaction with my father was such that his word was the end of the matter and no further discussion was required and yet, here in my hands, was this very same book. I was now made curious by this deceit and I opened this volume at the place where the sheet of paper had been inserted and yet it was not the text of the book that caught my eye but the writing upon this bookmark for it was in my father's hand.

That this folded page was torn from a notebook or journal I hold no doubt for one side was covered by his small and neat handwriting that is very similar to my own and indeed a stranger to both may not make a distinction between us. Upon the reverse, the paper was completely covered in unintelligible squiggles and marks that were, I believe, similar to those used in the Orient and yet I had no notion that my father could comprehend such a remote language for indeed he could barely manage a word of French. I sat in my father's chair to read and read again the portion of this journal that was written in English. As the tears welled up in my eyes, I spent an age staring at the aperture of the open window with a longing for the beautiful butterfly to return so that I might glimpse again its true and bold colours that looked so plain and desiccated with its wings closed up so tight.

My dear uncle, I now enclose a copy of this page of English for it recalls a distant occasion when two young brothers set out from London to Bristol on business and broke their journey near the town of Marlborough in Wiltshire. I am thrown into great confusion for I cannot recognise the father that I knew and instead I see a young man with a spirit that was once akin to my own. Sir, I would dearly wish to hear your recollection of this journey for it warms my heart to read of these exploits and it is indeed a found treasure to match any that may be recovered from the tombs of our ancient ancestors.

I must therefore gather together my pedestrian accoutrements; my hazel thumbstick, my pack and my snakecatcher's hat. I shall take with me the book Gulliver's Travels and also my mother's wedding ring for having picked it up I find that I cannot now relinquish it but I have returned the curl of hair so that it does not remain an empty box. Before dawn I shall depart for Wiltshire and follow in both your footsteps.

A portion from my father's journal dated May 1782
After boarding our coach at the George and Blue Boar in Holborn we

broke our journey at Beckhampton and walked back upon ourselves to the great green mound beside the Bath road. I was at first greatly vexed with my brother for he had suddenly demanded this halt in our progress to Bristol and it is again a challenge to my seniority and had our father been present then this circumstance would certainly not have occurred. When questioned he could not supply a satisfactory explanation to this behaviour and instead suggested that we were free men and could do as we pleased. Our luggage was deposited at the Beckhampton Inn and rather than sit in a crowded parlour to await the return of my errant brother I decided to follow on behind.

It was indeed a fine afternoon and my own curiosity grew as I approached Silbury Hill, for that is the name of this gigantic and mysterious upturned pudding.

James was seated at the base of the mound for he had spied my pursuit and insisted that we should make a wager of one guinea as to who would ascend the hill first and reach the summit. I felt compelled to establish my superiority and so together we made a rush upon the hill and with a deal of tugging and pushing I ensured that I was to become the eventual victor. James complained bitterly that I had acted unfairly to which I responded that no list of rules had been drawn up and I then demanded my guinea piece whilst fully aware that the wager had not been bound at the outset.

As we caught our breath and lay upon the grassy summit of Silbury Hill the purpose of our journey from Southwark to the bottle-glass factories in Bristol was soon to drift away like down upon the breeze to leave behind two indolent young men enjoying the sweetness of the air.

We were in time joined by a curious Welshman who made the ascent and was keen to attribute this mound to his Cambrian ancestors. James and I had not considered that this giant hill should be of human design at all and if it were so then by all means it should be our own

English pyramid. James was swiftly to his feet to take offence and said that the matter could be easily resolved and threw down his coat. By the look of this man's forearms I judged that he was used to heavy labour and was not at all a person to engage in pugilism. One hour before it had not mattered whether the Welsh or the English lay claim to Silbury Hill, for we had not yet arrived nor even knew of its existence. Our Cambrian friend ignored James' posturing and wished instead to debate the matter for his eloquence upon this subject was far more persuasive than his forearms could ever be. He had evidently contemplated the matter for many a year and passed this way often when walking between London and Bristol. He is a stoneworker and his name is Mr Edward Williams or indeed Iolo Morganwg. We had no mysterious second names by which to counter these claims or the barest consideration of the ancient activity of the English to redress the balance of the argument and so we lay about on the grass and listened to Mr Williams.

Before departing to continue his pedestrian journey to Bristol, our Welsh stonecutter cast his arm around in all directions to indicate the ancient activity that has occurred hereabouts. Indeed, at very close quarters to our elevated position the village of Avebury exists within an enormous entrenchment where vast crude stones have been raised and James queried whether these also were attributed to our friend's Cambrian ancestors. On receiving certain confirmation of this fact James sighed deeply and lay back upon the turf.

After saying farewell to the itinerant Welsh stonecutter my brother informed me that we were dull city dwellers and as we were in England and not Wales then it was beholden upon us to become familiar with these ancient haunts in case we met with another foreigner who availed to tutor us upon our own relics. I could but agree to this action and so we traversed back down the enormous man-made hill and spent a fine day discovering all manner of ancient curiosities. We later encountered jumbles of rocks that littered this green sward and did provide the material for the great stone circle in the village of Avebury and also, so we have been informed, the giant stones of Stonehenge. These are called "Sarcen" stones and how they came to be formed only adds to the plethora of mysteries that abound in this quarter of Wiltshire. James raised the question of how these tremendous stones may have been transported from their place of origin to the village of Avebury and indeed to the distant site of Stonehenge. The urge was then upon me to abandon my quest for the investigation of bottle-glass manufacture in Bristol and to make instead a journey upon foot to Stonehenge. I could not however break from the bond of responsibility to my father for he has finally given sanction to my idea of a bottle glass factory as an annex to Chalk's Brewery and the creation of our own bottled "Superior Stout", to rival any in London and indeed to export far and wide across the globe. Chalk's Brewery must come before any antiquarian ramble and so I urged James to accompany me to the Beckhampton Inn that we may collect our luggage and resume our journey to Bristol. We rushed a decent meal and it was necessary to ride on the outside of the next coach to Bath and then on to Bristol.

....And so ends this fragment of my Father's journal from May 1782

Friday 2nd September 1808

MY DEAR UNCLE,

This early morning I departed from London upon the Golden Cross coach where I was surely fortunate to secure an inside seat. In the darkness we settled together like chickens in a coup and I soon lolled into a skittish slumber to join the snuffling chorus of my fellow passengers. As the earth rotated in union with the grinding wheels dawn was reached somewhere near Slough and from thereon loud conversation intruded upon my wandering dreams. Eventually at the town of Marlborough I decided to abandon my precious seat, although I had paid to Beckhampton, for I was keen to feel the earth beneath my feet and begin life again as a pedestrian tourist. In truth, neither could I proceed for another minute in the company of a proud hangman by the name of Mr William Brunskill. There was not one condemned felon who had escaped the "drop" by the hand of this boastful executioner upon the gallows outside Newgate Gaol and each fatal episode was revisited for the entertainment of his fellow passengers. A pocket book, produced by Mr Brunskill, prompted the recital of this morbid litany and after being passed amongst us we were then informed as to the nature of the leather binding of this small volume for it was indeed a portion of skin from the cadaver of the notorious Owen Haggerty. One fascinated lady passenger was encouraged by the hangman to draw this vile relic across a large wart upon the end of her nose with a certain assurance that this disfigurement would soon be made to vanish entirely by such contact. I can inform you, my dear uncle, that Mr Brunskill is away from his place of work to invest his gallowside manner and tales of finality upon a dying relative in Bristol. After divulging his purpose, Mr Brunskill leant across to wink at me.

"Hope never made a rich man, did it ever Mr Chawk?" Thereafter, and for the remainder of the journey, I tried not to meet the hangman's eye.

The coach finally halted at the Castle Inn which is situated at the western margins of the town of Marlborough. After hastily collecting my pack and thumbstick, I had barely taken my first draught of sweet Wiltshire air when I spied before me a grand curiosity. Placed upon the valley floor and within a stone's throw of the Inn exists a huge mound that was partially concealed under a cloak of vegetation. A brief inspection revealed substantial terracing and it is unlike any Wiltshire barrow that I have yet encountered. I wonder as to the antiquity of this giant heap and confirmed aloud to myself that this could not be Silbury Hill for I have seen Mr William Stukeley's book of "Abury" where Silbury Hill is shown to stand alone upon open ground. I dutifully began to count my steps around the base of the mound and upon the near completion of this circuit I became fully distracted from my task by the approach of the hangman, Mr William Brunskill.

"Oh my gawd Mr Chawk..what 'ave I done? I've only sent me trunk on to the Beck..summat..Inn. Treat me kind Mr Chawk for I ain't done nuffink like this before."

At first I could not comprehend this circumstance as to why the proud hangman was not aboard the coach that I could now see departing with fresh horses from the yard of the Castle Inn.

"What 'ave I done?" repeated Mr Brunskill as he flapped his hat at a small host of late summer flies that had gathered above his head, "I says to myself, if I is to become a gent'mun then I must do's gent'munly fings and I sees you as a proper young gent'mun Mr Chawk, a proper young gent'mun, but I ain't got no boots I ain't."

I now regretted deeply, whilst aboard the coach, my expounding of the pleasures available to the pedestrian tourist for I knew not the consequence of this idle conversation. I could see no remedy to this

situation with the hangman entrusting himself to my company for the
journey ahead, until I was able to reunite him with his belongings at
the Beckhampton Inn.

I then produced John Cary's map of Wiltshire that is much travel
worn but still legible and I gauged that we had a walk of six miles ahead
to Silbury Hill and thereafter a short distance on to Beckhampton.

"Wos that then, Mr Chawk?"

I explained that it was a map of the County of Wiltshire and
that all pedestrian tourists should be in possession of a map.

"Ooh, then I must gets a map", confirmed the hangman to
himself.

At first I thought that if I struck out at a decent pace my already
perspiring walking companion would quickly reconsider his hasty
decision and return instead to the Castle Inn to await the next coach
to Bristol but Mr Brunskill dutifully trotted on behind, whistling
as he went, with his short arms dangling at his sides. The afternoon
was set fair and we soon crossed the gentle River Kennet by a narrow
footbridge where I made a halt. By shading my eyes against the sun,
I tried to establish the make up of the stones upon the river bed but
I soon became aware that Mr Brunskill was observing my posture
closely and he then emulated my stance to the extent of shading his
own eyes although he knew not what he observed.

"Very good Mr Chawk, very good indeed."

As I departed from the bridge the hangman paused to make his
own observation.

"Look see, an 'orse. A white orse up on the 'ill."

With a stumpy finger my uninvited companion eagerly gestured
towards the higher slopes of the valley to the south of the town of
Marlborough and I looked back with little enthusiasm to observe
the figure of a large horse engraved upon the hillside. Whilst turning
abruptly to continue on my way I stated that it had surely been created

by the removal of the overlying turf to reveal the gleaming chalk that abounds in this county and I could offer no account as to its purpose.

"A chawky 'orse," mused Mr Brunskill and he then chuckled to himself, "Mr Chawk on 'is chawky 'igh 'orse."

No amount of purposeful striding or lengthy pondering was sufficient to dampen the enthusiasm of the hangman for whatever my action, it was deemed to be appropriate to the business of pedestrianism and Mr Brunskill was now my attentive student. We continued by peaceful lanes to the village of Manton where I announced brusquely that we should leave the valley in pursuit of a view with a desire to ascend the downs that lay to the north of the Bath road. To further bemuse my walking companion, the downs were made to wait their turn for in a narrow meadow, placed between a twist in the river and the turnpike, we there stumbled upon three large recumbent sarcen stones to match in scale those found amongst the outer circuit at Stonehenge. I quickly set to, pacing about the place to inspect the length and breadth of these broad stones and also the degree of workmanship undertaken by the ancient stonemasons. There is also a large pit adjacent to these resting giants that tells of a fierce conflagration, not long occurred, with broken and blackened fragments of stone at its base.

Mr Brunskill soon found a perch upon one corner of a huge sarcen block where he puffed contentedly on his pipe whilst observing my antics. In my excitement I spoke of the late Mr William Stukeley for he laments the past destruction of the erected sarcen stones that abound in this mysterious land and decries this practice as an "atto de fe". If the stone stands erect then a pit is dug beside it and this stone is then made unstable by further digging. Loose rocks are placed in this execution pit and the condemned stone is then tugged and toppled to crash down upon them and a great fire of wood is started beneath the fallen sarcen. Once a tremendous heat has engulfed the giant, a line is drawn across the rock with cold water and this hissing mark is struck upon with great blacksmith's hammers and wedges are driven in to complete the task.

The hangman considered this statement at length before blowing out a stream of tobacco smoke that drifted steadily between us.

"Straw, Mr Chawk, not wood, straw."

I made a closer inspection of the pit and could now detect some residue of charred straw remaining at its base and confirmed that it would indeed make perfect sense to use straw at a time of harvest when, although still an expense, it was surely more plentiful than firewood.

Mr Brunskill then directed the long stem of his pipe towards my feet and shook his head slowly.

"Call's yerself a peddlestring tourist Mr Chawk? You needs the services of a good cobbla'."

I looked down and sure enough my stocking was there for all the world to see as the toe and the sole of my right boot had now parted company. To establish that it would take more than a damaged boot to deter my progress, we crossed the Bath road to explore the Downs.

In time we encountered an arrangement of sarcen lumps where a large capstone rests upon two irregular supporting stones and I have made a brief drawing for you my dear uncle.

I explained to Mr Brunskill that this was once a tomb and indeed I had seen others like it in Pembrokeshire, in South West Wales. Upon receipt of this information my curious walking companion nodded to himself as he now added this essential piece to his ever expanding inventory of prerequisites. As you well know, my dear uncle, the complete pedestrian tourist must at all times furnish the tales of his peregrinations with the casual and liberal inclusion of such far away places.

"Pem..burr ..oke ..shia," repeated Mr Brunskill, "very good Mr Chawk, very good indeed."

I peered beneath the capstone with no great expectation other than to meet the strong aroma of the sheep that had long sheltered here. Indeed, I was made to start violently, for the hangman had silently traversed to the opposing side of the structure and of a sudden forced his round head through an aperture to bark loudly in my face as if he were a mad creature.

"Grrrrahh."

In my surprise I clattered my head against the capstone as I recoiled from the tomb with Mr Brunskill making a low guttural laugh that became curiously exaggerated by the partial stone walls within the ruined tomb.

Unsettled by this wild-eyed unpredictability I hastened our retreat from the downs, preferring instead the security of the busy Bath road, but stating that the condition of my boot now made any further progress an impossibility. With a growing unease, I stumbled on as best I could with the hangman trailing close behind me. I wondered whether all was as it first appeared and my suspicions grew with every troubled step, regarding the purpose of this angel of death now poised at my shoulder. I have indicated, my dear uncle, that my good friends and colleagues have conspired to ensure my protection to see that I come to no harm for I have indeed given them good reason with my near burial in the flint pit behind the Winterslow Hut. There is also a silent concern that exists only in the expressions and glances between my adult protectors, although I am at a loss as to be able to identify this lurking danger. I confess that I pretend not to notice this clandestine mollycoddling but the circumstances surrounding the death of my father are a reoccurring whisper. To leave Southwark early with a desire to ascend Silbury Hill has laid me bare to whatever fate has in store and I now found myself alone in the company of a man who snuffs out life as one would extinguish a candle. Of a sudden the whistling had ceased and I had no means by which to gauge the hangman's proximity behind me. For a shocking moment I felt about my neck the hands of the executioner who quickly released his grip to thrust his short arms up further to clamp his hands across my eyes. As I called out in alarm the flapping sole of my boot caught a protruding stone causing me to sprawl upon the grass thereby releasing myself from the attentions of Mr Brunskill.

"Oh! Mr Chawk, oh my gawd."

The hangman was quick to lend his assistance and soon hauled me upright to set me down upon one of the ubiquitous sarcen blocks that populated the narrow valley in which we now found ourselves.

"There, there, Mr Chawk, you 'as a little rest."

The squat figure of Mr Brunskill sat down a short distance away upon another rock and dangled his shoes above the turf with his round face a picture of reassurance. After a moment he straightened his back and purposefully cleared his throat to break the silence.

"Good young Mr Chawk, I is 'umbly sorry for making you jump n' tumble n' squawk like a parrat. Old Brunskill's been finking about it and it ain't becomin' of one 'oo wishes to be a piddlestain tourist."

I stated that his action had indeed unsettled me for I was not prepared for such antics.

"It's wot they expects o' me Mr Chawk," exclaimed the hangman with a shrug, "if I ain't droppin' 'em at Newgate then I is scarin' 'em arf to deaf. It's wot I does."

I could only laugh out loud at this curious disclosure and Mr Brunskill chuckled also as he reignited his pipe.

"Then awl is now well, Mr Chawk?"

I confirmed that all was now well and we settled to look about at our surrounds to find that the grass here in this narrow valley was littered with rock and grazing sheep in equal proportions. There is indeed a similarity between wool and stone when viewed from a distance for it causes the curious illusion of sedentary mutton and shifting geology.

A small bird arrived and flitted from rock to rock until it settled upon one sarcen lump which had the added attraction of a natural sink of water in its pitted surface. Fine tail feathers lengthened this bird twofold and we watched as it bobbed about in its black, white and grey livery but with a scruffy face as if it were an unwashed urchin dressed to be a footman. This little visitor soon fussed in the water and gaily splashed about until it gave a haughty nod in our direction and dashed away in weightless flight, as if to mock our heavy earthbound existence.

"'Tis a good day Mr Chawk, a very good day."

I could but agree with the mischievous hangman after now dispelling my foolish doubts regarding his genuine interest.

"I believes that I shall makes a good puddlestrewn tourist Mr Chawk, in time, when I 'as got some boots, a map as you calls it, an' a stick."

I smiled to reassure the hangman that this would indeed be so but privately sir, I believe that a little restraint may be required if we are not all to jump from our skins when we least expect it.

Upon our departure from the rock strewn valley we took a lift with a carrier whose final destination was the town of Devizes that lies beyond the village of Beckhampton by some ten miles. We first diverted to the small villages of Lockeridge and West Overton before we finally rounded a corner and there before us rose the wondrous Silbury Hill and my stomach gave a giant leap for, as you will know, it is a truly astonishing sight. Ancient man has demonstrated that nature may be improved upon and that the gentle declivities of the Wiltshire chalklands required, in their estimation, an additional attraction. As the diminutive ant will gather in force to construct an anthill and so a forgotten population has mustered to build a gigantic mound, but under whose auspice this work was done makes a riddle to confound even the most diligent antiquarian. Plump Silbury Hill provides an ample target for any fool's bolt and the local wisdom offered by the carrier is that King Sel is buried here resplendent in a suit of gold armour and seated upon his horse. My dear uncle, if our enquiry proceeds no further than the acceptance of this tale then we might call this mound sepulchral and be done with it.

The carrier halted at the base of Silbury Hill and I was fully prepared to pay him a shilling for his trouble but Mr Brunskill would not hear of it and explained that he would now attend to the small business in hand. I was then forcefully encouraged to begin my assault upon Silbury Hill whilst the hangman struck a noble pose and declared his profession to the carrier with his foot firmly aboard the step of the cart to prevent any hasty departure.

"Deaf..'as bin my life," I heard the hangman announce cheerfully, as I crossed the turnpike with my boot now flapping open like the mouth of a panting dog.

There is a spur of ground that connects Silbury Hill with the adjacent road and I made my tentative approach by hopping upon a worn and narrow trail before this incline had me puffing greatly. I paused to catch my breath and then decided to dispense with my broken boot for it did more to hinder than to help. With my stocking slipping upon these mighty grass slopes, I was forced to crawl and tug my way to the summit of Silbury Hill. I confess that a great emptiness then descended upon me for I believe that I expected to find, revealed before me, two young men at liberty lying upon the grass enjoying the late afternoon sun. How ridiculous and impossible is this notion, my dear uncle, to follow with such expectation in my father's footsteps for I shall only ever catch up with him when I am dead? I then made a ponderous circuit of the broad plateau and looked out upon a vast panorama with unseeing eyes, thinking not of the view before me but all the while of my father. After retreating to the comfortable hollow at the centre of the summit of Silbury Hill, I took from my pocket the portion of my father's journal that described the scene played out upon this elevated stage over twenty five years ago. I had not read more than one sentence before Mr Brunskill's round head appeared on the horizon and having achieved the summit he staggered wildly, fanning himself with his hat. After his great exertion I thought that the hangman might expire before me as he took a succession of gasping breaths with the displaced phlegm of years gurgling in his chest.

"Mr Chawk...we musts ..'ave a little drink..come ..I 'as got money..on the account of sellin'..an inch of rope that 'ung 'Aggerty..to the lady wiv the fing on 'er nose in the coach..and a twist of 'Olloway's 'air to the country 'Arry . Come, ee's waitin' dahn the 'ill."

Mr Brunskill patted the coins in his purse and indicated for us to now continue on our way with the obliging carrier to the Beckhampton Inn.

"Piddlestrain tourists needs to sluice their gobs... same as any uva cove..'ain't that so Mr Chawk?"

I assured Mr Brunskill that I would soon follow on behind and catch him up at the Inn for I had some observations that I wished to attend to whilst still atop Silbury Hill.

"As you will Mr Chawk, as you will."

I watched as the hangman disappeared from view until all I could see from my hollow was the evening sky with its sparse high clouds now tinged with the golden hue of a retreating sun. I did not return to the reading of the page from my father's journal but instead let my mind wander until I became aware of voices and as I then believed that I would soon have company, I hastily raised myself and brushed away the late summer grass from my garments. It was soon apparent that the voices that I could hear came from the sloping fields that lay across the narrow valley where a team of men with great sickles were slicing their way through the ripened corn and I moved to the edge of my giant man made hill to observe this operation. As the corn stalks fell, they were gathered up by women with their backs bent to the task and these small bundles were in turn collected and propped together by labouring children into neat shapes and indeed the whole proceeding was conducted in an orderly and constant motion. This murmur of country voices bound together into a low moaning sound as if this tight gathering was but one weary machine moving slowly about the field. The periodic screeching of the sharpening stones across the long blades brought a brief halt to this labour and crooked backs were straightened before the invigorated steel again swept through the cornstalks to set this team into motion once more. Indeed, the harvest must be the zenith of all tasks in the agricultural calendar and now entering September the bulk of the prize is surely preserved in the farmyards and I wonder that the late August rain has caused some delay to the collection of these remaining acres.

My thoughts then settled upon Silbury Hill itself and there is a question that returns to me over and again when confronted by the great endeavour of our ancient ancestors; why are they so placed, these raised stones or giant mounds? I believe that we could today emulate our ancient ancestors by building a giant hill or by placing a stone lintel upon two upright sarcens, but there is a futility to this action for it is not bound up with the purpose of that forgotten time. Nor may we plant our modern antiquity in the correct place for we know not why one place is favoured above another. We may argue that Avebury is built at the place where sarcen stones naturally abide and yet Stonehenge lays some twenty miles to the south of this location. There is a chasm of knowledge that cannot be obtained by mimicry or indeed by sitting in quiet contemplation upon an anciently made hill, for that purpose is now lost and it shall not reveal itself.

Wisdom has not been gained by my clambering to the top of Silbury Hill and I am become overly sour in venting my frustration upon the study of our antiquities. Indeed, I now acknowledge that it was my father, or the pursuit of a relic of his once youthful character that has brought me to this place and the one mystery shall only compound the other.

Today the glorious sight of Silbury Hill signals the blowing of the post-horn of the west bound stage upon the Bath road to inform of their approach to the respective inns of Beckhampton. Just such a horn drew me from my reverie and so I began my slow descent to retrieve on the way my damaged boot.

At the Beckhampton Inn I was greeted with courtesy by the landlord and indeed my arrival had been expected for the celebrated principal hangman at Newgate Gaol had spoken very kindly of his new young friend. I enquired as to where I might now find Mr Brunskill and I felt a curious regret at the news that this same gentleman had just this minute departed for Bristol. I was taken aback when the landlord returned my thumbstick, for my walking companion had left it for me to collect and I knew not that I had mislaid it. I afforded myself a smile as I imagined the swaggering arrival at the inn of this novice pedestrian tourist, brandishing my thumbsick. I have perhaps acted unfairly in my dealings with the hangman and it appears as though he could wait no longer before continuing on his journey to comfort his dying relation. The landlord then produced a short portion of frayed rope and announced proudly that it had hung the evil Holloway and he excused himself to display this morbid relic to his other guests.

It is a problem at this busy inn to find a spare table corner upon which to write for everywhere is jostling, exasperation and impatience and I wonder how many travellers are expected to share a room and a bed in this place. A cobbler will attend to the repair of my boot in the morning and I must abide here at the Beckhampton Inn until his work is done.

Your confused but ever faithful nephew,

HENRY CHALK.

Saturday 3rd September 1808

MY DEAR UNCLE,

The day here at Beckhampton marches on without me for I am thwarted by the tardy cobbler as he deigns to keep me waiting and I am helpless without his attention to my boot. I have suffered a wretched night also as I have shared a bed with a seven foot giant who ensured that the trench in the centre of the mattress was his domain and my paltry share was but the sloping outer regions. The covers were also largely employed in the shrouding of this Man Mountain with only the flimsiest of sheet corners remaining for my comfort, despite my constant gripping and tugging. Indeed, a mountain is an inanimate thing so perhaps a volcano might better describe my bedfellow. During our nocturnal association we barely exchanged one word but at the breakfast table this same huge gentleman, observing the arrangement of my boiled egg in its cup, then remarked;

"Sir, I see that you are a Big-Endian, perhaps we should go to war over it?"

Indeed, it was true for his own egg was positioned in the opposing manner to clearly demonstrate his allegiance to the Emperor of Lilliput. To propose that such minor issues can lead to war is preposterous, but I believe that the author of Gulliver's Travels is of the opinion that the human race is not to be found wanting in that regard. Being unable to establish any common ground throughout the night we could now at least be reconciled in our admiration of Mr Swift's fine book and discuss the various merits of "Gulliver's Travels". As a consequence of my conversation with Mr Little, the name of this "Quinbus Flestrin", I am now greatly informed as to the sly satire that the author has concocted, for I knew not that the squabbles between Lilliput and Blefuscu referred to our own longstanding conflict with our troublesome neighbour France.

My gigantic bedfellow lowered his voice as he leant across the parlour table.

"You have encountered "A Modest Proposal", Mr Swift's most odious satire?"

With my mouth full I shook my head to indicate that I had not.

"A Modest Proposal for Preventing the Children of Poor People in Ireland from Being a Burden to Their Parents?"

This gentleman made no further explanation other than to nod grimly before dipping his egg and lowering the dripping finger of toast into his mouth, tearing and chewing slowly, whilst observing me through wide bloodshot eyes. At this display of provocative mastication I near choked on my food and protested that this was indeed an outrage, if I had interpreted his meaning correctly, and it was not at all a modest proposal.

"Indeed sir," agreed the giant, "it is a moral outrage that the author, who is himself of impecunious Irish origins, then turns upon the ruling government. It is satire at its most effective."

Of a sudden, I held no desire to complete my own breakfast and so I bid the enormous Mr Little a good morning and thanked him also for his illuminating instruction.

I have now taken a moment to consider that in six days time I shall be reunited with Miss Sarah Foster for it seems an eternity since our first and indeed our only meeting at Hindon on October last. Against my breast I have one of a pair of silver mounted flint hearts that were carefully manufactured in the workshops of Mr Henry Shorto of Salisbury. Flint is cold against the skin and as a consequence I can feel its presence in each and every waking moment. I confess that I had not considered this effect at the outset and did not wish such discomfort upon Miss Sarah Foster but she mocks my concern. In her letters that are by necessity written by her amanuensis, Mr Robert Foster, she states that she wears her gift always and only removes it if there is cause to make a spark for a fire or to skin a rabbit. Indeed, which other precious stone may be so useful and I am always greatly mollified by the fondling of my flint heart that hangs upon its silver chain.

In this hiatus there is perhaps an opportunity now to inform you of the events that occurred after my departure from the Winterslow Hut, for I have again been negligent in my correspondence to you my dear uncle. Is it not all or nothing with your errant nephew? I was still much confused after a blow to the head that I received as a consequence of my own foolishness in returning to the flint pit during the great storm. Mr Fenton has recounted to me how I attempted to depart upon my own from the Winterslow Hut but was found collapsed and insensible at the foot of the stairs. I wonder at the patience of my dear friends and also at the generosity of Sir Richard Colt Hoare, in permitting my convalescence at Stourhead. In due course the Baronet, in the company of Mr Fenton, then departed for a further tour of Wales and in the ensuing calm I was able to draft a small volume that I flatter myself may one day appear upon the shelves of the Baronet's great library. It will, in part, repay the dept of gratitude that I hold for Sir Richard Colt Hoare for there is as yet no book written on the purposefulness of flint.

Manufactured flint tools and their essential use in everyday life before the common availability of metal by the ancient people of South Wiltshire with an investigation into the likely sources of flint of the finest quality.

Or,

Life before the knife and fork

By

A Pedestrian

I was not to be left unattended at Stourhead and cherished greatly the visits of Mr Philip Crocker, who is the surveyor entrusted to the task of compiling detailed maps of South Wiltshire upon which each barrow, camp, British village or standing stone shall be charted. As a skilled draughtsman Mr Crocker has also to draw every drinking vessel, bead, brooch, lance, buckle, knife, battle axe and bodkin retrieved from the barrows to illuminate the Baronet's great work called "Ancient Wiltshire". After explaining his many duties, I then shared my modest notions of an investigation into the simple flint tools of the ancient common-folk for whom there are no raised barrows. Flint shall not decay and the scatterings of a remote stone industry may still be found amongst the plough soil today. I explained that I had found crude tools for scraping the fat from a hide, sharp blades to cut, points for piercing leather and all in the vicinity of Stourhead, whilst I walked the fields during my convalescence. A discreet visit to the game larder enabled me to test my theories and the flint scraper, which is perhaps the most ubiquitous of the finished tools to be found in the soil, shall gather up and collect the animal fat whilst not puncturing the valuable skin. Mr Crocker listened attentively to my theories before adding his own thoughts.

"The ancient past is indeed under our very nose Henry for we have been distracted by the chattels of the kings and queens. Perhaps these clusters of simple tools and chipped flint indicate where the common habitations once stood?"

He then cheerfully toasted me with a glass of sack and declared his support for this most worthy undertaking.

"To Mr Henry Chalk, in his search for the shadows cast in the soil by the ancient subjects of a forgotten king."

We both laughed openly at this exchange, which I take to be the signs of a burgeoning friendship.

I shall now put down my pen and again join Lemuel Gulliver upon his travels, for I now better understand the satire of this fine book and it is a comfort to know that my father once turned these very same pages.

*

My plans are profoundly altered and Avebury must remain idle and unexplored. I am embarked upon a journey that my father once contemplated before the bond of responsibility to his own father and to Chalk's Brewery determined that he should reject such distractions. Sir, you will have surmised by now that my destination is Stonehenge and I am resigned to the fact that I will not discover my father on the way. Indeed, I now smile at my own vain expectation that by some inexplicable means he should have awaited my arrival atop Silbury Hill.

Safe in the knowledge that I am no Pennant, Warner or Gilpin, it is not my intention to leave a trail of ink for others to follow but I can report that I am in or near the village of Marden, if I am reading Mr Cary's map correctly. I have before me yet another man-made hill that I shall soon attempt to record once I exchange my pen for a pencil. I hope in time to explain the circumstances of my repaired boot and to then praise the soaring profiles and swooping declivities of the high chalklands that lie to the south of Silbury Hill. There is also an extraordinary piece of flint retrieved from the sandy soils of this pleasant vale that requires explanation but such are the circumstances of a most unusual encounter, not long occurred, that all of the above must wait their turn.

My dear uncle, if you will consider a south bound pedestrian tourist now into his stride but ever susceptible to distraction and a giant cleric, brim full of purpose, pacing eastwards along the bank of a newly constructed canal, then surely serendipity will cause their paths to cross. I can inform you that these two beings did not collide and it was but curiosity on my part that sufficiently delayed my progress as I gazed down upon the idle waters of the canal from a fine new bridge and only then observed the huge gentleman ambling along the towpath towards me.

"Leaks, leaks and springs," announced the clergyman as he grew ever larger and then mounted the bridge with hand outstretched, "I am the Reverend Joseph Townsend of Pewsey and I inspect our portion of the Kennet and Avon canal weekly, for leakages between the towns of Devizes and Pewsey."

Before the act of wrapping his great hand around my own to grip and then shake it with some force, I observed curious ink characters written upon each fingernail and my face surely betrayed some puzzlement for an explanation was immediately forthcoming.

"Ah, you are familiar with Sanskrit? I propose that there is but one original language from which all others are derived but I must first explore these remote scripts. It is a means by which to learn for it is the very nature of fingers to remain visible at all times of the day."

I finally introduced myself to this colossus who I could now see at close quarters was indeed an elderly gentleman although his gait and motion were a country mile from any apparent infirmity. He possessed a great domed brow and a penetrating gaze that quite made me falter as I explained my own purpose which grew more insignificant with each word uttered. To lend gravitas to my tale I then seized upon the plight of the common labourer for I had been greatly troubled by their abject appearance, which is indeed the truth. As I passed from the high chalk lands and entered this level and sandy vale, I had witnessed the gleaners at their work. These are teams of women and children who scour the brushed golden stubble for any remaining ears of corn at the conclusion of the harvest. Indeed, harvesting and its aftermath is hard labour and it is no wonder that the country folk are bent and crooked of gait. Many are also gaunt faced and it is a crime that they are not better nourished when the production of victuals lies at the heart of their labour and a great deal of money shall, in the months ahead, be exchanged at the corn market. Thinking in part of Chalk's Brewery, I concluded by stating that all business requires labour but you do not underfeed your horse for it shall not have the strength to pull the dray, cart or indeed the plough and therefore I could not comprehend why the common labourers were treated so.

I was soon informed that the poor must exercise themselves in all manner of gainful work and the desire to eat shall sweeten even the severest labour.

"Mr Chalk, the poor cannot throw themselves upon the mercy of the parish and must instead help themselves. No man should seek assistance unless he has exhausted all means within his own power and it is the Poor Laws that are at fault for they only perpetuate the problem and must be reformed without delay."

The clergyman paused to shake his enormous head with his great brow rippled in consternation.

"The population will only exceed its natural bounds and charity without limits shall but increase the population and bring about a greater distress and dissipation."

I was now aghast for I detected not a trace of compassion for the common labourer and stated brazenly that I found these views to be most un-Christian.

At this the giant Cleric loomed towards me and I drew back to the parapet of the bridge. I was now entreated to a simple parable by which to demonstrate the struggles of mankind and a natural order from which the human race was not immune.

"Young Sir, if you will imagine a south sea island..you have read Robinson Crusoe? Good. Well, please dispense with Robinson and Man Friday for we require an uninhabited place save for a herd of goats that roam freely and their numbers increase for it is a verdant place with plenty for the goats to feed upon. One day a greyhound and a bitch are washed ashore," he held up his great hand to prevent the questioning of these circumstances, "the dogs breed and feed upon the goat population and at first there is sufficient for both the goats and their predators but in time Mr Chalk, the dogs become more abundant and the goats take to the mountains to ensure their survival, for the dogs cannot follow upon the steepest rocks and enter these craggy places. It is only the strongest goats that will survive this terrain and as a consequence it is only the fittest dogs that will still catch the goats and so a balance is met. The weakest of both species shall not survive and so a strong race of goats and greyhounds will populate the island."

The clergyman drew his inky fingers together and smiled benignly with the presentation of this gift of logic that surely reduced the human race to nothing better than a struggle amongst animals. My thoughts returned to the circumstances of my breakfast at the Beckhampton Inn when, in the company of another giant, I was informed of Mr Jonathon Swift's most lacerating satire. Before uttering my own parting gift, I carefully extricated myself from between the parapet of the bridge and the towering presence of the Rector of Pewsey.

"With respect I find yours a most *Immodest Proposal* and had Mr Swift concocted it then he would feel justly pleased with himself. Good day sir."

As I scuttled from the bridge, with all the while keeping an eye behind me, the Reverend Joseph Townsend turned abruptly about and uttered not one word but I could feel his hard stare until I was hidden from view.

My dear uncle, I am a poor reporter of useful information and had our discourse taken a different turn then I would surely be able to elucidate fully upon the exact progress of the new Kennet and Avon canal. It is indeed a bold and expensive venture and transportation between the cities of Bristol and London shall be greatly improved with benefits also to the many smaller towns and villages along the way. Earlier this year I suggested in all seriousness to Mr Gerrity, our brewery manager, that we should consider the establishment of tied houses beyond the environs of London and this notion was spurred on by my reading with interest about the new Kennet and Avon canal. I firmly believed that we should seize the opportunity presented by the canal before our competitors do so in our stead but Mr Gerrity was not to be so easily persuaded and stated that we should consider the great cost of acquiring the necessary property and also the very slow turn around of the casks. A further obstacle was the necessity for regular inspections of the beer by our collecting clerks and with my enthusiasm truly dampened I conceded that Chalk's Golden Pale Ale in bottle must be our sole new venture. I now make a silent vow that Chalk's beer shall one day pass under the new bridge, albeit in glass rather than wood.

No water had visibly leaked from the canal during my curious encounter but a valuable portion of time had ebbed from the day and my fleet footed departure was indeed justified in preserving the daylight hours for the business of pedestrianism. (Sir, as you will know by now pedestrianism also embraces feverish scribbling, amateurish drawing, idling, dreaming and disturbing the common order of places on the way.)

Here in the village of Marden stands the third enormous man-made hill that I have witnessed in this most curious quarter of Wiltshire and indeed it is a land to rival any visited by Lemuel Gulliver. The mound is sorely damaged as if a giant had spooned out its interior and destroyed the form of this vast upturned pudding. It is a place of great mounds, outlandish giants and giant white horses and I have named it Gorabhumlor. Perhaps my father was justified in expressing his caution as to the effects of my reading Mr Swift's extraordinary book when not yet fully grown to adulthood.

*

Sunday morning

My dear Uncle,

I have a tale to tell that will very soon make you cradle your head in despair at your avuncular association with this pedestrian tourist, for he is surely unrivalled in disturbing the common order of people and places. Perhaps there is also a book that should be penned on how flint shall cause a great deal of trouble in the hands of one Henry Chalk for there are chapters already writ and I will now contribute further to this record of irresponsible behaviour. From my position beside the river Avon I can hear the peeling of the church bells from up and down this broad valley for the sound travels well upon the water. I shall write and then rest a while for I have only slept fitfully since my arrival in Wiltshire.

I resume my tale in the small village of Marden where there exists a fine display of ancient activity for in addition to an enormous man-made hill there is a vast encompassing bank with a broad internal ditch and the winding river concludes the southern boundary of this earthwork. A walk about the village of Marden has revealed that a number of weighty sarcen blocks have been secreted about the place as the church tower sits upon a nest of these alien rocks, perhaps to prevent it from sinking into this sandy vale. At the mill also, the meandering river has large sarcen revetments set into these soft and vulnerable banks to assist in their preservation. I have today neglected the considerable ancient works about the village of Avebury, but I have before studied Mr William Stukeley's fine book dedicated to the antiquities of that place and the illustrations within ably depict that a large population of gargantuan sarcen stones are stationed within its own circular enclosure. I am left to wonder whether modern man has prospered here by the labours of the ancients for may not these most useful rocks, now beneath the church and alongside the river, once have adorned this giant enclosure at Marden in the same manner as Avebury? It is indeed a considerable distance from their place of origin, near Marlborough, but ancient man has already proved his tenacity in this regard, by moving these same pieces across Salisbury Plain to Stonehenge and Marden is but half that distance, according to Mr John Cary's map of Wiltshire.

As you may establish from my drawing the huge mound has suffered in recent times and I fear that there may soon be a level field where a great mystery once stood, if it is now the farmers will. I sincerely hope that this work was not undertaken in the name of antiquarian curiosity for reparation should rightly follow such intrusive investigation.

In time I left behind this gentle sandy vale and with the climbing of a long escarpment found myself upon the vast and elevated hub of chalk that is Salisbury Plain. I have been informed before that many a traveller has become lost upon the great plain and so it was with a degree of timidity that I chose to walk its periphery and thereby kept a reassuring view across the Avon Valley.

The sheep flocks are numerous and the shepherds are keen to seek company upon their lonely vigil and I have established that the great sheep fairs are soon to be held about South Wiltshire and so a greater massing of these flocks is to be expected in the following days. The sheep shall have their say and save for a gaggle of aggrieved geese these creatures are surely the most vociferous of all livestock for the contagion of a single bleat of alarm shall spread quickly to become an infuriating cacophony. It is indeed little wonder that the shepherds themselves are wild eyed and askew in their manner and cling to a passing stranger like a drowning man to a bobbing barrel.

On these elevated fringes of high chalkland I encountered the very last throes of harvest for I was drawn to investigate a large earthwork called Casterly Intrenchment, upon John Cary's map, and the internal acres were already turned to a golden stubble save for a scruffy twist of standing corn. The large band of harvesters were now engaged in song and good natured exchanges whilst reclining in the outer ditch and thus in their sunken position did not witness my arrival. Amidst this broad expanse of stubble a huge cloud of identical birds were engaged in their own act of gleaning and I observed as they traversed these cropped acres in a great rolling wave with those at the back leapfrogging to the fore until this great twisting black swarm departed for a neighbouring field. A good number of stooks of corn lay about awaiting collection, amongst which were strewn the harvester's tools and I picked up a sickle to feel its weight in my hand. It appeared negligent not to complete the final act of harvest when all about had been cleared and remembering the piece of fashioned flint that I had earlier in the day gleaned from the sandy soils of the vale, the opportunity now presented itself to test the keenness of this long blade. From end to end I gauge that it measures in excess of five inches and I shall not hesitate to proclaim it a broad blade for the greatest attention has been given by its maker to fashion the long convex curve

The Hangman at Devil's Den

The Hatfield Barrow

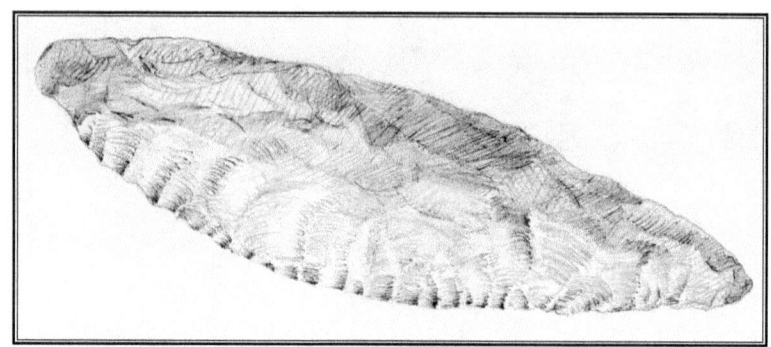

The Flint Sickle

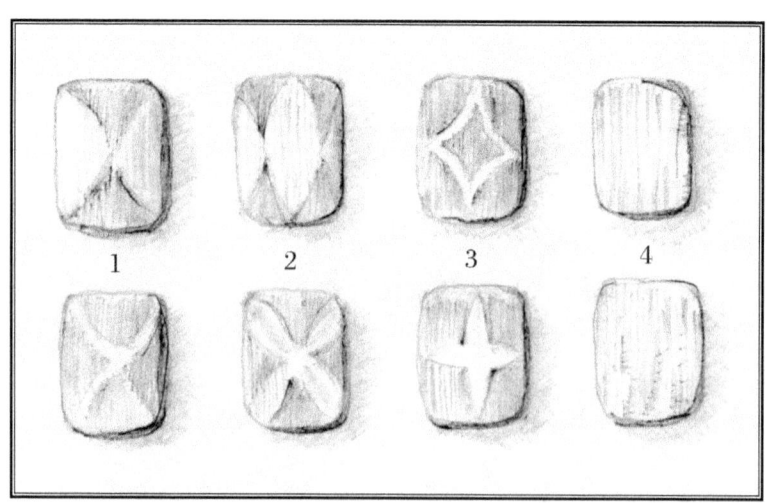

1 2 3 4

The Conjuror's Playthings

of its cutting edge. The most perplexing aspect of this piece is that it glistens along this finely made edge and I have never before witnessed such ancient magic. After removing my pack, I gripped firmly the sole remaining clump of standing corn to make it taught and then ripped at the foot of the plant with my flint and indeed I had some success in severing the stalks one at a time. I then held the piece with a straight finger supporting from behind on the opposing blunted edge and slashed at the remaining standing corn and found this a better means by which to operate with this ancient tool. As I stood amongst the stubbles with the final cut of the annual harvest gathered in the crook of my arm I wondered whether this was the true purpose of this crafted flint and that it was instead a crude sickle rather than a knife as I first thought and I had now fortuitously put the piece to its rightful use. I imagined it set in a cleft of wood for a handle and I also wonder that the glossy polishing of the cutting edge may have been caused by its repeated contact with the ripened corn stalks, if indeed ancient man grew corn as we do today.

As I juggled with these perplexing issues, I was spotted by the harvesters who to a man, woman and child quickly scampered from their sunny ditch to surround me in large number and the remnants of severed corn and also the flint piece were then hastily snatched from my person. By the look of anger and consternation upon these country faces I feared that I may now be dealt with harshly for the crowd of harvesters jostled and jeered about me whilst I knew not the cause of their grievance. A young woman broke free of the melee and held aloft the severed clump of cornstalks whereupon the throng of rustic voices called out as one;

"A neck, a neck we do 'ave un."

At the conclusion of this curious chant a great cheer was made but this distraction was short lived and a labourer with a dark and bristling beard turned and pushed me firmly to the ground and then spat upon his hands as if we were now to engage in a bout of pugilism.

As he gestured again for me to stand, I decided to remain amongst the stubbles whilst another call went up from the harvesters.

"Yerr's the Squire, the Squire's coom."

The belligerent mood amongst the harvesters now turned to panic as fifty or more of the labourers scampered amongst the remaining stooks of corn to collect their scattered tools. The galloping hooves of the Squire's mount resounded thunderously upon the dense chalk mass of the Plain as if it were not a man at all but instead a giant that was fast approaching. Wide eyed and ashen faced the bearded man stood with some reluctance to the fore of the cowering harvesters and removed his hat as the rider pulled up before him. The Squire glowered down upon the meek assemblage and his stentorian voice boomed out across Casterly Intrenchment.

"You bring shame to Widdington. Never in my father's day were we the last farm to bring in the harvest. We shall long hear the gibes up and down the valley. Your father was never late with the contract when he was harvest lord. We shall be a disgrace to both our father's names. Explain yourself man?"

The bearded labourer stammered that they had suffered badly with the weather but his excuses were soon disregarded by the mounted Squire.

"It is the same for all, the same for all...and who is that upon the ground?"

The Squire coaxed his horse to encircle the harvesters to examine this stranger in their midst. The gathering now recovered their voice and all clamoured together to describe the part I had to play in the disruption of the final act of harvest as if I were now in some way to be blamed for the protracted lateness of the whole.

"Ee did cut the neck, Zquire zur.. with thic vlint."

The Squire looked down upon me and his voice again boomed forth.

"What is your name sir and why are you cowering amongst the stubbles?"

I hastily stood and gave my name but was interrupted from any further explanation by the harvest lord in his attempt to regain some pride before the gang of harvesters.

"Oi did push un thur zur,"

"Aha, and a wish to bloody his nose I'll wager? Well get to it man. Mr Chalk, defend yourself."

With the arrival of the booming Squire I thought my prospects improved but he now appeared as keen as any to witness a fight and as I made no move to prepare for battle, the Squire drew closer with his horse.

"Are you a man or a boy?"

I declared that I was a traveller who did not wish to fight at all and apologised wholeheartedly for my interference with the last rites of the annual harvest, for I knew not that I had done wrong.

"It is done sir, for whatever the reason and now cannot be undone."

At this impasse the Squire frowned and the harvesters muttered amongst themselves whilst a wagon lumbered slowly towards us bedecked with ribbons.

"There are two things that must now occur," broadcast the mounted Squire, "if there is to be no honour established. You sir, must firstly pay a generous largesse toward the harvest celebrations to assuage for your interference here today."

The harvesters nodded vigorously and the harvest lord led a loud cheer at this welcome proposal.

"Secondly," announced the Squire, effortlessly silencing the excitable group with an extraordinary vocal power, "he who cuts the neck must sit at the table for our celebration of the harvest, for that is the custom. Mr Chalk, like it or not, you shall be joining us this evening. It is a situation of your own making."

The harvesters were audibly less keen on this second condition but had to concede the correctness of the Squire's ruling. The paying of the largesse was to be undertaken immediately and I knew not what sum was appropriate and looked to the Squire for guidance.

"It is a negotiation to be conducted between the passing stranger and the harvest lord. Mr Chalk you have blindly stumbled upon a custom that is centuries old."

I duly paid my largesse and my disadvantage was surely exploited by the emboldened harvest lord. The wagon now arrived carrying the very young and the very old to welcome home the harvesters and to collect the final stooks of corn. The all important "neck" was received aboard with great reverence and after further cheering I was then invited to accompany the final journey of harvest from field to farmyard. The Squire galloped on ahead and there was a deal of muttered explanation to the elders who had just arrived and ensuing scowls at this young stranger in their midst. I walked behind the laden wagon in silence wishing again that I had given more thought to my actions. A flask was thrust towards me by a young labourer which proved to contain cider and I was indeed glad to quench my thirst. There was an expectant mood amongst the harvesters with the knowledge that a feast lay ahead and neither a berating by the Squire at the lateness of the harvest or indeed my interference could subdue the weary labourers who sang with gusto under the open skies of Salisbury Plain.

I shall now rest a while before continuing on my way and in due course I promise to conclude the account of the harvest celebrations.

*

Sunday evening

MY DEAR UNCLE,

I am now comfortably installed at the George Inn in Amesbury with pen in hand whilst Mr John Fenton is playing a pleasing Welsh air upon his flute before the open window in the next room. There is still much to report and I am gratified also that there appears to be some distance between Beckhampton and Amesbury upon Mr John Cary's map for Mr John Fenton duly raised an eyebrow upon my arrival when I demonstrated the full span of my finger and thumb between these two places.

"Henry, your appetite for itinerancy is admirable but I understood that that you were to travel directly from Southwark to Amesbury?"

I explained that I had found a portion of a diary or notebook in my father's hand that described an unscheduled visit to Silbury Hill in the year 1782 when he and his brother James, my uncle, were travelling to Bristol upon business and it was indeed a flight of fancy on my part that caused me to follow in their footsteps. I was then scolded for behaving without responsibility and I am now bemused by this new concern for I have experienced before John Fenton's propensity for raillery. I am, however, pleased to be reunited with Mr Richard Fenton's eldest son who has informed me that he is still attempting to straighten his back after a lengthy journey from Pembrokeshire.

"I calculate that I have aged ten years in that wretched coach whilst you have a brightness in your eyes that speaks only of pleasurable travel. I believe that I must accompany you Mr Henry Chalk on one of your pedestrian excursions."

With this declaration John picked up my thumbstick and with a crooked back and ancient voice to match he embarked upon a circuit of the parlour tapping at the flagstones.

"I am old and cannot see..is young Chalk ahead of me?"

I know not whether this desire is genuine but I hold no doubt that Mr John Fenton shall require company this evening and so I must continue with my account of the final gathering of the harvest upon the eastern fringes of Salisbury Plain.

The destination for our noisy entourage was Widdington Farm which nestled comfortably in a valley below Casterly Intrenchment. A number of rotund corn ricks were already constructed in the farm yard and the scene was made gay with ribbons and green garlands. A large barn was to be the setting for the harvest supper and I clung sheepishly to the shadows of a broad elm tree whilst the final preparations were being conducted. The harvesters, who were not engaged in the building and thatching of the final rick, sat about in clusters drinking cider and singing rounds whilst the children played and danced.

The Squire now emerged from the farmhouse where he had paid a visit to the farmer who had been made absent from the proceedings as he was laid abed with a broken bone in his leg.

After inspecting the great bulging ricks, the Squire spied my attempted concealment in the shadows of the great tree and marched across the farmyard to stand before me with hands on hips.

"I recall Mr Chalk that I have not yet introduced myself. I sir, am Henry Hunt."

I had never before heard mention of this gentleman's name and simply offered my hand to be shaken but he at first ignored this gesture for he appeared bemused by my lack of surprise at his disclosure.

"Then you are not a gossip monger and as such shall form no opinion other than by your own judgement of the man that stands before you?"

"Indeed, I shall not sir," I replied.

I dared not ask the nature of such notoriety that should arm my prejudice and I explained instead that I was a pedestrian tourist who was to meet shortly with Mr William Cunnington and his family upon Stonehenge Down where a further campaign of barrow opening was due to commence. I explained that under the patronage of Sir Richard Colt Hoare a great deal of antiquarian investigation has already been undertaken to assist with this same nobleman's forthcoming publication that is to be titled "Ancient Wiltshire". I felt certain that these associations might help my cause in the eyes of the Squire but he was quick to undermine such presumptions.

"A fine distraction, I must say, from the important matters of the day. He made a negligent High Sheriff, vanishing into the wastes of Wales, when his duties were plainly at home in Wiltshire upon matters of national importance."

Surprised as I was by this accusation, there was no requirement for me to question this circumstance as Mr Henry Hunt gave a voluble and lengthy account of how he once addressed a public meeting of freeholders in Devizes to protest at the conduct of Lord Melville, who was then the Treasurer of the Navy. Lord Melville was implicated in defrauding the public of the monies entrusted to his position and all across the kingdom public meetings were being held calling for a full enquiry into the matter.

"Getting wind of the gathering storm the High Sheriff, your Sir Richard Colt Hoare, was nowhere to be found and I proposed a vote of censure upon such irresponsible conduct. Being young in politics at the time I was prevailed upon to withdraw my vote after receiving an apology. It was to be my first entry into public life Mr Chalk and I have since gained many friends and enemies along the way and amongst the latter shall sit the bloodsucking landowners of this county and those two corrupt factions the Whigs and the Tories. Amongst the former I count the oppressed and our Radical Reformers and indeed Mr William Cobbett for he frequently reports my various successes in his Political Register."

I had not heard of Mr Cobbett nor his publication and indeed my dear uncle you will know me to be one whose thoughts and aspirations are directed toward the past and I know little of political life and so I remained silent as Mr Hunt puffed out his chest and gave vent to his accomplishments.

Eventually he asked after my own affairs whereupon I made brief reference to Chalk's Brewery which sent this splenetic gentleman into a rage upon the dishonesty of brewers. He then boomed forth that his business venture in Bristol was recently made bankrupt where in attempting to brew fine and unadulterated beer he found the entire business racked with dishonesty, malpractice and skimping against which no honest man could compete.

"I suggest sir, that your business is no different."

My bile quickly rose to firmly defend Chalk's Brewery and I told this gentleman that the principals to which he claimed to adhere were identical to our own; hops and barley malt of the finest quality and indeed the purest water in all London from the new well that plunges six hundred feet below the streets of Southwark. I concluded that our family had been respected and conscientious brewers and that my father had proudly adhered to this tradition and I too, in my tenure, would now strive to do the same.

Mr Hunt nodded with approval, perhaps as much at my heartfelt and stout defence as at the description of our methods.

The convivial atmosphere in the farmyard was at odds with our heated exchanges and despite my apparent obligation to remain at the harvest celebration, I was to be no prisoner and would now challenge any that prevented my departure such was my anger. I had heard more than enough from the self-regarding Squire and was about to depart when a young maid with late summer flowers in her hair approached with two mugs of cider and offered them to Mr Hunt and myself. As I thanked the maid the Squire looked at me quizzically.

"Mr Chalk, am I to understand that you have succeeded your

father in the running of your business?"

I was taken aback at this enquiry but confirmed that my father had indeed died not eighteen months ago, an event which had projected me with some reluctance to face up to my responsibilities.

"Then please accept my sympathies at your loss Mr Chalk for you are still young."

The Squire then disclosed that it was the memory of his own father that caused him to make his infrequent returns to Widdington Farm for Mr Thomas Hunt had died eleven years ago and had been buried upon the eve of the "Harvest Home", the name given to this end of harvest celebration. Despite this gentleman's wind and bluster I now envy the fact that father and son grew up in accord and that Mr Hunt was at his father's side when he took his final breath and how I wish with all my heart that my own circumstance were the same. For all his propensity to enjoy the sound of his own booming voice, Mr Hunt listened to the tale of my abrupt departure from Southwark after the fortuitous finding of the page written in my own father's hand which led in turn to my divulging the tragic circumstances of his death.

"Then Mr Chalk we have found a common purpose for is it not our fathers that have brought us here today? We must now make a toast to their memory. I cannot assist with your perplexing tale and I was all for boxing your ears for disturbing the harvesters but now let all be forgotten. Our dear fathers!"

We both held a tear in our eyes as we raised our pots after which Mr Henry Hunt clapped me heartily on the back.

"Mr Chalk, you still appear bewildered by your presence here at Widdington. I should explain that the last sheaf of standing corn from the annual harvest is treated with great reverence by the harvesters and it has always been so. It is believed that the spirit of the harvest has retreated to those remaining stalks and such is their superstition that no man wishes to be responsible for this final act of severance or indeed meddle with the spirit for fear of endangering future yields. Despite the upheaval you have caused, and I do not wish to hear the reasons why, you have at least spared them this dread task and although none shall speak of it, to a man, woman and child they are silently relieved and of course have financially prospered by your actions. Sir, you may be at your ease this evening and no person here shall display any grievance towards you."

I felt a deal better after Mr Hunt's assurances and he now of a sudden excused himself to confront the parson who had just arrived in Widdington farmyard.

"Lo, it is the hungry parson."

Upon witnessing the Squire standing before him, the alarmed churchman briskly turned about his phaeton and departed from the harvest celebrations with the roar of Mr Henry Hunt's laughter ringing in his ears. Having emerged from the shadows to join the celebration, I and all present were now stricken and frozen in silence as the Squire's laughter faded and he turned to scowl at the harvesters.

"He is a parasite, you shall not clap eyes upon him from one year to the next for he lives not in Upavon and serves no person but himself. These swinging parsons must be made to lower their tithes, the landlords to lower their rents to the farmers and you must all receive a fair wage. To this end, nothing short of radical reform is required. Universal suffrage, freedom and free speech shall be denied you until there are honourable and independent men in government. I am such a man. I am a friend to the poor."

Mr Henry Hunt now stood alone in the centre of the farmyard as his booming pledge resounded about the valley causing the roosting colony of large black birds atop the giant elm to take to the sky and the lame farmer to hastily arise and close his bedroom window. We may be there still, every man, woman and child as if we were ourselves a cast of anxious faces captured in a painting with the athletic figure of Mr

Henry Hunt bestriding all at its centre. Our uneasy hiatus ended as the Squire clapped his hands.

"Fiddlers, where are you? Then fiddle and let us enjoy our Harvest Home."

I cannot say that the Harvest Home at Widdington Farm was as merry an evening that might have occurred for the presence of the Squire surely inhibited the pleasures of a rare and hearty meal for the harvesters. I gazed upon the rows of stiffly assembled rustics within the old barn that was bedecked with greenery and observed the crooked backs, stooped necks and the course hands that spoke of years of faithful toil in the fields about Uphaven. The very old were not forgotten and sat welcomed amongst the throng, their labours now spent but I witnessed the spectre of hunger upon these country faces, young and old together. It requires only a poor harvest for which the farmer will be set back but it is the labourer who shall survive upon the scraps of harvest. He also depends greatly upon the scraps of land that are now become enclosed by the quickset hedge as the progressive farmer seeks to embrace this efficiency as directed by the Board of Agriculture, for I have before read Mr Arthur Young's recommendations upon my visits to the British Museum library. I gave my plum pudding to a young brother and sister and stole away to the shadows to sleep amongst the remaining stooks upon the harvest wagon and left Widdington Farm after the cockerel burst asunder my dreams.

I encountered a dead horse upon the road in Figheldean with no person in sight and I could only surmise that arrangements were being made for its collection. To view a lifeless thing, it is a miraculous puzzle as to how life itself can animate a collection of muscle, bone, tendon, sinew, and organs. Beyond the village of Durrington I beat a path with my thumbstick to enable me to bathe in the river Avon for I was hot from the labour of carrying my weighty pack but also to remove the itching dust from my night in the corn wagon. The water had an earthy smell and was not overly deep but as I cannot swim, I was happy to spread my arms wide to float a while, tilting my head back to stare up at the drifting clouds. Amidst these conflicting but gentle motions it was as if my mind was being drawn in opposing directions and with no solid ground to affix me, I was instead suspended somewhere betwixt earth and sky. In time I was forced to walk upon the stony bed against the push of the river with a tangle of snaking weed about my legs to return upstream. Between the stinging nettle and the bramble there was no place to rest in comfort and so I chose instead the short grass in the field above the river bank to lay down and dry my skin in the sun. I may have lain naked for longer if it were not for a persistent and silent long grey fly that attacked my skin leaving raised lumps. There is a vast circular earthwork not one hundred paces from the river that sits upon ground tilted heavily to the east and indeed the entrance is at the lowest point on this eastern side. It is, I believe, called Durrington Walls and has a vast bank and inner ditch, much in the manner of the work at Marden where is enclosed the enormous man-made hill. There is no hill at Durrington but it is indeed a work of great magnitude and so close in distance to Stonehenge that I cannot believe that the two places did not have some ancient association. Upon the way to my destination, I encountered a lone sarcen stone recumbent in a field that does not readily explain itself other than perhaps it is a marker or indeed a runty straggler that did not complete its journey to the stone circle. The Cursus is then met, which is itself a huge ancient undertaking comprising of two parallel banks with a broad expanse of level ground between these boundaries. The work is ruler straight and exceeds a mile in length and was first identified by that keen seeker out of antiquities, Mr William Stukeley who thought it an ancient course for a chariot race and it has therefore become the "Cursus", whether it be intended for that purpose or not. There are many features that are given names but they only serve as a convenient nomenclature for their origins and titles are lost to us. Stonehenge is another such name, for we must call it something. Ahead I could now see the object of my excursion and I walked there directly from the eastern conclusion of the Cursus. There is a small valley between these two places where all sight of Stonehenge is lost but it rises again with powerful intent upon the horizon, for I had now joined the alignment of the ancient processional Avenue. On this occasion the shepherds were elsewhere and I shuddered as I entered the building, for it is indeed a great building my dear uncle. I rested upon the green sward with my back to one of the larger upright sarcen stones and there I began to weep. After fulfilling the walk that my father once proposed I had no further expectation of bridging the void between life and death.

Through a blur of tears, I then witnessed a flickering of bright colour and there briefly upon the grass before me alighted a butterfly with its wings spread wide to savour the warming afternoon sun. I rubbed at my eyes to ensure that it was not a trick of the mind but here with the same crisp scarlet and white markings imprinted upon black velvet was the butterfly that had prompted my early departure from Southwark. No sooner had it appeared then it fluttered away across Stonehenge Down and as the sheep began to drift back amongst the great standing stones, I left this sacred place with my heart soaring for in that brief moment all was as it should be and heaven and earth were in accord.

*

As tired as I am, my dear uncle, and with my bed beckoning I must hastily document an incident that occurred this evening. Upon joining Mr John Fenton for a late dinner and despite there only being the two of us in our small parlour, an occasion was called for. At the conclusion of our meal John announced that regardless of our lowly number, we were required to perform our antiquarian duty to determine the will of the god's with regard to our success at the opening of the barrows upon

Stonehenge Down in the morning. Our table was cleared of all but
our goblets that were filled to brim with wine and Mr Morgan, the
landlord, was sought with a request for a silver bowl that was placed
between us. From his pocket John produced four small tablets of bone
and I now understood the purpose of this preparation for I had heard
mention before of the Conjuror's Playthings. Not two years ago, under
the guidance of Mr Cunnington with the two Mr Parker's, a number
of barrows were opened upon Wilsford Down by the landowner Mr
Edward Duke of Lake. Amongst a plethora of the more expected
treasures retrieved during this short but prolific campaign, were four
unusual small engraved bone tablets of which replicas were made at
the request of Mr Cunnington. These facsimiles were dubbed "The
Conjuror's Playthings" by Mr Cunnington who presented the set
to Sir Richard Colt Hoare with a written description of the likely
outcome at the casting of these lots. They were now inexplicably in
the hands of Mr John Fenton who claimed to be looking after them
for his father. I requested to inspect these mysterious objects where the
original engraved design had now been replicated in red ink. Upon
each face of the tablets a different pattern was depicted apart from one
tablet that was blank on both sides.

John was impatient to get started whilst I wished to discuss
the significance of such a discovery for surely this was as close to an
ornament of ancient writing that had yet been brought to the attention
of the antiquary.

"Yes, yes Henry, place them in the silver bowl and we must
now stand and turn to the east..with our goblets in hand."

Whilst standing I read from the list of various permutations that
had been contrived by Mr Cunnington for the purpose of antiquarian
entertainment before embarking upon further barrow excavation.
I shall not record them all for you my dear uncle but a poor return
may state; "You will not attain your ends. Stay at home." whilst a

more encouraging indication of success might read; "Full completion
of your wishes". Once the bowl has been upturned it shall be the tablet
that settles farthest from the bowl that determines the outcome of this
mystical consultation.

After drinking deeply from his goblet, John vigorously cast
the Conjuror's Playthings from the silver bowl whereupon one tablet
tumbled from the table and despite our hasty examination of the floor
we could find no trace of it. At that moment the parlour door was
nosed open by the yard dog and being quicker in thought and action,
the animal spied the tablet of bone upon the flagstones and hastily
gobbled it up. The dog was then kicked back out into the yard by the
landlord with the parlour door slammed shut.

John slumped back into his chair and attempted to feign
unconcern at the loss of the tablet but was soon at the door peering out
into the dusk, hissing and making faces at the dog as it skulked in the
yard. I then excused myself for I had yet to conclude my account of last
evening and indeed of my journey today. Before departing I suggested
to John that it did not require a list of possible outcomes to know that
a dog eating the prophetic tablet was not at all a good omen. John
Fenton growled in response before refilling his goblet and continued
his vigil at the open door.

"Accursed animal, Henry is there a chance that the piece shall
reappear..in the morning..or perhaps I may be able to induce the thing
to wretch?"

I wish you a good night, my dear uncle, and I hold no doubt
that I shall sleep soundly in my bed.

Your weary nephew,
HENRY CHALK

POSTSCRIPT
There are two more issues that I must record to clear my mind and

to enable a blank canvas upon which to dream. My flint sickle is lost, despite my polite request for its return. I dared not mention it to the Squire and so it is left behind at Widdington Farm. May their future harvests be blessed and bountiful and perhaps the ancient flint sickle shall again perform the final act of harvest. In due course I will conclude a drawing that I began when the piece was in my possession so that you may obtain some idea of its form.

I realise also that I have not given an account of my repaired boot for I at first cursed the tardy cobbler in Beckhampton and I am now ashamed at my earlier impatience for the cobbler had been taken gravely ill and indeed it was his young daughter that completed the repair of my boot. Upon its return boots disparaged the quality of the finished work for it was perhaps not the neatest stitching but I believe that it will hold well enough and I gave boots a half crown for the cobbler's family, in addition to the cost of the repair.

Monday 5th September 1808

MY DEAR UNCLE,

It has indeed been a most eventful day and I can report that antiquarians far and wide shall marvel at the work undertaken upon Stonehenge Down by Mr William Cunnington and his two stalwart labourers Mr Stephen and John Parker.

After a comfortable night I arose very late from my bed and upon the completion of a fine breakfast I read a portion of Gulliver's Travels but in time I made my excuses to a fretful Mr John Fenton for I could no longer resist the urges of my feet. I explained that I would meet with Mr William Cunnington and his party upon Stonehenge Down although I hoped not to offend by my restless nature. John stated that he must await their arrival at the George Inn, lest there be any confusion on the matter and he wondered at their lateness for the appointed hour had come and gone with no sign of our friends. I had been informed that the day's activity lay to the outh of Stonehenge and so upon leaving the town of Amesbury and crossing the River Avon I sought a deviation from the toll road and was soon rewarded upon my ramble with a fine view across Stonehenge Down. It is no surprise to find a plump barrow at this location for it commands perhaps the highest aspect of the many tumuli that gather about Stonehenge. The stone circle stands dwarfed by its surrounds not a mile distant from this vantage point and is surely the hub of a vast and ancient graveyard. The tombs of these lost dynasties cluster together in mysterious affiliation upon the crests and elevations where Stonehenge must remain in view and to good advantage. A distant glimpse of whiteness, as the sun flared between passing cloud, signalled the position across the valley of the morning's toil by Mr Cunnington's two barrow diggers for the freshly exposed chalk shone like a beacon amidst the dry green hues of late summer. With this fortuitous guidance I left my lofty tree covered barrow and hurried to the conspicuous tumuli in expectation of witnessing the revealed secrets of the ancients. I found instead the two labourers laying in stillness, side by side, upon the summit of the barrow with the gaping excavation at their feet as if they themselves were awaiting burial. The gentle purring of contented sleep betrayed the notion of eternal rest for after the consumption of their victuals, Mr Stephen and John Parker, the two most experienced barrow diggers in the land, were now engaged in peaceful slumber. In my attempt at a stealthy retreat I tipped a nodule of chalk into the deep hollow with my boot, waking Mr John Parker with a start and he was soon to his feet in animated confusion, turning full circle upon the barrow for sight of Mr Cunnington and his party. Spying no one but myself he slowly retrieved his hat from the grass and employed it to give his father a gentle nudge.

"Bist git aan vather," said the younger of the two barrow diggers.

With reluctance Mr Stephen Parker relinquished the opium of pleasurable sleep and coughed himself awake before being hauled unsteadily to his feet by his son. I now felt at fault at this interruption to their rest and we stood in silence as the sun broke free into open sky to glare upon the chalk that surrounded us. I offered my name and explained that we had met before upon the chalk downs near Stourhead and the two men nodded together in sullen acknowledgement of this fact, touching their hats as they did so.

"Mizzer Chalk zur," they mumbled in unison.

The elder of the two labourers bent stiffly to gather his tools, adding his beer to the bucket and with a pick axe over his shoulder he plodded slowly away between the neighbouring tumuli. I felt bound to ask John Parker, as he collected his own tools, as to the prospects of the present excavation that lay open before us.

In response he retrieved some large shards of ancient pottery from a heap of spoil and held them out for my inspection, pointing to where they had been struck previously by a pick axe.

"T'wur avore we. Robbers zee, zo dwon't spec much wur no zense."

I have learned subsequently that the two labourers were surely deserving of their rest after leaving Heytesbury on foot in the early morning with their tools to commence opening barrows upon Stonehenge Down before I had stirred from my bed.

Stephen and John Parker now turned their attentions to the famous "Bush Barrow", so named for it displayed a crown of furze upon its summit and it was evident that a large portion of the tomb was already open and exposed to the elements. Father and son were still muttering to one another as to where they should begin their renewed examination within the open barrow when Mr Cunnington's carriage finally arrived and the quietude of Stonehenge Down was replaced by the fluster and hub-bub of greetings and introductions.

It was a pleasure to meet again with Mr William Cunnington who greeted me warmly as did Mr Philip Crocker. I was then introduced to Mrs Mary Cunnington and their youngest daughter Ann, whom I judge to be near to my own age. There followed a collective enquiry into my wellbeing after my near burial upon the plain behind the Winterslow Hut. I reddened as a consequence of this attention and Miss Ann Cunnington now suggested that I should be considered a fully fledged antiquarian after such heroic deeds. I answered that if it were also a requirement to be a fool then I assuredly did qualify in that regard.

"Fools are we all in the eyes of our detractors," stated Mr Cunnington, "and it is certainly a fool who neglects his own business to disturb the dust of our ancestors."

"Papa," retorted his daughter sharply, "you are never a fool and you must not say so."

I remained silent upon the subject of my own business that appeared to prosper well enough without my interference.

I was keen to enquire after Mr Cunnington's health for I am aware of the frequent and debilitating headaches from which he suffers. Mrs Mary Cunnington answered my concern by stating that their late arrival today was as a consequence of a poor night for Mr Cunnington.

"We are here out of fortitude Mr Chalk and it is no secret that I regard the demands placed upon my husband to be contributory to the frequency of these attacks."

Mr Cunnington took his wife's hand and tutted softly that she must not exaggerate this claim.

"I have yet to encounter a barrow or any place of interest to the antiquary where fresh air does not exist in plentiful supply and is indeed the best prescription for my condition."

He paused to take a deep breath as if to emphasize this statement.

"There, it is a fine day for opening barrows. Indeed, if we should have cast the Conjuror's Playthings, as is our custom Henry, then perhaps the God's may have granted us the full completion of our wishes."

Mr John Fenton having just emerged yawning from the carriage coughed suddenly in alarm at the mention of the Conjuror's Playthings and was quick to blame an intrusive fly for this outburst. He was equally keen to steer the subject away to new territories and suggested that he may soon play upon his flute, once he had wet his lips and also flushed the uninvited fly from his gullet and that a glass of wine was probably the best solution to achieve both these ends.

"John, you are become more like your father each time we meet," laughed Mr Philip Crocker.

Whilst our belated lunch was being prepared Mr Cunnington

consulted with the two Mr Parkers as to the outcome of their morning's labour and also how the renewed examination of Bush Barrow should now be conducted. Upon his return we made ourselves comfortable upon a patchwork of blankets beside the barrow and enjoyed a convivial lunch accompanied by the intermittent clomp of the pick axe and the slow scrape of the shovel. For my benefit our host described the frustration of the previous attempt upon this same barrow in July of this year.

"Henry, never before have I known a greater condition of expectation as existed upon that day for Mr William Stukeley in his great book of Stonehenge has drawn the attention of every antiquary to the singular presence of Bush Barrow."

Ann Cunnington then eagerly supplied the names of the esteemed company who had gathered together in such anticipation.

"The Reverend Iremonger from Wherwell and the Reverend Weston, Mr and Mrs Lambert from Boyton, Mr and Mrs Rackett and also the geologist Mr Sowerby."

Her father then lowered his voice to continue.

"John Parker in particular was greatly vexed at this failure before the eyes of our learned friends. Indeed, today he and his father are in a decidedly grumpy condition and I am at a loss to understand the cause lest it should be the memory of that day."

John Fenton stated loudly that it was now his duty to inspire our barrow diggers and also to appease the disturbed spirits of Bush Barrow by climbing the mound to play upon his flute. This musical offering soon prompted great billows of tobacco smoke to rise from within the tomb as if it were now of a sudden a smouldering volcano contemplating eruption. Having successfully accelerated the pace of the clomp and the scrape, John lay down his flute and Mr Philip Crocker enquired as to the details of my pedestrian excursion.

"Henry, I understand that you arrived upon foot from

Marlborough and not as we expected directly from London?"

Sir, you see that I am still to be mollycoddled.

I related the episodes of my excursion, lamenting that I could not show the fine flint piece that I retrieved from the sandy soils that exist to the north of Salisbury Plain. I then queried as to whether an antiquarian investigation had taken place into the huge mound situated in the village of Marden, whereupon I was informed that a full ten days of labour had been undertaken there last year by Mr Cunnington accompanied by the two Mr Parkers and a team of local men. Nothing but a few burnt bones, ashes and a slither of wood were retrieved after such Herculean labour into these unstable sandy soils but Mr Cunnington proposed that its purpose was indeed sepulchral.

"Others would have it as a Hill Altar but I maintain that we did not find the primary interment, Henry you have seen for yourself the size of the undertaking and it was akin to searching for a needle in a haystack. We could spend no more upon the great Hatfield Barrow and so I called the men from their work."

Mr Crocker stated in a serious tone that disaster was narrowly averted for without warning the great cutting within the barrow slumped down into the enormous excavation only moments after Mr Cunnington had called a judicious halt to proceedings.

"Indeed, Mr John Parker was reluctant to cease the work and would be down there still I fear. Sand does not behave like chalk Henry."

John Fenton reminded our gathering that I still managed to become buried under chalk nevertheless but agreed that good fortune and common sense had certainly prevailed at Marden.

I was then urged to continue with the account of my journey whilst there was a deal of questions I still wished to ask about Marden and its surrounds for Mr Cunnington strongly asserted that these ancient works were second only to Avebury and Stonehenge in their importance.

"Henry we shall visit together, on a good day."

I progressed to my meeting with the Reverend Joseph Townsend and now fully intended to reveal how the Vicar of Pewsey held the most unchristian sympathies toward the plight of the labouring poor. Indeed, I had not the opportunity to continue for Mr William Cunnington's face lit up at the mention of this gentleman's name for he clearly held the Reverend Joseph Townsend in the highest regard.

"He possesses an extraordinary collection of fossils and has found new examples amongst the greensands about the village of Pewsey. Henry, you no doubt discussed the origins of flint for it is a subject that is close to both your hearts? My good friend has informed me recently that the creation of this mysterious substance is due entirely to the decomposition of different marine bodies for it is these fossil remnants that universally form the nucleus of flint. This was a most fortuitous encounter Henry."

Mr Philip Crocker supported this view and spoke of his admiration for the Reverend Joseph Townsend of Pewsey.

"He surely informed you that he is the commissioner for all turnpike roads within the county of Wiltshire, though he may be unaware that he is referred to fondly as "The Colossus of Roads"."

Mr Cunnington continued the litany of achievements of this same gentleman.

"He has travelled widely and his publication "A Journey through Spain" is most enlightening in many regards. Did he not also invent a machine for the grinding of cocoa beans? I believe he did."

In turn Mrs Mary Cunnington confirmed her own appreciation for the broad talents of the vicar of Pewsey.

"He is a fine doctor to his flock and has published the most indispensible medical volume entitled the "The Physicians Vade Mecum" and I refer to it regularly and indeed no good home should be without it."

"I must correspond at the earliest opportunity Henry," confirmed her husband, "and I shall certainly send your regards to my good friend. It is well met, very well met indeed."

I hastily assured Mr Cunnington that it was a brief meeting and of little consequence for this gentleman would surely not recall a passing traveller when he has so much else to consider. Wishing to avoid all further reference to the Reverend Joseph Townsend, I hurriedly moved on to explain that I had met another gentleman on my journey who proclaimed himself to be a champion of the poor and indeed held aspirations to become a member of Parliament himself. I stated that if he were to succeed then surely he would gain the support of any decent freeholder, for the struggles of the labouring poor were plain for all to see.

"Indeed Henry," observed John Fenton, "then you have been busy socialising when I thought that you were engaged in pedestrianism."

Miss Ann Cunnington enquired as to the name of this gentleman and upon announcing him to be Mr Henry Hunt I may instead have stated that I was associating with the devil himself, such was the reaction of our party.

"That despicable man!" exhorted Mrs Mary Cunnington.

Miss Ann Cunnington shot her eyes wide in alarm and clapped her hands to her mouth to stifle a scream whilst Mr William Cunnington frowned deeply as glances were exchanged. He then addressed me kindly.

"Mr Hunt is not a person with whom you should associate Henry for he is a..a..a..I cannot say what he is..and..we shall not speak of him again."

Thus, the account of my journey ended abruptly as bulky white clouds cast great creeping shadows across Stonehenge Down and I was left to reflect that I am perhaps a poor judge of character. In the ensuing silence I withdrew to make a drawing to encompass the scene, whilst Ann Cunnington positioned herself at my shoulder in order to observe my humble efforts. As I sat with pencil in hand, Ann then took pleasure in whispering the deeds of Mr Henry Hunt who it seems tore his own marriage asunder and took another man's wife for a mistress.

"Mama would not like to think that I know of such matters but everyone knows how Mr Henry Hunt became persona non grata. No gentleman will entertain him though he holds a passion for sports of the field but his hunters stand idle in the stable and he may shoot no pheasant but his own. He has three children and the two boys are raised at the home of the mistress. He is handsome and Papa says he is a Jacobin and a very dangerous man."

To temper the obvious pleasure in relating such scandal I maintained a steady line with my pencil and a prudent silence but I cannot pretend that such close attention shall ever assist the artist however modest their aspirations.

We rejoined the party and I took my turn to climb the mound and observe the steaming backs of the two Mr Parkers for there appeared no end to the amounts of chalky soil to be moved from here to there. Miss Ann Cunnington had just proposed a game entitled "A Fool's Bolt" where we were obliged to provide a fanciful theory as to the origins of Stonehenge when Mr Crocker cocked an ear and indeed the steady clomp of the pick and slow scrape of the shovel had now ceased. As we listened to the silence upon Stonehenge Down there followed a single word of encouragement called out from within the tomb.

"Zurr."

Upon this one rustic syllable the expectations of our own party were now drawn and we hastened to gather at the rim of the excavation to find the two labourers kneeling upon the earth at a depth of eight feet or more in the very heart of the barrow. A number of ledges had been formed upon which the work had been staged and with Mr Cunnington and Mr Philip Crocker I was encouraged to descend as far as we were able until we stood pressed together upon a narrow ledge of chalky soil. A circle of soil stained bone had been revealed which indeed proved to be the skull of the occupant of Bush Barrow and the two Mr Parkers now cast aside their crude tools to adopt instead a pair of small trowels. I learnt that the patron for these antiquarian excursions Sir Richard Colt Hoare had presented father and son with these "barrow knives" especially manufactured for the task of delicate excavation and they were considered as badges of honour by the two men.

A discourse between John Parker and Mr Cunnington confirmed that the burial was placed upon the original surface of Stonehenge Down and not as expected within a grave or cist. John Parker now began to scrape at the soil around the skull and it was soon evident that the body had been lain with the head to the south. In an area between the skull and our own close position, a number of rivets were picked from the soil with also the fine remains of decayed wood and thin crumbling strips of brass. For the benefit of our party Mr Cunnington conveyed the information that an object had been placed above the head at the burial but had not survived. John Parker then shuffled along within the cramped hollow between the wall of chalk and the still submerged occupant of the tomb and now displayed a wide-eyed keenness for the task that lay before him. The deep shadow at this depth made it sorely difficult to view with any clarity and whilst John Parker worked with his nose to the soil his father sat back and lit a pipe to fill the hollow with tobacco smoke prompting Miss Ann Cunnington to cough and soon protest at this action.

"Mr Stephen there is little enough air to breath without the botheration of your pipe."

"Zurry miss."

The sound of metal striking upon metal made us lean forward

and as the soil was pared away from this new object, we could see it to be the head of an elegant axe with a broad splayed cutting edge. With care the axe was lifted upon the trowel and if any wood remained clad about the top of the piece it quickly crumbled away with the soil. The axe was passed to Mr Cunnington who held it flat upon his palm for us to view.

"The orientation of the body itself is most uncommon and neither is it contained within a cist as we might expect and now, we find an axe."

The piece was passed to Mr Fenton and it was in turn conveyed to Ann Cunnington who in preparation had a square sheet of canvas laid out upon the summit of the barrow to receive each newly retrieved object.

John Parker was now making short work of burying my boots beneath a mass of soil flicked from his trowel when a bright green object was revealed that appeared to glow in the shadowy light. The blade of a dagger had suffered from its exposure to the soil and this corrosion was termed "virdigris" by Mr Cunnington. A further piece believed to be the handle or its remains was also passed with care to the summit of the barrow. No sooner had one luminous green blade been extracted from beside the skeleton's torso than a longer piece was discovered which was deemed to be a lance for it was laid pointing upwards as if once attached to a shaft. John Parker now crouched low above the trowel and with the deftest touch revealed a small object that confirmed itself to be gold once the soil had been smudged away under his thumb. It is the nature of gold to remain unchanged in the soil and through our fingers passed an ornamented object that once adorned the occupant of Bush Barrow as a buckle or hasp, for there was a hook upon one face of the piece. Mr Philip Crocker stated quietly that gold is rarely found in isolation in such circumstances and amongst this southerly cluster of barrows on Stonehenge Down gold objects have already been retrieved which only served to fuel our sense of anticipation. John Parker continued with the steady removal of the soil beneath the delicate bones of the right hand where a further lance of brass was discovered but did not survive its extrication from the soil.

"Tes awl bruckley zur," lamented the younger excavator, looking up to Mr Cunnington as the piece dissolved before our eyes, the metal being so rotten that all structure was lost. John Parker sighed deeply and moved the point of his trowel to the collapsed ribs of the skeleton and the frustration of the decayed lance was soon forgot for there centrally placed upon the chest was an object that made our eyes widen in disbelief and we regarded one another in silent wonder. A large engraved gold breast plate in lozenge form that Mr Crocker later measured as six by seven inches had evidently been worn by the deceased at burial. The thin gold sheet was once attached to a wooden backing which had not survived the years, nor the remaining fragments from its extraction from the soil.

Mr William Cunnington pronounced that we should think now of our generous patron Sir Richard Colt Hoare for how he would have relished the conquest of Bush Barrow had he not been conducting a further tour of Wales with Mr Richard Fenton.

With the gold lozenge now glistening in the sun upon the summit of the barrow our attention was drawn again to what lay yet to be discovered and Mr Stephen Parker now continued down the right hand side of the skeleton from the skull and around the jumble of bones that once formed the backbone. Not a word was spoken and in due course the elder excavator was rewarded for his patience in revealing a stone mace head perforated by a central hole with a small metal ring that perhaps assisted with securing the piece to a wooden shaft. To accompany the polished stone a number of puzzling rings of bone were recovered that may have adorned a long vanished handle. With a hint of satisfaction Mr Stephen Parker straightened his back and held up a smaller engraved gold lozenge which proved to be the final success of the day, save for a jumble of beads retrieved from the soil.

As the excavators continued to reveal the remainder of the skeleton, Mr Philip Crocker measured the thigh bone and found it to be twenty and a half inches in length whereupon Stephen Parker proclaimed their subject to be "A gurt lanky zart o' a man".

Leaving the two men to complete their work we clambered shivering from the tomb to be enveloped by a warm and golden light with our shadows cast long across the plain. I paused at the summit to look down once more upon the scene below, at the crouched and soil tarnished fossil of a man and the two labourers charged with revealing his long buried secrets. Sir, I confess to be envious of their task for I have experienced once before upon the plains behind the Winterslow Hut, the pains and successes of such physical labour when the body is engaged but the mind shall rove freely. Mr John Parker has I believe an education born from his experience and the considerations of both Mr Parkers are sought by Mr Cunnington for he values greatly their ability and judgement in what I shall term a practical antiquarianism. I wished to engage with these taciturn countrymen but suspected that despite the fine success of the day, I had not yet been forgiven for disturbing their noontime slumber. The two excavators slowly emerged from Bush Barrow and as with all our party they appeared to relish the late afternoon sun after their time spent in the cold shadow of the tomb. I was soon to be left alone upon the summit and noted how this broad mound occupies a position of crowning glory on this swell of barrow populated down land to the South of Stonehenge. I then drew the attention of our departing party to some activity near the stone circle itself and what appeared to be the raising of small tents but none could offer an explanation until an approaching farmer upon horseback soon accounted for this mystery whilst we gathered about our carriage.

"Tus fer a game o'cricket on the morrow, yus."

The farmer then asked after our own activity and Miss Ann Cunnington displayed proudly the freshly revealed secrets of Bush Barrow to which he responded by scratching his head under an old felt hat.

"Wull, I know'd green burrow awl me loife but nuver did zee zich a thing avore."

Being a practical man, he pointed to the stone mace and pronounced it as the handle for a gimlet, making a screwing action with his wrist.

"Ah, vur a gimlet, if you asks me ladies and gent'mun."

At this we all departed for Amesbury with Stephen and John Parker travelling beside the carriage driver, leaving the occupant of Bush Barrow exposed to the dry air of these chalklands for the visit of Sir Richard Colt Hoare upon his return to Wiltshire.

Due libations were made at dinner and the buffed gold was presented at the table drawing much attention from a growing throng of cricketers and their supporters at the George Inn, with whom Mr John Fenton is now carousing happily. I have not imbibed greatly but slipped away to write my account of this truly astonishing day and prey forgive my indulgence in that regard.

I still crave correspondence from you my dear uncle and a single word or two would be sufficient to calm my great concern for your own well being, for it is a silence that dwells so heavily upon me with each passing day.

Your expectant nephew
HENRY CHALK

*

POSTSCRIPT.

Upon the removal of my boots I have found inside a quantity of fine soil and was able to pour out a small pile from each boot into my hand. I can only surmise that this occurred when Mr John Parker heaped the soil from his trowel about my feet and indeed the soil entered freely through the tops of my boots. Had I not noticed a curious glinting amongst this soil before the candle then I would have cast it out into the night from the window and so instead, in my stockinged feet, I sought out Mr Philip Crocker to borrow a glass to make a closer inspection. Mr Crocker explained that Mr Cunnington had the glass and we together knocked quietly upon his door and as they were not yet abed, we were invited in. To keep the soil from dispersing I had tipped it into my fob pocket and I now extracted a pinch to study under the glass and we found there to be a multitude of minute gold pins amongst the soil. I recounted the occasion of the burying of my boots by John Parker and that it had occurred at the recovery of the dagger and lance. Mr Crocker soon returned with the dagger and also the soil encrusted handle and a careful examination revealed that a portion of the wood from the handle remained intact and displayed a fine zig-zag design constructed entirely from a tight arrangement of these same gold pins. We all looked at one another for we could not comprehend the scale of this undertaking for no glass would have existed in ancient times and the pins were surely too small for the keenest eye or indeed the nimblest fingers.

Our host then summed up our thoughts at this discovery.

"We wonder at the most conspicuous achievements of our ancient ancestors with the creation of stone circles and the raising of great mounds and yet here is an undertaking of an opposing scale that is surely no less astonishing. Tomorrow we shall return and ensure that John recovers from the soil more of these extraordinary gold pins. Today the God's have indeed granted the full completion of our wishes to exceed perhaps even our greatest expectations, goodnight gentlemen."

I shall now read awhile from Gulliver's Travels for Mr Swift's tale is no stranger to such extremes in scale and perhaps it was after all a resident of Lilliput that was engaged to decorate the handle of the dagger.

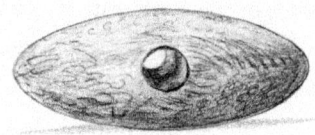

Tuesday 6th September 1808

MY DEAR UNCLE,

After the events of yesterday you may believe sir that my well of excitement is near exhausted but there is to be a game of cricket held upon Stonehenge Down and whilst at breakfast, I have been informed that I am to participate. The game is to extend for two whole days and Mr William Cunnington has graciously excused both John and myself from our antiquarian duties, such as they are, with the blessing that as young men we must enjoy ourselves whilst we can. Miss Ann Cunnington has stated that it is a fine distraction from the important business of becoming better acquainted with our ancient ancestors but she now wishes us success in our "frivolous pursuit".

I understand that two members of the cricket team cannot now attend the game and as John Fenton had spent a long evening extolling his virtues as a cricketer, we are now to join the home team. John has informed me that if any person should ask then I am to say that I am a cricketer also. When I enquire of John what shall be expected of us, he only shrugs his shoulders and complains of a heavy head and in the cold light of day he now confesses quietly to me that he knows nothing of the game.

There have been many new arrivals at the George Inn who are filled with talk of the game of cricket and this only serves to excite me further. The gentlemen of the opposing team are mustering in the parlour although they await the "Players" who I understand to be the experienced and regular cricketers. Indeed, there is some anxiety by our own side to establish the identity of these men and many likely names have been uttered. The Players in our home side are indeed not young men and I gauge by the mutterings of our own gentlemen, as the bowls of punch are circulated, that they are not known by reputation. I am now squeezed into the corner of the parlour and I shall report later, my dear uncle, on the events of the day.

Before I conclude there are now gasps of surprise, and indeed dismay, from our team with the news that Silver Billy has just this minute arrived at the George Inn. The opposing captain is as smug as a cat that has lapped the cream but as I know nothing of cricket or the men who play it, I can only surmise that Mr William Beldham, or Silver Billy as he is also known, is a fine player indeed.

*

Sir, I am just returned from Stonehenge Down and I have now hastily concealed myself in my room. There is much gloom and confusion amongst the participants of both teams for the outcome of the day has been most unsatisfactory and to some degree I am indeed culpable. As the Gentlemen and Players grumble and disperse from the George Inn, it will serve you best my dear uncle if I describe the events of the day in the order that they occurred. For once Stonehenge itself was not the object of our attention and it served only as the dramatic scenery for our most curious activity. Four tents had been erected in advance of our arrival with bunting and flags strung between them and indeed this festooned tentage gave the appearance of a small pageant. The day was set fair but with a gusty breeze that worked the flags and sent great white clouds scudding before a blue sky.

Cricket is neither a race nor a straight fight but it is more a chivalrous battle where the batsman is required to defend his battlements from the small hurtling red leather cannonball. The two "armies" have professional soldiers within their ranks who are well versed in all the elements of this warfare and they are termed the "Players". The gentlemen who comprise the remainder of the team, with the exception of the rustic "long stop", are surely superior in the natural state of affairs but in this egalitarian pursuit the advantage must be held by the best cricketers. The gentlemen, however, shall be at the top of the order when it comes to batting and such a list was posted before the commencement of the game. Indeed, I considered it a miracle that overnight I had of a sudden become a cricketer and felt emboldened by the sight of my name upon this list although I had never touched a bat or a ball in my life. John Fenton was placed at nine and I was to follow at number ten whilst the "players" in our team were positioned at seven and eight. John Fenton then stated that our lowly placements were due to our being late additions to the team and he then grumbled that we were only "making up the numbers".

Both teams must provide an "umpire" to stand upon the field of play beside the wickets and these men are the upholders of the laws of cricket once the game is set. The umpires have cocked hats and are also required to carry a bat and it is but another inexplicable facet of this game for they only lean upon these bats and they are not required to strike the ball for any reason. The score is kept by two men who sit in the outfield upon a bench and they record each run made with a notch cut into a tally stick. It is the simplest aspect of this game of cricket, for the team with the most notches at the end of the proceedings wins the game. The prize for the winning team is eleven guineas and eleven pairs of gloves but I understand that a great deal more than eleven guineas may be wagered with the bookmakers who are also present here on Stonehenge Down.

With the toss of a coin between the two captains, it was thereby determined that the home team should bat first and our gentlemen prepared themselves in the privacy of our tent. The opposing team then strode out onto the Stonehenge turf, smartly attired in colourful matching caps and received great applause from their supporters. Soon after, the two home batsmen appeared and they too were heartily clapped and encouraged by the burgeoning crowd. There was indeed now a wonderful sense of occasion and expectancy upon Stonehenge Down with this gathering of cricketers and their supporters and my heart raced with the thought that I would also be participating in this thrilling contest. Our "innings" however did not begin well for there are many ways for a batter to fail in his task and be judged "out" by the umpire and the gentlemen in our team soon explored all possibilities in this regard, whilst the supporters of both teams cheered and groaned respectively with the fall of each wicket. Our two "Players" spent a deal more time at the wicket demonstrating stout defence but did not add many notches to the tally-stick before they to were dismissed by the scuttling ball. John Fenton was summoned in a rush from the victual tent and had no sooner arrived at the wicket when he was "run out" without the bother of having to face the bowler at all. On his return he dropped the cricket bat at my feet and offered a word of caution before going in search of his glass of wine that had been hastily abandoned only moments before.

"Pray beware Henry for our man will not move one inch when there is a good run to be taken."

It is indeed a long walk to the wicket with the eyes of the opposing team upon you. One of the "Players" in our side had shown me how to stuff padding into the front of my stockings to protect my shins from the hard ball and I at first felt foolish with these lumpy additions protruding before me. My jovial partner greeted me at the wicket and appeared wholly unconcerned by our lack of notches thus far and then proceeded to list the viands that he would heap upon his plate once lunch was taken.

The bowlers begin their run with the ball held aloft and stride in with gathering speed to hurl the ball as might a man playing at skittles but with a greater elevation to enable the ball to land before the batsman. The scuttling ball must be kept out at all costs but my first delivery bounced away to the side and I spun around in a full circle as I followed its course but bat and ball made no contact. Some distance behind the wicket keeper is where the "long stop" stands and he is neither a gentleman nor a player but instead a rustic who is expected to dirty his knees in stopping the ball. From this distant position I could hear this countryman's voice calling out after my first failed attempt;

"Look at 'is 'ead up in the air, loike a goose."

As the bowler paced back to his mark, I pictured a honking goose in my mind and decided that I would instead keep my head low whereupon the long-necked goose was swiftly replaced by a snuffling pig. I now afford myself some mild amusement at these farmyard analogies but with my head down I was at least able to observe the ball as it hit the bat. At the fourth ball bowled I played it firmly away and a run was taken with plenty of time for my jovial partner to make his ground once I had arrived beside him and politely urged him to leave his position. I now faced the bowling of Silver Billy who had already accounted for a great number of our team. I heard it whispered by their captain that this was to be Silver Billy's final "over" before he was to be replaced by a new bowler and so I defended my wicket for all I was worth. With the fourth and final ball I then surprised myself by striking a pleasant shot straight back beyond Silver Billy and I pressed my fellow batter to run three and near caught him up upon taking the third run.

"Mr Chalk... Mr Chalk," he puffed, "such exertion before lunch.. is unwise."

At the next opportunity my red faced partner flatly refused to leave his crease despite there being plenty of time to make a run.

"Young sir, you have again kept me from feasting upon the ball and it is unfair. It is now my turn."

This gentleman was oblivious to the slender margins of his survival as the whistling ball shaved the wickets or bounced directly over the bail. With the bowler thundering in beside me I could but close my eyes and pray whilst the opposing side would groan in unison as my partner again swished at thin air, drawing cries of desperation from the field.

"A straight ball PLEASE bowler."

For the sake of our team, when I next faced the bowling, I decided to smite the ball as far as I could and on a few occasions it sped amongst the legs of the spectators and the cheering crowd parted to let the fielder to the ball whilst I urged my companion to keep running.

Finally, my jovial partner struck a ball high up into the air and stood craning his neck to admire this splendid effort until he gauged with some panic that it was about to descend from whence it came and land directly upon his head. With a great cry of anxiety, he leapt to the side to avoid this circumstance and as he lay sprawled upon the turf the ball was in turn caught by the wicket keeper and my companion was called out.

Our rustic long-stop was last man in and he trailed to the crease with the most doleful countenance as if he knew in advance the fate that was about to befall him. His first delivery then conspired to leap more than any previous ball of the morning and so struck the unfortunate man upon the head with a loud "tock", making him collapse back upon the three wickets and splay them in all directions. I helped long-stop Davis back to his feet with his brow now displaying a lump the size of a small egg and he staggered from the field shaking his head and muttering; "I knew 'twud 'appen".

With our first innings now concluded, the scorers announced that we had managed forty one notches of which my contribution was

twenty eight. I felt a pat on the back and turned to find that it was
Silver Billy who then shook my hand and studied me for a moment
before stating quietly that if it had not been for my efforts then our
score should be a paltry one indeed. A number of other gentlemen
repeated this gesture and the captain of the opposing team declared
loudly that;

"This young "goose" is far from cooked. Well done young Mr
Chalk."

Lunch was taken and in time we resumed the field of play as
belts were loosened and our captain ordered us to spread ourselves
about. The opposing gentleman batters fared no better than our own
men and notches upon the tally stick were scarce. The Stonehenge turf
accounted for a number of wickets until the arrival of Silver Billy at the
crease. It appears that Silver Billy is indeed the most heralded batsman
in the land and our opposing captain had paid dearly to secure his
services such was the import placed upon winning the game. My dear
uncle, to have Mr William Beldham in your team is akin to securing
the services of the late and beloved Admiral Nelson, may God rest his
soul, to participate in a gentleman's rowing match. Of a sudden the
game was no longer an even contest with our fielders never occupying
the correct positions to stop the ball and our bowlers were very soon
confounded. Indeed, wherever the ball pitched, Silver Billy was there
to pounce upon it with his feet moving like the most nimble dancing
master and with all the while a raised left elbow to lead the stroke.
The visiting supporters cheered each deft click as this master batsman
struck the ball to all parts of Stonehenge Down and they then urged
their man to run faster between the wickets.

"Tich and turn Billy, tich and turn."

The scorers notched upon the tally stick as fast as they were able
with the pile of wood shavings mounting rapidly about their feet. Runs
were taken with ease and our fielders retreated back to stand before the

crowd but still we had not enough men on the field to prevent the ball from passing us by. I was fully prepared to fling myself at the ball to prevent its escape into the crowd as it sped across the turf and on two occasions I succeeded. At first, I was unable to propel the ball back to the middle and our two Players had quick arms in this regard, but I was unable to emulate this method. I instead devised a means to lob the ball as if from an ancient battle machine called a trebuchet with my arm kept straight to whirl in a full circle alongside my ear and by this method some distance was gained.

Silver Billy had in turn punished all our regular bowlers so that none wished to meet the captain's eye and he scoured the field in desperation.

"You sir."

I looked behind my position to see to whom this gesture was intended and soon realised, with no small degree of alarm, that I was now being summoned to bowl. My protestations were ignored and I found myself with ball in hand and with Silver Billy poised and ready to deal with my novice efforts. My first attempt sent the ball sailing high over the batsman's head and it was returned by long-stop Davis. The second ball was also greatly elevated but within reach of Silver Billy who slashed it high and far until it came to rest in the ditch that encircles Stonehenge. There was some muttering by our own side at the wisdom of this choice of bowler and with the pair of batsman panting at their running of ten runs, Mr John Fenton duly trotted up to me with ball in hand and placed an arm around my shoulder.

"Henry, we shall forever be chasing leather at this rate."

He lowered his voice and counselled me on how I should abandon the accepted method of bowling and instead emulate the means by which I was able to send the ball in from the outfield.

"Yes Henry "the trebuchet", you may call it what you will but I implore you to try it now."

The Excavation of Bush Barrow

The Cricket Match at Stonehenge

As John Fenton returned to his position I settled at the end of my run before galloping towards the crouching silver haired batsman and with all my might I spun my arm over to release the ball. As a consequence of this great exertion I was sent sprawling upon the turf but was able to observe the trajectory of the ball as it speared in towards the master batsman's feet that had for once remained stationary at the crease, such was his surprise at the nature of my "trebuchet" delivery. Silver Billy let out a loud yelp as he dropped his bat and began to hop about clutching the toes upon his left foot.

"No ball, no ball," cried out the opposing team as they ran out onto the field to gather around their man.

"No ball", echoed the umpires belatedly as they too joined the growing throng around the now prostrate Silver Billy, whilst Mr John Fenton came across to haul me from the pitch and dust me off.

"You have certainly started something now Henry."

Fists were shaken in my face with calls of "cheat" by the opposition supporters who now rushed to the wicket with the cheering home crowd in close pursuit, casting their hats into the air as they went. Amongst this confusion a coach and four left the London Road and rounded the tents before rattling on across the turf to draw to a halt beside the grand melee in the centre of the cricket field. A smartly attired gentleman stepped briskly from the coach whereupon he ordered the coachman to fire his blunderbuss into the air to quickly restore order and to quell this fervent assembly of cricketers, supporters and bookmakers. It appeared that the owner of Stonehenge Down was issuing a writ against all the participants of the cricket match which would be enforced forthwith unless this unauthorised activity ceased with immediate effect. The unpredictable Fourth Marques of Queensbury had it seems not given his written consent for the match to take place much to the chagrin of our captain who claimed to have agreed the matter over dinner with the elderly Duke some months ago.

"I reminded him by letter only last week," he protested fruitlessly.

This unwelcome and unexpected news, delivered in stentorian tones by "Old Q's" official representative, had the effect of dousing the ardour of those who felt aggrieved by the outcome of the day for the cricket match and indeed the cricket field was no more. Orders were given for the wickets to be plucked from the turf and for the tents to be removed. Finally, the two perplexed captains shook hands and it was agreed that a match should be played, at a mutually agreeable location, perhaps next year and the prize would be preserved until such time that a winning team could be determined. All wagers made were now declared null and void due to the unforeseen abandonment of the game and indeed it was this circumstance that caused the greatest discontent. Silver Billy was helped to his feet and I sincerely wished to apologise in person for my action but still I dared not make my approach for fear of reprisal by the opposition supporters and instead accepted a ride in a carriage to the George Inn.

My dear uncle, I cannot undo what I have done and I am indeed thankful that the game was halted and yet I do not believe that my heinous crime upon the cricket pitch shall be so readily forgot. As I sit at the writing desk in my room before the open window, I can still hear the grumblings below in the yard as coaches are boarded;

"I believe gentlemen that we have been witness to the biggest travesty since Shock White arrived at the crease with his over–wide bat."

"I agree sir, a travesty of equal proportions. Let us hope and pray that we never again witness the over-arm ball."

*

My dear uncle, I had no sooner completed my account of the day when there was a knock upon the door and boots announced that Mrs Mary Cunnington wished to speak to me in the parlour. Boots assured me that all cricketers and their supporters had now departed the George Inn and I found all to be quiet in the smoke filled parlour with the exception of Mrs Mary Cunnington who coughed before speaking.

"Henry, would you care to accompany us to the river Avon as Ann intends to go angling this evening?"

I replied that I should welcome the opportunity for I had never before witnessed the catching of a fish.

"Then shall we depart, for there is a short walk to be taken?"

Ann awaited us in the courtyard where she held upright a long hazel wand with a number of wire hoops bound along its length and also a spool attached at the thicker end.

"Henry, please would you carry the rod and the net, there is also a small bag. I am so very fond of fishing that I insisted that I must bring my rod to Amesbury and papa has arranged with the farmer that I may try the river at Ratfyn."

As we walked from the town and made our approach to the River Avon, I enquired of the day's barrow openings for I was keen to establish whether there had been further astounding discoveries amongst the Stonehenge barrows. Miss Ann Cunnington explained that it appeared that the examined barrows had already received the attention of the tomb robber and therefore any content had been extracted and the information lost to the enquiry.

"We believed this to be possible at the outset, but Sir Richard requires of papa that we must be most thorough in our investigations."

It was now Ann's turn to question me upon the events of my day and as I carefully considered my words, Mrs Mary Cunnington interjected;

"It is a curious game that shows men to be boys at heart."

"Mama, please," admonished her daughter quickly as she reddened and looked away.

I apologised for not knowing that they had indeed observed the

game upon Stonehenge Down, for I should have wished to attend to
their comfort there.

"We walked across from the barrow opening," explained Mrs
Mary Cunnington, "and found it to be a very noisy affair."

"You were occupied with the bat in your hand Henry and we
wished to return to assist my father..for that is our purpose here this
week, is it not mama?"

We continued in silence until we met with the river where our
silence became more comfortable as stealth is indeed a requirement for
the successful angler.

"Mama, you can sit there," ordered her daughter in a whisper,
"and Henry and I will cross the hatches and return downriver for a
short distance."

Ann instructed me quietly that it was important to observe
the activity upon the river before we commenced. I knew not what
I should be observing and soon succumbed to the gentle gliding
motion of the water as it passed before us. I could sense no discernable
gradient to determine in which direction it should flow but the river
appeared certain enough of its origin and destination for there to be
any confusion over the matter. A large ripple upon the calm surface of
the river betrayed the position of a fish and also the nature of the fly
upon which it was happy to take its evening meal.

"Can you see the fly Henry? There are blue winged olives
aplenty this evening."

I could now detect the curious movement of these flies as they
jigged up and down and Ann was soon rummaging in her bag for
a feathery imitation of this species that was bound together with a
small barbed hook. This keen young angler spent a moment affixing
the fly to the final short length of fine silk thread and explained that
the remainder of the line upon the spool is of a weightier waxed silk to
enable it to be cast through the air.

Ann now raised herself to stand beside me upon the bank and having released a generous length of thread from the spool then flicked the supple hazel wand back and forth to enable the fly to arc repeatedly above the river. Once she was satisfied with her aim this feathery deceit dropped discreetly upon the surface to float gently towards the position of the fish. From his watery world the hungry creature quickly inspected this fresh arrival but then ignored the invitation. The fly was impatiently whisked away and after a further swishing through the air it once more landed gracefully upon the water and on this occasion the temptation proved too great. With the rod bending and line quivering in the hands of Miss Ann Cunnington, the ensnared fish fled downstream taking with it a deal of thread from the unwinding spool. With a firm stance upon the bank, the young angler lifted the hazel rod to retrieve the fish after its flight and by winding the thread upon the spool the resisting weight attached to the hook was drawn ever closer.

"Henry, the net."

I was able to just reach the struggling shape with the hooped net without myself entering the water and lifted out the weighty fish where it fought hard against this unwelcome exposure.

"Take the priest," Ann Cunnington then laughed out loud at the expression upon my face to this curious demand as she gestured to a heavy short wooden stick that had been placed upon the bank in readiness, "it is so called for it serves the last rites. Strike upon the back of the neck and then remove the hook. It is a fine trout."

I was not prepared for my complicity in this struggle but as instructed I carried out this most un-priestly act. After Ann reached down to remove the hook from the fishy lip, the creature inexplicably came back to life and quickly wriggled from my grasp to bounce from the grassy bank into the shallow waters where it made its escape.

"Henry!"

From across the river Mrs Mary Cunnington looked up from

her book at the sound of her daughter's raised voice and smiled before settling back comfortably against a tree, with the book now closed upon her lap.

"Let us try again Henry, and this time you may cast the fly and if you are successful then I shall ensure that the fish is thoroughly dealt with."

We walked a few paces further upstream until a new fish betrayed it's presence by disturbing the placid surface. Ann ordered me to stand beside her and she demonstrated how I must hold the rod and I practised the necessary flick with the hazel wand before attempting to cast the fly to the water. All was set and I made my cast but knew not where the fly and hook had gone.

"You have made a catch Henry," Ann covered her mouth as she laughed, "you have caught your hat."

I hastily removed the snakecatcher's hat and Ann carefully drew the hook from the desiccated snake hat band.

"It is a very curious hat Henry..and very old. I should like to accompany you to the gentleman's clothiers so that you may purchase a new hat."

Until today I had not experienced this close proximity with a young woman since that night in Hindon, where Miss Sarah Foster and I first met and circumstances dictated that we should conceal ourselves in a stationary carriage.

With the fishing rod now placed out of harm's way upon the bank we sat and observed the fish as they fed safely upon the unwitting fly as nature had intended and without our wily interference.

"Henry, you are young, as I am young..but are you now betrothed..for I have heard it said that you are?"

Of a sudden life all about the river paused, as birds perched and insects settled, the mammals ceased their activity in their bankside holes and the fish took no advantage of an easy morsel. In this complete stillness I awaited my own response to this most private of questions.

"I have indeed met..someone..and we correspond freely, but we have not yet openly pledged our troth."

"But your correspondence..is through another? It cannot therefore be..intimate?"

I swallowed and reddened at this close quarter and questioning.

"We are able to exchange..our feelings," I said.

"And those feelings..are they love?"

Ann turned to face me as if to demonstrate that looks alone could be sufficient in the conveyance of such a delicate subject. I construed by this intimation that if there were not this facility then there must be some failure or fault when eyes cannot meet and words must be spoken. I broke her gaze and as might a cautious fish, I drew back from taking the fly and changed my course entirely to find a deep sunlit pool where no barb may reach me. After a lengthy pause I cast a handful of bankside soil into the water and introduced a new subject for discussion to break the thread of a young woman's curiosity. Ann turned to observe this scattered interruption to the pristine surface whilst I proposed that the river before us was perhaps the receptacle for the ancient generations, when all but the Kings and Queens were buried in their prominent barrows.

Miss Ann Cunnington's brow soon puckered at this distraction.

"Pray explain yourself?" she said.

This abrupt change in her daughter's tone caused Mrs Mary Cunnington to waken from her brief slumber and lift the book from her lap to continue with her reading.

It is a notion that had not fully formed in my own mind but occurred whilst floating down this same river on Sunday afternoon. I reached down with my cupped hand to gather a small portion of the river and held it up before letting it trickle gently between my fingers.

"Observe the past, the present and the future," I said, whilst

Ann continued to frown as the final droplets of water fell upon the bank, "this river is born of distant springs that shall one day meet the sea. In turn the rain quenches the earth for the crystal waters to rise again and emerge as the infant spring. Suppose, if you will, that ancient man had not yet discovered our god but instead believed in the ways of the earth upon which his life depended; the changing seasons, the fruits of nature, the power of fire and the eternal river. By committing their dead to this eternal flow, the spirits of the ancestors shall join the spirits of the bountiful earth to become one inextricable tale."

Ann now visibly recoiled as she gathered her bag.

"Mama, we are leaving. Mr Chalk I do not like your ideas for the rivers would be thick with bodies and it would be revolting and please do not offend further by insulting the Almighty."

I cast a further handful of fine dirt into the water to confirm in my own mind that a pot of ashes would disperse well enough.

"Are you to remain here depositing soil into the river or will you now carry my rod?"

We returned in silence to the George Inn under a reddening early autumn sky with nothing to show for our labours beside the River Avon.

I wish you goodnight my dear uncle and I hope to dream of one whom I love dearly and who may indeed tolerate my idle thoughts.

Your wily nephew,
HENRY CHALK

Wednesday morning 7th September 1808

MY DEAR UNCLE,

All has changed and I am very soon to depart for Salisbury and I inform you now sir, in the event of you corresponding when I have already vacated this place. I received two letters this morning and I hoped in vain that you might have broken your silence but I found it instead to be a prosaic enquiry from Mr Gerrity at Chalk's Brewery. The second letter was a brief note from Mr Robert Foster to confirm the time that he and Miss Sarah Foster shall be arriving in Salisbury on Saturday 10th of September.

I awoke this morning with my stomach reminding me that I had forsaken dinner in favour of our angling excursion and I therefore sought to break my fast at the earliest opportunity. Mr Philip Crocker was already prepared for the day and he enquired of the events of yesterday upon Stonehenge Down and I believe that he enjoyed my account of the game of cricket with all its twists and turns.

"Poor Mr William Beldham. David has slain Goliath upon Salisbury Down, with a trebuchet rather than a slingshot."

Mr Crocker asked how I was able to perform with the bat when I had not before ventured onto a cricket pitch. I described my roving about the ploughed fields in search of fashioned flint for I have the habit of striking away each discarded flint with my thumbstick, once I have established that the piece has no merit to my investigation. Indeed, my stick is pecked by these repeated blows and I seldom fail in sending these odd shaped stones spinning away to all quarters. A hazel stick is narrow and the flint often small whereas a cricket bat is broad and a ball is the size of a fist.

"There are many facets to your study of flint Henry, yet this is surely the most fortuitous and unexpected."

Having completed our repast and with the downstairs of the

George Inn now a busy place, Mr Crocker suggested that we took the morning air to which I was happy to oblige. I soon confided in Mr Crocker that last evening I had accompanied Mrs Mary Cunnington and her daughter Ann who was keen to fish upon the river and that upon our excursion I was somewhat surprised by Miss Cunnington's curiosity regarding my own affairs and I knew not what to make of it. Mr Crocker halted and rubbed his chin thoughtfully.

"Henry, these are modern young ladies and they speak their mind and ask questions freely and directly. Ann is the youngest of the three daughters and is indeed the most precocious."

Mr Crocker looked about him lest there should be some danger of being overheard by the hedgerow and to be doubly certain he lowered his voice.

"I have the trust of this fine family for they are indeed my very dear friends and so I implore you to observe the utmost discretion with what I am about to tell you."

I assured Mr Crocker that this would be so as I am certain, my dear uncle, that you will not divulge these words to another living soul.

"Henry, it was Ann who proposed to her father that you might welcome a visit to Stonehenge Down to assist with the barrow opening. Mr Cunnington thought it an excellent suggestion in recognition of your genuine interest in antiquarian matters and so wrote to you upon that subject."

I confided in Mr Crocker, who has by this circumstance shown himself to be a true friend, that whilst Miss Ann Cunnington is both lively and interesting and indeed dedicated to her father's investigations, the course of my future is set and shall suffer no distraction. After a short silence between us I reached beneath my shirt and drew the fine silver chain above my collar that secured the dark flint heart in its mount of silver and displayed the piece to Mr Philip Crocker. I explained that at my request Mr Henry Shorto, who was a cutler in the city of Salisbury, had made an identical pair and Mr Crocker studied closely the fine workmanship and stated that he had not before considered that this common stone may be so beautiful. I informed him that in three days time the two flint hearts will again be reunited back in their place of origin whereupon Mr Crocker smiled and shook my hand warmly after he had digested the meaning of my statement. My companion's expression soon changed to one of concern when I stated that my plans had been thrown into confusion by the nature of our conversation and that it was now my intention to depart at once for Salisbury. I also explained that upon arriving I would again seek out my friend Mr Henry Shorto, for I believed that we held a mutual interest in the ubiquitous flint of this County and there was still much to discuss upon this matter since our first encounter in May of this year.

On our return to the inn I sought out Mr William Cunnington to explain that it was necessary for me to leave their company and depart for Salisbury and I apologised for this unexpected news. I thanked Mr Cunnington sincerely for the invitation to attend this latest campaign upon Stonehenge Down and that I was truly fortunate to be present at the conquering of Bush Barrow, for that was indeed a most memorable occasion. After they had completed their breakfast, I also thanked Mrs Mary Cunnington and her daughter Ann who stated that I was unlikely to ever become an angler to which I readily concurred. Ann then displayed less warmth in her dealings with me than hitherto and bid me a curt farewell. Mr Philip Crocker shook my hand firmly but with a look of consternation upon his face and Mr John Fenton appeared in the parlour to announce that he was to accompany me upon the coach to Salisbury. I explained that as an ardent pedestrian it was my intention to walk to Salisbury and not to travel upon the coach at all, whereupon Mr John Fenton looked aghast at this prospect and shot glances in all directions for guidance upon the matter. I believe that my sudden change of plan has caused some hasty consultation between Mr William Cunnington and Mr John Fenton to ensure that I should again be cosseted and kept safe from undisclosed dangers. As a consequence, my preferred means of travel has been entirely overlooked and Mr John Fenton is now to become a pedestrian tourist and once he has finally prepared himself, then we shall depart.

Sir, I shall communicate again when I arrive at Salisbury.

Your troublesome nephew
HENRY CHALK

Wednesday evening

MY DEAR UNCLE,

I should be much aggrieved with you and earlier in the afternoon this was indeed the case. I now regret deeply the thoughts that I held towards you for I since understand the circumstances by which you have deemed it necessary to publish my letters. I cannot describe the utter and profound shock of holding in my hand not one, but two books of my published correspondence to you; "A Tour in Search of Chalk" and "A Tour in Search of Flint". These small volumes were purchased in boards from a bookseller in Salisbury and they now sit before me upon Mr Henry Shorto's desk in his house in Rollestone Street.

Each idle thought and whim and indeed each expression of the love that I hold for another is now laid bare and I stand naked before the world. Shall the words I now write be themselves caught, bound and presented as A Tour in Search of Gold? Or indeed A Tour in Search of My Father's Soul?

Within the second volume entitled "A Tour in Search of Flint", I have read your "Letter to the Editor" and therein exists the sorry tale of a conspiracy held against you by those whom I had previously considered to be my friends. To know that you have written to your wayward nephew only for this correspondence to be withheld pains me greatly and I now sincerely wish to undo this injustice for you are my only living relative.

To publish all sir is to court disaster, for that is the circumstance that has most literally been so narrowly averted here in Salisbury upon this very afternoon but it has led to the abrupt departure of Mr John Fenton from my company. Sir, I shall explain in due course but I have sought the assistance of Mr Henry Shorto, who greeted me in his cutler's shop as a dear friend and I am very pleased to again make his acquaintance. Mr Shorto was most insistent that whilst I remained in Salisbury, then I should do so as his guest for his young family are away at Basingstoke for a number of days and he is not at all accustomed to an empty house.

Whilst my host is unavoidably detained this evening on Society business, I have the opportunity of recording the events of this most extraordinary and unsettling day.

I shall not bore you with the full litany of Mr John Fenton's complaints as we made our slow progress from Amesbury for my walking companion was not equipped with a pack but instead a green bag that has been borrowed from Mrs Cunnington. After exchanging this bag from hand to hand he very soon tired of carrying it at all and then deposited it heavily upon the road with a cry of exasperation.

"Henry, this is intolerable."

In truth I craved my own company and would happily proceed on my own but I took pity upon my companion for the quandary of his obligation was writ large across his face. I offered to hold one handle of the bag whilst he took the other and in this curious manner, we moved incrementally along the Avon valley. In time we made our way to higher ground whereupon Mr John Fenton cursed the interminable sheep flocks and the barren wastes before grumbling that he was now hungry. Without divulging my intentions, I directed our course not to Salisbury but instead to the midst of Grovely Wood and to the small domain of Peter Winter the charcoal burner and his boy Tam. Not one year ago I was shown great kindness by the charcoal burner and I wished to visit them again in their smoke filled world. We crossed the river Wylye at the village of Great Wishford and upon ascending the downs we encountered many souls carrying great faggots of brushwood back to their cottages, for it seems they are entitled to enjoy the largesse of the great sprawling wood that sits atop the ridge.

John Fenton had exhausted all complaints and now walked meekly beside me and made no comment as we entered Grovely Wood. I knew not the path that we should take and so followed a course that I hoped would lead in time to the ranging southern hazel coppices. We crossed a broad central drive and in time the taller trees gave way to a great succession of uncut and identical bushes and amongst these we followed a web of faint paths. A breeze rattled gently at the hazel leaves and brought notice of the smouldering combustion of the charcoal industry and we met with one charcoal burner at his work who upon hearing the name Peter Winter nodded and gestured to a path as though it were a thoroughfare in a busy city. The way ahead proved to be little more than an entrance to a further maze of flourishing hazel bushes and we soon became lost for I knew not which direction we should take. We halted to rest awhile and John queried whether it was ever our intention to visit Salisbury and complained bitterly that we had not a scrap of food to eat. I stooped to retrieve a freshly fallen hazel nut and my companion looked on in disgust as I broke open its shell with my teeth and offered the nut to be eaten.

"Henry, if I were a pig I might consider it."

With not a cracked twig to betray their approach we were taken aback as a band of gaunt and hollow-eyed nutters drifted silently

before us through the low wood as if they were weightless spirits
bound only to this earth by the ballast of their laden sacks. As the last
spectral figure vanished between the stands of hazel John dropped to
the woodland floor and looked aghast.

"Henry that shall soon be us if we do not find our way."

I urged John to get to his feet for I considered it my duty to
distribute some coins to assist these souls in securing food and lodging
for I believed them to be itinerants and not local men. As we lumbered
in pursuit of these ethereal figures, no sooner had we found our way
to a woodland track then we encountered a small but imposing figure
standing in our path. I soon recognised it to be Peter Winter the charcoal
burner and I was much relieved to again make his acquaintance but did
not receive the greeting that I expected. A dark storm quickly gathered
upon this little man's furrowed brow and before I could speak, he
flew at me causing John Fenton to hastily come between us. I have
described before the impediment to the charcoal burner's speech whilst
he strained to be understood and was clearly in a condition of great
anxiety but I could not comprehend the woodman's plight. Without
warning he turned about and urged us to follow and we were barely
able to keep pace whilst I caught sight of the band of emaciated nutters
passing from our view upon a different trail and I much regretted not
being able to come to their aid. In time we reached an encampment
where I fully expected to find the boy Tam and the mention of the
boy's name only served to agitate the man further as he rummaged in
his crude shelter. The encampment was not as before for it had moved
to a new grove amongst recently cut hazel bushes and a great orderly
clamp of wood was stacked and prepared for the making of charcoal
but was not yet lit. Peter Winter returned with the book Robinson
Crusoe, as he had done at our first encounter but he did not wish me to
read from the book and instead waved it in the air whilst pointing at
me and grunting in frustration. I knew that Tam lay at the heart of this

mystery and as I spoke his name again the little man nodded wildly
and pointed away into the wood as if directing us to the boy. To alarm
us further he then pretended to cast a noose around his own neck and
mimicked the death throes of a hanged man. Peter Winter threw the
old book to the forest floor and again urgently beckoned us to follow
him and at a trot we took a woodland trail until a broad track was
met and in time we emerged from the wood where a distant view of
Salisbury Cathedral now lay before us. There was no mistaking our
destination for the charcoal burner grunted and pointed to the slender
spire and chased us down the track for a short distance to hurry us on
our way to Salisbury.

As we descended towards Wilton, I breathlessly recounted to
John Fenton the circumstance of witnessing the apportioning of a
stolen deer at the New Inn and young Tam's complicity in that illegal
act. John's lethargy and resentment at his enforced pedestrianism was
now replaced by a growing curiosity and he stated that perhaps the
boy had again engaged in this illicit activity and was now residing in
the gaol as a consequence. At the Bell Inn we were fortunate that a
Salisbury bound coach was soon to depart and as three passengers had
disembarked to visit Wilton House, we were able to secure inside seats.
John Fenton and I sat with our luggage beside us to enable a hasty exit
at the gaol as agreed with the coachman, upon pressing two shillings
into his hand. We travelled in silence but all the while my head span
as I speculated upon the awful circumstances that might lie before us.
At the dread building that is Fisherton Gaol we were met with blank
expressions when I enquired of the boy Tam, for we had no surname to
offer. John Fenton soon pushed me aside.

"Gateman, we wish to know the fate of the young poacher who
took a deer from the wood at Wilton, by name of Tam."

This blunt demand did indeed meet with the acknowledgement
that the boy's name was Thomas Targett and not Tam at all and I

have again been fooled by the vagaries of the Wiltshire tongue. Upon
the release of another coin the gateman revealed that the boy was
this very day at the Petty Sessions where with two further men they
shall stand before the magistrate. Through the streets of Salisbury we
dashed to the new Council House where the usher informed us that
the Court had broken for luncheon and would resume upon the return
of the Magistrate. The official confirmed that Thomas Targett and the
two men would appear before the bench this afternoon and added that
their case was "Pecu'lar" in that the case against the accused had been
established by evidence contained within a book. I pressed the man to
inform as to which book could possibly relate such a tale at which he
rubbed his chin.

"Tis a Tur in Zarch o' Chalk, boi A Pudestrin' or zummat."

At first, I could by no means comprehend the gravity of this
disclosure and I enquired whether this book was on sale within the
City.

"Oi believes zo, yus zur."

The official closed the door upon us and whilst John Fenton
continued to question the relevance of a book to this case, a cold fear
soon overwhelmed me and I tried to gather my thoughts.

"John, I know not how it has come to pass but I sincerely
believe that it is a book that I have inadvertently written and it is my
own words that condemn young Thomas Targett and the two men."

I confirmed that this also explained the behaviour of the
charcoal burner for he had gesticulated towards me with a book in
a most accusing manner. John burst out laughing at my words as he
believed it a preposterous notion that one could write a book without
knowing of it.

"Let us go to the booksellers Henry, to find your mysterious
book."

After visiting three books sellers with John Fenton mimicking the Court Usher by requesting "A Tur in Zarch O'Chaak boi A Pudestrin'" and receiving nothing but puzzled expressions, upon the fourth attempt, to my great astonishment, we were successful. The bookseller presented us with a book in boards and my mouth was agape as I read its label;

"A Tour in Search of Chalk through parts of South Wiltshire in 1807 written in a series of letters by A Pedestrian."

The bookseller queried whether we required both books by the same author and before my eyes appeared not one but two books of my pedestrian adventures. As you well know my dear uncle, the second volume is entitled "A Tour in Search of Flint through parts of South Wiltshire in 1808."

"Henry, you have been busy. Give me your purse, we shall take both books," said John Fenton.

John demanded that we required fortification after this discovery and led me to the Plume of Feathers in Queen Street and soon placed a large brandy in my hands.

"You are certainly a dark horse Mr Chalk, or should I say Mr A Pedestrian. We must however think clearly and act quickly if we are to help the boy. Where in these books are the words that incriminate young Thomas Targett?"

I could not at first bare to touch these books and instead stated that it must be recorded towards the fore of the first volume, where I endured the hospitality of the New Inn below Grovely Wood and it was the night that I left my bed and chose instead to sleep amongst the straw above a stable. As John flicked through the pages of "A Tour in Search of Chalk", he at first confirmed that it was you sir who had initiated the publication of my private letters and I confess my anger grew with this revelation. John calmed me and stated that the most pressing business was to prepare a defence and my whimpering was not helping matters. I know not how long I sat staring blankly ahead before John slammed the book down upon the table making me jolt from my unpleasant reverie.

"This is what we must do. Henry you shall not appear at the court at all and you must place your faith in me. Until I return, under no circumstances, must you stray from this place and please will you now give me your word that this will be so?"

I muttered into my brandy that I would remain for I felt too shaken to do otherwise. Invigorated by a further brandy and the intrigue of the occasion, John Fenton snatched up "A Tour in Search of Chalk" and was gone in a trice whilst I stared at the remaining volume. I was at first unable to touch the book as if it were the most vile object but curiosity and perhaps vanity overcame me and with trepidation I opened the bare boards. Upon reading the Letter to the Editor, in your own words, it at once became clear your purpose in publishing my letters and indeed you knew that one day, I would hold these books in my hand and that your efforts would overcome those who wished to keep us apart. I believed that you may have abandoned your nephew and I cannot express enough my feelings of relief to find out that this is not so. My rage turned upon those so called guardians who purport to protect me from unforeseen dangers and from my own recklessness and surely Mr John Fenton forms part of this conspiracy. Despite any assurances to the contrary, for the circumstances had truly changed with this revelation, I arranged for our luggage to remain at the Plume of Feathers and hastened to the courtroom where the afternoon session had already commenced.

I was fortunate that there was sufficient interest in this case to attract a decent public audience in the gallery and I kept myself secreted behind two taller gentlemen. Thomas Targett looked pale and wide eyed as he peered from the dock, flanked by the Landlord of the New Inn and the man I once recorded as "Stoopid Martin". The Magistrate, one Mr Peter Maxfield Esq, was large and florid and scowled down at the accused as if their very presence in his court was sufficient to confirm their guilt. The crowd about me coughed, shuffled and muttered until the Magistrate lost patience and roared at the top of his voice.

"SILENCE. I must have silence or I shall throw you all out into the street where you belong. Pray excuse me, I do not direct this at you Mr Rammage, Miss Davies or you Mr Sheldrake."

The Magistrate now asked for the bookseller's assistant who had brought this case before the Court to be sworn in, whereupon the usher thrust a bible towards this overtly expectant witness and he duly swore an oath.

"Tell the Court your name sir."

"'Olford yer wurship."

"That would be Holford?"

"Indeed t'wud yer wurship."

"And you are in the employment of Priest's the booksellers in the City of Salisbury?"

"I most zertainly is yer wurship."

"And you present as evidence for the offence of deer stealing by the accused who stand before us, a book entitled..A Tour in Search of Chalk, by A Pedestrian?"

"I does yer wurship. Turrible doings."

"Mr Holford, will you refrain from rubbing your hands together whilst you address the court as it is most unseemly and one might argue that it is the author of this work who has recorded the crime and not yourself, that may be due the financial gain of one third of the penalty."

"Ah, but ee ain't ere an' I is yer wurship."

With this exchange I shrank down further in my concealment for I did not wish to catch Tom Targett's or the Landlord's eye for any recognition would spell disaster. I could not as yet see John Fenton's position in the court.

The Magistrate continued to question the bookseller's assistant.

"Do you read all the books that you sell Mr Holford?"

"I dun't read zo good zur. Twas a cust'mer did tell I n' I is only doin' me duty yer wurship."

"Usher, will you now read the relevant sections of this book to the court."

The usher now leant forward to whisper to the Magistrate.

"No, you certainly may not borrow my spectacles. I shall read it myself."

I felt sick to the pit of my stomach as the courtroom now resounded with my own condemning words and the accused looked at one another in expressions of dread horror as their secretive exploits were broadcast by the Magistrate.

"As the court will now be aware, these most serious events also record the complicity of the constable himself, but I have been informed that he is since deceased."

The Magistrate now turned to address the three accused who all looked down at their feet rather than catch his eye.

"This deplorable act is clearly beyond the powers of this court for it requires the severest of sentences and I hold no doubt that transportation awaits you. You shall therefore remain in Fisherton Gaol until the October Assizes."

The Magistrate was poised with gavel in hand when I heard John Fenton's voice.

"Sir, please excuse me."

"What is this?" exclaimed the Magistrate.

"I have evidence pertinent to this case which may prevent a grave injustice here today. I am a good friend of Sir Richard Colt Hoare who is perhaps known to you?"

"Indeed he is, he is also a Magistrate..but you must be sworn in and give your name sir, this is not a gentleman's club but a court of law."

John Fenton was duly sworn in and adopting his father's theatrical and stentorian tones he declared that until his arrival in Salisbury not one hour ago he had no knowledge of the existence of the book in question.

"I have made a cursory perusal and that is sufficient."

He then held up the first of the pair of books that we had just purchased and turned full circle to display the volume to all present within the court whilst I cowered down in my concealed position.

"I too appear in "A Tour in Search of Chalk". I shall not however be seeking recourse for the slights against my character contained therein. It is well known to the literate public that modest works such as this are but a vain accomplishment and a concoction plagiarised from the work of real travellers and real authors. It is perhaps the only shred of truth within the book where my own father, Mr Richard Fenton, who is himself a lawyer and dear friend to Sir Richard Colt Hoare, upon page one hundred and sixty seven, makes the following statement and I read; " You travel, you correspond, you embellish and then you publish". My Father is currently concocting just such a work for his own amusement. It shall differ in that it will grandly entertain and it is to be called "A Tour in Quest of Genealogy". Indeed, you may call it a satire upon such inferior works as the laborious scribbles of Mr A Pedestrian."

Once again my book was displayed to the court, as John Fenton paused in his delivery.

"Travel as we all know is tedium. Pedestrian travel is tedium in the extreme, sir, I know for I have suffered it myself, though not of my own choosing. Any flight of fancy or ripe anecdote from some adventurous tale will enrich the piece and indeed the printing presses in Paternoster Row are a blur of ink and machinery and the bookstands in the capital are creaking under the very weight of such vapid publications.

I now give an example that shall put beyond all doubt the validity of this work as a faithful record of events. Sir, you will no doubt be familiar with the name..Mr William Beckford of Fonthill and that it is well known that he will admit no persons to his Abbey."

"I have heard it said," agreed the Magistrate, "although it is the last place on earth that I should wish to visit and the last person on earth whom I should wish to encounter. The man is a fiend and an abomination, proceed Mr Fenton."

"Quite so sir, nevertheless, the young pedestrian purports to have entered the forbidden grounds belonging to the "Abbott" of Fonthill..yes It is a nomenclature that our mutual friend the Baronet also finds amusing. He then enters the building, meets Mr William Beckford, ascends the tower and flees with a pack of slavering dogs at his heals. It is the fare of a limited imagination. Sir, it was I who made a wager of five guineas with the author that he should carry out this trespass. It was conducted as a consequence of much libation but hands were shaken and a wager is a wager after all."

"Indeed it is, pray continue."

"It was perhaps three days after the wager was set that I met again with the author whereupon, in the presence of Sir Richard Colt Hoare at his home in Stourhead, we listened to an admission of his failure to fulfil the terms of the wager. Sir, if you study the volume before you, and we have to endure one hundred pages until the account is given, of how our Pedestrian succeeds in his mission to ascend the tower of Fonthill Abbey. I shall gladly request of Sir Richard Colt Hoare that he fully endorses my account, if it is the wish of the Court."

The Magistrate stated that he would not wish the Baronet to be troubled by such matters.

"Sir, I should like to conclude," said John Fenton, "that the incident of deer stealing is no less a fabrication than the entering of the domain of Mr William Beckford. It is a fine example of the embellishment recommended by my own father. It shall give colour to a bloodless tale for who wishes to read of the padding feet of a timid pedestrian and that, your worship, is all I have to say on the matter."

"Mr Fenton, the Court has, I believe, established that the anonymous author is known to you?"

"He is sir, but he is also an acquaintance of Sir Richard Colt Hoare and I would not wish to further sully the name of our noble friend by revealing such unfortunate.... connections. Indeed, it would be best for all concerned if the remaining stock of this inferior work were to be destroyed, to avoid any future indiscretions. I shall recommend this action to the author when we next meet."

"Quite so, quite so," declared the Magistrate, before scowling again at the accused, "hmm, I do not doubt that these two men and that boy are capable of such deeds for one only has to look at them. Tut tut..their day shall surely come. I am very grateful to you Mr Fenton for your timely intervention. The book is poorly writ. Case dismissed."

As the Magistrate banged his gavel upon the bench, he again raised his voice.

"We are not yet finished. There is a question of costs. Mr Holford, will you stand?"

The bookseller's assistant now rose slowly to his feet with his shoulders drooping as he glowered across the Court towards the victorious John Fenton.

"Mr Holford, in bringing this most insubstantial case before the court you shall pay five shillings."

I rushed from the gallery for I sincerely wished to explain and apologise to Thomas Targett and the two men for the great trouble that I had caused but found only John Fenton strolling proudly from the Court and he turned sharply as I called out to him.

"John, where are Thomas and the two men?"

John Fenton dismissed my question and instead berated me loudly for not remaining as I had promised at the Plume of Feathers. I informed him that I could not care less what he thought and my concerns were for the accused men and the boy Tom.

"They have fled Henry for caged foxes require little encouragement to bolt for freedom. I have averted disaster here today and yet you do not thank me?"

I could not however contain my rage and declared my abhorrence at witnessing John Fenton's pleasure in the condemning of my words and most private thoughts at which he protested most vehemently.

"I have done today what all good lawyers do. I have said what needed to be said and without falsehood. I wished to spare you any public humiliation hence extracting beforehand your sincere promise that you would remain at the inn. You did not do so you and have brought this pathetic and ungrateful indignation upon yourself. I am shot through the heart and shall return immediately to Pembrokeshire. You can meet with whom you like at Salisbury Cathedral and your friendly cutler, Mr Henry Shorto can guard over you for I am done with trying to help Henry Chalk. I am very hungry and where is my wretched bag?"

I informed John Fenton that his bag was safe at the Plume of Feathers whereupon he swiftly turned on his heel and left me standing outside the Council House. I now realise that even Mr Philip Crocker has broken my confidence as I have told no person other than he of my plans to meet with Mr Henry Shorto. Mr Crocker has related the details of our private conversation to John Fenton and it seems that none can be trusted whom I once considered to be my friends. No persons have been informed either of my meeting with Robert and Sarah Foster at Salisbury Cathedral and so Mr John Fenton has surpassed himself in the reading of my correspondence at the George

Inn this morning. Perhaps whilst I walked with Mr Crocker, Mr John Fenton was in my room reading my private papers. What is private now my dear uncle?

Mr Henry Shorto has no such allegiances and has just returned home therefore I now conclude my sorry tale for I have much to explain to one whom I may trust without reservation.

Your faithful nephew,
HENRY CHALK

Thursday 8th September 1808

MY DEAR UNCLE,

Despite my comfortable bed I have had a restless night for I have been unable to stop my mind from churning over the events of yesterday. Last evening I explained to Mr Shorto all that has occurred and he thinks it a most extraordinary tale. Sir, I am now caused some embarrassment for my meeting with Mr Shorto in May of this year is also recorded in the second volume of my published letters and he has referred to my departure from his house in the early morning.

"I better understand your action Henry from the reading of these pages. At the time I confess to being greatly disappointed for there was much that I still wished to discuss."

This morning after studying me across the breakfast table he interrupted my reverie.

"There is a simple antidote for your condition Mr Chalk. My family are not due to return until Saturday, when you also have a meeting in Salisbury. I propose a short pedestrian excursion, not a grand tour but a modest ramble, once I ensure that there is no outstanding business that cannot await my return."

I could see that my host was barely able to conceal his excitement at the prospect of becoming a pedestrian tourist and so I welcomed this suggestion.

"Henry you are better associated with the world outside the boundary of this city than I. My old boots must suffice and I require a pack so if you will excuse me, I shall return as quickly as I am able."

Whilst Mr Shorto attends to his affairs, I must inform you of an issue upon which my mind is already set. Sir, I invite and welcome you to join Chalk's Brewery as a partner and no longer will you be cast as a spectre in the shadows by those who do not know you. We shall go forth in business together and banish our estrangement for it is a circumstance that I cannot comprehend and one that I am now most fervently unwilling to perpetuate. Indeed, when I gather my thoughts, I shall write to the trustees of Chalk's Brewery to insist upon this arrangement with instructions that it be carried out forthwith. I hope and prey that you will accept this proposal.

My dear uncle you have gone to the trouble and expense of publishing the accounts of my wanderings with the intention of ensuring our reunion. I do however remain aghast at the discovery that you have broadcast to the world my most private thoughts. When my letters went unanswered I did become less guarded in my words for it was as if I were writing only to myself. Indeed, you are vindicated by your actions but others have read these books as I witnessed only yesterday in the Courtroom in Salisbury. I now also understand better the antics of the pedestrian tourist who found my spyglass upon the long barrow and put it to good use before returning it to me at the Winterslow Hut. I was at the time perplexed by his intimate knowledge of my previous ramblings but all is now explained for he possessed a copy of "A Tour in Search of Chalk" when I did not know that such a book existed. As I had become inspired by your book "A Pedestrian Tour of North Wales, 1805" and so this fellow had decided to follow the course of my first pedestrian adventure. Sir, there are consequences that have already arisen and may yet arise from your actions. Before Mr Shorto returns I have perhaps one hour to visit each and every bookseller in Salisbury to purchase all remaining copies of these first and second volumes of my published letters for I intend to destroy them. They have served your purpose my dear uncle.

Your nephew and forthcoming partner in business,
HENRY CHALK.

Thursday evening.
The Glove Inn

Mr Shorto and I did not leave Salisbury as early as we might but nevertheless have enjoyed a fine afternoon. We are this evening staying at the Glove Inn and you may recall that it is a place that I have visited before at the foot of Whitesheet Hill. It was not my intention to record the details of our excursion but Mr Shorto is now engaged in corresponding to an unsuspecting relation, no doubt to inform of his new life as a pedestrian tourist. I warned my friend that he may soon find his words in print and so to manage his subjects well and with discretion.

There is always a pleasant expectancy when departing upon any ramble and today in Mr Shorto's company his eagerness was palpable but he assured me at the outset that he would not talk all the way.

In time we gained the elevation of the raceplain and observed from a distance a noisy cluster of humanity and the bright colours of a race meeting soon to commence. Rather than gamble our money away, I directed Mr Shorto to a hazel bush beside the turnpike where I used his penknife, indeed a tool manufactured in his own workshop and with "Shorto Salisbury" stamped upon its blade, to cut a stick as befits a pedestrian tourist. I explained my preference for a stick not with a cleft at the top and instead it must be the thick end which should be held in the hand. The opposing and narrower end shall serve one better in all regards and I demonstrated to Mr Henry Shorto how with this whippy stick brambles and nettles may be severed at a blow whilst it is still stout enough to support the weight of a man. This narrow end may prize out a buried flint for inspection or test the depth of a bog before entering. It shall poke, prod, push, scrape, slash or strike and once broken it is easily replaced with another. An old dry stick may preserve fond memories but a green stick will bring vigour and I proclaimed it to be the weapon of choice for the pedestrian tourist. In response Mr Shorto brandished his new hazelstick as might a fencing master.

"En garde Monsieur Chalk."

Our sticks now clashed together as we engaged in battle to the great amusement of an overflowing carriage of passing racegoers who called out their encouragement.

From the lofty raceplain we followed the ghosts of the Roman Empire and you may find useful reference upon the construction of Roman roads in the second volume of my travails, my dear uncle, for I am covering old ground.

There is a thread of life that has long existed in the valley to the south of the raceplain with the gentle river Ebble at its heart. The grand old church of Bishopstone stands in near isolation for the new village of Bishopstone has inexplicably moved away to a new location further up the valley. The old village is but a series of humps and bumps in a grass field and my walking companion paused as we gazed out upon this conspicuous desertion.

"Where once the cottage stood, the hawthorn grew
Remembrance wakes, with all her busy train
Swells at my breast and turns the past to pain."

I complimented Mr Shorto on his recitation, for such fine words along the way shall serve him well in his ambition to become a pedestrian tourist.

How perfect for the keeping of life is the crystal clear river Ebble? The mills and constructed meadows shall compete for its bounty, to push the paddles or to drown the fresh grass. As a consequence of a discussion with Mr Philip Crocker during my convalescence at Stourhead, I now understand better this fine system where in the early months of the year the water shall protect the young grass in the meadows from the deadly frost. The water is encouraged to float down these slight gradients from the intricate raised channels thereby covering and protecting the nub of the grass root. It is the job of the "drowner" to work his meadow by blocking with a turf here or releasing the flow elsewhere. During the day the sheep may now feed upon this early season bite of grass and the shepherd will at night pen the flock upon the sides of the valley where they shall enrich the soil. The hazel hurdles that form these pens must be moved daily to ensure that each arable field enjoys its share of the "golden hoof".

My companion listened avidly and encouraged me to continue with this calendar of life outside the city walls.

I described how the ploughman turns the enriched soil and the sowers cast last harvest's seed. Boys will then rattle at the birds as the green shoots show and at the end of summer the harvesters bend their backs to bring in the prize, to the satisfaction of the wealthy landowner. As winter steals the daylight hours the corn is threshed

in the dusty barn and a weight of water is held back before the mill
for the faithful river to again serve the landowner well. The old mill
splashes and rumbles into life with the rotation of paddles, gears and
the grinding together of great millstones. In addition to the bulk of the
Squire's harvest, many a smallholder would require the services of the
mill. The cart or packhorse would make this journey upon paths and
ways born out of necessity, hauling the corn and then grumbling home
with the flour after begrudging the sly miller his dubious share of the
smallholder's annual toil.

My walking companion considered this short account of rustic
life.

"Imagine Henry, if life in England beyond this horizon one day
ceased altogether. Could not this gentle valley continue as it always
had and there would be enough for all?"

I stated that I should like to consider that this was once the
way of it in simpler times but that now our entire globe shall be the
new horizon. I explained that it was my ambition to export Chalk's
Pale Ale far and wide across the continent in glass bottles, but first
the barley must come from somewhere such as these cultivated slopes
above the gentle river Ebble. My friend again considered the words of
Mr Goldsmith:

"A time there was, ere England's griefs began
When every rood of ground maintain'd its man
For him light labour spread her wholesome store
Just gave what life required, but gave no more."

We had now drawn to a standstill as if walking and discussion
were not compatible bedfellows and I encouraged my friend to bring
his thoughts with him for we must make progress on our ramble.

There followed a lengthy silence as we climbed from the Ebble
valley to gain a ridge to the south to follow a broad drover's path on
our westerly course. I thought back to the cycle of life in the Ebble

valley and also to a song that I heard the harvesters sing over and again upon the occasion of the harvest home at Widdington Farm. Now with breath to spare I gave voice to this song, although I have had little experience of singing in company. As I completed the first few verses, Mr Shorto listened intently and then joined in with the chorus with his rich and deep voice supporting the melody like the solid foundations of an old barn. The song is I believe called John Barleycorn and is in keeping with the suspicions and mystery bound up with the cutting of the last sheaf of the harvest. Every means is taken to try to kill poor John Barleycorn but he returns with vigour and it is a blessing for without his sustenance we should ourselves surely die of hunger. John Barleycorn is now incarcerated within the great ricks across the land and despite the blades, forks and the beating with crabtree sticks before the eventual grinding between great stones, he shall survive. Mr Shorto paused to produce a penny loaf from his pack and we chewed upon a crust in celebration of John Barleycorn and once we had swallowed him, we began the song again and so a brewer and a cutler idled away their afternoon in a pleasurable rhythm of song, conversation and observation.

In due course our progress was interrupted by the most extraordinary vista to the south of our ridge which caused us to stand in acceptance of the time required to explore the diminishing scale of fields, hedges, valleys and woods. A rising twist of smoke here and there flagged some degree of conflagration in a cottage hearth or woodland clearing but with the harvest now over we could detect little other human activity from our lofty perch. In regular formation a fleet of plump white clouds floated gently above this late summer mantle of the county of Dorsetshire and perhaps Hampshire also and in the far distance the sea glistened like treasure laid out in the sun. I speculated that it must be the chalky cliffs of the Isle of Wight that we could discern beyond the shimmering sea and I lamented that I had not brought my spyglass for fear of mislaying it again. Our contemplation was disturbed by a large flock of sheep being driven towards our position and rather than become engulfed in livestock we were forced to stand aside. The surface of this way is pock marked by the hoof and we encountered two more great flocks of these horned sheep as we continued on our westerly course.

In time, I now discouraged my friend from making an inspection of the views to our north until we had gained the highest elevation upon our ramble and I pointed ahead towards the clump of trees that was to be our goal. To humour me, my fellow pedestrian then refrained from commenting on the eye catching tower of Fonthill Abbey that so dominated this brooding Vale.

"So, Henry, you had a purpose and a destination all along?"

I explained that it was at this same clump of trees, in May of this year, that I had realised the loss of my spyglass for I saw it glinting from a distant long barrow. Upon reaching this vantage point we then drew breath and I cast my arm to the north where the dark and wooded undulations of the Vale of Wardour offer a broad interruption to the ubiquitous chalk ridges and plains of South Wiltshire. With the uniform chalk layer disturbed and removed by some distant upheaval, it is a place of exposed rock, clay and water seepages where the River Nadder collects its sandy and snaking character, before conforming to the rules of the river Avon beside Salisbury Cathedral. I advised my friend that as you wander the dark and deeply incised lanes of this mysterious vale, the mischievous sprites of earth and stone shall dart about amongst the shadows and cause the visitor many a backward glance. Despite my best attempts to distract, it was inevitably Mr Beckford's conspicuous tower that drew my companion's attention.

"So, there it is, Fonthill Abbey. Henry from what you tell me of Mr John Fenton's presentation in court, I know not whether you gained access to the tower and therefore the deer stealers were indeed guilty or whether all is embellishment and justice was fairly seen to be done by the two men and the boy?"

I stated that I chose not to answer his question and neither did I wish to approach the Abbey and from my answer he must draw his own conclusions.

Our stomachs informed us that we must soon eat and so we made our way towards the Glove Inn and skirted around the grounds of Ferne House, lest I should again meet the daughter of that place.

Mr Shorto has now concluded his correspondence and so I must put down my pen for there is more to life than a perpetual record of one's existence.

*

Through Mr Shorto's vigilance and curiosity a mystery has been unearthed. My companion had opened Gulliver's Travels at an arbitrary place and it was the chapter from Gulliver's adventure in Laputa, the flying island. I had not yet progressed this far in the story and Mr Shorto chuckled to himself as he read but upon turning the page he paused.

"Henry, will you please show me again the curious script in your father's hand?"

There was an urgency to this request not in keeping with the pensive nature of my walking companion and I swiftly did as he asked. Last night I had shared this mystery with my host explaining how my departure from Southwark was hastened by the discovery of this single sheet of paper inserted inside the book, causing me to follow in my father's footsteps.

"Look here at this diagram on page one hundred and sixty two, for it contains a multitude of squiggles and see how they compare with your father's script."

When the two pages were gathered before the candle there was indeed a similarity but I stated that there were many more characters in the table than were written upon the page. With a pen and paper he proceeded to try to make sense of this new conundrum but after a lengthy period he sighed and put down his pen.

"There must be some order to this Henry or perhaps our own alphabet is coded amongst this table but where to start?"

I now wondered at my father's denial that he possessed a copy of Gulliver's Travels and that it was not after all a fear that it may corrupt and offend but instead that it contained a greater mystery that he did not wish me to encounter. We must now sleep upon this puzzle and in the morning we shall venture forth into the dark vale.

*

Friday morning
At Wardour Castle

A dense fog occurred in the night and greeted us as we strode away from the Glove Inn. I decided that we should seek out the long barrow, where I had before mislaid the spyglass and we soon left the turnpike and made our way up Whitesheet Hill. The fine mist clung to our clothes and caused the multitude of spider's webs to sag under this drenching and we still did not rise above the fog even with our clambering upon the ancient tomb at the crest of the ridge.

Mr Shorto requested the second published volume of my letters and upon extracting it from my pack I was about to speak when he smiled and held up his hand for me to remain silent.

"Here it is, page fourteen."

My friend read in silence for a short time and then closed the book.

"My dear A Pedestrian, it is one aspect of having your words and thoughts in print for you no longer have to repeat yourself. You suggest Henry that a chronology may be established and you have witnessed with your own eyes the fine and rare metals extracted from Bush Barrow, which you inform me is a round tomb. We must not forget that every past era had a past, present and a future and for these stone dependent peoples, who rest beneath our feet, the appearance of metal was beyond their horizon. One can only speculate at the arrival of the first metals, perhaps brought by strangers to our shores. Indeed, the occupant of Bush Barrow was fairly replete with metals and he may be adjudged to be a foreigner, a magician, a king or indeed the architect of Stonehenge itself, such is the proximity of his tomb to the great stones from your description Henry.

To present a piece of gold to the occupants of our long barrow would indeed mystify but its softness renders it useless to a hunter or a rudimentary farmer. It is an adornment and its rarity still implies wealth and power today so I propose that the occupant of bush barrow is more of our world than that of his stone dependent ancestors."

I could but agree with the insight of a cutler for my companion offers a fresh and insightful view into the mysteries of the past and I suggested that he will one day make a fine antiquary.

The sun appeared to be in no hurry to assert itself but as we speculated upon the distant past a pale blue sky slowly emerged through the dying miasma to confirm that a fine day was in prospect. We followed the old abandoned turnpike in an easterly direction for a short distance before scaling down the grassy slopes of this ridge to cross the new road and in time passed under a rock arch to make our approach to Old Wardour Castle. Settled in its comfortable hollow there is sufficient misty light remaining to assist with the picturesque splendour of this ruin and my walking companion is now immovable from this spot and he draws whilst I write. I have before established that Mr Shorto is a fine draftsman and I have just interrupted him to make a compliment as his drawing nears completion.

"Drawing, painting, observing birds, poetry and now, since meeting you Mr Chalk, pedestrianism and a curiosity regarding flint. These are the subjects that preoccupy me whilst my trade is that of a cutler."

I shall now take the opportunity to study again my father's curious script and compare it to the table of squiggles in Gulliver's Travels to see whether I can make any sense of it.

*

Friday evening
Rollestone Street, Salisbury

So, we are now returned to Rollestone Street and I can barely consider what tomorrow shall bring for Miss Sarah Foster arrives in Salisbury with her brother Robert. Mr Shorto has blisters on both feet and as he hobbled into the hallway, he proudly displayed his hazel stick to the housekeeper who tutted about what Mrs Shorto would have to say on the matter.

We were required to ride on the outside of the coach from the village of Hindon to the Deptford Inn this afternoon and we there had two hours to wait before we secured seats aboard the Salisbury coach. We did not arrive at Mr Shorto's house until nine o clock and after a bath and a late supper I now dare not let my mind wander and so I shall conclude the tale of our ramble.

Mr Shorto has already proved that he will make a better pedestrian tourist than I for he recites poetry and is a splendid draughtsman and I believe in time will become a respected antiquarian. From old Wardour Castle we meandered towards the village of Tisbury which is surely an old habitation for it lies at the natural heart of a vale that appears as old as time itself. The church displays an ancient importance on its site beside the river Nadder and there is a hollow yew tree of extraordinary age and girth in the churchyard.

There are many stone quarries in Tisbury and it is a trade that must depend upon the outlying web of small lanes for the twisting river is not navigable. The stone for Salisbury Cathedral has its origins in this quarter of South Wiltshire and the challenge of transporting such huge volumes of freestone, before the advent of any turnpike road, speaks of a powerful determination. A traveller in this county is able to view Wiltshire's rich geology displayed upright within the fabric of its village buildings and it is uniformly the very local materials that are torn from the valley sides, collected from the fields or dug from the ground that are gratefully utilised. Only the most ambitious undertakings demand the ostentation of imported materials and Salisbury Cathedral and Stonehenge shall command our respect and wonder in this regard.

In one small quarry I found a dark and glassy substance that has the character of flint but is perhaps more course. I have struck it and it breaks like flint and is sharp enough to warrant the effort, should there be no flint available. Mr Shorto has retrieved a piece for he intends to make a collection of flint to enable a study of its origins and this substance is close enough in character to justify its transportation back to Salisbury.

The lure of Fonthill Abbey gnawed away at my walking companion and also guided his feet for in the airless late morning we followed a brook from Tisbury in the direction of Mr Beckford's domain. We soon found ourselves entering a deep and narrow valley where the ground was slippery under foot for this is a place of many springs, heavy clay and water seepages.

"Observe the alder tree Henry that prospers here and the horsetails for they both require an abundance of water."

With Mr Henry Shorto by my side, every natural thing that we encounter now has a name and I have learned much from my companion. The burgeoning hedgerows are becoming an untangled mystery for the ripe berries of the briar are indeed pleasantly sweet to eat whilst the sloe of the blackthorn is sour and unpleasant for Mr Shorto playfully encouraged me to bite into this tempting black fruit. Also, the handsome butterfly that fortuitously guided me to inspect Gulliver's Travels in my father's study is known as the red admiral, a summer visitor to these shores. I have explained the significance of this bright and fluttering creature to my friend and he suggests that I shall forever think on my father when I spy a red admiral on my travels.

"Butterflies are surely the greatest adornment of the English summer Henry and the red admiral is perhaps the most striking of all."

The hot sun bore down as we made our steady way up this windless and deeply incised valley and above the tree tops, upon the near horizon, small white clouds bubbled up as if we were immersed in a great frothing pot. A jay and then a green woodpecker passed noisy judgement before us, with first a screech of alarm to be seconded by the mocking laugh of the woodpecker as Fonthill Abbey again revealed itself. My stomach tightened with the memory of my clandestine visit to that place and I wished for some grand distraction to enable us to take a different course and forget entirely about Fonthill Abbey. The sprites of earth and stone kindly afforded my wish for in the most unlikely manner a distraction was stumbled upon. At a place where the infant brook wound through an open meadow, we knelt beside the stream to splash cool water into our hot faces. My friend released the cupped water from his hands and from the bed of the shallow stream he removed a flat slab of stone to observe it more closely.

"This is no ordinary stone. What do you see?"

I accepted the heavy and dark dripping lump and before I could make my own observations, Mr Shorto demonstrated the cause of his interest.

"See how it is formed. It has the appearance of once being a liquid for the flow is curiously preserved. Henry Chalk, it is now my turn to surprise you."

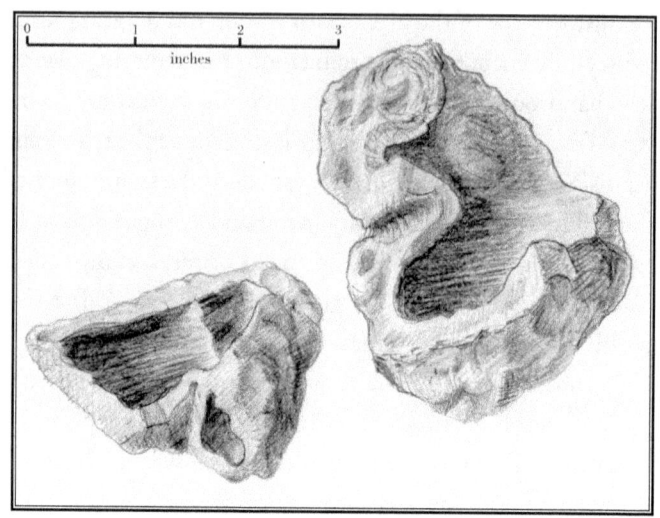

Tisbury Iron Ore

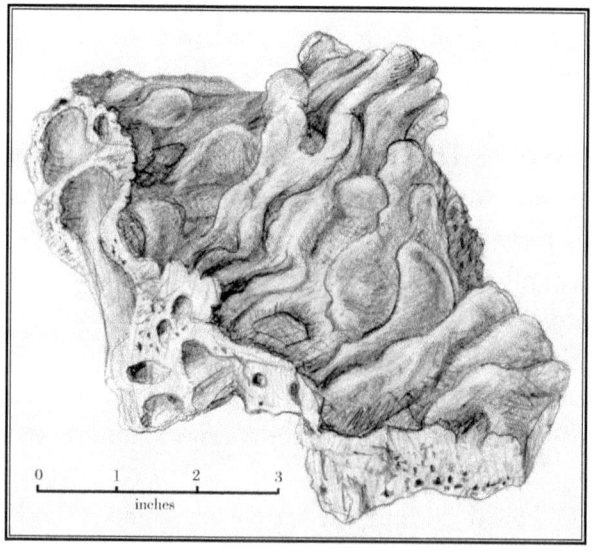

Tisbury Slag

I could see by the excited expression upon the face of my companion that he was indeed certain of the origins of this piece and I urged him to inform me of the nature of his discovery.

"Iron has been made upon this very spot. This piece is the waste residue, perhaps from the early manufacture of iron."

I looked about at the quiet narrow meadow for it appeared a world away from dark industry and ironworking but before I could question Mr Shorto further he raised himself and urged me to follow.

"Come, somewhere close at hand we shall find iron ore for you cannot make iron without it."

With the commencement of our search for iron ore I now embraced this most welcome distraction for it drew our attention to the ground beneath our feet and away from the conspicuous edifice that was the creation of the Caliph of Fonthill, Mr William Beckford.

Amongst the stubble in nearby fields we soon encountered further pieces of the dark grey residue from the iron making process but also the heavy crimson and rust brown pieces of iron rich stone from which iron is formed and we began gathering it up as if there were indeed some purpose to this action. In time we rested upon a large bank in the shade of a mighty oak tree to view the haul of stones at our feet.

"Well, I have been in your company not two whole days and I am now a fervent collector of stones. It is a consequence of being abroad with Henry Chalk."

I questioned my companion on what was to be done with this heap of heavy stones and Mr Shorto feigned his surprise;

"Why to make iron of course for South Wiltshire iron must be a rare commodity indeed. I will one day return to collect our pile and I shall know where to find it, for our old friend here shall not be moving far."

Mr Shorto slapped his hand upon the rugged bark of the great oak tree beside us.

"In truth Henry I do not understand the process of iron making that was employed here. I have witnessed upon my excursion to Ironbridge the same early residue for it is found in places where iron is produced today. Indeed this "cinder" or "slag" as it is termed can be introduced to the blast furnace for it still contains a good proportion of iron. Is it not heavy in the hand?"

There ensued some speculation upon the birth of iron making and Mr Shorto adjudged that iron ore would be combined with charcoal and a simple furnace might be constructed to produce a small volume of wrought iron. There must also be a supply of oxygen to increase the temperature of this operation and to this end a pair of bellows should suffice. Here at Tisbury, with the final formation of the iron, the slag has been made to drain from the raging furnace and flow sufficiently so as to form the quick to harden residues that remain for us to find in the stream bed and the soil. The wrought iron bloom is gone from this place for that is the prize.

"The making of iron began in a simple way, as must all things Henry. I cannot say whether we have today encountered the cradle of an ancient industry but neither do I see the remnants of the blast furnace."

I stated to Mr Shorto that iron objects were indeed absent from the South Wiltshire barrows and the discovered metal pieces were confined to brass, copper and gold. My friend confirmed that brass is a combination of copper and tin and so some ancient understanding of the transformation and the alloying metals was therefore understood.

"It is curious Henry, with the apparent ubiquity of iron ore in our country, that iron was not the first metal to be produced. I can only surmise that the greater temperatures that are required for the manufacture of iron were beyond the capabilities of these first ancient metalworkers."

We both lapsed into a thoughtful silence and lay back upon the bank to observe the colossal oak tree with its mighty girth, prospering here in the iron rich soil. If ever a natural object should possess the wisdom of years then surely within this majestic tree with its great spread of trunks and finer branches, heartwood and root there is a power forged through countless seasons. To sit in its welcome shadow is to be touched by a presence that is greater than the objects formed by man's intervention. I have scaled Silbury Hill and walked amongst the raised stones of Stonehenge but they do not readily whisper their purpose. A tree surely has no purpose other than to live and to promote life about it and yet our reverence is surely better directed towards a grand and ancient tree rather than an anciently adjusted stone. I sensed that Mr Shorto was also reluctant to move from this close affiliation with nature and his mood was reflective after long and silent meditation.

"Henry, consider if you will all the iron and steel that is deemed essential to our existence in the world today and here at our feet is heaped the earthly fruit that enables such enterprise. Ancient man once sought the best quality flint, as you have recently discovered, in the mines behind the Winterslow Hut and flint was once indispensible. Man will make progress, for such is our restless nature and so the following generations have abandoned one stone in favour of another."

I lamented the passing of the distant flint era and suggested that there was once a simplicity to the requirements of ancient man that is now lost to us.

"This was surely once a more brutal world Henry and that is not an attribute that I readily associate with you."

After considering this statement I confessed that as I was unable to deal a fatal blow to a fish for fear of hurting that creature then perhaps Mr Shorto was correct in his judgement.

As the sun dappled through the gently rustling leaves of the giant oak tree Mr Shorto dug deeper into my soul and I could but listen to this pervading wisdom.

"Henry, I have read in your own words how your eminent friend Sir Richard Colt Hoare sought sanctuary in the study of ancient antiquities as a distraction from the grief that he bore from the loss of his dear wife Hester. I adjudge that you are finding a similar distraction in a study of the flint age. The death of your father looms large as does the earlier death of your dear mother and the study of anciently worked flint is a comfortable world away. You are soon to meet with Miss Sarah Foster and it is surely time for the affairs of the heart to come before the commonplace business of the brain. You are young and there is time enough ahead for the study of old things."

I now helped Mr Shorto to his feet and we bid our silent farewells to the ancient tree and set off slowly for the village of Hindon, where I first met Miss Sarah Foster in such fortuitous circumstances. The conundrum of the lost era of Tisbury iron must await the arrival of the industrial antiquary to establish a satisfactory resolution but my host and I are in agreement that we have by chance undertaken "A Tour in Search of Iron" and such was our toast at dinner at the Deptford Inn.

I wish you goodnight my dear uncle and trust and hope that weary limbs assist with a swift passage to unhindered sleep for otherwise there is much to keep me tossing and turning in my bed.

Your faithful nephew
HENRY CHALK.

Saturday 10th September 1808

MY DEAR UNCLE,

I have indeed slept better than I expected and at breakfast I sent a note to the George Inn in the High Street, advising Mr Robert Foster of my address in Salisbury. Within the hour Robert Foster was standing before me and I could not take the smile from my face as I introduced Robert to Mr Shorto. There is so much that I need to convey to my good friend and not least the discovery of the publication of my private correspondence but all must wait until there is time enough to do so. My host suggested that it was akin to the meeting of two brothers such is the familiarity that exists between Robert and myself and he confessed that it has warmed his heart to witness such friendship. Robert has assured me that his sister has promised not to stray from their accommodation whilst he is absent for you will no doubt recall that it was just such a circumstance that caused the meeting between Miss Sarah Foster and myself in the first place.

"Mr Shorto, you will know by now that whither Mr Chalk goes then disruption shall soon follow."

My host stated that we had last evening returned safely from a short pedestrian tour and the acquiring of blisters upon his feet was the only mishap to befall us so perhaps their mutual friend was changing his ways.

"Sir, let us hope so. Henry, to avoid any confusion on the matter, please will you confirm that you are to meet with Sarah and myself at 3 o'clock within the northern porch of Salisbury Cathedral?"

My heart gave a giant leap upon hearing these words and I swiftly gave Robert my firm acknowledgement that this was indeed my intention and he checked his watch by Mr Shorto's longcase clock who confirmed the accuracy of this magnificent timepiece.

Our visitor now appeared impatient to depart and displayed not the usual ebullience that I associated with my friend. I now asked for Robert's assurance that all was as it should be and after a pause he admitted to an unsettling circumstance that had not long occurred upon leaving the George Inn to find his way to Rollestone Street.

"Henry, you will recall at the Winterslow Hut where across the hallway from your door lay the ailing doctor who on the night of the great storm stole a horse and saddle and then vanished into the night?"

I stated that despite the blow to my head I could remember clearly this circumstance although I never encountered the man who purported to be a doctor. I added that a number of other private possessions had gone missing and their loss was attributed to this same man.

"Well, whilst his door was open, I did enter his room to ensure that all was well as I thought his illness genuine and although he soon waved me away there was sufficient light to see his features clearly enough. I am blessed Mr Shorto for once I have seen a face I never forget it and today, Henry, on my way here, I have just passed by this same man in the streets of Salisbury. It took a further twenty or more paces for me to recall where I had before encountered this man and I then turned about to seek out this thief in the crowded street. To my surprise I found that this man had already paused at the corner to observe me and as a consequence of my looking back our eyes met for the briefest of moments. In a flash he was gone and I hastened to retrace my steps but upon rounding the corner and amongst the busy street I could find no trace of this rogue for he was quick to step into an alley or a shop doorway to avoid my interest. Henry, I do not believe that he is at all a good man for I witnessed malevolence in those staring eyes.

Please forgive and excuse me gentlemen for I am perhaps overly anxious on this day and it is all the fault of Mr Henry Chalk. I promised Sarah that I would not linger for she knows well enough my propensity for chatter so a messenger I must be. We shall meet again Mr Shorto. Henry, I look forward to the appointed hour."

Mr Shorto suggested that he would now escort Robert Foster back to the George Inn to ensure that all was well with a curious request that in his short absence I should not stray from the house. I am left to wonder at the identity of the ailing doctor and the wrong doings he may now be embarked upon in Salisbury.

I still await Mr Shorto's return but I have nothing more to add for I shall only confess to my fretful condition before the time has come to again meet with Miss Sarah Foster.

After this day my dear uncle it is my intention to return to Southwark where I shall make all the necessary arrangements for you to soon join me at Chalk's Brewery as my partner in business.

Your devoted nephew,
HENRY CHALK.

Correspondence to Mr Richard Fenton of Glynamel,
Fishguard, Pembrokeshire.

Wednesday 24th May 1809

My dear Mr Fenton,

I thank you sir for your kind and sympathetic correspondence and now humbly apologise for my lengthy silence. Indeed, it is Miss Foster herself who has encouraged me to be receptive to your appeal to again take up my pen after all these months and I draw upon her strength and support to steady my hand. I must learn from the course of my father's life and I shall not enter that cold and dark place called despair and by the recording of that fateful day and the ensuing turmoil I may yet begin to purge a great evil from my life.

My dear friend, I must not procrastinate further and I now cast my mind back to the events of 10th September of last year and return in my thoughts to Mr Henry Shorto's house in Rollestone Street where I am in a condition of great excitement for I am soon to meet with Miss Sarah Foster and her brother Robert at the northern porch entrance to Salisbury Cathedral. If I were a magician, I should alter the events upon that dread day and report instead that we drank tea at the George Inn for the duration of the afternoon or even examined with interest the silver gravy boats in Mr Shorto's shop in Queen's Street. It was not to be.

Mr Shorto assured me over and again of the accuracy of his longcase clock and also that he should soon be required to replace his worn floorboards after my incessant pacing up and down.

"Henry let us instead wear out the footways in the city if you are to continue in this manner. My family are not yet due to return and so, if you are agreeable, I shall accompany you and we may occupy ourselves until the time of your meeting."

I readily accepted Mr Shorto's suggestion and without explanation we left not by the front door but instead by the rear entrance of his house. I followed my host through the confined Three Cups Chequers to emerge into Winchester Street where we met with the outgoing tide of the gradually disbanding Saturday market. Small driven herds and gaggles of livestock and birds together with pedestrians and carts were now departing from their chaotic congregation in the market place and we crossed between a number of these straggling processions to make our way to St Ann's Street. Hats and eyebrows were raised upon the occasion of the esteemed cutler Mr Henry Shorto treading with care along the back lanes of the city. My companion stated that it was his intention to visit St Martin's Church but Salisbury Cathedral now loomed majestically in the opposing direction and I confessed to being helplessly drawn to the appointed meeting place despite there being a good hour at our disposal. Mr Shorto soon acquiesced but stated that if I had no objection, he would accompany me until the arrival of Robert and Sarah Foster. Forgetting that my private affairs had been scattered about the bookstands like washing left out to dry upon the hedgerows, I stated with some reticence that Miss Foster had been made sightless from an early age and I wished to inform my friend of this fact before introductions were made. Mr Shorto gripped my arm and halted before addressing me earnestly.

"My dear Henry, I have spent a restless night considering this circumstance after reading again the account of your first meeting with Miss Foster in Hindon. Love shall overcome such obstacles and you know this to be true with all your heart. Indeed, if any uncertainty exists then Miss Foster shall soon dispense with it and I shall eat your snakecatcher's hat if I am to be proved wrong."

I could only smile at the return of my oft repeated pledge and thanked my good friend for his concern but stated plainly that I harboured no such doubts.

Upon entering the cathedral close through St Ann's gate, Mr Shorto could now barely contain himself at the prospect of my meeting again with Miss Sarah Foster and was irrepressible in his chatter and he recommended many interesting features within the cathedral that we should seek out including the tomb of D'Aubigny Turbeville who was once a great oculist of this city. I was not required to ask after the deeds of this eminent gentleman for the plight of the unseeing world was now perhaps at the forefront of my friend's thoughts and I was hastily supplied with every detail and learnt that his most effective treatment was to extract iron splinters from the eye with the aid of a lodestone. The afflicted came from far and wide and from such remote quarters as the West Indies in search of the services of D'Aubigny Turbeville and it was once common to witness visitors in the streets of Salisbury with green silk over their faces or one or more eyes bandaged.

My friend then looked aghast and hastily apologised for his tactlessness in referring to such matters for he did not wish to cause offence.

"I am sorry Henry for I believe that I am nervous and am talking for the sake of talking so please forgive me."

We turned a corner and Salisbury Cathedral was soon revealed, rising from its spacious grass surrounds with the sporadic elm trees dwarfed by this breathtaking fulfilment of medieval vision. My heart dropped to my boots at this sight and I now believed that I had made a gross error for how could words alone convey to Miss Sarah Foster the awe experienced by the viewer or indeed the scale of such endevour. Upon reaching the northern porch Mr Shorto insisted that we tucked ourselves inside and did not loiter in plain view although in my distracted silence I cared little where I was positioned and so did not question this action. I now realise that this clandestine behaviour in concealing ourselves from view and by earlier leaving Mr Shorto's house by the servant's entrance was brought about by a degree of caution as to the presence in Salisbury of the mysterious ailing doctor. Indeed, it was kept from my ears at the time that this rogue upon meeting Robert Foster's gaze in the street, did draw his finger across his own throat in a most threatening manner before disappearing from view. Robert was unsettled by this action and did caution Mr Shorto to be on his guard also.

In the northern porch my racing mind was now directed to other matters and I welcomed the distraction of a small wandering dog as it entering this roomy antechamber which provides the main public entrance to Salisbury Cathedral. This scruffy four legged visitor soon cocked its leg and then appeared to enjoy the sound of his own voice enlarged inside this high stone porch and barked once more before leaving with an air of satisfaction and renewed importance.

A man with a crooked back and an ancient long grey wig then stumbled over the departing dog and uttered an unholy curse before taking a swipe at the animal with what appeared to be a hazel stick. The dog easily evaded the swinging blow and the irascible fellow continued towards the door of the main building muttering to himself and tapping furiously at the flag stones with his stick. By the opening and closing of this internal door there was released briefly into the porch the ethereal voice of a lone chorister amplified by the vastness within and it is a sound surely intended to transport even the most casual of visitors to believe that they are in the presence of angels. With the door closed I could now barely detect the heavenly voice and yet I was struck by the drifting notes of the chorister and indeed even by the short echoes of the barking dog from a moment before, for are these not sounds enhanced by the fabric of the building and its architecture? More visitors to Salisbury Cathedral came and went and Mr Shorto was required to smile politely and bid good afternoon to the respectable natives of Salisbury but refrained from explaining as to why he should be standing in the shadows of the northern porch. He consulted his fob watch and stated quietly that there was still three quarters of an hour until Miss Foster and her brother Robert were due to arrive and that his jaw now ached from having to smile at every passing acquaintance. To the long suffering Mr Shorto's consternation I suddenly announced that I now intended to dash to the city to make an important purchase thereby causing him to plead in whispered exasperation to explain myself. My friend appeared blank faced as I described the occurrence of a sudden epiphany by my listening to the amplified sounds of this cavernous stone building.

"Henry, I do not readily understand the connection between choristers and barking dogs and what is it that you need to purchase in such a rush? I beg that you pause .. and then take a breath before commencing for you shall only confuse me further. Good afternoon ..Mr and Mrs Gosling."

I did as instructed and gathered my thoughts before speaking.

"You have informed me that you have read again the account of the circumstances of my meeting with Miss Sarah Foster. Do you not agree that we conducted ourselves upon equal terms until daybreak informed of Sarah's condition?"

My friend nodded in agreement and then smiled wearily.

"Mr Bye..it is indeed a fine afternoon..Henry this is intolerable, pray continue."

"I believe that you thought me not listening when you described how those visitors to Salisbury seeking the treatment of D'Aubigny Turbeville wore green silk to cover their eyes? Without realising it you have provided the solution to my dilemma for although I have no such affliction, I shall now wear my own blindfold so that I may depend upon the remaining senses whilst we enter Salisbury Cathedral. Every soul who visits this place is humbled by the scale of this edifice and it is through both the eyes and the ears that this shall occur. Neither Miss Foster or I have before set foot inside Salisbury Cathedral and so there may yet be a condition of equality upon our visit, but I must delay no longer if I am to execute this plan."

Mr Shorto was now in a further quandary for he did not wish me to be at large upon the streets of Salisbury and by his expression he questioned the sense of my proposal whilst I also wondered whether Miss Foster would herself ridicule this contrivance.

"No, I shall go Henry and you must stay here and do not move from this spot. I have just time enough to dash to Rollestone street and return before the appointed hour. Mrs Shorto has a collection of silk scarves. Pray do not move."

I thanked my friend for his understanding and he now departed briskly, perhaps with some relief that he was no longer required to greet each Salisbury resident as they passed through the northern porch.

I now realised that my boots had collected a deal of mess from walking the back lanes of Salisbury amongst the market traffic and so I used the iron boot scraper at the entrance to the porch to remove this unpleasantness before I was to soon enter the Cathedral. It was necessary to support myself upon the smooth marble pillars of the stone archway whilst scraping the sole and heal of each boot and as I did so I felt a bump from behind. I turned to find the irascible gentleman with the ancient grey wig who in passing from the building had paid no heed to my presence and uttered a curse upon encountering me in his way. I hastily apologised but the crooked man continued on his muttering course, prodding his stick before him and with head down he proceeded to turn the corner to the west of the building.

Having cleaned my boots I dutifully returned to my position to wait and hope that brother and sister would not think me a complete fool and in nervous preparation I now closed my eyes. With my hands concealed behind my back I let my fingers explore the cold texture of the stonework whilst I listened to the ingress and egress of visitors to Salisbury Cathedral.

My dear Mr Fenton, I have never before disclosed the circumstances of Sarah's blindness and she herself remembers but little of the severe fever that struck on the occasion of her fifth birthday. Robert has informed me that he recalls the dark room in which his younger sister lay when even the smallest inundation of daylight caused distress and pain to the feverish child. Mr and Mrs Foster were unremitting in their bedside vigil and in time the fever abated with their daughter joyfully reclaimed from those deathly regions. That any intruding daylight no longer caused distress to the severely weakened child was at first considered a symptom of her recovery but Sarah was unable to gaze upon the anxious faces at her bedside. With the return of the visiting medic he proclaimed the patient to be blinded by the fever and so the young girl had now emerged into a world of darkness. The family did not give up hope that Sarah's eyesight would soon return and as she grew stronger every treatment was sought and applied. In the following weeks and months Mr and Mrs Foster saw their young daughter suffer the leeches, cupping and a variety of mercurial remedies until they eschewed all such treatment as causing sickness and undue distress. Sarah herself wished not to be cosseted but instead displayed a wilful determination to find her way in a sightless world often to the alarm of her parents with the many bruises of her venturing forth evident for all to see.

Sarah's plight has indeed directed the course of her elder brother's life as he has thrown his wholehearted support into the very recent formation of the West of England Eye Infirmary in the city of Exeter where he will very soon study under the oculist William Adams. Robert hopes that it will become a most progressive institution and that new research shall one day alleviate his younger sister's condition.

For some considerable time, Robert did not disclose the purpose of his restless travel to every hospital and specialist up and down the country and to Edinburgh also to establish the best science that may be applied to assist with the recovery of Sarah's eyesight. Miss Sarah Foster is, however, as sharp as a pin in her understanding and did permit her brother to believe that she knew not of his tireless pursuit but now all is discussed openly for the events of this day have caused our world to be turned upon its head.

By the time of Mr Shorto's return my eyes had long since reopened with my thoughts racing hither and thither and I now entertained grave doubts as to my intended course and had all but abandoned the notion of applying a blindfold at all. My companion announced that Robert and Sarah Foster awaited me outside upon the lawn for he had accompanied them from the High Street. Rather than rush to Rollestone Street he had instead purchased a green silk scarf from a haberdashers and also a length of silk ribbon that may assist in binding ourselves in some way as we conducted the tour. I thanked Mr Shorto for his consideration and that I would later reimburse him for the cost of these purchases, whilst I thought that I might now conceal them in my pocket and make no reference to Robert and Sarah of my earlier notion. My friend now bit his lip in consternation.

"My dear Henry, upon leaving the haberdashers with the silks in my hand I near collided with Robert and Sarah in the High Street. Introductions were made..and indeed Miss Foster is very beautiful and it did quite disarm me. I explained that I was fulfilling an errand for you Henry and when Robert suggested that if these silks were not a gift for his sister then perhaps they were intended for another admirer.. I found myself reddening at this good natured flippancy .. and so, I uttered the truth for I knew not what else to say and I make a very poor liar. Upon hearing my explanation Miss Foster laughed and said; "Trust Henry Chalk to think of such a thing". Robert then stated that they were very early in making their way to the Cathedral as Sarah had grown impatient of waiting at the George Inn and at this disclosure he was scolded by his sister for always talking too much."

Mr Shorto now appeared quite forlorn as he explained these circumstances as if he were in some way at fault.

"Henry, before I depart to soon welcome my own family on their return to Salisbury, I must inform you that Miss Foster has since requested that if it is indeed your intention to apply the silk scarf then it should be done before you are to meet. I will assist if you wish. I believe that Sarah fully respects your desire to restore the equality that existed at your first meeting and I do not think that she will mock you at all."

With this reassurance I folded the green silk scarf over and over and placed it before my eyes and turned about to enable Mr Shorto to tie it tightly from behind. He then pressed the length of silk ribbon into the palm of my hand and I thanked him warmly for being a true friend.

"I will be thinking of you Henry and good luck. I shall ask Robert and Sarah to enter the porch so that you may now conduct your tour. I would still advise caution when you are at large upon the streets of Salisbury and do not walk alone lest the ailing doctor is still lurking and as neither you nor I know his face then be careful of any that approach you."

I could hear Mr Shorto's departing footsteps and as I strained to listen to other movement within the porch it was my own short and rapid breathing that filled my ears. The first voice in the darkness was that of Robert Foster.

"Well Henry in true fashion you have indeed done the strangest thing. Sarah is here beside me."

"Good afternoon Henry, so shall it be the blind leading the blind?"

To hear Sarah's voice again, after the passing of almost an entire year, caused my mouth to become dry and my whole body to quiver with excitement and anxiety in equal measure. So much has been written with Robert the conduit for all that has passed between us but nothing shall supplant hearing again the voice of one who has occupied my thoughts night and day since the time of our encounter in Hindon. There was indeed no apprehension in Sarah's voice and for all the world I wished to tear the silk from my eyes and look again upon her face but her good humour and understanding did embolden me to have faith in my contrived sightlessness.

I shall try also to document my own words so that there shall be a parity of dialogue to make some sense of our encounter.

"Good afternoon Sarah, I am so very pleased that you have come but I dare not move from this spot without guidance. Mr Shorto has purchased a length of ribbon that may assist.."

"Then I shall take Robert's arm and we may both hold the ribbon and, in this way, proceed together."

With her brother placing one end of the ribbon in his sister's hand I gripped the opposing end firmly as if my life depended upon it.

The lone chorister's voice had now ceased by the time that we entered the main building and I felt a sudden vulnerability as we progressed slowly in our curious triumvirate. The close comforting references were our own footfalls or a swish of clothing but beyond there existed in the darkness only a soft cacophony of blurred disturbance. To be denied the sounds of middle distance ensures that no plan or map may be formed in the mind and all is therefore confusion. For the sightless I now believed it to be a place of intimidation and this cavernous building even reduced the English voices of the shuffling tourists to a conspiratorial babel where I could not discern one familiar word and I wondered what I had caused Sarah to endure by my suggestion.

Robert soon assuaged my discomfort as he informed us that we were now at the western end of the Cathedral and before us stood a succession of great columns linked by fine pointed arches and these flanked the broad and empty nave. Further tiers of columns and arches soared heavenward and below the distant vaulted ceiling harmonious lines of long clear glass windows cast down a flood of white light to illuminate this main body of the Cathedral. An elegance of gothic design and repetition could now be imagined but I held a picture of the exterior of this extraordinary structure in my mind and so my task was made all the easier. For Sarah's benefit her brother suggested that he described the form of the gothic arch upon the back of her hand with his finger to which she consented. After Robert's subtle demonstration of such gargantuan load bearing design upon his sister's skin and her laugh as he confessed to being no draughtsman, I was tugged into motion by the silk ribbon.

"Keep up Henry or we shall leave you behind."

Sarah's voice caused me to forget my concerns and I wrapped the ribbon around and around my finger bringing me ever closer to Sarah so that her scent now enveloped my senses and any mustiness of this building or the tobacco ridden odours of passing tourists were now expunged by her close proximity. Sarah had indeed reciprocated in keeping the silk ribbon taut between ourselves and I gauged that she too had twisted it tight around her own finger. The tightness of the silk ribbon caused my finger to throb but to feel the presence upon the opposing end of our attachment was all that concerned me and my heart soared ever higher with each transmitted motion.

Robert now described how there were tombs positioned along the length of the nave between the great stone columns and some of these carved recumbent statues were perhaps the early Bishops of Salisbury. I was content to pass by these stone figures and continue on our sedate procession for all eternity but Sarah was drawn by Robert's comment that one subject had suffered greatly at the hands of the tourists for the tomb displayed an array of graffiti. Sarah expressed a desire to examine it for herself if such a thing was permitted and her brother considered that there should be no objection as long as she did not intend to contribute to this disfiguration. He added that neither did there appear to be any officer of the church in sight to request such permission. Our guide explained that these tombs were positioned upon a plinth that first must be negotiated.

"Then assist dear brother and show Henry also where he must step."

Robert guided Sarah and myself to climb up a full step to reach the tomb and once elevated we positioned ourselves on either side of the recumbent figure with the ribbon falling slack between us.

"Thank you Robert."

It was as if this were a signal for our chaperone to remove himself from our immediate company whilst we explored with our fingers the effigy of the long dead gentleman who lay before us.

"I shall now examine the choir stalls," announced Robert, taking empathetic note of his sister's wishes but he added that we should not move from this plinth for the flag stones below would be most unforgiving.

As Robert departed, I heard a brisk tapping upon these same flagstones accompanied by an incomprehensible muttering and I judged this to be the same irascible gentleman in the ancient grey wig passing close by and I afforded myself some silent reassurance by this unsighted recognition.

"Our figure is much worn Henry. His fingertips have crumbled and many visitors have inscribed their names upon him."

I explained that the carving was made easily into a soft stone and it was perhaps alabaster. I could judge by her response that Sarah was smiling.

"Trust you to have a word on the stone. And what stone would you wish to be carved from when you are gone, it should perhaps be chalk?"

I laughed at this whispered suggestion in the darkness and listened to my response as if it were another's voice and not my own.

"Then my features would wear all too quickly. Sarcen stone would tax the sculptor and all but the most persevering tourist would not scratch their name upon me. I do not like to think of when I am gone from this world, for I believe that my life is just begun."

As we roved the cold and smooth effigy before us our finger tips brushed together and we both gasped at this contact. Of a sudden the Cathedral clock commanded three resounding chimes from some unchartable position above our heads and I waited for these great bells to cease their hum whilst I gathered my thoughts.

"Sarah, you will recall in the carriage once the dawn had intruded upon our special journey when you read my features with your tender touch? I shall not, for as long as I live, forget that moment."

My fingers explored the nose and mouth of the supine figure before me in vain hope that I might again encounter warm skin rather than cold alabaster.

"Sarah, have I spoken out of turn? Or reminded you of something that you wished to forget?"

I could not bear this close silence and I believed that Sarah had been offended by my blundering in the darkness. With my heart racing I slowly lowered my arm to make the ribbon taut once more so I might again locate Sarah's reassuring presence but the ribbon was weightless and unattached and I hastily gathered the full length of silk between my cupped hands. As if I were drowning in an unseeing world, I pulled down my blindfold and found myself alone upon the plinth.

My dear Mr Fenton I cannot truly recall the order of my panic at the realisation that Sarah was no longer before me and connected by our length of silk ribbon. With the freedom of sight all was incomprehensible and my eyes struggled against an assault of daylight and gothic grandeur amidst which I only wished to locate Sarah and restore the calm intimacy of our meeting. I did not call out her name for this was surely a game of hide and seek or a trick played out upon the unsuspecting Henry Chalk with Robert an accomplice to this charade and both would soon reveal themselves. Even the tourists had receded to the extremities of the Cathedral and I was left alone, turning in circles, at the very centre of the building beneath the great tower and spire. I looked in turn behind the choir screen but found no persons there and ran also the length of the nave before passing through the northern porch and outside to the open lawns but of brother and sister I could find no trace. I told myself to return to where I last heard Sarah's voice and I inspected all around the figure of Sir John Cheney but to no avail and I soon found myself again standing directly beneath the spire not knowing what to do.

A small pale object caught my eye as it drifted slowly through the air to rest upon the stone floor of the spacious northern transept. I took the thirty or more paces from my central position to retrieve and examine this curiosity and found it to be a once white handkerchief but now worn and discoloured and spotted with fresh blood. My instinct was to hastily discard this soiled handkerchief but it must have fallen from somewhere and so it was that by raising my gaze I saw Miss Sarah Foster standing stock still upon the very edge of an upper tier of the higher reaches of this building.

I cried out as soon as I could gather enough air into my lungs.

"Sarah, do not move one inch forward. Please, oh please be as still as you can. I am coming for you."

By the time my words skewed to all lofty corners of the Cathedral's interior I was already in flight to seek a means by which to gain access to these upper levels. In the far corner of the northern transept I found an open door to a spiral staircase and I bound up these tightly arranged stone steps with only an infrequent narrow window by which to find my footing. I stumbled many times and rasped my shins against stone whilst my arms thrashed at the walls to haul me ever higher. I could not comprehend why Sarah would have wandered so or found her way to this most precarious position and I hoped in desperation that she would heed my words and not move even a fraction of an inch. Into the light I emerged and my eyes sought and found with relief the blessed figure of Sarah standing upon the ledge with a great void between us and the open floor of the northern transept far below. I dashed before the extraordinary stained glass windows with their many bright colours flickering in my vision and once upon the same side of the upper transept I slowed to a walk and confirmed my intention to come to her. Still she did not move and I reached out to take her hand talking all the while though I know not what words passed my lips. As she gripped my fingers tears of joy rolled down my cheeks in celebration of a tragedy averted but rather than withdraw from the edge Sarah stated quietly and calmly.

"Henry, we are not alone."

I could not comprehend these words nor the fact that Sarah was immovable from her position with the tip of her shoes protruding out into thin air. I turned about and from the shadows a figure advanced slowly towards us across this broad upper floor whilst I peered to see who this might be that was inexplicably the cause of Sarah's immediate peril. The face that slowly emerged was a distant memory ravaged by time and when he spoke his voice was known to me and a paralysis gripped my body.

"You appear worried my dear nephew, well I suppose you have good cause."

The man halted behind Sarah and I listened to the disbelief in my tremulous voice.

"Uncle James, is it you?"

"It is indeed your dear uncle, or the "ailing doctor" you may call me what you will."

Without turning about Sarah took a deep breath before asking in a whisper after her brother.

"He is..resting..in the choir stalls, troublesome fellow that he is. He shall not I fear witness the tragedy of an impossible love when two lovers leap to their deaths bound by a pledge of eternal love and a silk ribbon. Henry you really have made my task all the simpler. It shall be clear to any that try to resolve this..tragedy that the lovers wished their chaperone to be indisposed whilst they make their leap to find peace and equality in another world. Well, that is how I view it. I shall take good care of Chalk's Brewery for I am the sole remaining eligible relation, as you well know. Think on it as a moment of liberation, you no longer have to write your interminable letters and I no longer have to read them whilst I plot your demise. Now, I shall not detain you. Henry you have the silk ribbon still in your clutches and I shall thank you for the return of my handkerchief. We could not wait here all afternoon my dear nephew for you to find us and so my handkerchief drew your attention, as I knew it would. You will note that the little vixen drew my blood whilst we made our acquaintance. Henry stop shaking and pull yourself together. Tie the ribbon to Miss Foster's wrist and then attach it to your own."

In this nightmare I was compliant to my uncle's every instruction for he only had to press his hand into Sarah's back to send her to her death upon the flagstones below.

"Kneeling down would be best, Henry help the lady, have you forgotten your manners? Now pull your blindfold back into position. There are tourists wandering below, let us hope that none look up just yet. You may say your farewells."

As I write these words the sickness that I felt in the pit of my stomach now returns but I shall take a sip of brandy to continue. My uncle's voice haunts me and there is barely a night that passes where I do not awake in a sweat before seeking the reassurance of my flint heart on its chain that I wear always around my neck.

As we knelt side by side upon the ledge, bound by our silk ribbon, neither did Sarah or I utter one word and the silence was broken by a bird as it landed in a fluster beside us.

"Shoo, be off, a wretched pigeon in the house of God. Flight is a most enviable ability, do you not agree? It is however wasted on such creatures."

Assisted presumably by my uncle's boot, the pigeon clapped its wings together and departed noisily into the wide open space before us.

"I almost forgot Henry, your mother's ring? Sadly, it shall never encircle the finger of your beloved. You may keep the silver clad flint hearts for I am fair sick of flint my dear nephew. You kindly informed me when you left Southwark that you took the ring from the heart shaped box upon your father's desk. Dear, dear Hannah, kept in that dull house with her dull husband, my prissy brother good riddance to him. It is perhaps in your fob pocket?"

The fingers of my right hand went to my fob pocket and inside I felt not a ring but instead a quantity of fine powder. It was indeed loose soil and the minute gold pins from the Bush Barrow excavation that the younger Mr Parker had directed towards my boots and I later retrieved to keep for examination. I gathered as much of this fine mixture as I could until I had a small heap within my palm.

"Henry, the ring? Hurry boy."

I mumbled that I could not at first readily pick it out of my narrow pocket. Holding my clenched palm down low I gauged that to retrieve the ring this diabolic fiend would now reach over me to prise the gold ring from my grasp. In my head I counted to three before casting the handful of soil and minute gold pins upwards and backwards and by the exclamation of distress and surprise that followed, I knew that I had hit my target.

In this same instant I shouted to Sarah to draw backwards and it was as if she were reading my thoughts, for I felt the silk ribbon that connected us tug in one motion. I ripped the blindfold from my face and with panic in my fingers I unravelled the ribbon from my wrist before charging at this demon as he clawed at his eyes to clear the fine dusty soil and minute gold pins. I forced him back against a pillar and smelled the rotten expelled air from his lungs as he gasped into my face. His red and watering eyes half opened and he regained his stance before pushing me backwards towards the edge. He now drew a razor from his pocket and flipped open its blade as he advanced towards me. At my back was the precipitous fall into the northern transept and whilst Sarah cried out for help there was no place for me to go but towards the slashing blade.

Behind the dread figure of my villainous uncle, to my great surprise and relief, another person now occupied our ledge and it was the irascible gentleman with the ancient long grey wig who, of a sudden, appeared with stick raised. He brought down his hazel stick across the back of the head of the advancing devil causing him to crumple momentarily and drop the razor to the floor which in turn skidded across the ledge to clatter down upon the flag stones below.

My uncle James now turned upon the irascible fellow and dealt him a blow to remove the ancient grey wig before gripping him by the throat.

I cried out in amazement at the revealed sight of John Fenton who had all this while been present in the cathedral.

"John, it is you, how..?"

"Never mind Henry..get this..murderous..fiend..from my..throat."

Before I could move to assist John Fenton, he was cast to one side whilst my uncle made his escape ducking around a pillar and disappearing with his footsteps resounding behind him.

I rushed first to Sarah and she gripped my hands whilst assuring me that she was unharmed but feared desperately for her brother's life. In this same instant John Fenton proclaimed that he could see Robert walking with some uncertainty across the floor below our position. This was good news indeed but I wasted no time in imploring John to assist Sarah in being reunited with her brother and to keep them both safe until my return. Sarah in turn pleaded with me as I rushed from her side to let my uncle go and not to pursue him but I was now blind with rage and knew what my action must be.

My dear Mr Fenton, I can write but little more at the present time and I shall dispatch this full and most painful account to you so that you might read for yourself all that occurred. You may be assured that Robert has made a full recovery from the blow to the head that he received at the hands of my despicable uncle and that Sarah has survived the horror of her abduction by this same fiend. I would not be surprised if both brother and sister and the entire Foster household wished for no further association with this troublesome suitor but that is not the case. The inner strength of Miss Sarah Foster has kept me from madness and despair and the love between us has been made all the stronger as a consequence of this dreadful ordeal. Miss Foster is indeed a remarkable woman and I hope that we shall all meet together before too long but I may not, at this stage, state the purpose of this celebration.

I wished above all to praise the actions of your son John for he did surely save the lives of both Sarah and myself by his timely and most surprising intervention. You have assuredly heard his version of events but I consider this full account to be my humble duty to describe his brave and valiant efforts. We parted not on the best of terms outside the Salisbury Court after his successful defence of Thomas Targett and the two men from the charge of deer stealing. I gave him not the credit that his efforts deserved and I was foolhardy not to heed his request for me to remain at the inn and I instead crept into the public gallery to witness his clever dissection of my published letters, to dismiss them as merely a work of fiction. John then departed for Pembrokeshire but unknown to me before leaving the city he purchased, for your perusal, a copy of both "A Tour in Search of Chalk" and "A Tour in Search of Flint". With nothing better to entertain him in the pauses on his journey he read these books from cover to cover and found to his horror, embedded in my words, sufficient evidence to establish a most malign intent towards me from my sole remaining relation. There was indeed a grave and growing suspicion as to the character of my uncle James, shared between my good friends and I include you sir to the fore of this number. I have learned subsequently that he had written letters to Sir Richard Colt Hoare and to the trustees of Chalk's Brewery, demanding in ever more threatening tones that he be made aware of my whereabouts stating that the responsibility as to my well being was his alone and not that of others who bore no Chalk blood in their veins. At the time I suspected an unspoken concern amongst my friends and I know now that my brazen wanderings brought anguish to those who wished me only to be at large in trusted company. I do not consider for one minute that any knew of the extent of the evil that long fermented in the twisted and rotten heart of my uncle James. He who I wished to invite as my partner at Chalk's Brewery.

John pieced together these known suspicions and they were then confirmed to him in black and white upon the page. Knowing that I supplied my uncle with word of my every move he presumed correctly that I had told this villain of my forthcoming meeting with Sarah at Salisbury Cathedral. If a trap were to be set then there was time enough for this villain to creep from his lair to deal me a final blow and dispose of the obstacle that stood between him and the security of Chalk's Brewery. Of course, my own foolish antics by applying a blindfold played into the hands of my murderous uncle to make his task all the easier. I could now be dispatched with my beloved Sarah and lo, a pact of self murder would be pronounced by the Coroner. John has informed me of his regret at making himself scarce upon seeing Sarah and myself standing at the tomb for he did not wish to intrude or pry at this most intimate moment and so took instead a turn around the cloisters. As the ancient clock struck three, Sarah was forcefully and silently abducted and she has told me that the most unspeakable threats were made if she cried out and did not walk with him in a manner so as not to attract unwanted attention from bystanders in the Cathedral at that moment. That Sarah bit my uncle's finger is no small surprise for she is not a meek person given to easy submission but he did smuggle her away to the higher levels of the building and awaited my arrival. Robert Foster was dealt a violent blow upon the head and was laid out in the choir stalls until he awoke in a very giddy condition but mercifully there has been no lasting damage and he is back to his robust self once again. Whilst Sarah and I were perched high up upon the ledge, your son John searched frantically to all points of the compass within the great building and it was but the noisy flight of the departing pigeon that had settled briefly beside us that caused him to look up and so he saw Sarah and myself kneeling in preparation to fall to the stone floor far below. To his horror he thought he may yet be too late to save us but he did not call out for surprise was still on his side and finding the means by which to reach this level he timed his arrival to perfection. Indeed, for the rest of my days I shall be eternally grateful to your eldest son John. He has since described how he found the old wig at an inn upon his return journey where it had apparently been resting on a peg for the last ten years and the hazel stick was torn from the hedgerow once a plan of disguise had been born. Your mischievous son could not resist his play acting whilst I waited at the northern porch and rather than reveal his presence to me, he enjoyed the role of the irascible gentleman, even bumping into his quarry and cursing all the while.

I must now put down my pen although I have more to relate to you, for I have told you nothing of the pursuit of my wretched uncle during which your son again played his part.

Please extend my best wishes to Mrs Fenton and inform of John's heroic deeds although I feel certain that he will already have done so himself. I hope to visit you again my dear friend when business at Chalk's brewery permits but I shall correspond further to conclude my tale as soon as I am able. I do not have the fortitude now to write another word for it pains me greatly to relive this nightmare.

Your most humble and grateful friend
HENRY CHALK

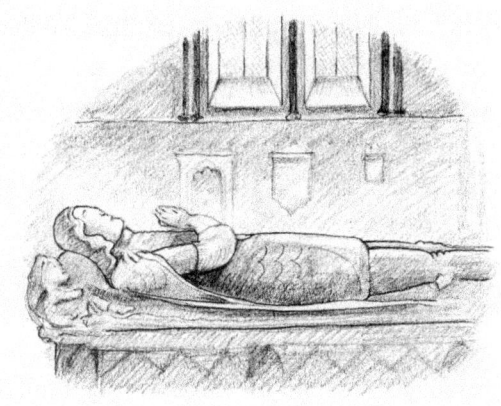

Thursday 8th June 1809

MY DEAR MR FENTON,

Thank you for your kind words and also the encouragement for me to now complete my tale. In the two weeks since I dispatched my lengthy tract to you, I have received some very special visitors. Two days ago Miss Sarah Foster and her brother Robert arrived to take tea with me and indeed a tour of Chalk's brewery ensued. A pall has hung over the brewery but it has been lifted by the effervescent Robert Foster and by his sister Sarah who has won the hearts of many with her smile and also her genuine curiosity into the business of brewing. Brother and sister were able to sample the very first production of Edward Chalk's Golden Pale Ale for which the hard water from the new well is ideally suited and it shall be exported in bottles that have been manufactured especially. My father once abandoned his notion to produce a bottled stout but I have named this pale ale in his honour and memory for I believe that he would have approved of this endevour.

Sarah was then drawn to visit the dray horses for they were now stabled after the day's exertions and she tied a ribbon upon her favourite but there were treats for all the horses that Sarah met.

It is by her guidance that I have placed some of my own books upon the shelves about the house and also in my father's room. Sarah has informed me that it is now my room and will think of me sitting at my desk when I next write. Indeed, she believes it to be a good house and perhaps with this blessing the ghosts will one day rest in peace and be no longer bound to pursue me about the place, to the relief of all concerned. Sarah then asked, with a knowing smile, if I were now embarked upon the "steady middle ground through life" that my father would have wished for me or whether I still craved "the peaks and troughs of adventure"? These were indeed familiar words and phrases that I recalled from the book "Robinson Crusoe" and indeed I had quoted the very same myself when corresponding with my uncle on my first pedestrian adventure. I now scowled at Robert who protested that it was his sister's demand that he should read aloud from the two published books of my letters and he was only following instructions. Again, my every thought and deed is blown into the air like threshed chaff.

I am due this evening to attend the theatre with Robert and Sarah and I am saddened that they are to return home tomorrow after this brief visit to the capital.

As you know sir, I am due to meet again with Robert and Sarah in one month's time for you have initiated a visit to Holnicote, which is situated not five miles from Minehead, and is the home of Mr and Mrs Martin Fortesque. I sincerely look forward to meeting again with you sir and perhaps John also and I have before heard Sir Richard Colt Hoare speak with tenderness of his sister's family and their estate and so it is with great anticipation that I now wait for these intervening days to pass.

I have been blessed with another visitor and Mr Henry Shorto has departed after taking luncheon at my house. His business caused him to travel to London and he thought it rude not to call and, whilst he was about it, to also inspect my cutlery. I was therefore able to repay, in a very small part, Mr Shorto's hospitality for he has spent the night under my roof and in the morning I conducted him upon a tour of Chalk's brewery. He has long been fascinated by the story of the digging of the great well and requested that he be allowed to drop a small pebble into the darkness and await the sound of broken water echoing up from the depths. Upon his arrival at my house my friend presented me with a small coloured illustration of a red admiral butterfly that he himself has drawn. I could not keep the tears from my eyes when he revealed this gift and I thanked him wholeheartedly and stated that it would now sit upon my desk and forever remind me of my father. Mr Shorto has also given his encouragement for me to put pen to paper and hopes one day to read all in another volume of Henry Chalk's adventures and in doing so he believes that I shall "remove a great burden from my mind". He has instructed me to proceed as before and record events in the order that they occurred and for once I will do what I am told.

I shall now do my best to breath life into a sorry tale and so I recommence where I left off in our position high above the northern transept in Salisbury Cathedral. It was my own rage that compelled me to leave Sarah and her brother Robert in the care of your son John and pursue my uncle whilst he was hindered by having the soil dust and minute gold pins from the Bush Barrow excavation cast into his eyes. Along high passageways and up tight and winding stone staircases I chased my sole relation whilst I could hear scampering footsteps ahead of me as ever upwards, we traversed this great gothic maze. At the base of the tower I encountered the ancient clock whilst the afternoon sun blazed through the long clear glass windows, illuminating a web of structural ironwork but I had no thought to inspect such features and hastily returned to the enclosed dark staircases as I continued my ascent. At the next level I peered briefly at the giant bells but I was now convinced that I was gaining upon my quarry and so I soon burst out of my staircase to where the giant windlass is housed, directly beneath the spire itself. Now puffing heavily and wild eyed, I ordered the startled windlass operators to confirm that a man had just this minute passed this way and to a soul the three men looked heavenward. The interior of the spire is a great confusion of ancient timbers crossing back and forth between the tapering stonework and in the gloom I could now detect a figure ascending the succession of narrow wooden ladders. I hurled myself upon the rungs of the first long ladder and I was soon bouncing and springing as I reached its centre but I cared not for my own safety. As I climbed ever higher, I thought of every element of my uncle's evil, the pieces that your son John had so astutely assembled from my published correspondence. In the village of Hindon, upon the night of the election, across the glowing brazier I met with the evil stare of Joseph Barklay, who was a bad man in my uncle's employ and he then pursued me but was deterred by the presence of Mr Beckford's dwarf and his henchmen.

I considered also my nocturnal departure from Stourhead House after the foolish butchery experiment that I was encouraged to conduct upon Sir Richard Colt Hoare's deer by your son John and I then took flight to ensure my return to the Stourhead Inn before midnight. Awaiting me at the gatehouse with his knife at the ready was the murderous Joseph Barklay but he was foiled in his work by my youthful haste and his heart then stopped as he gave chase.

I now dwelt upon the night at the Winterslow Hut when I was drawn to entering the room of the ailing doctor just when my candle had become extinguished and there was a period of grave vulnerability before the arrival of Robert Foster. In the darkness I had paused before the open doorway and there I sensed a time from my youth when my uncle had appeared from a darkened room and my mother could be heard sobbing inside. It is but a distant memory but the house was quiet on that day for it was the event of the great hop market in Southwark which was a very gay and popular occasion. Upon seeing my uncle, I had fled to the kitchen and he found me clutching at the apron strings of Mrs West and adopting a pleasant manner he then proposed an excursion to the Port of London and we departed soon after. My uncle never again set foot across our threshold and indeed he left me at the front door upon our return from the port. Neither was my mother's laughter heard again within these walls and I now recall that her golden hair was cut short and remained so until the birth of my dear sister. Soon after, both mother and daughter then passed from this world to leave our house a place of perpetual sadness.

Finally, upon the occasion of the great tempest, once Robert had departed from the Winterslow hut, I did foolishly return to the flint pit and laboured in the deluge to reveal the secrets of the ancient miners. As I lay bleeding upon the floor of the pit, I thought the vision of my uncle standing above me a trick of the mind but indeed it was he that cast down the extracted flint tools upon my head. It was only by the return of the quick thinking Robert Foster that I was retrieved from my chalky grave after my uncle had departed upon a stolen horse for he thought his work done.

To return to the Cathedral spire you may imagine me, my dear Mr Fenton, leaving daylight far below as I ascended each creaking ladder whilst I was forced to grope before me to find the foot of the next ladder. A curiosity caused me to halt for a moment for a pin prick of light entered the darkness through a minute aperture in the mortar and of a sudden I was aware of my position high up in this jumbled wooden frame and shrouded only by a thin cloak of freestone. Perhaps with no fury in my veins I may have become meek and fearful but the creaking and clattering above me spurred me on and I called out the most vile threats into the constricting darkness. I heard my own voice spit out that I should have no mercy when I got my hands upon him and that I wished him dead and in response I heard a whimpering from above. Of a sudden daylight poured down upon me where a small hatch had been opened and I was able to propel myself ever faster now that I could see my way ahead. My quarry now attempted to climb from this aperture whilst I dashed to grab a trailing leg and then pulled with all my might. I heard a scream as I clawed the figure back inside the spire and I continued pulling until the man's terror was plain to see but I had the greatest shock for it was not my uncle's face.

"You are not my uncle," I now gasped.

The man was speechless and appeared to be awaiting the fate that I had promised.

"I apologise with all my heart sir, for I thought you my murderous uncle and now I find that you are not he."

We both now gulped air for a good minute after our exertions before I introduced myself and established that the man's name was Marchant and with shaking hands he lifted up an object that transpired to be a horn, tied upon a piece of string around his neck.

"I blow's me 'orn see."

The man put the instrument to his lips and gave a faint puff that barely caused a note to emerge. He stammered that for a wager he had climbed the spire and was to blow his horn as proof of his deed to those awaiting below. I now put my own head out of the hatch and was required to rub at my eyes before I could see the sky, the far horizon and the city of Salisbury, as if it were comprised only of toy houses and by leaning out as far as I dared I peered down towards the base of the Cathedral. My dear Mr Fenton it was as if I were now Lemuel Gulliver bestriding the diminutive Lilliput and yet for all that there was to feast my eyes upon in this strange land, I was drawn instead to observe a minute figure crossing with perceptible haste the green handkerchief of grass far below. In vain hope I bellowed forth my uncle's name but my voice travelled no distance at all from this perch amongst the clouds and I hastily thrust the startled man towards the open hatch.

"Quickly man, blow your horn. Blow as if your life depends upon it."

Mr Marchant now popped his head out into the sky and blew with all his might and blew again and again.

I forced myself alongside the horn blower and sure enough this figure that had not long emerged from the body of the Cathedral now paused briefly to peer up towards our position at the tip of the spire. I looked down helplessly as this one ant, amongst a scattering of stationary ants, now hastily continued on its way and in my heart, I felt that my villainous uncle had made good his escape whilst I had pursued the wrong man.

I again apologised to Mr Marchant but reminded him that he had after all fulfilled his wager at which he perked up and produced a small flask of brandy from which I gratefully took a sip before we commenced our descent.

Once I had finally returned to the floor of the Cathedral, I found John pacing up and down with Robert sat cradling his head beside the tomb of Sir John Cheney and Sarah, who had been standing with her back to me, now turned before I could announce my arrival. There was a palpable relief at my safe return and an urgent enquiry into the whereabouts of my wretched uncle. Three further persons were also gathered and John explained that the Cathedral vergers had been alerted by the commotion within the northern transept and the Close constable was summoned once John had described the events of the afternoon. I explained to this gathering that I believed I had witnessed my uncle scurrying from the building as I had looked down from an open hatchway at the top of the spire but I was helpless to act and now he may be anywhere in the city or beyond. I confirmed to the church officials and the Close constable that I knew not where in Salisbury my uncle may have secured a room but that he lived in Exeter and I gave his address and declared that this was indeed the extent of the information that I could usefully provide. The two vergers and the constable muttered together whilst I attended to Robert Foster who assured me that he would live but stated that he could recall nothing of the blow that he received for it had been administered from behind and he awoke in the choir stalls with his face pressed against a hassock.

The Close constable stated that he would now speak with the city constables to see what may be done outside the walls of the Cathedral Close and we explained that we would remove to the George Inn in the High Street so that Robert Foster might rest and recover from his assault. Once we were installed in a parlour at the George Inn, Robert was able to properly assess the damage from his attack and demonstrated that a large egg shaped lump had appeared upon the side of his head.

"Better a lump on the outside my dear sister, than on the inside. I shall survive."

John now enquired as to how I had managed to make an ascent of the Cathedral spire in the fruitless pursuit of my uncle. With some embarrassment I explained that like a confused blood hound I had followed the wrong trail that had caused me to clamber to the very tip of the spire. I then admitted to terrifying an innocent man who was at the same moment ascending the spire to fulfil a wager and I described how I had cursed and threatened at his heels up each of the ten ladders. John looked on with an incredulous expression on his face as he imagined the scene. I concluded my account by stating that the poor fellow was about to cast himself out of a small hatchway at the very top rather than suffer the appalling litany of punishments that I had pledged to undertake and it was only once I had dragged the poor man back inside the spire by his leg that I realised my gross error. John gave a loud snort of laughter and was soon unable to help himself and such was our sense of relief in being safely gathered together that this outburst quickly spread like an infection to Robert Foster who cradled his sore head whilst squeeking with painful yet uncontrolled laughter.

"John..stop...I implore you ...please no..."

Sarah at first admonished her brother for such a display but was soon attempting to stifle her own mirth and I was next to follow for the contagion of laughter can be irresistible and it was after all a ridiculous tale. It was perhaps a good antidote for everything that had just occurred and our nerves were assuredly the better for this most inappropriate behaviour.

In the hiatus that followed, for the gravity of the situation was soon to return, I now composed my apology to all present but especially with Sarah in mind for she had suffered a most terrifying ordeal at the hands of my cruel relation and her abduction had been made all the easier by my own voluntary blindness. Before I was permitted to begin my pathetic address, John slapped his hand down flat upon the table causing us all to jump from our chairs;

"Henry you have the address of this fiend. We must reach his lair before he does and I'll wager a guinea to a penny that he will rush there now. His game is up here for he has played his hand and we need to be on the next Post to Exeter."

With this he dashed from the building and returned in a short while with two tickets not aboard the Mail but instead The Mercury.

"We depart at eight and let us hope that we can obtain seats upon the inside."

With this next course of action now decided I stated that I must inform Mr Henry Shorto of the hideous drama within the Cathedral and the true nature of my villainous uncle to whom I had entrusted my every thought and deed whilst abroad upon my pedestrian adventures. It was then by Mr and Mrs Shorto's insistence that Robert and Sarah should stay in Rollestone Street until Robert was fully recovered and fit to travel. This was duly arranged and before John and I departed aboard our coach, we enjoyed a good meal in the company of Mr and Mrs Shorto who were indeed appalled at the relating of the events within Salisbury Cathedral.

Mr Shorto insisted that he would take up our cause with the Justices in Salisbury and inform them of our plans and he also suggested that upon our arrival in Exeter we should seek this same assistance for we were now certain that our quarry was a very dangerous and unpredictable man.

So it was that John and I gathered ourselves in order to meet our coach at eight o clock in the evening at the Council House but before departing from Rollestone Street I had taken Sarah to one side to ensure that she was recovered from her ordeal. I was about to state that after the events of this day she must surely question her association with me but I was quietly dissuaded from voicing these uncomfortable thoughts.

"Sssh, I know what you are about to say and I wish for no

such thing Henry. We are both stronger than that. I am unharmed and Robert shall have an aching head for a day or two. You have had the greater cause for distress for the one that you once trusted has displayed their evil intent towards you and your very foundations will be shaken by this. If you are to pursue this...your uncle... then do so with care and return safely to me."

I took Sarah's hand and she squeezed it tightly and there was no requirement for us to exchange another word before my departure. I sincerely hoped that Robert would not suffer unduly from his blow to the head but he assured me that he fully expected to be able to return to Minehead shortly and he insisted that I should visit their family home there once the business in Exeter had been attended to. Robert, in turn, cautioned me to take the utmost care for this blackguard appeared capable of the vilest deeds and he was indeed now a most desperate man and all the more dangerous for it.

Mr Shorto escorted us to meet the coach and he brought with him two thick coats in case we were required to travel on the outside. There was by good fortune one seat available within the coach for a ticket had been purchased from Salisbury to Exeter but no traveller had arrived to lay claim to it and so in the blink of an eye John installed himself within the coach and closed the door. I thankfully accepted both of Mr Shorto's coats with a promise to return them and I clambered up to take my place aboard the roof of the coach. Before we departed John reopened the door to call up to me that we would exchange seats at Dorchester and so I settled down for an uncomfortable night. I bid Mr Shorto farewell and as the coach lurched forward a thought occurred that it was perhaps my uncle that had purchased the unused ticket but at our arrival had shrunk back into the shadows cursing his luck for he was unable to take his seat with John and I present. I wished to alert Mr Shorto of this possibility and so I called back to him to be on his guard and to make haste back to Rollestone Street without delay.

"He is still here, I am certain of it. Beware for your own safety."

My friend looked back, unable to hear my words above the clattering of hooves but raised his hat before continuing on his unhurried way. I could do nothing but pray that no further harm be inflicted upon my friends and hoped instead that it was now a race to Exeter that would preoccupy my malevolent relation.

I shall not describe our journey sir, save to say that Dorchester came and went and with every change of horses I returned to my perch upon the outside of the coach. I can recall looking back to witness the sun breaking free of the horizon into a cloudless sky and we appeared to outrun a fleet of warships upon the English Channel that were becalmed upon their westerly progress by an absence of wind, but of the stops and places that we passed I can give little account. In truth I cared not whether I rode inside or outside for I had been made numb by the events that had occurred in Salisbury Cathedral and I shuddered over and again at the thought of Sarah standing upon the ledge high above the northern transept. John had travelled to Wales and then straight away returned to Salisbury to save the day in the guise of the irascible old gentleman and so it was by my insistence that he should have some degree of comfort within the coach.

We breakfasted at Bridport and it gave me the opportunity to formally thank your eldest son for his quick thinking, bravery and indeed his friendship. John silently considered my words before suggesting that if I really was that grateful then perhaps he may have the piece of untouched gammon that was laying idle upon my plate. As John concluded both our breakfasts he asked about my uncle and whether he had always been a rogue and how could such a man have gained my trust?

I explained that I had no contact with my uncle from the age of seven but one day a surprise package arrived at the brewery and contained within was a small volume entitled "A Pedestrian Tour of

North Wales, 1805". Inside there was a dedication to me from my
uncle James Chalk and also a note with his address in Exeter but he
counselled against speaking to my father about the book or of our
renewed contact. He referred to a "misunderstanding" for which the
blame had been unfairly apportioned upon him and these were the
events and concerns of an adult world that should not trouble the
relationship of an uncle with his only nephew. As I could not speak
easily with my father, either upon matters of business or in our home,
I welcomed the approach of my uncle and so I began some occasional
correspondence and indeed it was the adventurous spirit of the book
that caused me to set forth upon my own pedestrian excursions. I
admitted that I when I first left my home in Southwark for South
Wiltshire with the scent of adventure in my nostrils there was no other
person that could be the recipient of my correspondence.

John listened patiently and concluded that my uncle's motives
were clear from the start and that I was just an obstacle to his achieving
ownership of Chalk's brewery.

"Your uncle had a plan Henry but he has been thwarted and let
us hope that we find further damning evidence at his quarters and that
the rogue shall be quickly apprehended and punished."

On the Sunday afternoon we arrived at our destination and put
up at the New London Hotel although John and I were required to
share a room. We were informed that the inns in Exeter are frequently
overflowing with travellers and so we counted ourselves lucky to find
a bed at all. We wasted no time in asking directions to Guinea Street
and soon found ourselves in a quarter of the city in which the poorest
inhabitants lived and worked. Indeed, these same circumstances may
be found in any city in England but I had no notion when I dispatched
my letters that they would arrive in such a place after their collection
from the Exeter Postmaster.

We observed from across this grimy street a small property

situated next to the Old Golden Lion ale house that appeared to be a tailor's shop and the sign above the door simply read; "Howson". Being a Sunday, it was closed but we had not the time to wait for Monday morning to arrive and so John crossed the street to knock loudly upon the door. An old face appeared at the window and mouthed an obscenity and the small figure gestured for us to go away. John knocked again and on this occasion the bolt was drawn and the door opened sufficiently to enable a little wizened head to appear and the obscenity was now audibly repeated.

By placing his boot in between the door jamb and the door John prevent its immediate closure but provoked a further stream of curses from the unpleasant little man.

John demanded to know whether a Mr James Chalk resided at this address whereupon the man's eyes narrowed tellingly before he spat in John's face and as John recoiled the door was slammed shut. I offered John my handkerchief to wipe his eyes and guided him back down the narrow street. I suggested that the filthy little man was surely not about to cooperate and so we must return to our lodgings to enquire where we may find a constable or indeed a Justice of the Peace to give authority for a search of the premises in Guinea Street. We soon established that there was no prospect of speaking with a Justice of the Peace on a Sunday and a constable was equally elusive and so we soon found ourselves again observing the lowly tailor shop from a stinking alleyway across the street.

"Henry I cannot stand here for a moment longer for I will surely wretch."

I stated that I would offer the old tailor money if it would gain his cooperation and so I now banged on the door and a young man's face leered briefly at the window and I was required to knock again and on this occasion the door opened sufficiently for the face to peer out at us. The young man said nothing and held no expression in his face as I explained that we were seeking Mr James Chalk. I then held up a guinea piece and the simple fellow tried to take it from my hand but I withdrew it before requesting that we be permitted entry and he then may have the money. The man looked crestfallen at the disappearance of the golden coin in my closed palm and he opened the door to reach out further into the street. John now seized the opportunity to push open the door at which the fellow stood tamely to one side but with his mouth open and both hands cupped before him to receive the coin.

"Henry do not waste good money on him for he is a simpleton. Let us do our work before the filthy old man returns as I'll wager that the boy is here on his own for the time being."

I could not now renege on the offer of parting with a guinea and so I dropped it into the young man's cupped hands and he stared at it whilst we left him at the open doorway. The ground floor was indeed a shabby tailor's shop and upon a small shelf at the foot of a narrow stairway John spied a pile of letters addressed to Mr J Chalk, 6B Guinea Street Exeter, Devonshire.

"Henry, I recognise your handwriting. We have the right place."

My most recent letters had evidentially been collected from the Postmaster, perhaps by the simple fellow, in readiness for the return of my uncle and I despaired anew at trusting my every thought and deed to one who had long wished me dead.

John now darted up the steep and worm eaten ladder to the next floor and here evidently was the accommodation of the tailor whilst the young man slept in a cot in the shop and I had never before witnessed such squalor and found it hard to imagine how a life could be conducted in these circumstances. Upon ascending a further ladder, we now encountered a locked door and John stated that this was surely the room where my uncle James Chalk now resided. The simple fellow had followed us to the top of the small premises and looked on spinning the gold coin around and around in his fingers as we rattled at the door to no avail. He now stooped down in the passageway and placed his hand in a hole in the rotten wall and extracted a large key and then placed it upon the floor beside us.

John snatched up the key and after fumbling with it in the lock it made a heavy click and as he pushed open the door the simple fellow gave a loud shriek beside us and fled down the ladders and after slamming the front door behind him we could hear his heavy footfalls disappearing down the street. My heart was in my mouth as we entered the place of habitation of my uncle James Chalk and the floorboards groaned loudly under our cautious feet. A single clouded window permitted only a gloomy light by which to view the room and indeed at first there appeared to be little to see for it was sparsely furnished with only a bed, an old writing desk, a simple chair and a large trunk that proved to be locked. Upon the desk under a shroud of dust a number of books were piled up including my uncle's own "Tour of North Wales, 1805", but also books and earlier tours of this same area. Upon inspection I found passages underlined, scribbled marginalia and even whole pages torn from books and it was apparent that there was nothing original about my uncle's book and that it had indeed been plagiarised from existing sources. The two books of my own published letters gathered dust also beneath a pile of my correspondence and John sneezed loudly at the disturbance of so much dust. In a simple drawer I found one of my toy soldiers and I recalled my uncle, upon an early visit to our house lining up these soldiers before I would knock them all down again. At the back of the drawer I found three further objects and upon my realisation of their significance, I slumped forward upon the creaking chair and I confess that I wretched upon the floor at my feet. Sir, it is with the heaviest of hearts that I now describe the confirmation of how my uncle, to whom I once entrusted my every private thought, has been a wreaker of lives and the cause of great evil. As John looked on I at first picked up my father's fob watch with his initials EHC engraved upon the back. This is the watch that was taken from my father as he expired in the street after falling under the coach on Fleet Street and it could mean only one thing, that my wicked uncle was present at that very moment and was surely the cause of his death. The second object was a small round wooden box with a tightly fitting lid and within was a curl of golden hair and this sent my fingers trembling further for I knew it to be my mother's hair. Beside this box was a folded card with a broken wax seal and upon the front was my father's name Edward Chalk and inside a fine curled lock of the same golden hair was sealed to the page with a small blob of wax. Also was written "9 'o clock tonight at the Temple Church". Here was the note that was delivered on the evening when my father departed from the house and I was never to see him again, for he died later that evening in the street under the wheels of a coach. The Temple Church off Fleet Street was where my mother and father were married, as my mother's family had some association there. I now began to shake in the chair as if a fit had overwhelmed me for my very worst fears had been confirmed before my eyes.

John assisted me from that wretched room and we returned to our lodgings at the New London Hotel where I flung myself upon the bed in despair and could make no sound at all as if my uncle's hands were gripping me firmly about the throat. I awoke still in my clothes and at first believed that I had experienced the very worst of nightmares but to quickly dispel this notion John burst into our room and parted the curtains with a flourish to admit the early morning sun.

"Henry, I have engaged two constables to escort us back to the tailor's shop and I have informed them that it is a murderer that we wish to apprehend. There must be no delay."

I leapt from the bed and poured some water from the jug to splash into my face before following John to meet with the two constables and we then made haste to Guinea Street and to the tailor's shop beside the tavern. The door was already ajar and the constable's knocked loudly and also called out for any persons to present themselves. Receiving no reply, they now entered the building and John guided them to my uncle's room and this door was also open and it was soon apparent that the large trunk, the books and any remaining clothes had been removed. Of the simple fellow or the tailor there was no sign and the constable's searched high and low and also roused the landlord of the Old Golden Lion tavern to enquire whether any persons had seen a large trunk being removed but all to no avail. With their fruitless search concluded the constables shrugged and now excused themselves and so we returned to our lodgings with John lamenting that my devious relation had successfully evaded our attentions.

"It would indeed be a grave injustice if your uncle were not punished for his crimes. I sorely regret that instead of sleeping in a chair I did not last night return to stand vigil in Guinea Street for he was surely close upon our heals had we but realised it. I fear that he has now fled the city and there is no knowing where he might be."

John then expressed his concern that I should succumb to a severe melancholy given the great tragedy that had befallen my family but I was able to reassure him that my thoughts were now directed towards the future.

"There is hope within my heart that a condition of happiness awaits and my mind shall not become sick on his account nor my spirit diminish. He is forever gone from my life."

We ate a good breakfast in silence and after pushing away my plate I confirmed that I must now travel to Minehead where I would visit the home of Mr and Mrs Foster, for I had arranged to meet with Robert and his sister Sarah there. I knew not how I should be received by this family for all the trouble that I have caused but go I must. John declared that he would accompany me to Minehead for he could then take a packet ship to Milford Haven where it was but a short distance on to Fishguard.

So it was that we left Exeter behind us and I have told you all I know about my wretched uncle and to this day I know not of his whereabouts. He is indeed a wanted man in Exeter, Salisbury and London but with every passing day I now fear less for the safety of my friends or indeed for myself although, if pressed, I cannot readily explain this circumstance.

Sir, I cannot sufficiently convey the gratitude that I hold for your eldest son John. You will know well enough his penchant for raillery and indeed there have been occasions when I have presented an irresistible target for his amusement but I feel that we have both grown to be men since we first met and I now greatly value his friendship. Perhaps one day I may be able to reciprocate for all that he has done. My dear Mr Fenton you also have been a rock that I have been able to cling to in a stormy sea and I look forward to meeting you again shortly at the home of Mr and Mrs Fortesque in Holnicote. Mr William Cunnington and his family have extended the hand of friendship and I greatly value Mr Cunnington's common sense and the ability to see things afresh and adjudge for himself the significance of each of his antiquarian discoveries. Indeed, he explores uncharted territories and I look forward to the publication of his Patron's great work "Ancient Wiltshire", for within shall be described the invaluable contribution of Mr William Cunnington and his stalwart barrow diggers, Mr Stephen and John Parker and of course their surveyor and draughtsman Mr Philip Crocker. I would also include you sir, as part of this most special assembly for your passion is that of the most committed antiquarian and your presence upon such excursions brings a lightness of heart when the excavation of bones and dust may instead become a dry and sombre occasion. I wish you well with your own literary endeavours; "A Historical Tour of Pembrokeshire" that has required many years of study and travel and also a work of satire; "A Tour in Quest of Genealogy", that John informs me that you have been encouraged to complete by the reading of my own two published volumes. I am indeed flattered but I shall never know whether John is being serious.

Of Sir Richard Colt Hoare, I cannot speak highly enough for he has entertained this callow youth and given sanctuary and encouragement to my own investigations and I one day promise to contribute to his great library with my own modest work;

_____"Manufactured flint tools and their essential use in everyday life before the common availability of metal by the ancient people of South Wiltshire with an investigation into the likely sources of flint of the finest quality."

I am perhaps a fool to value the ubiquitous flint above the allure of precious gold but it is my conviction that flint has enabled ancient man to survive and prosper for countless millennia, whilst gold is a most divisive and corrupting material. Indeed, it is not the fault of gold for every species upon this earth has been content to leave it untroubled amongst the streambeds or in its buried seams and it is only mankind that have become enslaved to this rare and beautiful metal.

Please do as you like with this correspondence and indeed John informs me that he collected all my remaining letters from my wretched uncle's abode. I have no use for them.

Your faithful and most grateful friend,
HENRY CHALK
or, if you should prefer, A PEDESTRIAN.

POSTSCRIPT

Sir, I have this evening received news of the fate of my uncle James Chalk. Mr Gerrity, our brewery manager, arrived with correspondence from his twin brother who crossed the Atlantic five years ago and has a printing business in Philadelphia. There is a cutting before me upon the desk from the "Philadelphia Aurora" newspaper reporting "The execution of an Englishman" and informs of events that occurred some weeks ago. In summary, the man was tried and convicted for the stealing of a horse and saddle and upon the scaffold he declared that his name was not as he had previously given; Robert Foster of Minehead, England, but instead; James David Chalk of Southwark, London. The felon concluded that he could not depart from this world bearing a false name and he deeply regretted the course that his life had taken and he now implored the hangman to be swift about his work. The hangman duly complied and at half past ten o clock on the morning of Wednesday April 26th 1809 the Englishman James David Chalk was executed.

The pen shakes in my hand and of a sudden I am a child once more. There have been days when I have convinced myself that my uncle's evil deeds were a consequence of an illness, indeed a malign tumour that did grow and grow until all goodness was forced aside by an all consuming and parasitic evil.

I am left to contemplate the wreckage of the Chalk family and try as I might to piece together these broken fragments, I am now denied a confession from my uncle as to the full extent of the evil deeds that he has orchestrated. I shall never know the circumstances as to how my father was led to his death, to be pushed under a carriage on Fleet Street. Was there a pursuit of my uncle from the Temple Church, where they were to meet after the delivery of that fateful note and did my uncle have an accomplice? Perhaps Joseph Barklay was employed to assist in executing my father's murder, as he had attempted my own. All are dead now.

After our flight to Exeter my uncle was close upon our coat tails and whilst our backs were turned, he removed his trunk and remaining belongings and fled. His whereabouts have been the subject of much speculation but tonight I have learned that he sought refuge in Philadelphia and after committing further crimes was caught and did pay the ultimate price. That he used the name of my dear friend Robert Foster makes my skin crawl, for to take a good man's name and to only confess to this deceit upon the scaffold indeed confirms the unscrupulous nature of my uncle.

As a consequence of this news I have forfeited a night at the theatre and I did send word immediately to Robert and Sarah Foster that circumstances had determined that regrettably I could not attend. I hope that I have not spoiled their pleasure this evening but my world is again turned upon its head.

I would be gratified if you could communicate the news of my wretched uncle's demise to our mutual friends for none have been spared the anguish of these last few months.

When I read again, as I have just now done, the page written in my father's hand that tells of an unscheduled visit to Silbury Hill in May 1782 by two young brothers, I cannot see the man that my uncle became nor foretell that he would one day take the life of his elder brother. There is still the mystery of my father's coded message on the reverse of this same page and many have tried to unlock this secret but have failed to do so. It assuredly contains, within this curious script, the dark burden that my father carried for the remainder of his life, from the time of their excursion to Bristol now twenty-seven years ago. It is perhaps best for all that it shall remain a mystery.

As I look up from my writing, I see Mr Shorto's beautiful

illustration of the red admiral butterfly upon my desk and it warms my heart. My dear Mr Fenton, I shall forever treasure the memories of my mother and my father and of late, in my dreams, they appear as a young and happy couple for that was surely their condition before my accursed uncle preyed upon their lives.

The door bell has just rung and my heart races for I can now hear Robert and Sarah in the hallway talking with the housekeeper Mrs Harrison and on my account they have forfeited an evening at the theatre.

Sir, in many ways, I am a fortunate man.

The Coded Message

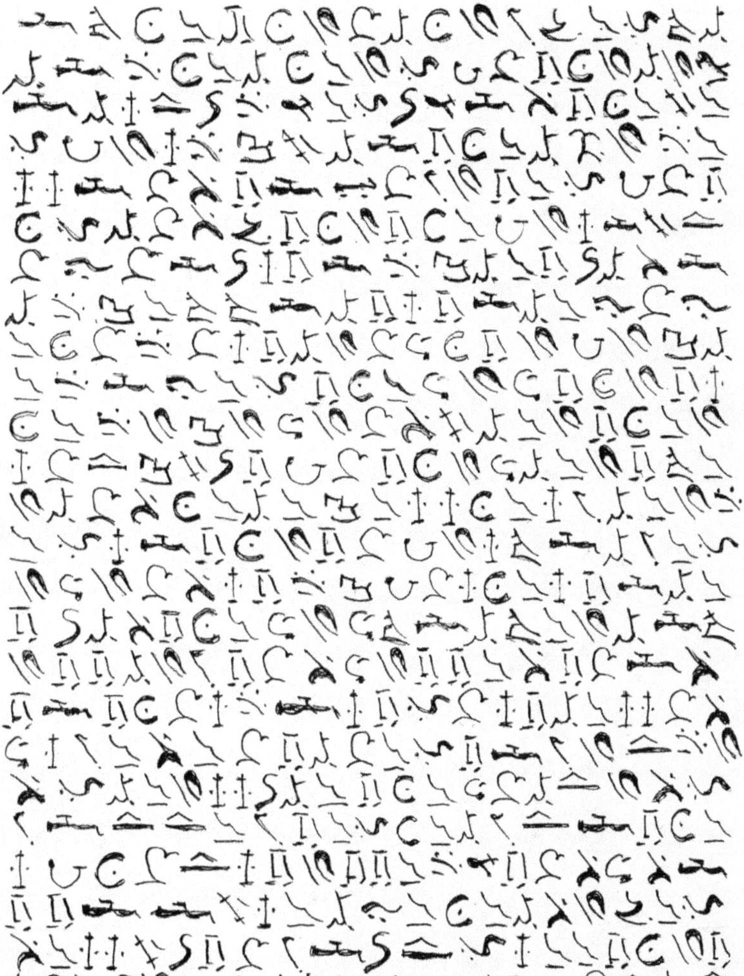

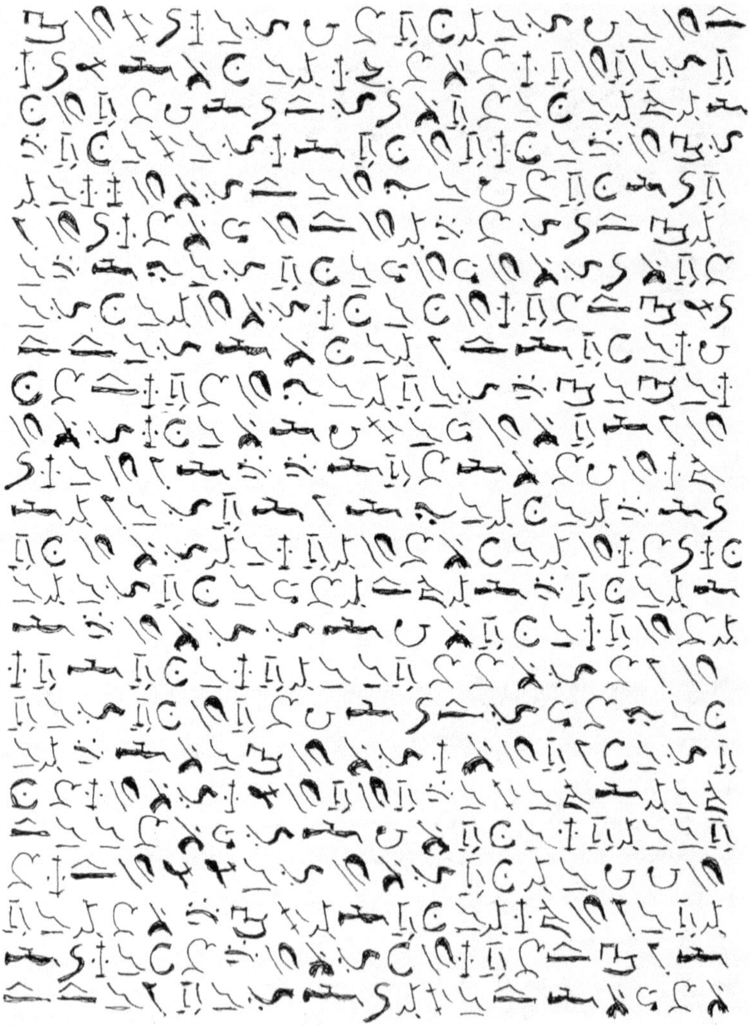

REAL CHARACTERS AND DIGRESSIONS

THE ANTIQUARIANS AND THE PRODUCTION OF *THE ANCIENT HISTORY OF SOUTH WILTSHIRE* (1812);

SIR RICHARD COLT HOARE (1758 – 1838)

As Heywood Sumner suggests in his book 'Local Papers' (1931), when appraising Wiltshire's earliest archaeological benefactors; 'A fox-hunting squire who gives up the chase in favour of hunting for earthworks and antiquities is of rare occurrence.' In 1785, Sir Richard Colt Hoare inherited Stourhead from his grandfather, Henry Hoare 2nd, on the condition that he was to have no involvement with the family banking business, thereby protecting the estate and its properties, should the banking business run into future difficulties. Tragedy soon struck however with the loss of his wife Hester in that same year, after giving birth to their second child, who also died. Seeking distraction from a desperate sadness that was to haunt him for the rest of his long life, the Stourhead heir then embarked upon extensive European tours, before returning to explore the antiquities of Wales during many summer excursions.

William Cunnington's early antiquarian investigation in the vicinity of Heytesbury had drawn the interest of the MP H.P.Wyndham and also William Coxe, the rector of Bemerton and later Stourton, with both men successively harbouring desires to build upon Cunnington's work and publish their own books on the antiquities of Wiltshire. With Colt Hoare himself becoming increasingly curious about the ancient history of his adopted county and after being introduced to Cunnington, he then offered to take over the reins and the funding of this previously uncoordinated enquiry. From the outset his aim was to produce and publish the pioneering Ancient History of South Wiltshire, which was to be written up by Colt Hoare but this ambitious project required a team of experts and second in command was to be his new associate William Cunnington, a wool trader from Heytesbury. A young surveyor, Philip Crocker, was to produce accurate maps of each 'station' or area and would also illustrate all the finds from the barrows. The barrow diggers were William Cunnington's men, father and son Stephen and John Parker from Heytesbury, who had already been digging a number of barrows under Cunnington's instruction.

Once 'The Ancient History of South Wiltshire' (hereafter referred to as AW vol1) began to take shape then Colt Hoare sought out James Basire 2nd, one of the very best engravers, to produce the plates from Philip Crocker's maps and illustrations. The end result is a huge and stunningly produced catalogue of ancient artefacts, drawn together by Colt Hoare's breezy descriptions of his exploratory excursions on horseback, providing the reader with an open-air sense of riding out and joining in the hunt, to explore together the activities of our ancient ancestors.

Colt Hoare was steeped in classical learning and possessed possibly the best private library in the land and yet was aware that the answers he was seeking were still unknown and unwritten. Colt Hoare's work therefore became entirely dependent on Cunnington's assessment of every excavated barrow. With Colt Hoare 'barrow mad' by this time, the pressure was heaped upon Cunnington to come up with the goods, for the Parkers to open nearly 500 barrows and for Philip Crocker to constantly survey and illustrate. The main constraint upon Colt Hoare's ambition was the health of his 'co-adjutor' William Cunnington who at times was unable to do anything as the result of a long-term illness from which he eventually died in 1810, two years before the full publication of AW vol 1. It was William Cunnington however to whom this sumptuous first volume is dedicated, a baronet deferring to a tradesman, such was the fresh intelligence, discerning eye and judgement of the wool merchant.

Colt Hoare then went on to produce Ancient Wiltshire vol 2 (published in 1819), which dealt largely with the north of the county and was compiled with barely any barrow investigation, after Cunnington's death. Cunnington had been quite prepared to admit what he did not know and without his caution, more classically referenced theories were creeping in again, as Colt Hoare attempted to fill in the gaps. A third volume, focussing on the Roman era was published in 1821 and was largely an account of the Roman roads and settlements or 'stations'. Again, old and tenuous sources were applied but it did include some new fieldwork by Philip Crocker, establishing previously unrecorded Roman roads such as that from Old Sarum to the Mendip lead mines.

Later in life and with Ancient Wiltshire now out of the way, Colt Hoare then focussed on The History of Modern Wiltshire and coordinated a countywide campaign, producing a complete set of volumes between 1822-1844. A practised delegator by this time, he joined forces with a variety of men from different backgrounds to compile the historical records of Wiltshire. The Stourhead library was made available and comfortable topographical gatherings were arranged annually where each division of the county could be accurately investigated and recorded. Again, Philip Crocker was the surveyor and produced maps of the various Hundreds (archaic minor divisions within the county), upon which these large volumes were based. The final volume was produced six years after Colt Hoare's death.

Sir Richard Colt Hoare was never going to be content as solely a 'fox-hunting squire'. His broad cultural and artistic education, gained on the Grand Tour in his earlier years was followed by a deep immersion into the study of medieval texts before his focus and ambition was drawn towards ancient and modern Wiltshire. He has left behind an extraordinary legacy and there is a fine memorial to the Stourhead baronet in the northern transept of Salisbury Cathedral.

PHILIP CROCKER (1781-1840)

An essential member of the team that produced AW vol 1. He cut his teeth assisting the Ordnance Survey to compile 1-inch to 1 mile maps of Wiltshire before working for Colt Hoare in 1807 as his surveyor and in 1812 he finally resigned from the Ordnance Survey to become the steward at Stourhead. His father Abraham Crocker moved to Frome as the Master of the Bluecoat School in 1783, also setting up as a land surveyor and running a family printing business. In 1806 he produced a text book for schools and students 'The Elements of Land Surveying', which I recall seeing at an antiquarian book fair and regretted not buying. It seemed to be a valued educational book as it ran to a number of editions. Philip Crocker, one of four sons, may well have contributed to its production although by this time he already had enough on his plate. Seeking out references for Philip Crocker some years ago, I recall reading about him in Stuart Piggott's book 'Ancient Britons and the Antiquarian Imagination'. I have just checked it out again; 'Crocker's plans of earthworks were something new, but they hardly served knowledge, as they were surveyed unintelligently by someone who, however conscientious, had no understanding of what he was recording'. This is a particularly curmudgeonly assessment of Crocker's contribution which has made me want to seek further opinion and I found it in Mark Corney's paper on the 'Hillforts of Wessex'. Mark Corney worked for years as a Senior Landscape Investigator for the Royal Commission for Historic Monuments of England, so he really knows his stuff. He redresses the balance well; 'The superb surveys produced by Philip Crocker on behalf of Sir Richard Colt

Hoare. These plans are a remarkable and accurate record of many monuments including hillforts....the first 'landscape' plans specifically executed to record extant archaeology'.

Without Philip Crocker's contribution then AW vol 1 would have no foundation, no visual aids, no accuracy and certainly no beauty. In Devizes Museum library I once requested to see the book of Crocker's original watercolour plates of all the artefacts displayed in AW vol 1 (From which James Basire made all the engravings for the published book). The Society had not long purchased it at great expense and Lorna Haycock, the then Sandell librarian and archivist, staggered in with this enormous and heavyweight book. I must add that Lorna was inspirational in her role, incredibly knowledgeable, patient and above all helpful in directing people towards source material. It was she that read the manuscript for 'A Tour in Search of Chalk' and immediately rang me up on a Saturday afternoon to say that I must send it to John Chandler at Hobnob Press. She knew that John would be interested and sure enough he was and agreed to publish it, without me even asking him. Thank you Lorna. To put the icing on the cake in 2005, after 'A Tour in Search of Chalk' was published, Lorna catalogued the paperback book and placed in the old wooden, glass-fronted bookcase amongst all the original books that had inspired it. Sadly, Lorna died last year. Philip Crocker's original material, all in colour, is beautiful and it would be wonderful to see a facsimile one day. I can still visualise the electric greens of the verdigris on the bronze daggers from the oxidation of the copper content. There are issues with determining the scale of different objects that are illustrated together on the same plates in AW vol 1 so, in that sense, scientific accuracy has suffered for the sake of design, but Colt Hoare had artistic sensibilities and obviously desired to produce a very aesthetic and attractive book. There are certainly scales included, either in chains or yards, for some the more detailed plans of camps or earthworks.

Philip Crocker also undertook a variety of incidental drawings and paintings such as capturing Stephen and John Parker at work in a watercolour during a dig 'South of Stonehenge' when Colt Hoare and Cunnington were also present. Seeing this original painted image is like witnessing the opening scene from an old film, a book opens and a frozen image comes to life, animating father and son to the task at hand, hearing the slow scrape of their tools and sensing the sweat of their labours. There is another image of William Cunnington's house in Heytesbury which shows the three Cunnington daughters in the garden, who were good friends of Philip Crocker and also essential participants in the AW vol 1 project.

All in all, I think Philip Crocker did an incredible job, especially considering the tug of war that was going on for his skills between Colt Hoare's urgency to complete his project and Colonel Mudge, of the Ordnance Survey, for the systematic mapping of Wiltshire, West Sussex and Hampshire at a time of national conflict.

WILLIAM CUNNINGTON (1754 – 1810)

Wool merchant and pioneering archaeologist. William Cunnington was a native of Northamptonshire but moved to Wiltshire in his early teens to begin as an apprentice in the drapery trade in Warminster, after an arrangement by his father. Before he was 20, and now in a business partnership, he moved to Heytesbury where he was to live for the rest of his life. At 33, he married Mary Meares from Frome and although there is no record of a dowry, he was soon able to set himself up on his own and became a successful wool merchant, mercer and draper. An intelligent and studious man, unencumbered by a classical education, he was able to cultivate his own antiquarian and geological interests through reading, corresponding widely and observation. As his business grew, he still found time to focus on these nascent studies and undertook enough fieldwalking to find a stone 'celt', or axe, some ten years before his first barrow investigations took place. Paradoxically, the real impetus to his antiquarian activities was an illness that was to increasingly debilitate him until causing his death in 1810. It could be reasonably stated that without William Cunnington's illness then AW vol 1 would not have happened and nor would so many of South Wiltshire's round barrows have been excavated. The disease was acromegaly which causes an abnormality in the pituitary gland (normally a pea sized gland at the base of the skull), which then produces too much growth hormone. Today it can be clearly recognised by the obvious physical effects to the body; enlarged facial features, swollen hands, enlarged feet, thickened skin and a strong body odour. By very intricate modern surgery to reduce the size of the gland, in combination with a course of steroids, acromegaly can now be treated very effectively. In William Cunnington's case it was the accompanying debilitating headaches and persistent tiredness that caused him to consult his doctor. There was no understanding 200 years ago of this illness or of its treatment and the blunt prescription from the medic to his patient was 'to ride out or die'. Fresh air was the only perceived solution and William Cunnington did just that, taking to his horse across the south western portions of Salisbury Plain with its enormous amount of conspicuous archaeology to wonder at. It was at this stage that he began to explore beneath the turf, employing local labourers to excavate the prominent barrows in the neighbourhood, drawing the attention of other likeminded gentlemen and ultimately Sir Richard Colt Hoare, who drove the investigation to a whole new level.

Throughout William Cunnington's earliest antiquarian associations, as he found his feet, the more he heard from those with a 'classical' understanding of the ancient past, the more caution and reasoning he then applied to his own assessments. He had soon learned enough by his own investigations to doubt the perceived wisdom. Roman sites and their engineered road system were tangible and this physical evidence was underpinned by the written accounts of Caesar and Tacitus. Nearby Pit Meads, a prestigious Roman villa in Norton Bavant, had been known about for some years, and before Cunnington's time had offered up four different mosaics, none of which survived their extraction from the soil or the component parts then became lost afterwards (there are drawings apparently). It was however a chance to become acquainted with the domestic building residue of Roman sites and also the coinage, pottery and any remaining tesserae. These were objects that could be accurately associated with a comprehensible, if rather broad, period of roman occupation. There was much speculation about what could be attributed to the Saxons or the Danes, such as the numerous hillforts that studded the higher chalklands, on the periphery of Salisbury Plain. Then there were the huge long barrows which H.P. Wyndham considered as being 'battle barrows' containing the dead from conflicts between the presumably victorious Saxons and the post Roman Britons with both parties buried 'promiscuously in this common tumulus'. We can now attribute long barrows to the Early Neolithic and the hillforts to successive stages of the Iron Age. Certainly, after Colt Hoare began financing and directing proceedings, with long barrows taking many days of expensive labour and turning up nothing more than a few bones, heaped up flint and some blackened earth, attention quickly turned to the much more productive round barrows. It has to be said that, in archaeological terms, the manner and haste of the investigations caused significant and irreparable damage and neither were certain records regularly kept, such as the skeletal or cranial details. There were many occasions when it was discovered that barrows had already been visited by the tomb-robber but with hindsight this is comparable to the antiquarian interference, with the exception that the grave contents were retained and preserved. Ultimately, there was still no chronology that could be applied, other than to name the types of barrow and to distinguish between those that contained the early metals and other more sophisticated goods and those that produced only crude pottery, cremations and bones. It was not until 1836 when Thomson, a Danish antiquary, set out the notion of successive stone, bronze and iron ages. Bronze goods were described as 'brass' in Cunnington's era, hence this reference in the Henry Chalk trilogy. As the great variety of grave goods began to accumulate, they were displayed in an especially created structure in William Cunnington's garden called the 'Moss House', where a great many fascinated visitors signed the visitor's book. There is an invaluable account in Richard Fenton's 'A Tour in Quest of Genealogy' of his visit to the Moss House, which provides the only contemporary account of this astonishing collection on display.

As the barrow investigations progressed, William Cunnington kept Colt Hoare informed and up to date in a steady succession of reports and assessments that were so crucial to Colt Hoare's forthcoming publication. Pivotal to all this were William Cunnington's three daughters; Mary, Elizabeth and the youngest Ann. Not only was one of the three always in attendance with their father, when he was present at an excavation, but they also undertook all his correspondence from an early age. Receiving a good education in Bath, the three girls had neat and legible handwriting and after 1801, all letters were dictated by William Cunnington and any on archaeological matters were written in duplicate, with one copy retained for their father's records. Due to his illness and the resulting debilitating headaches and tiredness, he could never have coped with all this administration and I can visualise the father cradling his head as he formulated and uttered the words, with one of his three daughters beside him, scratching the ink onto the page. I believe also that it would also have been the three daughters who helped arrange the artefacts inside the Moss House, even perhaps guiding any visitors around the displays, being fully conversant with the details after so much of their father's dictation. In the account of the visit to the Moss House in Richard Fenton's 'A Tour in Quest', he records that; 'Nothing could be more curious or systematic than the arrangement of the museum: the contents of every tumulus was separate and the articles so disposed as in the case of ornaments, such as beads, in such elegant knots and festoons..'. The strings of faience glass, jet and amber beads and shale rings were not extracted from the soil in that condition but had been painstakingly and prettily arranged for the sake of display. William Cunnington could not have done this but his daughters would have enjoyed the task, designing their own versions of ancient decorative necklaces and he describes as much in a letter to William Coxe, earlier in the campaign; 'My daughter has washed the beads, rubbed a little sweet oil over them, and strung them in a neat manner. They will make a very pretty necklace, perhaps two thousand years old.' The festoon to the fore of Ancient Wiltshire (and the cover of this book) also incorporates beautifully crafted barbed and tanged flint arrowheads and the mysterious 'Adder Stone', and is effectively a prehistoric jumble of attractive pieces, all wired together. It was very much a team effort. Mary Cunnington, with her increasing concern for William's health, would accompany her husband in the field, particularly when he was to stay away from home. Meanwhile, Colt Hoare was single-mindedly driving on the campaign, demanding more and more from his 'co-adjutor', not appreciating quite how ill he was. William Cunnington was slowly dying and without the loving and dedicated support of his family, AW vol.1 would never have taken the form it did. In May 1810, the first of the three parts of AW vol 1 was printed, although the entire book was not available until 1812, but at least William Cunnington did get to see the project in print and underway. He also got to see his own portrait as the engraved frontispiece, which had been a well-kept secret by Colt Hoare, after persuading William Cunnington to pose for the artist Samuel Woodford, when he and Mary were visiting London in 1808. Colt

Hoare was insistent that the unwilling Cunnington should oblige 'to secure a portrait of the primary and chief investigator of our British antiquities'. This painting now hangs in Devizes Museum, and it is due to the thoroughness of Colt Hoare that this visual record exists. In his portrait, the physical effects of Cunnington's acromegaly can be recognised, albeit not as exaggerated as in the most severe cases, but his large facial features and prominent jaw are typical diagnostic indicators. William Cunnington died on 31st December 1810 with Colt Hoare still complaining that his last two letters had remained unanswered. He was not to know how serious his 'co-adjutor's' condition had deteriorated. Even the close friends and neighbours, the Lamberts at Boyton, were unaware with Aylmer Lambert writing to thank his friend for the fine haunch of venison that the Cunnington's had sent over and for the accompanying letter from 'Miss Cunnington' to which Lambert replies; 'I am sorry to find you are again not quite so well'. Five days later William was dead. Colt Hoare wrote a very sincere letter of condolence to the family, stating that; 'I participate most cordially with you in the heavy loss you have sustained as a parent and a husband; and myself as a worthy friend and co-adjutor.' William Cunnington was buried in Heytesbury churchyard with a tablet on the wall inside the church, that was perhaps composed by Colt Hoare; '..By his decease the literary world has lost a persevering antiquary and skilful geologist, the community of Heytesbury a good neighbour and active fellow citizen, the poor a humane advocate and charitable protector, his own family an affectionate husband and indulgent parent.'

After his death there was some dispute as to the ownership of the great accumulation of artefacts in the 'Moss House'. The fossils were bought by a geologist from Bath with Mary and the three daughters considering that they now owned the antiquities also, with Colt Hoare only securing the intellectual rights to publish all that had been generated by William Cunnington's invaluable contribution. Then there was the detrimental effect on his business, whilst he had been trying to keep up with Colt Hoare's demands, during those last few years leading up to his death. In 1814, the eldest daughter Mary wrote to Colt Hoare stating that; '..my sister's and myself have always expected to obtain for them at least six hundred pounds-for this I am confident you would not blame us if you were aware of the loss which as a family we have sustained from the close application of our father to the study of Antiquities, and from his having frequently expressed an opinion that the collection might after his death be a means of remuneration to us.' Despite funding the entire barrow digging operation, in 1818 Colt Hoare eventually paid £200 for what was to become the 'Stourhead Collection'.

With the antiquities removed to Stourhead, they were carefully preserved by Colt Hoare but after his death they then languished in boxes in the cellar until the collection was finally loaned to Devizes Museum and eventually purchased in 1878 by the Wiltshire Archaeological Society for £250. The Stourhead Collection can be viewed today in Devizes Museum, presenting a unique and stunning array of largely Early Bronze Age grave goods with many recovered from the heavily barrow populated Stonehenge landscape. William Cunnington is certainly remembered as a proto-archaeologist and it is significant that he questioned and cast doubt upon the classical and also the modern wisdom of his era. In correspondence to Philip Crocker, with whom there was no reticence in challenging the accepted views of classically educated men, he writes; 'Having described what I have seen (after the excavation of the giant Hatfield Barrow at Marden), it only now remains for me to sum up the evidence, and lay the whole before a jury who have washed in the Cam or the Isis, and for them to determine the nature of the work. The period when such works as Abury, Stonehenge, and many other British works were raised is so certainly remote that after wading through all that has been written by the ancients with Olans, Wormius, Stukeley, Borlase, King, etc among the moderns, we have at last nothing but conjecture to rest upon.'

RICHARD FENTON (1747 – 1821)

I have not listed Richard Fenton amongst the contributors to Ancient Wiltshire vol 1 (see above) and yet it was probably this aspect, above all others, that set the ball rolling to write the trilogy in the first place. I will attempt to explain, as briefly as I can. Colt Hoare first met Richard Fenton in 1793 when the baronet was touring in Wales, taking his annual summer excursion. Colt Hoare had a property at Lake Bala, in what is now termed Snowdonia National Park but he would ride out to explore widely and met Fenton in Fishguard in Pembrokeshire, where Fenton lived, after a recommendation from a mutual acquaintance. Colt Hoare, like all British tourists who were no longer able to visit the continent due to the Revolutionary and Napoleonic wars, now turned their gaze towards domestic travel and in the baronet's case it was Wales in particular (also Ireland in 1806). In time he was drawn to annotate and illustrate the 13th description by Giraldus Cambrensis of Archbishop Baldwin's earlier journeys throughout Wales in 1188, which was published in two volumes in 1806. Richard Fenton, now a retired lawyer, was embarking upon his own ambitions to write a History of Pembrokeshire and by 1804 a firm friendship had been formed and Fenton now regularly joined Colt Hoare on his summer excursions. This friendship extended towards Fenton visiting Stourhead and also spending the early season in London with Colt Hoare, theatre going, playing cards and socialising. Once Colt Hoare had embarked upon his Ancient Wiltshire campaign then Fenton and his son John, were regular attendees at the barrow openings.

Richard Fenton, in his earlier metropolitan life, had published a slim volume of poetry, to which both Goldsmith and Sheridan subscribed, with some of the poems addressed to Garrick and Dr Johnson. These are rather tenuous associations and any later biography of Fenton makes a great deal of these lofty connections but there is little doubt that Fenton was a minor poet and a minor player amongst literary heavyweights. He continued to write poetry but it is as if his innate sense of humour reduced everything he wrote to mild satire and any gravitas is lost. I believe that it is exactly this quality that could raise the spirits of Colt Hoare, with Fenton supplying the humorous to alleviate the melancholy that seemed to dwell inside the Baronet throughout his life, after the loss of his wife Hestor in 1785.

As AW vol 1 was nearing completion, in this flurry of readiness to publish, Fenton managed to publish two books himself in 1811. The first was 'A Historical Tour through Pembrokeshire', a hefty volume and could have been an invaluable work, with Fenton a native of the county, if it had not been so discursive with the author more interested in who he had met on the way. Colt Hoare undertook a series of very proficient water colours that were engraved to illustrate the book, demonstrating his own commitment to his friend's undertaking. The other of Fenton's books to surface in 1811 is 'A Tour in Quest of Genealogy through several parts of Wales, Somerset and Wiltshire.' I bought an original copy at end of the last millennium and as consequence, here I am still writing about Richard Fenton twenty years later. I made a study of this book over a period of two years, exploring every thread and avenue in a fertile period of tangential and haphazard research. This was my portal into a world of two hundred years ago. I had already begun collecting old books relating to South Wiltshire (my 'patch' at work, looking after the public rights of way) and here was an anonymous book, attributed to 'A Barrister', and stuffed full of fascinating references. The digressive qualities that undermined his Pembrokeshire history is exactly the stuff that I found so interesting in 'A Tour in Quest'.

Also, in 'Quest', are a number of Fenton's poems, this book being a receptacle for all his gathered interests, woven together into a playful pastiche of the Domestic Travelogue that I refer to in the introduction. The question that eventually intrigued me was, what was Fenton's contribution, if any, to Ancient Wiltshire vol 1? There is poetry in Colt Hoare's book but not Richard Fenton's. It is instead William Lisle Bowles who gets a page and a half romantically describing the lightning flashing from the excavation tools as the party cowered within the opened barrow during a thunderstorm at Oakley Down, just over the border in Dorset. This is absolutely Fenton territory but then Lisle Bowles had the kudos, having received the approbation of Coleridge and Wordsworth after his 'Fourteen Sonnets' was published in 1789. More mystifying there is a poem in AW vol 1 on the subject of the 'Glain Neidyr', a small bead with a hole in the centre that turned up in a barrow excavation at Winterbourne Stoke. Colt Hoare states; 'This very curious bead has two circular lines of opaque sky blue and white, which seem to represent a serpent intwined round a centre, which is perforated'. It was romantically named the 'adder stone' and the supporting associations are from Welsh bardic literature, again perfect Richard Fenton territory and yet 'Mr Mason, the poet' is given a couple of very ordinary stanzas expounding its druidic importance. For the record it is a Saxon glass bead and it appears on the cover of this book at the very bottom, as part of the threaded festoon design that I have shamelessly lifted from the frontispiece of AW vol 1. So, if there is no room for any of Fenton's poetry in AW vol 1, what is the contribution of Colt Hoare's best friend towards this major work? In the end I concluded that it was levity. Richard Fenton's good humour, enthusiasm and spirit raising character that Colt Hoare found so uplifting and supportive in their friendship can, I believe, be detected as grand phrases and mantras in the text of Colt Hoare's book and I'll eat my snakecatcher's hat if I'm wrong.

As for Fenton's own publication, 'A Tour in Quest', it is a beautifully crafted satire on the Domestic Travelogue, containing real people and real events. It may even have been inspired by Colt Hoare's own 'Tour of Ireland' published in 1807, a tour undertaken in 1806 with his son Henry rather than Fenton. Colt Hoare never seems to make mention of 'Quest' after it was published 1811, was it really so much of a mickey take that Colt Hoare chose to ignore it? After studying this book over a two-year period, extending to five crammed notebooks and realising that I am not wired correctly to write an academic study of Fenton's contribution towards AW vol 1, I instead followed in Fenton's footsteps and concocted my own Domestic Travelogue.

I have not yet referred to Eloise Fenton, Richard's wife of whom I know very little. Whilst researching Fenton I came across an account of how they supposedly met in London and that it was Oliver Goldsmith who had initiated the meeting. Eloise was the daughter of a Swiss aristocrat who had been a colonel in the French army. Whilst out walking in London with Goldsmith, Richard Fenton spied a garden party taking place and became captivated by the sight of young Eloise. Goldsmith then stated that he would make an introduction and boldly entered the garden, as if he were a family friend, stating that Fenton was a celebrated Welsh poet and they were then invited to join the party. Upon leaving, it transpired that Goldsmith had no idea who these people were and just had blustered his way in but the important introduction had been made and Eloise later became Fenton's wife. It is recorded that Richard and Eloise spoke in French to each other throughout their married lives, which gives some credit to Fenton as a linguist. However, I then read an entirely separate account in Washington Irving's 1877 biography of Oliver Goldsmith, where it was Richard Glover the poet and dramatist who apparently entered a London garden party uninvited and then introduced Goldsmith to the daughter of the host. Even the same dialogue had been used describing the scene. I suspect, as with most of Fenton's supposed London literary and theatre associations, they were given more weight as time went on so that when his grandson, Ferrar Fenton gave his account in 1903, they had been buffed up considerably.

Richard Fenton died in 1821 and his loss was deeply felt by his wife Eloise but also by his best friend, Sir Richard Colt Hoare.

JOHN FENTON (1786 - 1864)

John Fenton as a character is obviously essential to the story, Henry Chalk's nemesis but also his saviour. By the time that I began the trilogy most of the real characters were fully formed in my mind, as I had researched and thought about them before even realising that I was going to write the books. Looking back now, as I compile these informal biographies, at John Fenton and all the characters, have I wandered so far away from the known facts? John was Richard and Eloise Fenton's eldest son, followed by Richard and Samuel. In his father's 'A Tour in Quest' the author has a constant companion on his travels, referred to as 'H Jones', a bright younger man who is a good foil for the older author and is also an accomplished musician who plays the flute. It is 'H Jones' who writes the dedication at the front of the volume, explaining that it has fallen to him to see to the publication of his friend's letters, the author having vanished abroad with a broken heart. The fact that John Fenton was a regular companion to his father during, in particular, the Wiltshire barrow investigations where it is recorded that he would play pleasing Welsh airs on his flute, is helpful. Neither could I find any reference to a 'H Jones' anywhere in what evidence there is relating to Richard Fenton's life, or perhaps more specifically in any of the collated correspondence between Colt Hoare, Cunnington, Richard Fenton or Philip Crocker, all of which is catalogued in Devizes Museum library. Then, looking more closely (with a magnifying glass) at my copy of 'Quest', which has a number of small engravings throughout the book, I established that they had been attributed to 'J Fenton'. An 'advertisement' to the fore of the book, explains that the publisher had taken the decision to include them as he happened to have a few available from a 'periodical publication'. It all adds up to a bit of playful Richard Fenton subterfuge and I concluded that John Fenton had made the original sketches or watercolours for the engraver to utilise and more significantly it was John Fenton who was the young companion throughout 'Quest' and not 'H Jones'. There are also a couple of illustrations of artefacts from barrow excavations in Richard Fenton's original 'A Historical Tour through Pembrokeshire' that were undertaken by John Fenton, a beautiful flint axe with a ground and polished edge, demonstrating drawing skills on a par with Philip Crocker.

As to John's character? Some years ago, I had located a copy of an article included in the Journal of the Pembrokeshire Historical Society number 7 (1996-97), dedicated to Richard Fenton and there is also a biography of Richard Fenton, written by his grandson Ferrar Fenton, from a reprint in 1903 of Fenton's 'A Historical Tour of Pembrokeshire'. It seems as though there had been a falling out between father and eldest son. After the publication of 'Quest', probably through William Owen Pughe's influence, John had become a follower, or a devotee, of the fanatic and 'sham prophetess' Johanna Southcott, much to his father's alarm. John also hurriedly married Elen, the daughter of Owen Pughe, at St Pancras church, all these events causing distress to the Fenton household. Richard Fenton had plans to build a church in Lower Fishguard, to serve his tenants and the neighbourhood. John, as the eldest son and potential inheritor of the estate, strongly opposed the idea stating that; 'If you do father..I will turn it into a dung-hill to fling the stable muck into.' This was the final straw and John was disinherited in favour of the second son Richard. John's career developed however and he held a post, described as the 'Permanent Head of the

Foreign Corresponding Bureau', whatever that means. His nephew Ferrar Fenton records that he was 'a man of dissipated life, learnt in the circle of Carlton House and association there with the Prince Regent and his companions'. Sadly, it seems unlikely that there was ever any reconciliation between father and son. Upon Richard Fenton's death, the house and estate passed to his second son Richard but he, deeming this unfair, then sold its reversion back to his elder brother John for a nominal consideration. It also seems as though John Fenton was unable to manage the estate, bringing it to the verge of ruin until it was sold off to a button manufacturer. I was however intrigued to find that John Fenton had undertaken some antiquarian investigation in South East Dyfed, in South Wales. In April 1850, a now elderly John Fenton and the landowner opened two barrows, accurate details of which were recorded by John Fenton, particularly with regard to the skeletal and cranial remains which were measured and recorded accurately. This is a much-lamented feature of Colt Hoare and Cunnington's work that this information was not made available for succeeding archaeologists. Interestingly the study of skulls, or craniometry, was very much in its infancy and it was not until 1865 that John Thurnam published his pioneering contribution to Crania Britannica, attempting to categorise and distinguish ancient ethnicity through skull size and shape. So, from somewhere, John Fenton had realised the importance of this information that earlier antiquaries, including his father Richard, had not appreciated. John must therefore have been attuned to the latest thinking of the time, towards the advancement of archaeological and scientific understanding. This is small but also a very positive footnote in the life of John Fenton.

So, is my characterisation accurate? It is a punt that you have to take, fictionalising the nature of real people but I think it sad, to now be reminded again, of the discord between father and son.

STEPHEN PARKER (1749- 1817) AND JOHN PARKER (1781 - 1867),
FATHER AND SON BARROW DIGGERS.

Stephen had been employed as a barrow digger by William Cunnington before Colt Hoare's involvement and then he and his son John became the established and trusted team as the decade progressed, opening nearly 500 barrows between them. During this active six or seven years, they were paid very well by Colt Hoare which would have been way above any agricultural rate at the time. It is also recorded, on one occasion, that Colt Hoare intended to give the Parkers a Christmas bonus of 10s/6d, with the proviso; 'if they mend their manners'. With the death of William Cunnington however, all excavation then ceased and father and son were back where they started, living on scarce labour at very low rates. There is some evidence of John's sporadic employment by Colt Hoare thereafter, but this was very occasional at best.

William Cunnington had obviously built up a very good and trusting relationship with the two men, who were often left on their own to conduct excavations and would then report back with their findings. Their experience of repeatedly digging down from the top of so many barrows can only have informed their practical knowledge of what to expect, the varying strata, whether the tomb robbers had got there first and the imminence of reaching the cremated remains or interments when finer tools would be employed. Colt Hoare had 'barrow knives' made in Salisbury for the two men and Cunnington records that John Parker was very proud of his 'Badge of Office'. The two labourers would also make use of a mason's trowel for the finer excavation (as noted by Cunnington in 1808) and this could be the first ever reference to a specific tool being employed on an archaeological excavation. John would also accompany Philip Crocker on his surveys, dragging the surveyors chain, or the 'Devil's Guts' as they were known, due to the use of the 22 yard chain in measuring out the agricultural enclosures to the benefit of the landowners, often robbing the villagers of any scraps of land that they could utilise to sustain themselves. There are some very prominent archaeologists today who did not receive a formal university education but effectively learnt on the job. By surveying the field archaeology with Philip Crocker, John Parker would have built upon what he had already learned through excavation so was perhaps the most practically educated of them all, by the end of this short period. John would certainly become vexed if a dig was unsuccessful, particularly if there was an expectant body of gentleman onlookers, such as at the first attempt at Bush Barrow in July 1808. Cunnington, as a respected tradesman, could certainly relate well to the two labourers although for the titled Colt Hoare, this was a gulf that could not be bridged. There is an occasion when John was left to survey on his own in Stourhead and encountered pottery and brick flues in a cultivated field, evidence of habitation, and he obviously told Cunnington about it but not Colt Hoare. Upon hearing of this later, the baronet clearly felt aggrieved and wrote to Cunnington; 'John Parker seems to increase in stupidity as he grows in years, for he said nothing to me about his discoveries in Bonham'. Cunnington wrote back defensively stating that; 'John thinks you blame him wrongfully because you told him that you knew of everything around your house.' William Cunnington also interceded in 1802 when Stephen Parker approached him, requesting help after his eldest son Stephen had been sentenced to death at Winchester for stealing a pig (or a sheep, there are conflicting accounts!). Cunnington wrote to William a'Court, the Heytesbury squire, asking whether he would speak to the judge on behalf of the Parkers. As a consequence, the sentence was commuted to transportation to Australia.

Stephen Parker died in 1817 at the age of 66 but John lived until he was 86, surviving by whatever employment or poor relief that he could obtain. The 1841 census records John as an unemployed labourer, living in nothing more than a shack in Heytesbury churchyard. A later census reports that he was then living in Heytesbury Almshouse and dependent on charity but by the time of his death he had relocated to nearby Knook and was over two years behind with the rent. John Parker did receive an obituary in 1867, in a local paper, where it was recorded that he was William Cunnington's 'Principal pioneer'. It is pleasing to think that he had been remembered so long after his active contribution as part of the team that produced AW vol 1.

The archaeologist Paul Everill has done a great job unearthing the known facts about the two barrow diggers from Heytesbury and his paper; 'The Parkers of Heytesbury: Archaeological Pioneers' can be found in The Antiquaries Journal 90, 2010.

Richard Fenton included a poem in 'Quest', which is effectively a roll call for the Ancient Wiltshire vol 1 team. The much longer poem is titled 'A Barrow Opening at Everley, Autumn 1806'. I have included a small shovelful;

'In the chorus, got by heart
Let Stephen and John bear a part;
Illustrious barrow pioneers
Who never yet have had their peers.'

BECKFORD EPISODES:

WILLIAM BECKFORD (1760-1844)

At the age of 9, William Beckford inherited Fonthill in addition to one and a half million pounds and £70,000 per year, all accrued from sugar and slavery in Jamaica. Described as the richest commoner in the land, he inherited none of the machismo of his father Alderman Beckford and was instead an effete, brilliantly gifted youth with an overwrought imagination. His infatuation with young Lord Courtenay of Powderham Castle, who was 11 at the time, grew to become a life defining scandal for Beckford. Lord Courtenay was present at Beckford's extravagant 21st birthday party at Splendens, the house his father built at Fonthill. Beckford was also conducting an affair with his cousin Louisa at the time and James Lees-Milne describes the Arabian Nights atmosphere of the event: 'For several days and nights on end the exclusive party indulged in an orgy of acting, music and love-making'. In 1783, with his emotional entanglement with 'Kitty' Courtenay still burning fiercely, Beckford married Lady Margaret Gordon and they immediately travelled to Switzerland for their honeymoon. They returned to Splendens and after losing one child, two daughters did survive but Margaret died of a fever shortly after and Beckford was genuinely heartbroken. Leaving his two daughters in the charge of his mother, with the British press at his heels, blaming his wife's death on 'his flagitious behaviour', he fled the country. Initially intending to visit his Jamaican properties, instead he reached Madeira and diverted to Lisbon. His Portuguese journals, as Beckford tried to become accepted by the Portuguese court, paint an extraordinary portrait of royal life and the monasteries at Sintra were to enthral and influence his future building plans.

Much has been written about William Beckford, not least about the scandal that caused him to be ostracized by English society, which in part provoked the later building of the audaciously prominent Fonthill Abbey, with the intention of excluding all but a few select visitors. It is however neither his predilections nor his building that defines the cultural legacy of William Beckford, but instead it is his writing and his visionary art collecting. His journals contain some of the very best travel writing of any period and his gothic novel 'Vathek', written in French at the age of 21, is an extraordinary flight of imagination, horror and oriental brilliance. James Lees-Milne suggests in his biography of William Beckford that Beckford's prose was 'devastatingly sharp and amazingly modern. Like Byron,

Beckford antedated the sophisticated satire writers of recent times, Wilde, Firbank and Evelyn Waugh.' To read his translated journals and to enter Beckford's world is to stand upon the brink of becoming strangely mesmerised and you either have to withdraw or else succumb to an uncomfortable fascination.

As a collector Beckford had the most astute connoisseur's eye and was unconstrained by conventional intellectual prejudices. Being ahead of his time he cultivated an interest in early Italian Renaissance paintings and Asian and Islamic art which in turn influenced future collectors such as Prince Albert. With visionary ability he selected many astonishing and now iconic paintings, drawings and prints, a library of rare books, exquisite furniture and he also commissioned many object d'art to adorn his surroundings. Rivalling the Prince Regent in the scope and extravagance of his collecting, Beckford took great pleasure in arranging and re-arranging their display, despite having so few visitors at Fonthill to witness its magnificently furnished interiors. He commissioned JMW Turner to paint a number of landscapes with the Abbey dominating from all quarters, many of which went on display together for the first time in the wonderful 'Turner's Wessex' exhibition at Salisbury Museum a couple of years ago. Beckford's interests were not only confined to the buildings and their content but extended to the landscaping and planting of his walled estate at Fonthill, expressing many European influences from the extensive travelling in his youth.

Beckford's exclusion to all but a very few select visitors to his domain only served to increase public speculation about Fonthill Abbey, with rumours abounding such as being able to drive a carriage and six horses to the very top of the tower. By 1820, Beckford's financial situation had become critical due to another fall in the price of sugar and also many legal issues with his West Indian agents, the Wildman brothers, and in 1822 William Beckford put Fonthill Abbey and all its contents on the market. The scale of public interest at the time can be measured by the 72,000 copies of the sale catalogue that sold at a guinea each. Then there was to be the public viewing, prior to the sale, with anticipation now at fever pitch people flocked from far and wide at this most unexpected opportunity to see for themselves 'the Caliph's abode of treasure', after being excluded for so long. With the sale only two days away, the expectant public were then stunned by the pinning of a brief notice on the gate stating that the estate, the house and all its contents had been sold by private treaty. The purchaser, for £330,000, was gunpowder magnate John Farquhar, who had made his fortune by supplying powder to the East India Company and was now determined to live like a gentleman. Beckford stated that 'I am now rid of the Holy Sepulchre...which no longer interested me since its profanation', by which he meant the public crawling all over Fonthill Abbey, during the days before the aborted public sale. Beckford could now pay off his debts and Farquhar, evidently an eccentric in his own right, could live like a gentleman for a couple of years at least, until the tower of Fonthill Abbey fell on the afternoon of 21st December, destroying the Great Western Hall and the whole of the Octagon, beneath the tower. Miraculously no-one was injured although by the incredible force of air caused by the collapse, a servant was blown thirty feet down a passage, like a pellet through an air gun. Farquhar seemed unbothered by the whole event, stating that the house was too large for him to live in anyway and there was plenty remaining standing for his needs. One significant loss was the sight of Fonthill Abbey tower and I have often tried to visualise its dominant position, looming above the darkly wooded Vale of Wardour.

After the sale of Fonthill Abbey, Beckford moved to Bath where he bought two properties in Lansdown Crescent and built nearby Lansdown Tower. He once stated; 'Some people drink to forget their unhappiness...I do not drink, I build.' Beckford died in 1844 and his tomb lies amongst the jumbled cemetery adjacent to the tower.

There are a great many books on Beckford, too many to list, and the Beckford Society still flourishes.

FRANCHI (1770-1828)

Gregorio Filipe Fransisco Franchi. Beckford met Franchi in Lisbon after hearing the 17 year-old playing the harpsicord. This led to clandestine visits by Franchi to Beckford's residence where they played sonatas and sang together. Beckford recorded in his journal that; 'Franchi came sneaking in at tea time. I felt confused and guilty,' and 'at tea time Franchi came in and we played like kittens.' Franchi entered Beckford's service and remained for 40 years, travelling widely as agent and factotum, dealing and negotiating on Beckford's behalf, purchasing art and rare books for the Fonthill collections. The Wiltshire neighbours called him the 'Portuguese Orange' but, by all accounts, he was a cultured and faithful confidant with an 'outstandingly sweet character', according to James Lees-Milne in his book 'William Beckford'. He had a wife and family in Lisbon for which Beckford had granted a generous annuity but Gregorio Franchi rarely returned home. Despite a genuine friendship and interdependence, as Franchi lay dying in his Baker Street lodgings in 1828, Beckford deserted him. Boyd Alexander in his short monograph on Franchi 'From Lisbon to Baker Street' records this as the saddest episode in all the Beckford papers; 'It seems typical of so many of the rich and powerful that their most faithful retainers are abandoned in their hour of greatest need.' It was the Duchess of Hamilton that paid the £10 for Franchi's tombstone 'since Beckford could not bear to be involved with sickness and death'. Before his death Franchi, obviously in dire straits and to repay debt, had sold back to Beckford for £3,000 the original annuity that he and his wife had been granted. Unaware of this transaction, the grieving Barbara Maria de Castello De Laage Franchi hastily wrote to Beckford from Portugal, pleading for financial support. Did she get a reply?

PIERRO THE DWARF

Also referred to by Beckford as; Perro, Pierrot and sometimes Nanibus. Swiss by birth, Pierro was rescued by Beckford on his travels from 'wretched circumstances' in Evian. He remained with his Master for 40 years and is constantly mentioned in Beckford's correspondence, often with affectionate amusement. James Less-Milne states that; 'He had a grim, determined manner, was faithful, cunning, grubby and rather smelly.'

JAMES WYATT (1746-1813)

Fonthill Abbey architect; His father Benjamin was an architect and young James was one of four of seven brothers who also became architects, but it was to be James Wyatt of this dynasty that would become renowned. From the age of 24, after winning a prestigious competition to design the conversion of the Pantheon in Oxford Street, which gained many influential plaudits, he was to be in constant and often overwhelming employment thereafter. Beckford's initial instruction to James Wyatt in 1795 to begin a small structure 'which should contain a suite of rooms small, but amply sufficient for the enjoyment of a day whether sunshine or shower', rapidly grew in ambition to become the great Gothic folly that was Fonthill Abbey. Despite this increase in scale, it was still not Beckford's intention to create a place of habitation but more importantly the decorative effect that this structure would impose upon the surrounding landscape. James Wyatt always seemed to be expected elsewhere as he often overstretched his commitments but Beckford was more demanding than most clients, even the King with ongoing building operations at Windsor Castle. The change to make Fonthill Abbey now the new home for William Beckford required wholesale reconstruction with its timber and cement replaced by stone from the demolition of 'Splendens', the earlier house at Fonthill built by his father. Despite Wyatt being required to oversee the project, the haste and cutting of corners of the building process meant that as a structure it was unstable. Beckford sold Fonthill in 1822 and three years later the great tower collapsed.

Wyatt's other local involvement was of course the decluttering of Salisbury Cathedral which won him many critics, particularly after his death when he seemed to have been blamed for everything that the Chapter and the Bishop had demanded. It was the sepulchral interference that riled the antiquaries most and during the works Horace Walpole in correspondence to Richard Gough states; 'I shall heartily lament..the demolition of those beautiful chapels at Salisbury. Should I get sight of Mr Wyatt, which is not easy to do, I will remonstrate against the intended alteration; but probably without success, as I do not suppose he has the authority enough to interpose effectually: still I will try.'

The list of Wyatt's major projects in the appendix of Antony Dale's 1936 publication 'James Wyatt' is astonishing, ranging from gothic Cathedrals to overhauling Marshalsea prison. Here was a man in huge demand from Northumberland to Dublin and the distances undertaken in viewing, revisiting and overseeing his work would have taken their toll. Ultimately, James Wyatt even met his death on the road, hastening to yet another job when the private carriage he was travelling in overturned and he died of head injuries shortly afterwards. Writing in 1872 C.L.Westlake said: 'No English architect has perhaps been so much overrated by his friends, or so unfairly abused by his enemies as James Wyatt.'

SAUNDERS, THE CIRCUS BOY

A young tightrope-walker at the Circus Royal who captivated Beckford. Beckford writes to his agent Franchi; 'So if young S----d-rs wants a change of air (and perhaps of habits too) let him come to this bosky shade 'to cool his fever''. Young Saunders was part of a troupe that was soon to leave for Ireland. Henry Chalk's appearance at the great front door of Fonthill Abbey was timely and caused a deal of confusion.

INDIVIDUALS:

WILLIAM BELDHAM (SILVER BILLY), CRICKETER (1766-1862)

Even as a young man his batting exploits were widely talked about; 'Safer than a bank...wherever the ball was bowled, it was hit away in the most severe, venomous style.' He played for the Hambledon club upon Broadhalfpenny Down in Hampshire, England's leading cricket club until the formation of the MCC. As a bowler he was equally destructive through his accuracy and guile and his fielding displayed extraordinarily fast reactions and coordination. Long before the titans of cricket; W G Grace, Victor Trumper, Jack Hobbs and Don Bradman, stepped out upon the field of play, William Beldham had already set the bar very high. Some would say that his achievements have never been surpassed. In these early years of the sport, a number of cricket matches were played upon the Stonehenge turf and another significant local venue was Perham Down near Ludgershall.

WILLIAM BRUNSKILL, HANGMAN

Well. There was a hangman called William Brunskill who operated at Newgate Gaol but whether he bore any resemblance to the character Henry Chalk encountered is unknown. I saw it as a blank canvas and had fun filling it, with the unsettling combination of executioner and practical joker.

WILLIAM HAZLITT (1778 – 1830)

A brilliant essayist. Born into a dissenting family in Maidstone Kent which led to his viewing the world from the perspective of an oppressed minority. He later abandoned his London training towards becoming a Unitarian minister after discovering metaphysics, painting and the theatre but still maintained a passionate commitment to fight for the liberty of the individual. Coleridge described Hazlitt as; 'A thinking, observant, original man. Brow-hanging, shoe-contemplative, strange.' Whilst Charles Lamb comments; 'Hazlitt does bad actions without being a bad man. In his natural and healthy state (he is) one of the wisest and finest spirits breathing.' He met Sarah Stoddart through Charles and Mary Lamb in London, where William and Sarah married and then moved into her small cottage in the village of Winterslow (the Stoddart family were from Salisbury). Their firstborn died in July 1809 and after moving back to London their second child William survived, unlike their marriage which was finally annulled in 1822 through a Scottish divorce. Hazlitt writes of marriage generally in his 'Advice to a Schoolboy'; 'If you ever marry, I would wish you to marry the woman you like. Do not be guided by the recommendation of friends. Nothing will ever atone for or overcome an original distaste. It will only increase from intimacy.' From reading Stanley Jones' biography of Hazlitt, it does seem that Sarah Stoddart and William Hazlitt were an odd couple and also, in differing ways, at odds with the world around them, so a happy union was perhaps unlikely. Later in life the son William commented of his parents that although they were 'both of the kindliest nature (towards him),' they had 'no more notion of managing children than the man in the moon'. Hazlitt was hopeless with money and never checked bills and although he must have earned a good deal through writing and lecturing, he died poor in furnished lodgings. His distain for money is demonstrated by the story that he would often give his young son a pound note and tell him to get rid of it as soon as possible, either spend it or give it away in whatever manner he pleased.

William Hazlitt did return to Winterslow, where he could 'listen to the silence', staying at the Winterslow Hut for prolonged writing seclusion and extremely long walks. (The Winterslow Hut latterly became the Pheasant Hotel until it closed and is now private apartments.) His essays 'My First Acquaintance with Poets' and 'The Fight' are stunning examples of Hazlitt's prose.

HENRY HUNT (1773-1835)

Known to generations of revising school pupils, preparing for their history exams, as 'Orator' Hunt, the radical speaker at the infamous Peterloo Massacre in Manchester on 16th August 1819. How he came from wealthy Wiltshire landowner to incendiary reformer advocating one man one vote, secret ballots and annual parliaments is a very interesting tale, as is his fiery political relationship with William Cobbett. I can thoroughly recommend the book 'Two Cocks on the Dunghill' by Penny Young (Twopenny Press) for a full account. Henry Hunt's autobiography is also available as a reprint, to get both barrels of his splenetic self-aggrandisement. His legacy, however, was very real and he was an important influence upon the later Chartist Movement. Rather than conspire Jacobin subversion, Hunt was very open about his support for democratic radicalism, becoming the MP for Preston in 1830. He opposed the 1832 Great Reform Bill, on the grounds that it did not go far enough and, also in 1832, he presented the first parliamentary petition in support of women's suffrage, which was received with much ribald laughter by the House.

HENRY SHORTO (1778-1864)

That Henry Shorto suddenly developed a fascination for flint and the fossils in the chalk, local to Salisbury, should come as no surprise after his fictional encounter with Henry Chalk! From 1811 onwards he amassed a large lithic collection and corresponded widely on the subject, even presenting a letter to the Geological Society of London regarding his theories on the formation of flint through the transportation of dissolved silica from the sponges present in the calcareous sedimentations. A recorded minute from the meeting of March 1814 does briefly record the content of the synopsis but attributes it to 'Mr Henry Sports'. The fact that Henry Shorto did not publish his ideas, combined with the loss of his substantial collection of flint and fossils after he died, has meant that his geological contributions have been unheralded. It is plausible that his collection became absorbed into the Blackmore Museum in St Ann's street Salisbury, as there were family associations with its founder William Blackmore. There is a fine and extensive account of Henry Shorto's life and his geological contributions in The Wiltshire Archaeological and Natural History Magazine vol. 83 1990 by H.S. Torrens. I was very pleased to note that in later life Henry Shorto spent his time watercolour painting and composing poetry. In Salisbury Museum there are some fine examples of Salisbury cutlery, including pieces from the workshop of Henry Shorto. The giant pen-knife that hung above the shop doorway in Queen Street is also on display. It was not until the 1850's, after a cholera epidemic, that the open drains in Salisbury were replaced by an underground sewerage system and the mortality rates in Salisbury then dropped dramatically. For all things Salisbury, 'Endless Street', by John Chandler (Hobnob Press) is a comprehensive and very enjoyable account of the city's evolution and later history.

REV JOSEPH TOWNSEND OF PEWSEY (1739-1816)

A man for whom the word 'polymath' could have been invented. His principal interests are referred to in 'A Tour in Search of Gold' but it is significant that he was present in the company of William 'Strata' Smith as they set about recording, in tabulated form, the basis of Smith's geological observations that 'The same strata are found always in the same order and contain the same peculiar fossils'. Townsend greatly encouraged William Smith to produce a geological map of England and Wales which was finally published in 1818, two years after Townsend's death. Townsend's influence as a political economist was also very significant. In 1786 he published a paper entitled 'Dissertation on the Poor Laws by a Well-Wisher to Mankind', which was intended to expose the harmful effects of the Poor Laws in England, stating that this artificial support was 'unnatural and forced', leading to a growth in population that was unsustainable. Townsend's ideas gained a broader exposure by influencing the writing of Thomas Malthus and later on Charles Darwin in his 'Origin of the Species'.

EDWARD WILLIAMS (IOLO MORGANWG) (1747-1826)

The stonecutter that Henry Chalk's father Edward Chalk and Uncle James met on the summit of Silbury Hill in 1782. Williams was an influential figure in Welsh bardic culture, even to the point of forging medieval Welsh literature to bolster the Welshness of South Wales. His imaginative tampering with the Welsh texts has taken a great deal of unravelling by later historians. A curious mix of labourer, poet, fantasist and antiquarian. There is a great account of Edward Williams in the Wiltshire Archaeological and Natural History Magazine vol 97 2004, from which I gleaned most of my information. Looking at it again now, I recall reading of his laudanum addiction which he took from his mid-twenties for a 'troublesome cough' and continued to take for the rest of his life which might explain, in part, his bardic flights of fancy.

HARRIET GROVE (1791-1867)

Daughter of Ferne – cousin of Percy Bysshe Shelley (1792-1822) Although only briefly encountered in 'A Tour in Search of Flint', Shelley's poetic amours to Harriet Grove, in the mislaid letter picked up by Henry Chalk at Ferne, set the young pedestrian's mind racing as to how love should be transmitted on the page. 'The Grove Diaries' edited by Desmond Hawkins, gives Harriet's diary extracts from 1809, when she was already in correspondence with her sixteen year-old cousin 'Percy'. This young but intense romance ended abruptly in September 1810, after the publication of Shelley's early poetry in conjunction with his sister Elizabeth entitled; 'Original Poetry by Victor and Cazire', in which Harriet's sister Charlotte is referred to unfavourably. This caused sufficient offence for Harriet to cease corresponding with Percy, combined with his increasingly unsettling views on religion and the sanctity of marriage. Harriet's attentions were soon elsewhere however, as demonstrated by her marriage to William Helyar of Sedgehill in November 1811.

PETER WINTER

I did not realise it at the time but revisiting 'Stig of the Dump' by Clive King, after all these years whilst reading it to my 7 year-old granddaughter Scarlett, the caveman in the chalk pit and the charcoal burner in Grovely are probably related. This wonderful book also enters into a world of chalk and flint in the first few pages. It's funny how stuff works itself out.

ACKNOWLEDGEMENTS

Having taken so long to complete the trilogy, many people have been exceptionally kind and helpful at various stages along the way. Dr John Chandler has shown great faith and patience in publishing my books and the quality output of Hobnob Press, over so many years, has greatly enriched our knowledge and understanding of Wiltshire and the surrounding area. Dr Martin Green has been incredibly generous in sharing his archaeological knowledge, which has in turn formed the backbone of my understanding in all things flint related. Witnessing Jake Keen replicating the earliest forms of iron smelting has been inspirational and prompted the finding of the early iron making site in Tisbury. Salisbury and Devizes museums for being special places to gain inspiration, educate and promote wonder and a big thank you to all the staff and volunteers. Phil Harding for casting his eye over my earliest fieldwalking returns and for endorsing the first volume. Dr John Gosling for lending an ear and imparting wisdom. Wiltshire Council, for giving me the job of looking after all the public rights of way in South Wiltshire, I hope that I gave enough in return. Alex Howson, who had to listen to me banging on about story ideas when we were erecting kissing gates and for his thoughtful input after reading the manuscripts. Leah Scott for reading the draft of the biographies and offering gentle guidance. My mother, who has read, corrected and encouraged my writing throughout, I am very grateful that we could share in this together. Finally, Lindsay, for enduring the whole process and reminding me that real life, family, fun, friends, food and music are even more important than my obsessions.

www.ingramcontent.com/pod-product-compliance
Lightning Source LLC
Chambersburg PA
CBHW050120030726
47505CB00007B/1955